LITTLE GIRLS

Kate Medina has always been fascinated by the 'whys' of human behaviour, an interest that drove her to study Psychology at university and later to start a crime series featuring clinical psychologist Dr Jessie Flynn. She has an MA in Creative Writing from Bath Spa University and her debut novel *White Crocodile* received widespread critical acclaim, as did *Fire Damage* and *Scared to Death*, the first two books in the Jessie Flynn series.

Before turning to writing full time, Kate spent five years in the Territorial Army and has lectured at the London Business School and the London School of Economics. She lives in London with her husband and three children.

f Facebook.com/KateMedinaAuthor
🐦 @KateTMedina

Also by Kate Medina

The Jessie Flynn series
Fire Damage
Scared to Death

Standalone novels
White Crocodile

TWO LITTLE GIRLS

KATE MEDINA

HarperCollins*Publishers*

HarperCollins*Publishers*
1 London Bridge Street
London SE1 9GF

www.harpercollins.co.uk

This paperback edition 2018

3

First published by HarperCollins*Publishers* 2018

A catalogue record for this book
is available from the British Library

ISBN: 978-0-00-821403-6 (PB)

Typeset in Sabon by Palimpsest Book Production Limited,
Falkirk, Stirlingshire

Printed and bound in Great Britain by
CPI Group (UK) Ltd, Croydon, CR0 4YY

MIX
Paper from
responsible sources
FSC™ C007454

This book is produced from independently certified FSC™ paper
to ensure responsible forest management.

For more information visit: **www.harpercollins.co.uk/green**

For Isabel and Anna,
my two little girls

1

Though the summer holidays had ended for most, there were still a few children playing on the sand, their parents – holiday-makers, she could tell – setting out windbreaks and unpacking the colourful detritus of a family morning at the beach. Others, local mothers in jeans and T-shirts, walked barefoot with friends and dogs, keeping a roving eye on their offspring.

The sun was shining, but the air felt laden with the threat of rain and Carolynn could make out the dark trace of a sea storm hovering to the south of the Isle of Wight, misting the horizon from view. Would it rain or would the sun win out, she wondered. Would the storm come in to shore or blow out to the English Channel? Who knew; the weather by the sea, like life, so unpredictable.

Raising a hand to shade her eyes from the sunlight knifing through the clouds, she watched three little girls in pastel swimming costumes throwing a tennis ball to each other, a small dog – one of those handbag dogs she'd never seen the point of – running, yapping between them.

It was a good sign that she had brought herself to West Wittering beach this morning when she knew that families with children would be here. Evidence of her growing strength, that she could stand to watch little girls playing, listen to their shouts and their laughter.

She was healing. Except for the nightmares.

On the edge of a carefully constructed calm, aware though that her heart was beating harder in her chest – *but still softly enough to ignore, and she would ignore it, she could ignore it, she wouldn't have another panic attack, not now* – she slithered down from the dunes feeling the talcum-powder sand between her bare toes, the warmth that it had soaked up from the long summer. A ball streamed past her feet, followed, seconds later, by a little girl, the youngest of the three, nine years old or so from the look of her, just a year younger than Zoe had been. She bent to pick up the ball, flicked a sandy knot of hair from her face and smiled up at Carolynn as she walked back to her sisters. Carolynn watched her go, transfixed by the shape of her body in the pale pink swimsuit; still pudgy, no waist, puppy fat padding her arms and legs – just how she remembered Zoe's limbs, a perfect dimple behind each elbow.

She realized suddenly that the little girl had stopped, was looking back over her shoulder, pale blue eyes under blonde brows, wrinkling with concern. Carolynn forced a quick smile, felt it flicker and fade. She dragged her gaze away from the girl. She wouldn't want her to think that there was something wrong with her, that she was anything other than a mother out for a walk on the beach, just like the little girl's own mother. That she was someone to be feared. A danger.

Pushing off against the wet sand, each footstep leaving a damp indent behind her, Carolynn walked on towards the sea. Ever since she was a girl herself, the outside, nature, had been her escape, her way of letting her mind float free. Over these past two years she had needed its uncomplicated help more than ever before. Today of all days, she needed it desperately.

A massive hulk appeared in her peripheral vision: a ship, loaded three storeys high with a coloured patchwork of rusting steel containers, grimly industrial and incongruously man-made against the backdrop of sky and sea and the seagulls swirling overhead.

Another memory, surfacing so violently that she caught her breath at its intensity. *A good memory, though. Don't shut it out.* Standing at the top of the sand dunes with Zoe, two summers ago, looking out over the Solent and watching a huge container ship glide past on its way to unload at Southampton docks. Zoe had been awed by its sheer size, a floating multi-storey tower block that the law of physics said should just turn turtle, flip upside down and be swallowed by the sea, it was so ridiculously top-heavy. The questions bursting from her without a break, words mixed up, back to front in her excitement to ask everything.

Where does it come from? Where is it going to? What's in all those big coloured blocks on the ship, Mummy? Why don't they all topple off into the sea? How does the ship stay upright, Mummy? Mummy? Mummy? Mummy . . .

Carolynn's gaze had found the writing on the side of the ship's hull. *China Line.* All the ships that cut through the Solent seemed to be from China these days.

Toys, darling.

Toys?

Zoe's brown eyes saucer-wide, terrified she might miss the answers if she blinked for even a millisecond.

The day had been changeable, much like today. Grey clouds skipping across the sun, but still warm enough to walk in T-shirt and jeans, a cool breeze blowing in from the sea, the sand warm under their bare feet, holding the summer's heat. The last day of their long-weekend break.

'Can we watch the ships next time we come here?'

Reaching for Zoe's hand, feeling the spangles of sand on Zoe's skin grate against hers, squeezing tight, so tight. 'Of course we can, darling. If you're good. But you must try *very* hard to be good.'

They had driven back to London that night, she remembered: Zoe fast asleep in the back seat, exhausted by the fresh air, a layer of sand coating her bare legs and arms and pooled around her on the seat, as if someone had sprinkled icing sugar through a sieve; Roger miles away as he stared through the windscreen, exasperated by the weight of Sunday traffic, his mind already fixing on tomorrow's workday.

She shouldn't have come to the beach today. It had been a stupid mistake.

Next time.

She might go for hours with the sense that she was finally getting to grips with her grief, and then suddenly she'd be visited by a memory, an image so intense that it would take her breath away. And even the good memories hurt so badly.

Next time.

There hadn't been a next time.

She raised her hand to her mouth, pushing back a sob. *How could anyone believe that I murdered my own daughter?*

2

Jessie reached for the green cardboard file of loose papers on her desk, but her fingers refused to obey the command sent from her brain, and instead of gripping the file she felt it slide from her left hand, watched helplessly as a slow-motion waterfall of papers gushed to the floor and spread across the carpet.

Shit.

She sank to her knees, feeling like a disorganized schoolkid, ludicrous, unprofessional. How the hell was a client supposed to trust her judgement when she couldn't even persuade her useless, Judas hand to grasp a simple file? The disability constantly there, goading her. She should have stapled the papers, but she didn't like to. Liked to be able to spread her patients' – 'clients', the majority of them were called now, she reminded herself – files out on her desk, look at the pages all at once, her gaze skipping from the notes of one session to the notes of another, nothing in the human brain working in a linear fashion, so why should notes be laid out linearly, read sequentially? It made no sense.

'Please, just sit down. I can get them myself.' Trying to keep the edge from her voice.

'I'm happy to help.' The tone of the reply too bright, too jolly for such a benign statement. Everything that Laura said tinted with that Technicolor tone.

Even down here on the floor together, scrabbling to collect Jessie's spilled papers, Laura wouldn't meet her eye. Five sessions in and Laura had never looked her directly in the eye, not once, not even fleetingly. She wore a sober grey skirt suit and cream pussy-bow blouse, work clothes, from a life before her daughter's accident, but Jessie noticed a fine layer of sand, like fairy dust, coating her bare feet in the sensible, low-heeled black court shoes. She had been to the beach before she came here. Outside. Nature. Jessie wouldn't know until they started talking whether that was a good or a bad sign. Laura had told her in that first session, five weeks ago, that nature – immersing herself in nature, walking, or more often running now – since her life had changed in that one fleeting moment two years ago, was the only way she could force her mind to float free. To give up its obsessive hamster-wheel motion, if only temporarily.

Two years today, wasn't it? September seventh? Jessie glanced down at the scattered pages, trying to find the notes from Laura's first session to check, knowing, as she looked, that looking was unnecessary, the date cast in her memory. Seven, randomly, her favourite number. When she was a child, she used to change her favourite number every year on her birthday to match her age. At the age of seven, she had been old enough to understand that a favourite number wasn't favourite if it changed annually, and so seven stuck. It was only when she was older that she realized she'd happened upon 'lucky 7'. Seven days of the week, seven colours of the rainbow, seven notes on a musical scale, seven seas and seven continents.

Seven for Laura, a number forever wedded with tragedy. The day that her daughter, spotting her best friend across the road, had pulled her hand from Laura's and been hit by a courier's van.

Laura held out the papers she'd collected.

'Thank you,' Jessie said, taking them.

They rose. Clutching the file to her chest with her left arm, Jessie sat down in one of the two leather bucket chairs that she used for her sessions. She had positioned the chairs in front of the window, as the bucket chairs in her old office at Bradley Court had been positioned. No discs in the carpet yet, from their feet, to knock her sense of order off-kilter if patients nudged them out of line, the office and her life outside the army too new for such well-worn, comfortable grooves. She glanced over to the window, her gaze still trained to expect the wide-open view of lawns sweeping down to the lake, saw instead a brick Georgian terrace. Her ears, tuned to birdsong, heard the hum of traffic. The architecture was beautiful, the road narrow, quiet, but this new environment was grating all the same. Grating, Jessie admitted to herself in her more honest moments, purely because it wasn't Bradley Court. Wasn't her old life. A life that she hadn't voluntarily surrendered.

She looked down at her left hand. The scar across her palm from the knife attack was still a gnarled, angry purple. Two finer, paler tracks ran perpendicular, where the surgeon had peeled back her skin to repair the severed tendons, a row of pale spots either side of the main scar where he had sewn her palm back together, each stitch identical in length and equidistant, a triumph of pedanticism, the best job that could be done, given the severity of damage to her extensor tendons, he had assured her. It still felt as if it belonged to someone else – the grotesque hand of a mannequin. Occasionally it obeyed her; more often it didn't.

She sensed Laura watching her, looked up quickly to try to catch her eye, saw her gaze flash away.

'We can sit at the desk, if it's easier,' Laura murmured.

Jessie shook her head. The barrier of the desk was too formal, too divisive for such a tense, skittish patient. 'How was the beach?' she asked.

'Huh?' Laura's eyes, fixed resolutely on a point just to the left of Jessie's, on a blank spot of wall, Jessie knew without needing to look, widened.

'Sand. Your feet.'

Laura glanced down. 'Oh, I thought you were a mind reader for a second.' A tentative, distant smile. 'I'd hate you to actually be able to read my mind.'

Jessie returned the smile, watching Laura's expression, listening to the nuances in her voice. The forced jollity, like a game-show host worried for her job, always, irrespective of the subject matter.

'So how was it?' she prompted.

'What?'

'The beach?'

Laura took a moment, and Jessie noticed the apple in her throat rising and falling with the silence, as if the answer was sticking in her craw.

'Fine . . . good.'

Using the oldest trick in the book, Jessie acknowledged her words with a brief nod, but remained silent. Dipping her gaze to Laura's file, she tapped her fingers along the papers' edges, smoothed her fingertips around the corners, perfectly aligning each sheet with the others and the edge of the file.

Laura's voice pulled her back. 'There were . . . there were children there. Girls. Little girls. Three, playing with a ball.' Laura let out a high-pitched, nervous bark. 'And one of those dreadful little dogs. The type that Paris Hilton carts around in a handbag.'

'How did you feel?' Jessie asked gently.

The apple bobbing, sticking.

'Fine . . . OK.'

Jessie had learned over the five sessions not to probe too actively. The woman in front of her was tiny, blonde hair worn up in a chignon and liquid brown gazelle's eyes made huge by the persistent dark circles under them, roving, watching – always watching, taking everything in, but never engaging. They reminded her of Callan's eyes the first time she had met him, recently back from Afghanistan, the Taliban bullet lodged in his brain. The wary eyes of someone for whom the prospect of danger is a constant.

Laura's file said forty-one, but she looked at least five years older than that, late, rather than early forties, every bit of the pain she had lived through etched into the lines on her soft-skinned, pale oval face.

'The girls were, uh, sweet. They were sweet. One ran past me.' Laura's skeleton hand moved to cup her elbow. 'She had dimples, here. Puppy fat—' She broke off, the internal tension the words had created in her palpable.

'The storm held off?' Jessie asked, changing the subject to relieve the pressure.

'It went out to sea. It was nice. Not hot, but warm, sunny.'

Her gaze moved from the blank wall to Jessie's scarred left hand. It was clear from her questioning look that she

9

wanted to know how the scars came to be there, but Jessie wasn't willing to share personal information with a patient. She'd had colleagues who'd been burnt in the past, letting a patient cross the line from professional to personal. However much she sympathized with Laura and felt a shared history in the traumatic loss of a loved one far too young, she had no intention of making that mistake herself.

'I have scars too.' Laura gave a tentative smile. 'And not just psychological ones.' Slipping off one of her court shoes, she showed Jessie the pale lines of ancient scars running between each of her toes. 'I was born with webbed feet, like a seagull. Perhaps that's why I like the sea.'

They both laughed, nervous half-laughs, grateful for the opportunity to break the tension, if only for a moment. For both of them the subject – scars, psychological scars – was minefield sensitive.

'Will it ever stop?' Laura croaked.

What could she say? No. *No*, it will never stop. Your dead daughter will be the first thing you think about the second you wake. Or perhaps, if you're lucky, the second after that. During that first second, still caught by semi-consciousness, you may imagine that she is alive, asleep under her unicorn duvet cover, clutching her favourite teddy, blonde hair spread across the pillow. But you'll only be spared for that first second. Then the pain will hit you, hit you like a freight train and keep pace with you throughout your waking hours. This is now your life. Over time, a long time, it will lessen. One day you'll realize that instead of thinking about her every minute, you haven't thought of her for a whole hour. Then a day. But will it stop? No, it will never stop. Jamie never stopped, even for me, his sister. And for my mother? No, *never*.

'It will fade,' she said lamely.

Laura's fingers had found the buckle of the narrow black patent leather belt cinching her skirt at the waist, the only thing preventing it from skidding down over her non-existent hips, the skirt having been designed for a figure ten kilos heavier.

'It has been two years.'

'I know.'

'September seventh. It's supposed to be the luckiest number in the world, isn't it? Seven?'

Seven dwarves for Snow White, seven brides for seven brothers, Shakespeare's seven ages of man, Sinbad the Sailor's seven voyages, James Bond, 007.

Laura's eyes grazed around Jessie's consulting room, minute changes of expression flitting across her face as she absorbed the salient details: no clutter, no mess, spotlessly clean, the single vase of flowers – white tulips, Jessie's favourite – clean and geometric, arranged so that each stem was equidistant from the next. The sunlight cutting in through the window lit tears in those liquid gazelle eyes, Jessie noticed, as her gaze flitted past.

'Except that the bible doesn't agree,' Laura said.

Seven deadly sins.

'It was my fault.'

Jessie shook her head. 'No. We've talked through this, Laura.' *Countless times.* And they would, she knew, countless more. 'It was an accident, plain and simple. An accident with horrible consequences that you would have given everything to be able to prevent, but still an accident.'

'That's a mother's job, isn't it, though? To protect her child from harm. That above anything else, the one and only vital job. You can fail at all the others, but not that

11

one. *Not that one*.' Laura rubbed her hands over her eyes, smearing the welling tears across her cheeks. 'I succeeded at everything else. All the stuff that I thought was so bloody important back then. Writing her name before she'd even started in Reception, reading level 4 Biff and Chip books by the Christmas holidays, number bonds to ten by Easter, even though learning was such a struggle for her. But it wasn't important, was it? That was all a big fat lie.' Her face twisted with anguish. 'And the one thing, the only thing, the only critical job was the one I failed at. The job of keeping her alive.'

Jessie had faced her fair share of grief, her own and other people's, patients', in bland consulting rooms like this one, but the grief pulsing from this woman felt different. Like the grief she had felt from her own mother when her little brother, Jamie, had committed suicide. Grief and guilt. The overwhelming emotion – guilt. And something else too, something she couldn't put her finger on. Why wouldn't Laura look her in the eye, even momentarily? Still?

'Laura.'

She nodded. She looked worse than the last time Jessie had seen her, just a week ago. Exhausted, thinner, if that was possible in such a short time, the black rings under her eyes so dark, they looked as if they had been charcoaled on. She reminded Jessie of a pencil sketch: there, but almost not.

'It wasn't your fault, Laura. None of it was your fault.'

3

The woman screwed her eyes up against the rain and the wind that drove it horizontally into her face and lashed the wet dregs of her blonde hair around her cheeks. She was alone on the beach, and that was how she liked it.

The gunmetal sea lapping the sand was deserted also; certainly no pleasure boats out this afternoon, but no ships either that she could see, visibility misted to a few hundred metres offshore, the primary colours of the rides at Hayling Island funfair across the mouth of the harbour resembling washed watercolour strokes on grey paper.

Weather like this caused holiday-makers to bolt for shelter. Duck into the cafés and restaurants on Shore Road, their steaming waterproofs draped on the backs of chairs while they had tea and cake; or potter around the pound shops in East Wittering village, throwing a fiver at their kids' boredom until the rain stopped or the shops closed, whichever happened first. There were too many people during the summer months, which was both a curse and a bonus for her. She watched them with suspicion and they watched her with more, used to seeing tanned, long-limbed girls in surfer T-shirts and board shorts at the beach, not the kind of woman they'd expect to see begging for coins around train stations in grotty town centres or rifling through the 'past sell-by date' bin in budget supermarkets.

She had mixed feelings now that the summer holidays were nearly over. She despised the tourists who arrogantly commandeered her beach with their hoards of possessions and their loudly advertised happiness. She hated them, but their presence occasionally brought her a windfall: things deliberately discarded, others left accidentally, having slipped from overflowing beach bags or dropped from baggy pockets. Items she could use, barter or sell. Days like this were good, rain following sun. She didn't mind the miserable weather because it cloaked her in solitude. Solitude was comfortable to her – she knew nothing other than loneliness. There had been only a brief period in her life when she hadn't been on her own, a wonderful, fleeting time that had changed everything.

The woman looked from the stormy horizon to the little girl lying in the dunes at her feet. The sand was white, the little girl's skin whiter, as if she had been washed sparkling clean by the rain. The tinny tune of a washing powder advertisement from years ago, from when she had used to be parked in front of the television for hours on end as a girl herself, chimed in the woman's dulled brain.

Little girl, far away in a world of your own, in a world built of dreams that are yours and yours alone.

She had wanted to be the girl in that advert. That perfect, soft focus blonde child playing in a meadow full of wild flowers. She had wanted, so desperately wanted, the crisp white broderie anglaise dress the little girl was wearing. But though she was blonde and fair-skinned, she had never owned a dress like that, never seen a field of grass, just the scrappy patches of dirt dotted around the tower blocks where she lived, where kids skidded their bikes and teenagers smoked and fucked. She had never seen a meadow, cows, sheep, horses; had never seen any animals aside from the pumped-up dogs dragged around on studded leather leads and the rats that scurried around the bins at night.

The eyes of the girl with the perfect white skin were open, staring fixedly up to the sky as if her gaze had been caught by one of the seagulls hovering above them on an updraught. They were cloudy green like the sea on a cold, clear day. Her hair was brown and curly, so dark against the sand and her own white skin that it looked as if her head had been caught in a halo of dirty seaweed.

Little girl, far away in a world of your own, in a world built of dreams that are yours and yours alone.

A doll lay next to the girl. A nasty plastic doll dressed in a cheap pink ballerina dress, with eyes that the woman knew would move if she lifted it. The doll's eyes were green like the girl's.

You've always been a quiet one, but I don't know, it doesn't seem to keep you any cleaner.

Shells ringed the child and the doll in the shape of a heart, a heart even whiter than the sand and the little girl's washed white skin. It was so long since the woman had considered love, felt love, that the shape of the heart knifed, just for a second, into a part of her that she had long since shut and padlocked. She shook her head, trying to shake off the memory and the feelings the sight of the little girl and the perfect pale heart surrounding her had brought to the surface.

15

Extending her foot, she nudged her toe against one of the shells, knocking it out of kilter, against a second, third and fourth, kicking them out of line too. She smiled to herself, a small, satisfied smile. The heart was broken now and that was better. A broken heart reflected the life that she had lived. The life this little girl would doubtless have lived, had she lived. Real hearts were for television advertisements and soppy songs written by fools.

Bending down, she fingered the necklace around the girl's neck. It was a silver locket; antique, from the look of it, engraved with two sets of footprints: those of an adult and, next to them, the smaller prints of a child. The silver was cold and her thumb pushed the wet from the engraved metal and left a dull print that was swallowed by raindrops the instant she pulled her thumb away. It would be worth something that, but she wasn't going to take it. She had her reasons for not stooping to that. For not taking a necklace off a dead child. Beneath the necklace's chain of silver coiled another, the thick dark chain of a bruise. Apart from the bruise, starkly black and purple against the soft white skin, the little girl looked untouched. Alabaster.

The woman stared down at the dead child and thought that she would feel something.

Sadness? Horror? Anger?

Or nothing? At least – nothing.

But what she felt was worse. It was a feeling that she recognized as satisfaction. Satisfaction that someone else would hurt the way she hurt every moment of every day. *Cruel.* When had she become so cruel as to enjoy someone else's grief?

Little girl, far away in a world of your own, in a world

built of dreams that are yours and yours alone. Though I cannot share your dreams, you are still my very own.

A small part of who she was – who she used to be – hated herself for the feeling. But that person was so far gone that she existed in another life, a life that had happened to someone else, and the tiny nugget of self-hatred was easy to ignore.

She looked down at the bruised tracks on the underside of her forearm, the soft skin there almost as white as the dead child's, the needle marks dark as the snake of bruises coiled around the child's neck. The woman had lived by the sea all her life and she recognized weather patterns like she recognized those self-inflicted patterns on her arm. The rain had set in for the evening, at least. There would be no one else to disturb the quiet of the dunes today, walking where she had walked. She didn't need to rush. There was no urgency to tell the police. The little girl was dead. She would stay right here in her heart of shells and the doll with the matching eyes would keep her company.

Pushing herself to her feet, stepping carefully around the prone child, the woman walked on, the wet sand clinging to her bare soles, rainwater slopping around her toes. A packet of cigarettes caught her eye, damp, sodden, but she could dry them. Bending, she slipped them into the pocket of her jacket. A little further on, a two-pound coin, spilled from a purse or pocket. Lucky. A lucky day, for her at least. September seventh. Lucky seven.

Straightening, she walked on, eyes grazing the sand for treasure, leaving the dead child behind her alone in the dunes, staring up at the sky, staring up at nothing.

4

Icy water stung Carolynn's cheeks as she fumbled the front-door key into the lock with one hand. The plastic handles of the grocery bags cut into the wrist of her other arm; usually she would have set them down on the ground, but the path at her feet was sodden. It hadn't been raining when she'd left the house mid-afternoon for her run, but the sky had been a uniform ceiling of grey, so she had slipped her waterproof cagoule over her lycra tights and tank before she'd set out.

Roger's car wasn't on the drive so he must still be at work. Though she preferred it when he wasn't home, the thought of stepping into that oppressive little house, alone once again, made a sick feeling balloon in her stomach. Today of all days, she couldn't bear to be out among the crowds – couldn't trust herself to be in enclosed spaces with families, bracing herself against the sound of children's voices rolling in from down the street, or from another aisle in the supermarket. But now that she was alone, with no external stimuli to distract her, her mind was flooding with memories, pictures so vivid that she felt faint, knocked sideways with the pain.

Unbidden, an image from her visit to the beach that morning rose in her mind: the little girl in a pastel pink bathing costume. Where would she be now? With her parents and sisters, eating Nutella pancakes at the surf café? Tucked up on a sofa in a rented holiday home watching cartoons? Playing board games in a hotel lounge? Normal rainy-day holiday activities that she would never again do with a child of her own. Her goal when building her family had been to have pretty, bright, well-mannered children, to want to spend quality time in each other's company, to relish every single, simple moment. The thought of that dimpled little girl on the beach hurt like a weeping sore.

It wasn't my fault, she screamed inside. *You need to believe that it wasn't my fault.*

Grocery bags knocking around her bare ankles, she staggered into the kitchen and laid them on the clay-tiled floor. On a dull early evening like this, even with all the ceiling spots on, the kitchen was unbearably claustrophobic. Dirty cream walls and dark wood kitchen cabinets topped with black laminate work surfaces shrunk it to half the size it actually was, making her feel as if she'd squeezed herself into a cardboard box.

The house was a rental. A small white house jammed between the gate of a static caravan park on one side and a boarded-up, crumbling bungalow on the other. It was right by the sea, but you wouldn't know it, except for the stream of tourists wandering past in the summer, shouldering beach bags and clutching ice creams, and the brutal weather that rattled the window panes in winter. From the kitchen window, she could see the road and beyond that the concrete sea wall that wouldn't have looked out of place bordering a military bunker. It had been built head high and a metre thick to prevent the sea from eating up more land, but she couldn't see the point of being by the sea if you couldn't appreciate its beauty. And she did love the sea. Cheap and faceless, this was a running-away-to house, a hiding-away-in house. They had only planned to be here a couple of months until the furore surrounding the court case had died down and they'd decided how and where to rebuild their lives. But their London house hadn't sold – prospective buyers put off by having seen it on television for all the wrong reasons – so their hands were tied.

Hauling the fridge door open, Carolynn listlessly filled it with the shopping, every bend and straighten a gargantuan effort. She felt physically and mentally exhausted, wrung out like a damp dishcloth. She had eaten nothing all day and yet she wasn't hungry, was rarely hungry these days. She had to force herself to eat enough to keep her body grinding along.

As she flicked the kettle on to make herself a cup of tea, the cat jumped on to the island, leaving a trail of dusty paw marks from its litter tray across the black laminate surface. Revolted, Carolynn fought the urge to swing the full kettle from its stand and knock the bloody animal to the floor with it. The cat had been Zoe's, a Burmese, bought for her by Roger's mother because 'every child needs a pet'. Carolynn hadn't needed to ask the subtext. Every child needs someone or something they can love unconditionally, that loves them back without reserve or judgement.

Didn't your husband become so alarmed about your ambivalence towards your daughter that he asked his mother to move into your house to look after her?

No.

And did his mother not live with you for a full eighteen months, from when Zoe was a year old until she was two and a half, until her husband, your father-in-law, became ill and she had to move back to her home to look after him?

No. *It wasn't like that.*

She'd tried hard to put her struggle with motherhood, all those negative feelings she'd had, behind her by the time Pamela bought Zoe that repulsive cat. She was four then. Pamela had used her fourth birthday as an excuse for the purchase, but Carolynn knew the real reason. Why were people – her own mother-in-law, for Christ's sake – still treating her as if she couldn't manage, couldn't be a proper mother, even then? And why did Roger let Pamela behave like that? Shouldn't he have supported her, his own wife?

Thereafter, did your husband not employ a full-time live-in au pair, even though you were not employed yourself? I put it to you that it was because he was worried about his daughter's safety if he left her with you alone. With her own mother.

That's not true.

You had severe depression, didn't you, Mrs Reynolds?

No. No, I didn't.

The prosecuting solicitor had kept interrupting her. Arrogant. He was so arrogant, he wouldn't let her speak.

Absentmindedly, she reached out to stroke the cat, but it arched its back, bared its teeth and hissed at her. *God, even the cat hates me.* The cat who'd been bought precisely because Burmese cats were as loving as dogs. She'd see it sitting on the garden wall, letting every damn stranger who walked up the street pet it, rubbing its head against their hands; she could hear its purr even through the glass window. And yet it couldn't abide her.

You were referred to a specialist mental health team because you had such severe depression.

Making a huge show of putting on his glasses, letting the jurors' minds linger on the words 'specialist mental health team', as if she was mad. He wanted them to think that she was mad. He hadn't understood. None of them had understood.

Depression brought on by motherhood. Isn't that true, Mrs Reynolds?

There was nothing strange about postnatal depression, so why had they used it against her in court? Tried to insinuate that she was crazy? Mental health was an issue for many people. Some philosopher she'd read had summed it up beautifully. She couldn't remember the exact words, but it was something about most people leading lives of quiet desperation. Life was mainly struggle, wasn't it? Hardly surprising then that so many people succumbed to depression, as she had done. She *had* found motherhood tougher than she had expected it to be. She hadn't fallen crazily and unconditionally in love with Zoe. Those weren't crimes.

Reaching for a tea towel, she flapped it at the cat, which arched and hissed again and then leapt to the floor, scooting a wide path around her legs to dodge the kick she launched at it. She'd find a furry patch on one of the cream sofa cushions in the sitting room later, no doubt. Have to wrap Sellotape around her fingers and pat her hand across the patch to collect up all the stray hairs, pick up the few that had stuck, like pine needles, in the cream cotton with her nails. Roger liked the house clean. *We both do – it's not just him.*

The kettle had boiled and she made herself a cup of green tea, paced as she sipped it, too stressed and upset to sit down, sit still.

September seventh.

Lucky seven.

Seven detestable sins.

She hadn't told Dr Flynn in her session this morning that, besides Roger and the odd impersonal interaction with people in shops around the village, she was the only living adult Carolynn spoke with all week. That she would talk properly to no one, bar her husband, until next week's session. That the sessions were rapidly becoming a beacon of light for her; her only beacon. She recognized a kindred spirit in Jessie Flynn. Flynn wouldn't tolerate a filthy cat padding over the surfaces in her kitchen. Those surfaces would be spotless – spotless and bright white. Everything in Flynn's house would be white, Carolynn imagined, and immaculate, just as her own house had been, back when they lived in London.

Though she was sure that Jessie would be able to disguise her Obsessive Compulsive Disorder from less perceptive patients, she couldn't hide it from her. Carolynn recognized OCD when she saw it, shared that desire for cleanliness and order, even though she wasn't a fellow sufferer. She would like to be friends with Jessie. She needed a friend, desperately. Someone who she could talk to, someone who would *understand*. They couldn't just keep running and hiding. Keep telling lies.

5

The seagulls were agitating Detective Inspector Bobby 'Marilyn' Simmons, unsettling him. There was a flock of them, circling overhead, like vultures orbiting a carcass, as if they knew there was a dead child inside that tent, as if they could smell the blood, sense death.

Later, he would accept that they were attracted by the people, himself included; a Pavlovian response after a summer of beachgoers tossing chips, burger buns and the fag end of sandwiches in their direction. But the sight of them, that ear-splitting squawking, made his nerves and the hairs on the back of his neck stand on end. He was tempted to grab a handful of stones and hurl them up into the sky, throw stone after stone until every single one of the vile creatures had scattered, but that would give the smattering of reporters who had got the early wire about the little girl's murder exactly what they wanted: DI Simmons demonstrating he was taking this case far too personally. Day one, an hour in, and already it had burrowed right under his skin. Even if he could continue to kid himself that he wasn't yet drawing parallels with Zoe Reynolds' murder – two years ago today, he had realized a microsecond after he'd heard that the body of a young girl had been found on West Wittering beach – the press wouldn't be so forgiving. They would forensically examine in print any actions on his part that weren't entirely by the book, seizing on anything that could be interpreted as proof that he wasn't coping, that he couldn't be objective.

Stripping off his overalls and overshoes and handing them to a CSI officer, Marilyn turned his collar up against the spitting rain and slid down the dunes on to the tidal flats, sucking the salt-laced air deep into his cigarette-ravaged lungs, grateful to be out of that claustrophobic InciTent and away from the sad, desecrated little body. Her green eyes were clouding over with a death film already, wide open, but seeing nothing, recognizing nothing.

Though civilization was barely five hundred metres away – £5,000,000 houses owned by city bankers who had cashed in their chips and retired down here with their families for the quiet life, others heading here at weekends – it always surprised him how startlingly remote this peninsula was, tied to the main stretch of the beach by a narrow bar of sand and extending like a bloated finger into the mouth of Chichester Harbour. Fifty acres of silky soft sand dunes topped with knee-high marram grass where children could play for hours, disappear for hours, even when the beach in front of the dunes was packed with holiday-makers. The local police had fielded many calls over the years from frantic parents whose children had gone missing on this stretch of coast. Most turned up an hour or two after they'd disappeared, having simply lost track of time. Years ago, when he was starting out in the force as a PC, before he'd had his own children and experienced parental worry first-hand, he'd done his fair share of trudging through these dunes, sand penetrating his brogues and gritting between his toes, calling out Noah or Amelia's name, itching to clip the little sod's ear when he or she was finally found.

The location should have been God's gift for footprints, but that forensic avenue had been frustrated by the time of year and the weather: a rainy afternoon following on from a sunny morning and a string of sunny days before that, at the end of the summer holidays. Adults and children's footprints criss-crossed his crime scene as if a herd of demented cattle had passed through; it would have taken forever to process each and every one, had the rain not obliterated the whole lot.

What was the little girl doing all the way out here anyway? Had she been in the dunes when she met her killer? Had she come under her own steam, playing with friends or wandering alone, or had she been brought here? And if she'd come with her killer, had she done so voluntarily, or had she been bribed or coerced? Easy to bribe a child of that age with sweets, easy to force them with threats. Simple for an adult to convince a child who knew them well to come and play on the beach for an hour.

According to the initial estimate from Dr Ghoshal, the pathologist, she had been dead for between one and two and a half hours, which meant that she had been killed sometime between three-thirty and five p.m. Whoever the child's killer was, he or she had chosen well, both in terms of location, weather and timing.

He didn't even know who she was. Only nine or ten years

old and yet no one had come forward to claim her. For Christ's sake – what kind of home did the poor little mite come from?

6

Just one glass. There was nothing wrong with having a small glass of red wine before Roger came home. It was a quarter-to-seven – perfectly respectable. She used to drink all the time in her old job: nip to the pub at lunchtime with her colleagues, pop out for drinks after work on Fridays as a reward for making it through another emotionally draining week dealing with all those traumatic cases.

Cupping the wine glass, she wandered into the sitting room and switched on the television. It was an early-evening chat show, five glossy women with expensive highlights, dressed in clothes that Carolynn would have worn for a night out in central London, in the days when she had friends to go out in the evening with, sitting behind a pink panelled desk. The women, all her age or older, looked immaculate even under the harsh studio lights; they were so removed from the image she saw in the bathroom mirror every morning, they might as well have been aliens from another planet. She had looked like that once though, hadn't she? Dewy-skinned, bright-eyed and sleek. Before the pain took its toll . . .

At the sound of the front door, her shoulders stiffened, the muscles under her skin bunching into tense knots. Roger's footsteps echoed across the tiled hall as he walked into the kitchen, then stopped. She heard the sound of his breathing and, though he said nothing, she knew he was surprised that she wasn't in the kitchen preparing dinner. A good meal was important to him after a long day at work. Uneasy, Carolynn looked quickly for somewhere to stow her wine glass, out of sight. But before she'd taken a step, she sensed rather than heard him standing in the lounge doorway, felt his eyes on her.

'I, uh, I didn't expect you back,' she murmured, pasting on a poor impression of a smile as she turned.

A shadow crossed his face when he saw the glass in her hand. 'I left early so that I could be with you. Because of . . . you know.' *Because of today.*

Carolynn nodded, feeling like a reformed drug user, caught sneaking a hit. 'I . . . I just fancied a small glass,' she said.

'It's a bit early, Caro.'

They stood, facing off against each other across the living room. 'It's nearly seven, Roger, and it's only a small glass.' Her tone sounded like that of a child defending the state of their room.

'I don't think you should be drinking alone.'

'It's just one.'

'One leads to two, then three.' He puffed air into his cheeks and blew noisily out of his mouth, like a balloon deflating. 'What did you do today?'

I went for a run. I go every day. You couldn't expect me not to go today of all days.

She didn't say it. She had changed out of her running clothes, as she did every day before he got home from work,

29

had taken a shower, put on a dress. He liked her to look pretty, feminine. He hated to think of her punishing her body with that obsessive running. He didn't realize how much she needed it, how it was the only thing keeping her sane.

'I popped to the supermarket,' she said. 'I bought steak for dinner. I thought it would be nice to have something tasty, expensive.'

'I'll look forward to that.' His tone was flat.

When had their relationship become more about what wasn't said, the undercurrent, than the words actually spoken?

Carolynn chewed a fingernail. 'I want to integrate a bit, Roger,' she said. 'Make some friends . . . a friend, at least.' *Dr Flynn. Jessie.*

His forehead creased. 'We came here precisely because we didn't want to integrate.'

'I know, but I'm lonely.'

'You have me, Caro.'

'You're out at work all day.'

He shook his head. 'We have each other.' There was an edge to his tone. 'You don't need anyone else.'

Carolynn nodded, feeling like one of the spring-necked plastic animals in the box on the counter in the pound shop, placed there to tempt small children as their parents were paying at the till.

'We came here to escape, to protect *you*. I can't keep you safe if you make friends. Friends ask questions, they need to know about your past, your history. What would you tell them?'

The vexed tears that had been poised behind her eyes since the moment they had snapped open this morning, were creating a film across her corneas now, furring Roger's face, softening the uncompromising light in his eyes.

'And I think that you should stop seeing that psychologist. She's too close.'

Carolynn gasped; couldn't help herself. In the short time that she had been seeing Jessie Flynn, she had come to live for those sessions, looking forward to them days before they happened and sinking into depression the day after at the prospect of another week dragging by before she'd get to chat again. Really chat.

'Maybe just one more session.' That plaintive tone again; she hated herself for it. That tone wasn't her, she never used to be this needy and dependent.

'After today, you won't need to.' His voice was firm.

After the second anniversary of her death, was what he meant. As if life would miraculously return to normal when they woke tomorrow morning. As if life would be wonderful for the 364 days that followed, until the third anniversary, the fourth . . .

Carolynn dipped her gaze to the swill of burgundy liquid in the glass. 'I've been careful,' she murmured. 'She doesn't know who I really am. But I think we could be friends. I'd like her as a friend.'

'A friend?' He laughed, a bitter sound. 'You're paying her, Caro. Actually, let me correct that: *I'm* paying her. That's why she's listening to you. A woman like that will have loads of friends.'

How did he know what Jessie Flynn was like? *Oh*. She remembered now. He'd collected her after her third session. It had been Flynn's final appointment of the day, and she'd walked out with Carolynn. Roger had been leaning against the car, warming his face in the late afternoon sun, and she'd noticed even then, though she hadn't liked to admit it to herself, how his eyes widened when he clocked her psychologist.

'Christ, I might book a few sessions with her myself,' he'd muttered, half under his breath, as they drove away.

She shouldn't have been surprised at his reaction. Jessie Flynn was stunning. She even made those women on the TV chat show look ordinary, with that jet-black waist-length hair and those spectacular ice-blue eyes.

'I'm only protecting you, Carolynn. You know that, don't you?'

She gave a faint nod, tuning him out. She *could* be friends with Jessie Flynn. Tons of her old friends had been like that – cool, edgy, beautiful – when she had lived and worked in London, before motherhood, before Zoe. *She* had been like that too. Before.

'Let's save the wine, eh?' Stepping across the carpet, he laid his hands on her shoulders. 'I'll change out of my work clothes, have a shower and we can have a glass together.'

As he dropped a hand to take her glass, the words on the television cut into Carolynn's consciousness. She hadn't even noticed that the chat show had ended.

'. . . *The body of a young girl has been found at West Wittering beach. Details are still coming in, but police believe that her death was not due to natural causes. A doll was found by her side. Detective Inspector Bobby Simmons of Surrey and Sussex Major Crimes has warned parents to be vigilant.*'

The wine glass slipped from her fingers, every rotation in its tumble to the carpet freeze-framing in her mind, like individual pages in a flip-book. The glass hit the cream wool and cartwheeled, once, twice, red liquid fountaining out of it, spraying Roger's pale mustard boots, peppering the wall-paper, coating the carpet in blood red. A sliver of her brain registered the damage and knew that Roger would be furious about wine stains on his brand-new nubuck Timberlands, but all she could think was:

Another dead girl. Another doll.

7

The figure in the background was unmistakable, his black suit and hair so stark against the white quartz sand that he resembled an overgrown crow. His presence made it impossible for her to take in what the reporter speaking to camera in the foreground was saying.

West Wittering beach, wasn't it? Jessie recognized it from a couple of months ago, when Callan had booked them a day of kite-surfing lessons. It had been a disaster. She had been unable to grip the bar properly because of her ruined hand and had ended up storming off in a fury – blaming Callan, of course, transferring all her frustration, her anger at her own impotence, on to him.

It was raining down there too. The sky above the beach was metallic and wetly luminous, water pooled in shallow dips in the sand. Her eyes moved from Marilyn to the InciTent, where Tony Burrows, his lead CSI, toddler-rotund in his white forensic overall, was massaging his bald spot with a latex-gloved hand. Though she had only met him once, she recognized the tic as tension. Yellow 'Police Do

Not Cross' tape flapped in the wind, sealing a section of the dunes off from the press and a handful of local gawkers.

So, it was suspicious death or confirmed murder – must be, to get the police and press out there. Christ, that will keep Marilyn happy, she thought cynically, recognizing a moment after the notion entered her head how the last six months had coloured her attitude to everything, hating herself for that negativity. She was good at helping her patients move on from trauma, pitifully poor at heeding her own lessons. *Physician heal thyself* – what a joke that was.

' . . . *the body of a young girl has been found in sand dunes at West Wittering beach . . .*'

Oh God. A dead child. Now I really hate myself.

The picture switched suddenly to the Channel 4 News studio and Jessie froze. The view of the beach on the screen behind the presenters had been replaced by a photograph of a woman. A confident, healthy-looking woman, late-thirties, size ten or twelve, a sensible weight, blonde hair cut in a glossy bob, clear brown eyes focused on something just to the left of the camera. Her head was tilted and she was smiling, showing a perfect row of pearly white teeth.

The name displayed beneath the photo – Carolynn Reynolds – was not the name Jessie knew her by. The face and body had changed, too. In fact, the woman in the photo was barely recognizable as the woman Jessie had seen five times in her consulting room, the fifth time only this morning; the woman who had never met her gaze directly with those lightless brown eyes.

Nevertheless, she was sure that it was Laura. She had spent five hours studying her facial features, every nuance of her expression, her body and its language.

'Do you want a glass of wine?'

Laura.

She held up a hand to silence Callan. 'Shhhh, I'm listening.'

'I'll take that as a rude, ungrateful yes,' he muttered, planting a soft kiss at the base of her neck, which made her shiver despite her focus on the television screen. Then he padded barefoot into the kitchen, naked except for a pair of white boxers, his sandy blond hair dishevelled from bed. He'd worked forty-eight hours straight on a trafficking case, had got home at lunchtime and retired to bed for the afternoon. When she'd got home from work, she had stripped off and slid under the duvet, waking him up by sliding her hand into his boxers. They had made slow and languorous love before he had crashed and she had pottered downstairs in his dressing gown to flick through some patient files with the television turned on in the background.

Laura.

' . . . *the death of this young girl echoes that of little Zoe Reynolds, whose body was found in the dunes at West Wittering beach two years ago today, only a hundred metres from where this child's body has been found. Zoe's mother, Carolynn Reynolds, was tried for Zoe's murder, but acquitted nine months ago due to lack of evidence. No one has been charged with Zoe's murder. Detective Inspector Bobby Simmons of Surrey and Sussex Major Crimes, who led the investigation into the murder of little Zoe and is now on the scene at West Wittering beach, told us that it is too early to confirm a connection between the two cases.*'

Jessie scrambled for the remote to freeze the screen on Laura . . . Carolynn's photograph so that she could study it, be sure, only remembering, as her finger jabbed impotently at the pause button, that the news was live. *Shit.*

36

' . . . *we will update you as soon as we have more on this story.*'

The woman's photograph was replaced by the picture of a graph in freefall, the story something financial that Jessie immediately tuned out.

'Callan.' She still called him by his surname, even though they had been dating for nearly six months and he had virtually moved into her tiny farm worker's cottage. Gulliver in Lilliput, still hitting his head on the door frames, when he wasn't concentrating. 'One of my patients . . . clients was just on the news.'

A glass of Sauvignon and a bottle of beer in his hands, he came to stand next to her, passed her the wine.

'Did you hear what I said?'

He smothered a yawn with the back of his hand. 'Yes. What? Some woman? There's only one woman I'm interested in and she's not on the TV.' He planted another lingering kiss on her neck, which she twisted out of, but not before she'd shivered again at the feel of his lips on her skin.

'Stop trying to distract me and listen,' she said, nudging his bare stomach with her elbow. 'It's the woman I saw this morning, the one who is so weighed down by guilt that she can hardly force herself to grind through the days.'

She flicked through the TV channels on the remote, BBC1, BBC2, ITV and Channel 5, all showing other programmes or advertisements. Switching to BBC News 24, she laid the remote on the coffee table, aligning its long edge with the edge of the table, corner with corner, before she straightened.

Callan noticed, said nothing.

'The woman whose daughter died in a car accident?' he asked, stroking his hand down her arm, lacing his fingers through hers, the movement casual, sensual. But she knew why he'd done it.

Glancing at the remote, she felt the tension rise, the electric suit shiver across her skin, bit her lip to stop herself from pulling her hand from his so that she could adjust its top a few millimetres to the left, align it perfectly, absolutely perfectly, with the table edge. It was catching her eye, dragging her attention from the television and she needed to concentrate for when the child murder story, Laura . . . *no* . . . *Carolynn*, cycled around again. Her OCD had worsened, driven by the stress and disappointment of the past six months. She was making up for the lack of control over her life's bigger picture by controlling what she could, the minutiae of her environment, tidying, aligning, ordering. But the knowing didn't help with the stopping.

'Are you talking about the woman whose daughter was killed in a car accident?' Callan's voice pulled her back.

'Yes, but Zoe didn't die in a car accident. She was murdered. Laura— *Jesus*, Carolynn . . . she's actually called Carolynn, lied to me. She lied about her identity and she lied about the death of her daughter.' She looked over her shoulder and met his searching amber gaze. 'But why? Why lie?'

8

'It could be a copycat, sir,' Workman said, in a tone of forced calm. 'Zoe Reynolds' murder was a fixture in the press for months, and the spotlight was shone again when Carolynn was on trial. You'd have to have spent the last two years living in a mud hut in Papua New Guinea not to have read about it, not to know all the details.' A pause. *'Everything.'*

Eyes fixed on the misty hummock that was the Isle of Wight fifteen kilometres across the Solent to the south, the curved grey back of a breaching whale, Marilyn nodded, hoping she wouldn't notice that his hands were shaking.

Everything.

Workman was right. The column centimetres the Zoe Reynolds case had occupied would add up to kilometres, every sordid bloody detail raked over countless times, however hard he had tried to keep some things back, just a few elements of the poor little girl's murder, to preserve some dignity for her memory if nothing else. *Zoe Reynolds.* That name forever seared into his memory as if it had been cattle-branded on to his temporal lobe. The statistics of child abductions and murders in the UK branded there also, from the many hours he'd spent trawling through the data, buttonholing experts, interviewing convicted paedophiles to try to understand their thought processes, eliminating paedophilia as a possibility, cycling back again and again to the conviction that it must have been the child's mother, that he had been right to pursue her as hard as he had done, despite being unable to amass enough evidence to nail a guilty verdict.

In the twenty-two years since he joined Surrey and Sussex Major Crimes, Zoe Reynolds' murder was the only case that he still took to bed with him at night; his own personal abject failure. Around two hundred children were unlawfully killed in the UK each year, with at least three quarters of those deaths due to abuse or neglect by a parent – filicide – or other close relation. And those were only the reported cases. The woman he'd spoken with at the National Society for the Prevention of Cruelty to children had told him that the statistic was an under-estimation, that each year some parents literally got away with murder. Not all parents who kill their children live on benefits in some sink estate, she'd told him. Affluent parents have tempers too. Affluent parents lose control. The inference wasn't lost on Marilyn: fall down the stairs in a middle-class household and you've slipped; do the same in a tower block with alcoholic parents and your mum or dad threw you down them.

'A copycat,' he murmured, finally acknowledging Workman's comment, yanking on the knot to loosen his tie, lessen the tightening in his airways. Copycat crimes were far from uncommon. *Two years to the day.* 'Yes, it could be.'

The soft sigh that he wasn't supposed to have heard over

the shore breeze told him that she had noted the lack of conviction in his tone. She'd been by his side throughout that first case, had been affected by little Zoe's murder – in truth, even more than he had been. She hadn't, though, shared his dogged conviction that the mother, Carolynn Reynolds, was responsible. Despite knowing the statistic on child murders as well as he did, she found it hard to accept that a mother *could* kill her own daughter. Not *that* pretty, polished mother. Not *that* daughter. Not in that cold-blooded way. Given Workman's personal history – her struggle to come to terms with her own childlessness due to infertility – he had doubted her ability to remain objective. He'd come close to having her sidelined for the duration of the investigation, but eventually decided against because losing DS Sarah Workman would have been akin to hacking off his right arm. He had needed her support, particularly with so public a case, his work under such close scrutiny, so he'd kept her with him but monitored her closely, tempering her opinions with a spade full of salt. He'd caught her a few times, studying the crime scene photographs of the dead child, wallowing unhealthily in them, he'd thought at the time. He'd done the same, but privately, and even as he was looking for the umpteenth time, he knew that what he was doing was mentally destructive, the visual equivalent of sticking needles under his fingernails.

'We owe it to this little girl to—'

Marilyn raised a hand, cutting her off.

'We do indeed. And we will.' He dropped his hand to her shoulder. 'And I don't need a lecture about objectivity, thanks, Sarah. Come on, let's leave Burrows to it, get back to base and brief the team. I'll start jibbering if I don't get away from the noise of these bloody seagulls.'

* * *

41

The journalists who had thronged the crime scene on the beach seemed to have made it back to the station in Chichester quicker than he had, which, given he was still driving his beloved Z3 – sixteen years old, 143,000 miles on the clock and performing to every bit of its age and mileage – he had to acknowledge wasn't surprising.

Monitoring police radio frequencies 24/7 for the first whiff of a heinous crime, the press piranhas had gone into a frenzy the moment they found one. Marilyn was engulfed as soon as he stepped from the car: voice recorders and cameras, like the black eyes of Cyclops, shoved into his face. Shouldering through them, he made it to the concrete steps into the station, where at least his back was covered by the closed front door. Stopping, he turned under the stone arch, squinting against the sinking sun's rays, knowing that he might as well face the pack now than delay it. Pain now, double pain with bells on later when they'd had a chance to feed off each other, speculate, the process always made more creative, the conclusions more fantastical and inflammatory when they had no factual information to work with. He wasn't a natural politician, preferred just to get on with the job and let his success rate speak for itself. He didn't want to become one of those policemen who always had their eye on the main chance, on creating good impressions over delivering results, on the next promotion, but even he'd realized, in a flash of deeply uncomfortable clarity out on the beach, that he would need as many people on his side as he could get, given the high-profile disaster that the Zoe Reynolds case had been. *His* personal high-profile disaster.

Moreover, he would never forgive himself if this little girl's killer escaped justice as Zoe's had. One ghostly child remonstrating with him in the early hours was already one too many. He held up his hand to silence the chatter and still the jostling.

'The body of a young girl was found in the sand dunes at West Wittering beach by a passer-by late this afternoon. Dr Ghoshal, the Home Office pathologist, estimates her to be nine or ten years old.'

Shouted questions:

'Who found her?'

'Where exactly was she found?'

'How long has she been dead for?'

'How was she killed?'

He noticed a few elbows connecting with ribs as they vied for the best spot. No raised hands or other such decorum, the press pack aptly named. Stray dogs being tossed a roast chicken would behave better. Ignoring the questions, he pressed on:

'We have not yet identified the child and so far no one has come forward to tell us that their daughter is missing. My first priority is to identify her.'

Questions coming thick and fast:

'What does she look like? Hair colour, eye colour—'

'How are you going to identify her?'

'What kind of family do you think the kid comes from if no one has noticed she's missing?'

Fair question that one, but he ignored it too. It wasn't his job to speculate or criticize. His ex-wife would fall about laughing if she caught him casting judgement on bad parenting on television.

'How was she killed?'

'Are there any suspects?'

And then *the* question, the one he knew would come:

'Do you think that this second girl was murdered by the same person who murdered Zoe Reynolds? It's too much of a coincidence, surely, otherwise? A couple of hundred metres from the spot where she was found, two years to the day?'

Two years ago, to the day.

. The visceral memory of coming upon Zoe's strangled body, that vile doll lying beside her, black felt-tip marks around its neck aping the strangulation bruises on Zoe's. The image visited him often, with unrelenting clarity, as the image of this second little girl's body would no doubt visit him also.

Another dead child. Another doll.

The same doll – make and model – he was sure of it. The doll's image was something he'd never forget. It had been so lifelike, but at the same time not, like one of the countless bodies he'd seen on dissecting tables, a lifelike carcass without life or soul. The doll's eyes, particularly, had stuck in his mind. Brown – the same colour as little Zoe's eyes.

And the doll found beside this child?

Green.

It hadn't occurred to him at the time, back on the beach, but both the child and the doll had green eyes. He saw them now in his mind's eye: the child's eyes a deep sea green, already clouding over, the doll blinking its glassy green eyes at Burrows as he lifted it with gloved hands and slid it into an evidence bag.

Brown to match Zoe's eyes. Green to match this second little dead girl's eyes. *Jesus, what the hell am I dealing with?* Had that detail been in the press? Would a copycat know? Or was it just coincidence that the dolls' eyes matched the girls'?

Coincidence?

Whatever he was about to tell the press in an effort to defuse tension around the possibility of a double child murderer being on the loose in this sleepy seaside town, he didn't believe in coincidences.

The restless increase in volume from the press pack brought him back to the moment.

'It is far too early to make any judgements as to whether the murder of this little girl and the murder of Zoe Reynolds, two years ago, are connected. However, I would like to speak with Zoe's parents and would ask them to get in touch with me as a matter of urgency.'

Holding up a hand to signal that the impromptu press conference was over, receiving a barrage of new questions in reply, he backed up the stairs, still facing them. *Never good to turn your back on a journalist, unless you want a knife between the shoulder blades.*

'We will hold a full press conference in due course to update you all properly on the progress of this case,' he concluded. 'Now if you will excuse me, I have a child murder to solve.' *A second child murder . . .*

9

Carolynn turned the taps on full force in the downstairs cloakroom, though Roger would know that the rush of water was to mask another sound, the guttural sound of her retching. Her stomach heaved and she vomited again, a stream of hot bile the colour of buttercups running over her fingers. Sitting back on her haunches, she sucked in a breath, locking on to the feeling of the cold floor tiles against her legs, holding that sense of chill calm in her mind as her stomach heaved again, heaved and settled.

Pushing herself to her feet, she reached for the hand towel, catching her reflection in the bathroom mirror as she did so. *Lollipop*. A pasty, wan, lollipop. She and her friends used to laugh at women like her, women they called lollipops because their heads were so ludicrously oversized on their emaciated bodies, rail-thin models who posted pictures of themselves on Instagram clutching plates of pizza in an attempt to convince people that they *really did* eat. Just as she now kept the fridge filled and cooked meal after meal to convince Roger that she was eating, to keep him off her back, though the reality was every mouthful tasted like cardboard and she ended up tossing most of the food into the caravan park's bins so Roger wouldn't catch her out.

She swiped a hand across the mirror, leaving a streak of bile across the glass, fuzzing her own grotesque image from view.

Back in the sitting room, the silence jarring, Carolynn realized that the television was now off. Roger watched her gaze track to the blank screen.

'I switched it off,' he said, matter-of-factly. 'We don't need to see any more.'

'What are we going to do, Roger?'

'Do?' His eyes registered surprise.

'I need to understand what the police are thinking.'

'You were acquitted, Carolynn.'

She nodded, concentrating hard on the brown vines twisting through the wallpaper like strings of DNA, not meeting his searching gaze. She hated this room, had always felt claustrophobic in it, and now she felt as if the vines were coiling around her, squeezing her throat with each rasping breath she managed.

'That detective inspector—' Even now, nine months since the collapse of her trial, since they had fled down here to anonymity, she couldn't bear to say his name. The man who had hounded her, who was convinced of her guilt, still, no doubt. She had caught his eye as she'd left the Old Bailey a free woman, had recognized the cynicism and anger in his look. He would never stop hunting her.

And now. Now he had another reason. A second dead child. High-octane fuel to his fire.

'That detective inspector said on the news that he would like to speak with me . . . with, uh, with us.'

'He has to find us first, and he won't be able to do that. Nobody knows where we are. We left no trace. They won't find us. They won't expect us to be living here in Bracklesham Bay, so close to where Zoe was murdered. It was a clever choice.'

Carolynn nodded distractedly. The location, a sprawling seaside town crammed with tourists and seasonal workers in summer, shuttered and battened down, locals retreating inside to their hearths and their television sets in winter, provided perfect anonymity. Roger had read about the beautiful, kilometres-long white-sand beaches that stretched from Bracklesham Bay to East and West Wittering in *The Sunday Times* a few years ago, and they had spent a long weekend here every September since, a last hurrah before Zoe went back to school.

'My photograph was on the news. It will be in every paper. I can't face it again. I can't face that whole process, being treated like a side of meat.'

My body, the searches – they said that they wanted to make sure I didn't have any hidden drugs, but really they just wanted to dehumanize me, remove every shred of my dignity.

'I could never go through that again, Roger.' Her voice shook. 'I couldn't—'

Complete strangers screaming at me in the street, calling me a child murderer, dragging at my clothes and hair, spitting in my face.

'You won't have to, because they won't find us,' he said firmly. 'You don't look like you used to. Your hair is different, your face, your body. There's nothing left of your body.' He emitted a brief, heartless laugh. 'Remember that book we used to read to . . . to Zoe?'

Carolynn flinched at the sound of Zoe's name on his lips.

'Stick Man. Do you remember it, my Stick Lady love?' His fingers and thumb pinched the skin of her upper arm. His grip left two white indents, which she knew would turn black. Was she bruising more easily these days? 'You are virtually unrecognizable now, Carolynn.'

She tried to suppress the involuntary shudder as his arms slid around her waist and he stepped forward, closing the gap between them, pressing himself against her. She wanted to shove him away, dismiss him, but she couldn't. She needed his support, his complicity. They were in this together.

'And this little girl's death is totally different,' he murmured, his breath misting hot and damp against her ear, making her want to shudder all over again. 'You were nowhere near West Wittering beach this afternoon, were you?'

She had been the one to find Zoe dead in the sand dunes of West Wittering beach two years ago. She had left footprints all over the crime scene, her DNA had been all over her daughter's body – *Well, it would have been, wouldn't it? I'm her mother* – her fingerprints on that disgusting doll with the moving eyes and the black marks around its neck. Roger was right. This *was* different.

'You have an alibi. You were here, at home.'

Carolynn gave an uncertain nod.

'Weren't you?' he pressed. 'Apart from that quick trip to the supermarket?'

'Yes,' she lied. 'But I was alone.'

'It was dull, rainy. You had the lights on in the kitchen when I got back. Someone would have seen you through the window. Someone from the caravan park.'

'Yes,' she murmured listlessly.

She had been out running again, on the beach, down to

49

East Wittering and further, to the west, pounding along the sand, the rain peppering her face, the beach deserted. Only a kite-surfer zipping backwards and forwards two hundred metres offshore, too far away to attest to the identity of anyone on the beach. Her breath caught in her throat. *Oh God.*

'What?' Roger asked.

'Nothing.'

His eyes remained fixed on her face, weighing, judging.

'Really, Roger, it was *nothing.*'

She pressed her hands against his chest and levered him away from her, trying to keep the relief she felt at the widening space between them from telegraphing itself to her face.

'Take some of your pills and go to bed early. Stay away from the windows, away from television. An early night will do you good. And tomorrow . . . ' He paused. 'Tomorrow everything will look better.'

She nodded dully. The last thing she needed was to sleep, to dream. She wanted to think. The news of the little girl's death had brought back something about the day she had found Zoe's body, something that was hovering at the edge of her memory, just out reach.

Roger left the sitting room and she heard him jogging up the stairs, returning a moment later, two small white pills nestled in the palm of his hand. Flunitrazepam. He had bought the pills, liquid, every possible method of sedating her, off the Internet from Malaysia, had had them delivered to a PO Box in Chichester, which he had opened under their new false identity.

She looked at the pills and shook her head. 'I might go for a run.'

'Are you serious, Carolynn. Now? With that police and media circus out there? You're upset and you need to calm down.'

They stood, facing off against each other across the sitting room. Carolynn chewed at the skin around her thumbnail.

'Stop that, Carolynn. You'll make your hands look ugly.'

Dropping her hand, she nodded dully. He was right about the nail-biting, about the pills, about staying inside. He was always right these days. He hadn't used to be, when they first got married, but now she could see that he was. Always. When had the tables turned? Since she had been accused of Zoe's murder, since the trial? Or earlier than that? Since becoming a mother had leeched her energy and her happiness?

But she longed to experience the feeling of endorphins coursing through her body, the euphoria, however temporary that came with utter physical exhaustion. Sometimes when she returned from her runs along the beach, something had shifted inside her and she found some small measure of peace. Often though, only her body was changed, the miles she'd run registering themselves in physical exhaustion, but everything else, her mind, the thoughts that haunted her waking hours, unchanged. Still, running was like a drug to her now, her only hope of respite, however temporary.

'Here.' He held out his hand. 'Take your pills.'

Obediently, Carolynn extended her right hand for the pills, her left for the water. He watched as she popped first one and then the other into her mouth. His eyes tracked the movement of her hand as she raised the glass to her lips and took a sip. Tilting forward, he planted a soft kiss on her cheek, grimacing, she could sense without even seeing his expression, as the downy white lanugo hair on her face tickled his lips.

'I can't go back,' she said again, when he had stepped away, aware of the thread of desperation in her voice. 'I can't go through all that again. I *can't*.'

'You won't need to, but you have to listen to me, do what I tell you.'

She nodded. No matter how hard she looked into his eyes, searched for something there, all she ever saw was emptiness. It was the same emptiness she saw in her own.

'That means no friends, for starters. And no more visits to Dr Flynn.'

She started to speak, to object, but his fingers moved to cover her mouth, cutting her off.

'We can't risk getting close to people, Carolynn. You know that. Not now. Not with this second little girl dead, so close to where you found— where Zoe was found. It's too much of a risk. They'll find us and then they'll find out . . . they'll find out the truth this time and we just can't take that chance.'

The truth.

He left the sitting room and she spat the pills into her palm and slipped them into her pocket.

10

Marilyn stood at the front of the incident room and contemplated the hastily assembled team. Sarah Workman had looked washed-out on the beach, but he'd put it down to the light filtering through grey clouds; now, under the harsh fluorescent strips, her skin was a sickly pale grey and she looked even worse. Already the stress of the case was taking its toll, and there would doubtless be sleepless nights and soaring stress levels to come for all of them. He met her gaze and gave her what he hoped was a reassuring smile, but was more likely a maniacal grimace. Nothing about this case promoted a genuine smile.

'Good evening, everyone. I won't keep you for long, as we have a lot to do.'

A photograph of the dead girl was already tacked to the whiteboard behind him, where it would stay throughout the investigation. Once they found out who she was, it would be joined by one of her alive, smiling preferably, looking like the undefiled child she had been, reminding everyone why they were here, who the eighteen hour days were for.

'As you all know, the body of a young girl was found in the sand dunes at West Wittering beach earlier this evening.' He glanced down at the notes he'd scribbled, though he knew everything, what little they had so far, by heart. 'I don't have much to give you, I'm afraid. Dr Ghoshal will perform the autopsy tomorrow, but his preliminary assessment is that she was killed by strangulation. She was wearing what looked to be a school uniform – white shirt, navy-blue jumper and navy trousers, no identifying school badge – and her clothing wasn't disturbed, so it is unlikely that she was a victim of sexual assault, though of course the autopsy will confirm or refute that.' He paused. 'A doll in a pink ballerina dress was found by her side. The doll had black marks drawn around its neck with felt-tip pen. The black marks aped the strangulation bruise marks around the little girl's neck.'

His gaze scanned the assembled faces as they digested the information. A stranger could be forgiven for thinking them indifferent; Marilyn knew better, knew that the little girl's murder had touched them all deeply, just as Zoe Reynolds' had done two years previously.

Arthur Lawford, the exhibits officer, raised his hand. He had been with Surrey and Sussex Major Crimes longer even than Marilyn, a solid thirty years on the job and still a sergeant, a role he was more than happy to languish in until retirement. Not everyone could be the star player; not everyone wanted to be. Lawford had been the exhibits officer on the Zoe Reynolds case, and along with Marilyn and Workman he'd lived through the disaster it had become.

'A doll, sir?' The inference clear.

Marilyn nodded. 'Similar.' He paused. 'The same. Identical, except for the colour of her . . . of its eyes.'

Lawford frowned. 'Its eyes, sir?'

'What colour were the eyes of the doll we found by Zoe Reynolds' body, Artie?'

'I don't remember, sir.'

'Brown. They were brown, weren't they?'

Lawford shrugged. 'I don't remember.'

'Think about it, Artie, *think*. They were the same colour as the little girl's, weren't they? Brown? The same colour as Zoe's eyes?'

He scanned the room again. Its occupants stilled, the usual background noises – the shifting of bottoms in seats, crossing and uncrossing of legs, the rustle of clothing – had ceased. He knew what they were all thinking. Only DC Cara was new to the team. The rest had worked with him on the Zoe Reynolds case, had been party to his unswerving conviction that Carolynn Reynolds had murdered her own daughter, had watched him wilt, shrivel, as the trial progressed and it became clear that they hadn't secured enough evidence to convict. He couldn't afford to get emotionally involved in this second murder case, had to maintain a professional distance. *Easier said than done.*

'Check will you, please, Artie, and let me know,' Marilyn said as casually as he could manage.

'Yes, sir.'

Tapping the whiteboard behind him, Marilyn indicated the list he'd scribbled. 'Our priorities are to identify the dead child and interview her parents; interview the woman who found her body; get uniforms on the ground in the beach car park, the village centre, on the road in and out of East and West Wittering villages and on the knock to try to locate some witnesses. We need to construct a detailed timeline of the little girl's movements, from when she left her school – whether that was alone, with one or both of her parents, or with a friend or friends – to when she was killed. Most prep-schools finish at three-thirty, so there isn't a lot of time between her leaving school and her meeting her death. That suggests to me that the school is local to the beach, in Bracklesham Bay, East or West Wittering. There can't be many, so let's find out where she was a pupil quickly, based on her uniform. Lastly, we need to find Carolynn and Roger Reynolds, Zoe Reynolds' parents. Though this is something I won't be disclosing to the press, I would be very surprised if this second child's murder isn't linked to Zoe's. I made enquiries earlier this evening and it appears that the Reynolds have disappeared.' *Run.* He didn't say it.

'Are they suspects, sir?' a voice from the back of the room asked. 'Is *she* a suspect?'

A knock on the door saved Marilyn from having to answer the million-dollar question to which he hadn't yet formulated a balanced, unprejudiced answer. DC Darren Cara stepped through the doorway, holding up a piece of paper.

'I think we have a name for the little girl, sir – Jodie Trigg. Call just came through. The mother got back from work half an hour ago and found her daughter missing. Her bed looked as if it hasn't been slept in. The description of her daughter matches that of the dead child.'

'And Jodie Trigg's mother has just realized that she's missing now?' Marilyn said angrily. He glanced at his watch. 'It's knocking midnight. The little girl has been dead eight hours, for Christ's sake.'

Cara gave a slight shrug of his shoulders.

'What about friends and relatives?' Marilyn asked. 'Has she checked with them?'

'She has a sister in Bognor Regis, but Jodie isn't there.

The mother – Deborah, Debs Trigg, she's called – lives at Seaview Caravan Park in Bracklesham Bay. She called park security and asked around her neighbours and Jodie hasn't been seen since she left for school this morning. She's a pupil at East Wittering Community Primary. I tracked down the school's headmistress and she confirmed that Jodie was at school all day today, though she did mention that Jodie is not the best attendee and often turns up late. She also confirmed that the children wear a navy-blue uniform. Only the blazer has the school badge on it.'

Marilyn nodded. 'And the child wasn't wearing a blazer. Thorough job, DC Cara. Thank you.' His gaze moved from Cara back to the assembled team. 'Have we had any other calls about missing children?'

A mass shaking of heads. Marilyn raised a surprised eyebrow. Typically, when a serious crime made the news, their phones rang off the hook with people eager to get a slice of the macabre action. The over-helpful, the hoaxers, the gloaters, the ghouls and the common or garden nutters: the whole gamut. This was the reason he had only ever appealed one case on *Crimewatch* Zoe Reynolds, driven by utter desperation after her mother had been released and all other investigative avenues closed. A *Crimewatch* reconstruction could be useful for jogging memories, but it inevitably resulted in a deluge of information, most of it entirely useless. But he had been surprised, back then too, at how few hoax calls they'd received when Zoe's murder was re-enacted on BBC One: an unexpectedly compassionate response. It seemed as if this second murdered little girl – Jodie Trigg, he reminded himself, they had her name now – was engendering the same solicitude. The violent murder of a young child too tragic for even the crazies to wallow in.

Marilyn took the piece of paper that Cara was holding out to him and read: Jodie Trigg, mother, Deborah (Debs) Trigg, Buena Vista, Seaview Caravan Park, Bracklesham Bay. It was a sprawling park of rectangular static mobile homes, a beige-hued blot on the landscape, half a kilometre eastwards along the beach from East Wittering, a kilometre from West. At its centre was a huge entertainment complex, jammed with arcade games and slot machines and serviced by a huge restaurant and a couple of snack bars which served anything that could be fried to within an inch of its life. There was a nod to health and fitness in the form of a swimming pool, resplendent with fake palms and a tiled beach that sloped into one side of the pool. He'd taken his own kids there once, so many years ago that it could have been last century – *probably was* – and he still shuddered at the memory of curly hairs clogging the drains in the changing rooms and the stench of chlorine masking eau-de-kiddies'-piss.

Some caravans were holiday lets, others occupied by permanent residents whose number, he assumed, included Debs Trigg and her daughter Jodie. No mention of a father, he noticed, then immediately chastised himself for making an assumption about the structure of their family purely based on where they lived. He knew all too well that people held similar, uninformed prejudices about his own fifteen-year absence from his now adult children's lives. Well-justified prejudices, in his case.

'Listen up,' he said, refocusing. 'DS Dave Johnson will take the lead on organizing the uniforms. DS Workman and I will go to Seaview Caravan Park now to speak with Debs Trigg. Cara, you take the lead on the search for Carolynn and Roger Reynolds.'

'Do you think the two cases are linked?' Cara asked.

Marilyn shrugged. Another awkward question he'd happily duck. Privately, he was iron-clad certain, given the location of the murder, the date, and the arrangement of the girl's body in the heart of shells, an identical doll by her side, that the two cases were linked, but he wasn't about to share that certainty this early on, even to his team. 'It's too soon to say for sure, but as a courtesy, if nothing else, we should get in touch with them. They'll be seeing all this on the news and it will bring everything that they experienced two years ago straight back to the surface. I'd like to chat with them in person, reassure them that we haven't forgotten little Zoe.' It was an evasive answer, the best he was going to give at the moment.

'What about Ruby Lovatt, the woman who found Jodie's body?' Workman asked. 'She's still in an interview room downstairs. We could divide and conquer.'

Marilyn shook his head. After the Zoe Reynolds disaster, he wanted, *needed*, to be in on all the action on this new case. He couldn't afford to miss anything, any nuance.

'Send her home and ask her to come back first thing tomorrow, eight a.m. Cara, get a family liaison officer to meet us at the Trigg's caravan, will you?'

His gaze made one final circuit of the room and settled again on Workman.

'Steel yourself, Sarah. We have a difficult house call to make.'

11

Jessie liked to leave the curtains open at night, to let the stars and the moon come into the bedroom with them. It reminded her of Wimbledon: of the winter evening she and Jamie had wrapped themselves up in blankets and taken their mugs of hot chocolate outside, lain on their backs on the lawn, Jessie pointing out the bear constellations, Ursula Major and Ursula Minor, to Jamie and Pandy, his beloved cuddly panda; of standing at her bedroom window at night, when the rest of the house was asleep, tracking the stars that made up her star sign, Gemini.

When she'd lived with her father and Diane in their narrow terraced house in frenetic Fulham, all she had been able to see through her attic bedroom's skylight was the sodium streetlights' orange blanket, cloaking the moon and stars. She had hated the feeling, ever since, of being unable to see the night sky from her bedroom. Callan didn't mind. He liked the outdoors, was happy to leave the curtains open and let the night flood into the bedroom with them.

With the soft mattress underneath her, the warmth of

Callan's hard body next to her, she should have drifted easily to sleep, but her mind kept circling back to the television news, to Laura . . . *Carolynn*.

'What's wrong, Jessie?' Callan murmured, his lips moving against her ear. She could feel him, warm and semi-hard against her thigh. Half-sleepy, half-aroused. Shifting on to her side, she shuffled the gap between them closed and slid her arms around his neck.

'Nothing.'

'Sure?' His fingers moved absently-mindedly through her hair.

'Sure.' Linking her fingers with his, she guided his hand to her chest, placed it right over her heart. 'Your hand would be more gainfully employed somewhere around here, I feel, Mr Callan.'

Shifting closer, moulding her naked body to his, she kissed him deeply, her tongue teasing his, felt him harden, fully awake now. And though she tried to lock on to the feeling of his lips against hers, his thumb circling her nipple, the sensation firing hot in her groin, all she could think of was Carolynn, her face plastered all over the television screen. Carolynn Reynolds and two murdered girls.

I'd hate you to actually be able to read my mind. She had been a long way from a mind reader with that woman.

She felt Callan's hands on her shoulders, rolling her gently on to her back, and he moved on top of her, the muscles on his chest and abdomen hard against her breasts and stomach, his weight pinning her down.

Another little girl murdered in the same place Carolynn's daughter had been murdered two years ago. Two years to the day. September seventh. Lucky seven. Seven detestable sins.

61

Callan's knee eased between both of hers and she felt his hand stroke down her stomach, his fingers slip between her legs, slowly inside her. She gasped, moving her hands to his shoulders, simultaneously holding him away and digging her nails into his back, her body responding, her mind somewhere else, beyond her control, detached from the maelstrom of desire, obsessing.

Outside, the night sky, lit only by a sliver of moon, was so black that the stars dotting it seemed to be pulsing, alive with energy. The curtains framing either side of the window caught her eye. Caught and held it. The left curtain was flush against the window frame, but the right was half-drawn, truncating her view of the sky. The electric suit tingled against her skin.

'Callan,' she murmured. He was rock hard against her thigh now.

'Yeah?'

Usually, she loved making love with him, loved to mould herself around him as he moved inside her, loved to grate her nails down his back as she came. But now the curtains were lodged in her mind along with Carolynn's lies, two little dead girls, and the electric suit was hissing and snapping.

'Callan, I just want to, uh, to look at the stars quickly.'

'Huh?'

'I just want to look at the stars.'

'What?' Pushing himself up on to his hands, he stared down at her incredulously.

Tilting her head so that she didn't have to lock eyes with him, she slid out from under him. 'I'll only be a minute,' she said.

Rolling back to his side of the bed, Callan put his hands over his face and groaned. 'Jesus Christ, Jessie.'

'I'm sorry, but it's such a beautiful night. It's going to rain soon and then the stars will be obscured by clouds.'

Her excuse sounded ridiculous, even to her ears, but on the spot she couldn't think of anything more convincing. Climbing out of bed, she padded over to the window. Raising her arms as nonchalantly as she could manage, the electric suit hot against her skin, she ran her hand quickly down the edge of the right-hand curtain, pushing it back, aligning it with the window frame.

The left curtain was straight; the right still wasn't. She repeated the movement again, sliding both hands down the curtains in unison this time.

Again – three.

'What the hell are you doing, Jessie?'

'I'm just looking at the stars, like I said,' she managed. 'They're stunning tonight.'

The curtains were straight. She knew in her logical mind that they were straight, but the electric suit still hissed and snapped.

Four.

Quickly – five. Still no release.

Perhaps if she ran her hands down the curtains seven times, lucky seven, she'd know they were straight.

'Enough now,' Callan said, his tone one of suppressed anger. 'Come back to bed.'

'In a minute.'

She had to reach lucky seven, then the curtains would be straight, the electric suit would die down, she'd be able to return to bed, make love with Callan, not think about

Carolynn and the lies that she had told. Not think about two little dead girls.

'For fuck's sake, Jessie,' Callan muttered, subsiding back against his pillows.

How many times? Four? Had it been four?

She couldn't concentrate, knowing that Callan was watching her. Her rational mind acknowledged that her behaviour, the need, was abnormal, but the compulsion to perform the ritual was too strong to resist.

Four? No – *no*, five.

'I can see Gemini,' she managed, running her hand back down the curtain again. *Yin and yang. Light and dark. Good and evil.*

'Stop now, Jessie.'

Without answering, she shook her head.

She was pretending to look at the night sky, but Callan knew exactly what she was doing, recognized the compulsion that drove her to perform the ritual even as he found it impossible to understand. The curtains were perfectly aligned, but that didn't seem to matter. Her OCD had worsened since she'd been invalided from the army and he had no idea what to do about it, how to help her.

Seven. The heat from the electric suit died, as if she'd found the secret emergency 'Off' switch.

When she returned to the bed, Callan was lying on his back, staring up at the ceiling. Sliding under the covers, she shuffled across, closing the space between them and pressed her chilled body against his. Curling an arm over his chest, a leg over his thighs, she buried her face into his neck. His body was warm, but she could only feel his bones and the muscles that wrapped around them. Nothing yielded to her touch.

'I need to go to the bathroom,' he said, rolling away from her.

He locked the bathroom door and switched on the shower. His erection had died, but his balls were aching. Stepping under the jet of warm water, he tilted forward, resting one hand against the cool tiles, letting the water run down his back while he masturbated. Jessie would know what he was doing, but he didn't give a shit.

When he climbed back into bed she was lying motionless, staring up at the ceiling as he had been while she'd been fiddling with the curtains. Though he knew that the compulsions were out of her control, he felt unreasonably angry. He had been so ready to make love to her that it hurt.

'I'm sorry, Callan,' she murmured, shifting on to her side to face him. Reaching out, she traced her fingers across his cheek, to the scarred rose of the Taliban bullet wound on his temple.

'It's fine,' he muttered, not moving, not responding physically.

'I'm sorry,' she repeated. 'I'm a pain. I know that I'm being a pain. More than a pain.'

He sighed. 'It's fine, Jessie. I understand.' Though he didn't.

'I love you, Callan.'

Sliding an arm around her, he pulled her close and kissed the top of her head, the slight dampness left on his skin from the shower, warming between them.

'I love you too, Jessie. Now go to sleep.'

'Night, Callan,' she murmured.

Now go to sleep.

But would she? Could she? Her mind was starting to race again.

12

The only view that Buena Vista benefited from was a three-sixty of other static mobile homes, so close on all sides that a swinging cat would have had its head caved in. Buena Vista itself was dark cream, a tarmac parking area to its left-hand side, empty of cars, an ankle-high white plastic picket fence demarcating a narrow, rectangular garden to its right. Lights shone through grey net curtains that covered a full-width window at the near end, and other smaller aluminium framed windows dotted the caravan's carcass, casting yellow rectangles on to the surrounding mobile homes. Though nothing about him or Workman overtly said 'police', their combined forty-plus years in the force must have left some indelible external mark, because he sensed that they were being watched by multiple pairs of eyes as they skirted Buena Vista to locate the front door.

In the narrow garden, a rotary dryer sagged under the weight of washing, limp in the cool night air, and someone had planted a few perennials, most of them wilted from neglect. But it was the child's pink bicycle leaning against the concrete steps leading to the door that tightened Marilyn's throat. He plucked at the knot of his tie to loosen it, the result fruitless, the constriction in his airways undiminished.

Before he knocked, he glanced over his shoulder at Workman. Her expression was detached, her gaze fixed resolutely on what would have been his back, if he hadn't turned unexpectedly and caught her eye. She wasn't the only one who appeared devoid of emotion. As he turned back to knock, he met his own faint reflection in the rectangle of mirrored glass set into the door panel, recognized the studied expression of neutrality that he'd become so adept at fixing to his face when the situation required it.

The woman who yanked the door open before his fist had connected was a little over five foot tall, heavy in a solid, shapeless way. Her dark hair, pulled into a tight ponytail, was dyed a few shades too dark, accentuating the paleness of her skin. 'Indoor' skin, Marilyn found himself thinking, despite her living right by a stunning beach. Green eyes – the little girl's eyes, Jodie's eyes, Marilyn recognized immediately – ringed with red, met his. He raised his warrant card and Debs Trigg stepped back from the door, her face collapsing in on itself.

She had called the police when she had discovered Jodie's bed empty and unslept in, and seen Marilyn's appeal to identify the dead child on a news channel. She must therefore have had a strong suspicion that the murdered girl was her Jodie, but their poker-faced presence at her door was the final big nail in the coffin of her hope.

An animal yelp of pure pain rooted Marilyn to the spot. Jack-knifing on to the sofa, Debs Trigg scratched clawed fingers down her cheeks, raising bloody red weals in their

67

wake. Workman shoved past Marilyn, knocking his shoulder in the cramped space, and caught Trigg's wrists.

'Don't, love, don't do that. Please don't hurt yourself like that.'

He should have stepped forward himself, he knew, should have grabbed her wrists himself, but from the moment he had set eyes on her all he could think of was Zoe Reynolds, his mind spinning back to Carolynn on her knees in the beach car park cradling Zoe's limp body and howling, and later, sitting opposite him in the interview room at Chichester police station, so composed by then, so closed-down. He had been wholly unable to see anything in those dark eyes, or to decipher the secrets buried in the brain behind them. A second child was dead because of his ineptitude.

His gaze moved past Debs Trigg and Workman to the photograph of Jodie on the shelf behind the sofa, a ten by eight colour shot of a laughing child, arms spread wide, wind flapping her yellow summer dress around her thighs, the white sails of yachts in the background. Unmistakably West Wittering beach. Unmistakably the little girl he had seen dead this morning, a chain of bruises around her neck, that vile doll by her side, the last chink of uncertainty closed. Heartbreaking. Utterly heartbreaking and his responsibility. His fault. His failure.

It took Debs Trigg a long time to stop crying. Marilyn and Workman had exchanged tense glances and he had resumed staring through the nets at the blank white backside of the static caravan next door while Workman did her best to comfort the distraught woman. Slipping his mobile from his pocket, Marilyn fired off a quick text to DC Cara, asking him to chase the family liaison officer pronto. The sooner he could escape from this hellhole of emotion and get back to investigating little Jodie's death, the better for all concerned.

Rising from the sofa, Trigg scrabbled for the packet of Superkings on the table and lit a cigarette, sinking back beside Workman, hunching her shoulders and folding an arm across her chest – defensive body language, Marilyn recognized, inwardly allowing himself a brief, cynical smile at the knowledge and terminology he had absorbed from Jessie Flynn.

'It's definitely her, isn't it?' she muttered, on a stream of smoky breath. 'Definitely?'

'We'll need you or a relative to formally identify her, but yes, we're pretty certain that the girl found this afternoon in the dunes at West Wittering is your daughter, Jodie,' he said, in the businesslike tone he resorted to when faced with emotionally charged situations. 'She was wearing a navy-blue school unform, white shirt, navy jumper and trousers. She also had a pendant necklace, with two sets of footprints engraved on it, around her neck.'

Hauling smoke into her lungs through pale lips, Trigg nodded, tear-stained eyes fixed on the floor. 'She loved that necklace. Found it on the beach one day when she was walking home from school, she did, a couple of months ago. I told her she should hand it in, but—' she broke off with a shrug. 'You know, and she loved it an' all, so I just let her keep it.'

Workman pulled a black notebook from her pocket and Marilyn noticed her shift sideways, expanding the space between her and Debs, subtly re-establishing a professional distance. She made a note about the necklace in the book.

'I need to ask you a few questions, Mrs Trigg,' Marilyn continued. 'To help us with the investigation.'

'Miss. There isn't a Mr – though I think you already worked that out, didn't you, Inspector?' She took another tense drag of the cigarette. 'Ask away.'

'Why didn't you report Jodie missing earlier?

'I was at work, wasn't I.'

'Where do you work?'

'F & G Foods in Chichester, on the packing line.'

Workman wrote the name of Debs' employer in her notebook.

'What time did you get home?' Marilyn continued.

'I'm on lates this week. My shift is midday until ten p.m., so I didn't get home until eleven.'

'What did you do then?'

'I went into Jodie's room to check on her and found her bed empty. I could tell that it hadn't been slept in.'

'What time does she usually get home?'

'School finishes at three-fifteen.'

'And she walks home alone?'

Debs frowned. 'She's nearly ten years old, for Christ's sake – Year Five. So yeah, of course she walks alone. There and back. It's only half a kilometre along the beach.'

'Where is she a pupil?'

'East Wittering Community Primary.'

'So, she would have been on the beach alone yesterday afternoon?' Marilyn confirmed. 'Walking home from school.'

'Not down there. Not as far as West Wittering. School's East Wittering. West Wittering is a good kilometre further on, in the wrong direction to home.' Anger flared in Debs' eyes. 'If you're gonna have a go at me, you can get out.'

Marilyn saw her aggression for what it was: grief transfigured as anger. For a woman like Debs Trigg, every day would be a fight, for money, for food, for time, for a job that paid more than £7.50 an hour, subsistence living. Fight – anger – would be her 'go-to' emotion and it would be far easier for her to process than grief. Whatever her relationship with Jodie, which he had yet to clarify, he knew that she would be hit by a freight train of misery when they left. He wouldn't want to be in her or the family liaison officer's shoes for anything.

'Would Jodie have had any cause to go to West Wittering beach yesterday afternoon?'

Rubbing the back of her hand across her nose, Trigg sniffed. 'No, of course not. Like I already said, it's in the opposite direction to home.'

'Did she like to meet friends on the beach?'

'School friends, sometimes. They all like to hang out on the beach, don't they? What kid wouldn't?'

'We'll need a list of their names.'

'Fine. The school will know better than me.'

'What about adults? Was she friends with any adults?'

Her lip curled as she looked up and met his gaze with her tear-stained eyes. 'What, like nonces?'

Marilyn shook his head. 'Anyone.'

The lit tip of the cigarette glowed as Trigg sucked hard, her chest expanding as she drew the smoke deep into her lungs. Marilyn would have killed for a cigarette right now, but lighting up in the middle of an interview could hardly be called professional, whatever the interviewee was doing, and he was going to play this one by the book. Page, line, word and letter.

'People who work around the caravan park,' she murmured, exhaling. 'It's friendly like, and we've lived here since Jodie was born. She knows everyone on the site. The staff and full-timers, that is, not the holiday rental lot.'

71

Marilyn nodded. 'Do you give her a time she needs to be home by?' he continued, using the present tense deliberately, following Trigg's lead, to minimize her stress and upset. *Faint hope.*

'I tell her she needs to be home by eight, latest.'

'And you finish work at ten p.m.'

'Depends if I'm on an early or late shift, but yeah, yesterday was a late, ten p.m., and then it's an hour bus-ride home.'

'So, what does Jodie do between three fifteen and eight?'

'She stays out and plays with schoolkids on the beach, or kids from the caravan park. Sometimes she goes to hang out at the entertainment centre, watches people play the arcade games.'

Marilyn nodded. The list of people the little girl had known and the time that she had spent alone both seemed to fall into the category 'how long is a piece of string?' The only certainty: another murder of another little girl, two years ago, the link between them, in his mind at least, concrete. The colour of the doll's eyes a detail that he was sure hadn't been in the papers.

He was a pot calling the kettle black, pulling Debs Trigg up on her parenting skills, particularly as he recognized that she had little choice, but at least his own parental failings had been compensated for by his ex-wife, a caring, responsible woman. Even so, his daughter had gone off the rails. It sounded as if poor little Jodie had had no such stability and his heart went out to her, to her memory. Many nine-year-old kids he'd dealt with in his career had had it far worse, but he still felt that every child deserved a fairy tale childhood. Adulthood was tough enough, without hard times starting long before.

'Would she have gone to West Wittering beach voluntarily?' he asked.

Trigg gave an evasive shrug. 'What reason would she have to go?'

'I was hoping that you would be able to help me with that.' A sharp edge to this tone that he was struggling to suppress. 'She has four and three-quarter hours from when school finishes to when you expect her home and another three hours after that, before you actually get home. It's a long time.' *A very long time, particularly for a nine-year-old child.*

Trigg waved the stub of the cigarette towards the corner of the caravan. 'We've got the telly and often as not she's got homework.'

Marilyn nodded. 'But she could have gone down to West Wittering voluntarily. She could have been meeting someone without you knowing.'

Trigg's red-rimmed eyes remained fixed on the blank square of the television screen in the corner, looking but not seeing.

'Couldn't she, Miss Trigg?' he prompted.

'Yeah, I suppose she could 'ave.' The words drew a little jerk out of her, as if the effort of acknowledgement hurt her.

'I'll need that list of her close school friends and everyone else she knew and saw around here on a regular basis. Detective Sergeant Workman will give you a hand with it.'

Trigg gave a dull nod. All the aggression, the fight had leaked from her. Tears welled in her eyes and a barely audible voice came from the back of her throat. 'How was she killed, Detective Inspector? How was my baby killed?'

'She was strangled,' Marilyn said plainly. There was no benefit in sugar-coating, not for anyone.

'When?'

'Mid-to-late afternoon.' He glanced at his watch. It was half-past midnight. *Yesterday afternoon.* 'Thursday afternoon,' he added, probably unnecessarily.

'When I was at work then,' Debs muttered. 'When I was on the fucking packing line, knowing nothing, some bastard was strangling my baby to death.'

Marilyn didn't say anything. There was nothing to say.

'She wasn't . . .' Her body twisted with anguish at the question. 'She wasn't sexually assaulted, raped, was she?'

Though only Dr Ghoshal could confirm with 100 per cent certainty whether Jodie had been sexually assaulted, Marilyn shook his head, ignoring the look of chastisement that Workman shot him. He was getting good at ignoring her looks. He had seen the child's body in the InciTent, still dressed in her school uniform, shirt and trousers, none of her clothing disturbed. Zoe Reynolds hadn't been sexually assaulted and he would be happy to stake his professional reputation – what little he had left when it came to solving child murders – on the fact that Jodie Trigg hadn't either. Every fibre of his instinct told him that Jodie's murder, as with Zoe's, wasn't a sexually motivated crime. Every fibre told him, still, that Zoe's mother Carolynn was responsible for her murder. And Jodie's? He'd find out. This time he *would* find out.

'No, she wasn't sexually assaulted,' he repeated firmly. 'We'll know a lot more once the, uh, once the autopsy has been performed later today.'

At the word 'autopsy', Trigg began rubbing her hands convulsively up and down her arms, her clawed fingers leaving raw weals on her pale skin.

Workman caught one of her wrists again. 'Please don't.'

'Autopsy. Why? Why can't you just leave her alone? Give her back to me to bury in one piece.'

'It will help us to catch her killer,' Workman said gently. Her hand was knocked away as Trigg shrank into the corner of the sofa, looking from Marilyn to Workman and back, like a cornered animal.

'Look, I know this is difficult, Miss Trigg,' Marilyn said, measuring his tone.

'You don't *know* anything,' she snapped. 'You don't *know* me. You didn't *know* Jodie. Has your daughter died, Detective Inspector?' She caught his gaze and held it defiantly, tears streaming down her cheeks. 'So don't *fucking* pretend that you know anything about us, or anything about how I'm feeling.'

'Miss Trigg,' Workman said.

Trigg spun around, eyes blazing. 'Or you!'

'We're trying to help you, Debs.'

A sob washed over her. 'No one can help me. Jodie was the only good thing that had ever happened to me. No one can help me now.'

Workman's jaw was rigid. The colour had completely drained from her face. Looking across at her, sitting stiffly in the passenger seat next to him, Marilyn cursed himself for not bringing DC Cara with him instead. The death of a child was emotionally the toughest crime for an investigative team to deal with; he knew that from Zoe Reynolds. But it had to be easier for a twenty-two-year-old DC who'd never had his own kids and was aeons away from wanting any, than a forty-six-year-old woman who had tried everything to have them and failed. Her voice was thick and Marilyn realized, with horror that she was struggling not to cry.

His own coping mechanism relied on his focusing with blinkered efficiency on the investigation, the hard evidence. The emotional aspects he locked in a small box deep in his brain, stowing the key somewhere he hoped never to find. It hadn't quite worked out that way with Zoe. The little girl's ghost seemed to know exactly where he'd hidden the key, chose his weakest moments to unlock the box and unleash the flood of memories, the world of self-recrimination.

'I'm sorry, sir,' Workman sniffed, embarrassed.

Marilyn slid his arm around her shoulders, a move which they both found awkward in the cramped car. Dropping his arm quickly, he muttered, 'You're human, Workman. And so am I. Believe it or not, so am I.'

13

'Marilyn told me about the Reynolds case,' Callan said, slumping down on the sofa next to Jessie, coffee in hand. 'The murder of that first little girl.'

She glanced over and met his gaze. 'Zoe, you mean? When did he tell you about it?'

She had been watching News 24 for the past three hours, since four a.m., unable to sleep at all last night, a fact she wasn't about to share with Callan. She had risen six more times during the night to straighten the curtains, seven times in all, sliding her feet softly heel to toe on the carpet as she crossed the bedroom so as not to wake him, to avoid the inevitable, impossible explanations if he caught her. She had spent the rest of the night lying on her side, watching him sleep, feeling unbelievably lucky that she could call him hers, but desperately insecure at the same time at how her tenuous grip on normality might wreck what they had. He only had so much patience and she knew that, though he professed to understand her OCD, there was no way that he did, or could.

She had watched five half-hourly cycles of 'The West Wittering child murder', as the press were calling it, clearly at a loss for a snappier title. The little girl had been named an hour ago as Jodie Trigg, the last news update featuring footage of the press clamouring at the closed door of a static caravan, a uniformed police constable guarding it, trying to keep them at bay, kids in pyjamas jumping up and down in the background, trying to get their faces on television, their parents looking more suitably sombre.

'He visited me in hospital last December while you were in the Persian Gulf and unburdened his soul. He probably thought I was too drugged up to remember.'

'What did he say?' She tried to sound nonchalant.

'That she keeps him awake at night.'

'Zoe?'

'Yeah.'

'And?'

'That he was certain her mother murdered her.'

'She was acquitted,' Jessie said.

'Due to lack of evidence.'

'She was still acquitted.'

Callan frowned. 'It's not the same as being found innocent by a jury, as you well know.'

Jessie took the opportunity of the story cycling around again to break eye contact. Marilyn this time, exiting the police station, looking as rough as Jessie felt. His tie was crooked and his black suit – did he have any others, or was there a row of identical suits hanging in his wardrobe? – was crumpled. He raised his hands and the press pack fell silent.

'You need to tell Marilyn that you know where Zoe's mother is now living and what she's calling herself,' Callan said.

Jessie kept her gaze focused on the screen. 'I'm sure he already knows,' she said dismissively, as she heard Marilyn, clear as a bell, asking Carolynn and Roger Reynolds to get in touch with him as a matter of urgency.

Callan raised an eyebrow. Pressing mute on the remote, Jessie cut Marilyn off mid-flow and swung around to face him.

'He can find her,' she snapped. 'He's a policeman after all, so that's his job. Doing some work for a change will be good for his liver.'

Callan sighed. 'It's bloody hard to find someone who doesn't want to be found, and he has enough to be getting on with, investigating the murder of a child. The second murder of a *second* child.'

Jessie held his cool amber gaze unflinching, but she regretted what she'd said about Marilyn, knew it had been unnecessary, nasty. She didn't even know why she'd said it. Many of the things she said and did nowadays felt as if they were coming, involuntarily, from a new, alien part of herself that even she didn't like. She hunched her shoulders like a stroppy teenager.

'There is such a thing as patient confidentiality, Callan.'

'When can patient confidentiality be breached?'

'Never.'

'That's not true. There are conditions under which patient confidentiality no longer applies. Confidentiality is an important duty, but it's not absolute.'

'For me it is absolute.'

Callan's hands were clenched into fists and one of his legs jittered, a sure sign that he was angry, trying to contain it. 'You can disclose information if it's required by law.'

'Fine. When Marilyn has me in handcuffs, I'll 'fess up.'

She raised an eyebrow. 'Handcuffs. Now there's something we should try.' It was a feeble attempt to lighten the moment, another thing she regretted as soon as she'd said it. Neither of them was in the mood for pathetic flippancy.

Dipping his gaze, Callan shook his head wearily. 'I'm being serious, Jessie.'

'So am I.' She bit her lip. 'If my patients can't trust me, I'm nothing, I'm worthless to them. They come to me because they're desperate. I'm often their last port of call before suicide, or crime, usually after they've tried burying their issues with alcohol and drugs. Many of them have been let down by society so often that they have no one else to go to and trust no one. I can't just be another person who fucks with their minds.'

'This is different. The woman could be a killer. You could be putting yourself in danger meeting with her and you could be putting other people in danger by concealing her whereabouts.'

Jessie gave a snort of laughter. 'If you had met her, you wouldn't be saying that. She's a frightened, timid, traumatized, middle-aged woman who is so thin she could play hide-and-seek behind a broom handle. She's not a threat to anyone.'

'She's a very convincing liar, because she had you fooled.'

'I've been trying to help her out, not catch her out. *Find* her out.'

'Marilyn believes that she's guilty of her daughter's murder.'

'She didn't murder Zoe. I know she didn't.'

'Bullshit.'

'It's not bullshit.' She gave another teenaged shrug. 'I have a good sense of her. An intuition.' *Even though I fell for*

80

her lies about her daughter dying in a car accident. But generally, she *did* have a good sense of people, a sixth sense. It came with the territory of her job.

'So why is she hiding?' Callan asked curtly. 'Why is she lying, even to you? Someone she can trust, with whom all her conversations are confidential?'

Jessie threw up her hands. 'What reception do you think a woman labelled a child killer would have got? She would have been vilified, taunted, stalked, jeered at, chased down the street, pushed around, spat at. Even her best friends, her own family, her parents, if they're alive, her husband, for Christ's sake – even they would have looked at her differently, even they would have *wondered.*' She sought out his gaze, usually the colour of warm honey, now cold and cynical. 'You'd heard about the Zoe Reynolds murder, even before Marilyn told you, hadn't you?'

It was his turn to give a teenage shrug. 'I was in Afghanistan two years ago.'

'And I bet that you still heard. It made the *Sun*, the *Mirror* – all those quality papers you boys read when you're at war.'

He didn't reply.

'Callan.'

'Vaguely,' he muttered. 'I remember it vaguely.'

'So?'

'So what? The press moves on. People move on.'

'They don't though, not in such an emotionally charged and shocking case, and particularly not in one that wasn't solved. There's no smoke without fire, after all. And now – now that this second little girl has been found dead? Two years to the day after Zoe's murder. Can you imagine the press storm? You could see it on the beach last night.' She waved her hand towards the television screen, where Marilyn was now trying to force open the driver's door of his dilapidated Z3 against a jam of press bodies and cameras: 'You can see it now. Newspapers, TV stations – they're all there.'

Callan drained his coffee and set his cup on the table, rolled his eyes and picked it up again in response to Jessie's admonishing look. 'The two cases may not be related. This second girl could have been killed by a copycat. By a parent, a relative, an adult friend, someone she knew who took the opportunity to do what they've been wanting to do for some time.'

Pulling the sleeve of her dressing gown over her hand, Jessie rubbed at the ring Callan's cup had left on the spotless wood.

'Even if they're not related, this child's death will break open all the old wounds,' she said, looking up. 'Laura— Carolynn, whatever the hell her bloody name is, will be splashed across the front pages, forced back into everyone's consciousness to be the victim of that "no smoke without fire" speculation all over again. The stares, the gossip, the snide behind-hand remarks, the pushing and shoving in the supermarket, the Internet trolling – it will start all over again.'

'Perhaps there isn't smoke without fire. All those old sayings come from somewhere.'

Jessie rolled her eyes. 'From the mouths of idiots.'

Callan gave a wry smile. 'Thanks.'

Jessie sighed. 'Can you really not see why she went to ground?'

'Of course I can. But that doesn't detract from the fact that she may be a child killer. She may be dangerous and I don't want you to put yourself – or anyone else – at risk.'

Jessie bit her lip, didn't answer. She felt as angry as he did and she felt right. Righteous anger, a powerful force.

'Ever since you were invalided out of the army, you've had your finger firmly on the self-destruct button,' Callan muttered.

'Self-destruct button? What the hell are you talking about?'

He sighed. 'You know exactly what I'm talking about.'

She shook her head. 'No, I don't.'

But she did know what he meant. She just couldn't help herself. Couldn't help that mean new alien streak that made her feel as if she didn't care about anything or anyone – with the exception of Callan and Ahmose, her elderly next-door neighbour who was more family to her now than her actual family – and least of all herself. Couldn't help that her OCD, which she had worked hard to control until her army career was ruined, had resurged with a vengeance, and was now spinning out of control.

Digging her top teeth into her bottom lip, tasting the copper tang of blood, Jessie focused hard on the television. She could butt against Callan all day, argue, get nowhere, but what was the point? She had already made her decision. Hooking a leg over Callan's thighs, she swivelled around and slid on to his knee, facing him.

'I love you,' she said, stroking her hands down his bare chest to his stomach.

She planted a soft kiss on his lips. He tasted of coffee and warmth and for a brief, intense moment she would have given anything to be back in bed with him, making love. But she needed to get going. Shuffling backwards, off Callan's knee and the sofa, she stood.

'I need to go to work, unfortunately.'

'Don't do anything stupid, Jessie.' His gaze was interrogative. She held it steadily.

'I won't. I promise.'

And she would keep that promise. However, his definition of stupid was probably very different from hers.

14

The little girl's murder was already front-page news. It screamed at Carolynn from every paper on the rack displayed inside the sliding double doors of the Co-op and Tesco Metro, from the newsagent's window, from newspapers folded in shopping bags or tucked under the arms of everyone she passed on Cakeham Road. Eight a.m., a balmy feel to the morning and the East Wittering village centre was bustling, locals and tourists shocked out of bed early by news of the child murder, locked in tight knots, talking in hushed, funereal tones. Carolynn forced herself to walk slowly, *leisurely*, as if she was no different from anyone else here, fight-or-flight tension locked in every one of her twitching muscles.

Zoe's murder had precipitated the same news frenzy: a crowd of journalists outside the police station, camera flashes blinding her as she was taken in from the beach to be swabbed down and interviewed; as she was driven to the Old Bailey eleven months later in the blue police van, photographers standing on tiptoes and thrusting their cameras up to the tiny, blacked-out bulletproof windows set high in its walls, hoping to snatch a shot of her, handcuffed and cowering, her life over so many times by then that she didn't know which way was up and which down. Inconceivable nightmares yet to come.

Everyone was talking about the girl's death: How was she killed? Who could have done it? Was this death linked to the murder of that other poor little girl, two years ago? What was her name?

Zoe, Carolynn wanted to scream. *Zoe Reynolds. My daughter, Zoe.* Not just that other child. That other poor little dead girl.

Information, opinion, gossip leaked from every huddle she passed. How could a child have been killed in broad daylight on a family beach? What had she been doing out there alone anyway? Where was her mother when she was being butchered?

An elderly couple were sitting on the bench at the bus stop, heads dipped to the paper spread between them. Carolynn inched closer, ears straining to decipher their murmurs.

'The mother has finally come forward,' she heard the man say. *Come forward into her own personal nightmare.*

'How could a mother allow such a thing to happen to her own daughter?' the woman snapped. 'Why wasn't she there to protect her? Only nine or ten and out on the beach on her own to be murdered, poor little mite.'

A chill gripped Carolynn and she swayed, snatching at the back of the bench for support. The couple's heads whipped around as her shadow loomed over them, and Carolynn saw the surprise on their faces, surprise that morphed to concern when they saw how pale she was.

How could a mother allow such a thing to happen to her own daughter? Why wasn't she there to protect her?

She had heard the same, over and over. The antipathy she had felt towards Zoe, her postnatal depression, twisted by friends, acquaintances, people she'd overhear gossiping in cafés, by Internet trolls, by the press, into wilful neglect, into deliberate child cruelty.

At least this other mother had been spared finding her daughter's body. At least she wouldn't suffer those other nightmares – the shallow sympathy that morphed to accusation, the arrest, the trial, the brutal destruction of her hard-won life.

'Are you OK, dear?' the old lady asked.

'I'm fine,' Carolynn managed, pushing herself upright, finding a television aerial fixed to the newsagent's roof across the road, focusing hard on that one spot to keep herself from swaying, toppling. She needed to act normally, couldn't afford to attract attention to herself like this. What if people noticed her odd behaviour and worked out who she was? The old lady was still watching her quizzically. Carolynn met her look with a fixed smile.

'I'm fine, thank you.' The voice that spoke, her voice, sounded distant, as if it was coming from someone else. 'I've had a summer cold that went to my head and has been making me dizzy.'

She needed to get a paper, needed to know everything. She didn't want to know, couldn't bear to. She needed to not be recognized, felt an overwhelming urge to bolt, keep running until she had outpaced this nightmare.

Both supermarkets were full, people with too much time on their hands, lingering and gossiping, wallowing in shared shock and horror. Her chin welded to her chest, eyes cast to the ground, Carolynn ducked into Tesco Metro and snatched up a copy of the *Daily Mail*. Holding it in front of her, pretending to read the front page, she headed over to the self-service tills, a blur of tears obscuring everything but the huge black headline that screamed: SECOND GIRL MURDERED AT WEST WITTERING BEACH. A photograph under the headline showed the dunes, a white 'InciTent' – she remembered the term from two years ago – and that man, that horrid policeman, with the weird mismatched blue and brown eyes, an overgrown, malevolent raven in his black suit.

At the self-service till, she scanned the barcode, slid the paper under her arm and fumbled her purse from her bum-bag.

'Please put your product into the bagging area . . .'

She froze.

'Please put your product into the bagging area . . . please put your product into the bagging area . . .'

Oh God, everyone is looking at me. What am I supposed to do? Panic bloomed in her chest. She had never used one of these tills before, had only chosen it to avoid facing a shop assistant. She felt sick.

'The paper, madam.' A man in a blue uniform with a Tesco badge fixed to his chest had appeared beside her. 'You need to put the paper in the bagging area.'

Where was the bagging area? She should have just gone to the normal till; it felt as if everyone in the store had turned to stare. She *couldn't* be recognized.

'There.'

Without raising her head, Carolynn's gaze tracked down the man's arm to his extended finger. She dropped the paper on to the metal tray and the electronic voice ceased.

'Thank you,' she murmured. She sensed that he was still watching her as she fumbled her purse open and found sixty-five pence. She wished he'd just go away. 'I'm fine now, thank you,' she repeated, a cutting edge to her tone.

A balloon of air eased from her lungs as he stepped away, turned his attention to another customer. She slotted the money into the till and took her receipt.

'They'll need to find the first little girl's mother now,' a loud female voice chimed right next to her. 'The one who got let off due to lack of evidence.'

An answering voice, high-pitched and screechy. Uneducated – it was an uneducated voice – Carolynn couldn't stop herself from thinking.

'She's disappeared though, hasn't she? Says so, right here.'

Two women, she saw from the corner of her eye, both about her own age, early forties, overly made-up with brassy, box-dyed hair. They were both reading a red-top paper.

'What was her name? D'you remember?'

'Reynolds, wasn't it? Karen, Caroline, summink like that?'

A concurring murmur. 'Stuck up, she was, from what I saw on the telly. Stuck up and ice-cold.'

Carolynn's breathing was too loud, as if her lungs had been replaced by a rasping pair of bellows.

'I always thought she did it.'

They are all staring at me. I can feel Zoe's weight in my arms. Heavy, she's got so heavy these past few years. I haven't held her. I hadn't noticed.

There was a tear in the bellows that kept Carolynn from catching her breath.

'You could tell from the way she behaved that she was guilty.'

Her hair is a mess, caught with seaweed. I hate her looking untidy, but I can't untangle it because my arms are filled with her body and I can't stop, I must keep going forward. Why are they all staring at me?

'Well, you wouldn't go hiding if you was innocent, would you? I wouldn't if it was me, anyways.'

Carolynn let out a sob – she couldn't help herself.

'Are you all right, love?' The woman's forehead, under her choppy claret fringe, wrinkled with concern.

Carolynn nodded, fumbling her purse back into her bum-bag. She wanted to scream at them, to tell them how she had been haunted, unable to sleep without medication for two years, unable even to get out of bed for a month after Zoe's death. How she had lost everything: her job, her friends, her home, her life, her sanity. *Everything*. How she was afraid, terrified, that it was all going to start again. She turned away, aware that hot tears were running down her cheeks, unable to hold them back.

There is something around her neck. Dirt? Is it dirt? No, bruises. There are bruises around her neck.

'Hey, hold on, you've forgotten your paper.' The woman's eyes narrowed as she held out Carolynn's *Mail*. 'Are you sure you're all right? I don't mean to meddle, but you look awful, love.'

Shaking her bent head, Carolynn reached for the paper, mumbled a quick 'thank you', turned and bolted out of the supermarket and straight across the road.

Her eyes are open, she's staring up at me, but I don't think that she can see me. I'm not sure if it's the reflection of the clouds, but her brown eyes are milky.

The screech of tyres and a bumper collided with her thigh. She tumbled on to the tarmac, the paper spinning from her hand, white pages flapping and dancing in the road.

A man caught her arm. 'Jesus Christ, are you OK?'

Tugging her arm from his grasp, she nodded, her body transmitting a message of pain to her brain as she struggled to her feet. Her right thigh ached from the bumper and she felt as if her left side had been dragged down a cheese grater.

'The paper. I need my paper.'

She knew that he must think she was mad as she scrabbled to collect the spilled pages, grabbed the couple he collected from his outstretched hand. He was still watching her as she limped to the side of the road. Others had stopped too, to watch the skinny crazy in the jogging outfit who'd just charged headlong into the road without even looking.

Screaming. I can hear screaming. I think it's someone else, but the noise is so loud, so constant, like an animal in pain, and I realize that the noise is coming from me. It is me who is screaming.

15

The nausea had risen from Jessie's stomach to her throat. Lowering the window to allow cool air to rush over her face, she swung off the motorway at the next exit, reached a roundabout and turned off to join a country road. A hundred metres down, she bumped two wheels on to the grassy verge, shoved the door open, and projectile-vomited on to the tarmac. Stumbling to the verge, she vomited again, coffee-saturated bile filling her nose and mouth. She gagged and coughed, trying to clear her clogged airways, hating how the vulnerability of vomiting catapulted her straight back to childhood, wanting, for an acute second, her mother for the first time in as long as she could remember.

She hadn't been taking care of herself, she knew: not eating properly, downing coffee in the mornings to keep her mind focused on her patients, mainlining wine in the evenings, to take her mind off them. Stupid, self-destructive behaviour. Yet more stupidity to add to her burgeoning list. Resting her forehead on the cool metal roof of her car, she waited for the storm in her stomach to subside, remembering that she hadn't bought any water, that she'd have to live with a bile-coated tongue until the next service station.

As she straightened, her mobile rang, her mother's name flashing on its face, as if her fleeting desire for maternal comfort had travelled instantaneously the forty miles north-east to the sixties house in the quiet cul-de-sac in Wimbledon where she had grown up, where her mother still lived with Richard, her new partner, whom Jessie had met once and thankfully liked very much. He was just what her mother needed; everything her father hadn't been. Caring, solid, reliable. Not a self-obsessed wanker.

'Mum,' she croaked.

Her throat ached and the taste in her mouth was revolting.

'Are you OK, darling? You sound a bit bunged-up.'

'I'm fine, Mum,' she croaked again, ducking and wiping her mouth on the hem of her pale blue summer dress.

'How are you, Mum?'

'I'm good, darling.'

Their relationship still formal, too much left unsaid for it to be anything but. She wanted to get moving, get to the Witterings and find Carolynn. Encourage her to make contact with Marilyn without having a showdown as to why she'd repeatedly lied in their sessions, the duplicity that had been her and Jessie's professional relationship for the past five weeks.

'What do you want, Mum? I'm sorry, but I'm in a bit of a hurry.'

Even over the sound of her own rasping breath, Jessie heard the change in her mother's, quicker, lighter, betraying agitation. She'd hardly spoken – she couldn't possibly have offended her mum in only two sentences.

'I was calling to say that Richard and I are looking forward to seeing you later.'

Later? Her mind still blank.

'And his daughter is coming too, so you'll get a chance to meet her. She's lovely. A little older than you, with two daughters, four and six, but they're very sweet little girls. I'm sure you'll get on wonderfully.' The last sentence said as a plea. 'They're going to be our flower girls. I've booked a table for us all in the Fox and Grapes at twelve for lunch and the fitting is at two.'

Oh, shit. Shit, shit, *shit*. Now she remembered exactly why, a few weeks ago, she'd blocked out today in her diary. Blocked it out with a quick slash of her biro, late for a meeting, meaning to write lunch with her mum and Richard and the appointment with the bridesmaid's dress fitter in later, forgetting of course.

'I'm so sorry, Mum, but something's come up at work. I need to see one of my patients urgently.'

No reply, just that light, choppy breathing.

'I'm sorry,' she repeated, feeling another upswell of sickness. 'But it's an emergency. I have to see her.'

'I'll rearrange . . .'

'Yes,' she managed.

'When? The wedding's next Saturday. They do need time to make any alterations.'

She couldn't ruin her mother's wedding, but she couldn't think beyond today, beyond Carolynn, beyond two little dead girls.

'Monday, Mum.' It was Friday now. She'd be done by

tomorrow. Monday was safe. 'Monday, first thing. I'm sorry, I have to go.'

Jamming her finger on the red telephone symbol, she spun around and vomited again, pebble-dashing her sandals and bare legs with steaming yellow bile.

16

The woman on page five of the *Daily Mail* looked sleek and stylish, her hair cut into a glossy long blonde bob – a lob it was called back when she wore it; *God knows if it's still called that* – dark brown eyes holding the camera's lens with a flirtatious confidence, the contrast between blonde and dark striking, stunning, even if she said so herself. It was the photograph of a woman Carolynn no longer recognized. One of her old colleagues, a married man with whom she had engaged in an energizing but harmless office flirtation, had taken the shot at a work dinner.

She had been badly wounded back then, two years ago, when the photograph had found its way into the papers. She'd erroneously expected loyalty from friends and colleagues, only to realize, as successive pictures from friends' parties, from their weddings, from her godson's 'godparents and close family only' christening appeared in the paper, as her life crumbled, that loyalty was fiction.

She reached the shore and stepped from the concrete walkway down on to the pebbles. Why did she always seek out the beach when she needed comfort? The beach where Zoe had been murdered. It made no sense. Nothing made sense any more. Sense was for a life she used to know. Control was for a life she used to know.

The tide was out and a few people were walking by the water's edge, a couple of dogs chasing balls across the sand, but the pebbly section at the top of the beach, furthest from the water, was deserted. Sinking down, Carolynn unfolded the paper. Its pages were out of order, her photograph, page five, on top. She couldn't read until she had rearranged it, needed to digest the information in order of gravity, understand what the journalists considered most notable, what they were *thinking*. Because the journalists' thought processes mirrored those of their sources in the police, and of that detective inspector with the horrid, piercing eyes. It was imperative that she figure out what he was thinking, where his focus lay. Whether she could continue to hide here, in plain sight, or whether she needed to run again.

Apart from that clamouring headline – SECOND GIRL MURDERED ON WITTERING BEACH – the photograph on the front page could have been from two years ago, her own life stilled in black and white. The only difference, the journalists, even more this time, and the location of the white tent shielding the little girl's body. Back then the tent had covered the spot in the beach car park, where she, cradling Zoe's body, had fallen to her knees, where the screams of horrified beachgoers mixed with her own, the sirens of the police arriving, had finally brought her to a standstill.

Zoe is heavy, too heavy. I hadn't noticed that she'd grown so big. I need to stop, to put her down, but I can't, I must keep going forward.

Fat wet drops fell on to the page, blotting out the shock-faced uniforms standing outside the tent, the journalists lined up along the 'Police – Do Not Cross' tape. Wiping her sleeve across her eyes, Carolynn flipped the page.

I need the people to get out of my way. They are staring at me with such horror and such pity. I can't stand to be pitied.

Zoe's face stared back at her from the page, tear-stained eyes reproaching her mother for not protecting her, for letting her die. Carolynn forced herself to look at the photograph and felt a great weight pressing down on her chest.

It's not Zoe. It's not her.

She knew that the photograph wasn't of Zoe, that what she was seeing wasn't real. That another little girl was pictured under the headline: *Murdered Beach Girl Identified*.

Not Zoe. Of course, it wasn't Zoe. It couldn't have been. But she knew exactly who it was.

17

Ruby Lovatt was already seated in the interview room when Marilyn and Workman entered. She was leaning back in her chair, arms crossed under her breasts, which made her ample cleavage almost pornographically prominent in the thin, low-cut silver jumper. Head tilted to one side, a half-smile on her face, she was eyeballing DC Cara, who was standing in the corner, hands jammed into his pockets, shifting awkwardly from foot to foot as if he'd been stung by something. Marilyn smiled to himself. He knew Ruby of old, knew the tricks that she played. She was well accustomed to dealing with men, manipulating them. He had been a victim himself a few times when he was younger, greener. Ruby's gaze swung from Cara to meet his as he stepped through the doorway, narrowed as it shifted past him to check out DS Workman.

'DI Simmons,' she winked. 'Fancy seeing you here.'

'Good morning, Ruby.'

Signalling to DC Cara to leave, which he did at speed, Marilyn pulled out a chair and sat down, as did Workman, beside him. Placing the file containing the photographs of the crime scene and Jodie Trigg's broken little body on the table in front of him, closed for the moment, he placed flat hands on the tabletop either side of the file, met Ruby's gaze and smiled what he hoped was a pleasant smile that communicated nothing, gave nothing away.

'So how are you, Ruby?'

She opened her mouth and jutted out her chin in a way that told Marilyn she was about to make a suggestive comment. He braced himself, embarrassed for some reason by Workman's presence, as if she was an elderly relative who needed sheltering from the baser side of human nature. He wished now that he had come to interview Ruby alone, but this was an important interview, critical, and he knew that Workman would pick up on nuances that he might miss.

He was surprised when all Ruby said was, 'I'm fine.' A pensive nod. 'OK.'

Her nose was crooked – it had been broken at some point – and both of her front teeth were chipped.

'Do you mind if we record this interview, so that we have a verbatim record?' he asked.

'Do what you like,' she muttered.

Marilyn switched on the electronic recorder. He spoke the date and time and listed their names.

'What were you doing on the beach, Ruby?' he began.

'Looking for treasure.' She smirked. 'Like a pirate.'

'In the rain?' Workman queried.

Ruby's gaze switched to her. 'I don't dissolve.' She shrugged. 'I like it out there when the weather's bad. I like being alone.'

'Why?'

'Because nice privileged people who go to the beach with their nice privileged kiddies don't like to be around people like me. And I don't like to be around them.'

Workman nodded. 'What did you find?' she asked.

Ruby jutted her chin. 'Apart from a dead girl?'

Marilyn sensed Workman draw in a virtually imperceptible breath; realized, from the slight narrowing of her gaze, that Ruby had also sensed her discomfort.

'What time did you find her?' Marilyn asked, taking over the questioning.

Another shrug. 'You fancy giving me that posh watch of yours and next time I find a strangled little girl I'll be able to tell you to the second.' She was looking directly at Workman when she said it. This time, to her credit, Workman didn't react.

'Estimate,' Marilyn said.

'What time did the café call you?' Ruby muttered.

'Five-thirty.' He didn't need to check the file to know.

'So maybe I found her half hour before that.'

'Half an hour?' Even he couldn't hide his shock. The café was ten minutes' walk from the spot in the dunes where Jodie's body had lain; significantly less at a panicked run. 'What did you do in between?'

'Walked, looking for treasure, like I said.'

'Did you find any?'

'This and that. Bit of cash, couple of other things.'

'How far did you walk?'

'Through the dunes to the end and back along the beach.'

'Then you went to the café and told the manager about Jodie Trigg, and he called us.'

She nodded and leant forward, giving Marilyn a view of the pale swell of her breasts, the dark valley between, a

101

flash of red lace too shiny to be real. He felt a movement in his trousers, a tightening. Yanking his gaze away, he focused on Jodie Trigg's file, calling to mind the photograph of her inside it. Jesus, what the hell was wrong with him? He felt wrung out, crazily exhausted already and the little girl had been dead less than twenty-four hours. He knew that the feeling had less to do with the fact he'd been up all night, and more to do with the fact that the murder of a second child, two years to the day, so close to where Zoe Reynolds' body was found, had kick-started every self-flagellating emotion he possessed. He needed a caffeine hit. He needed to bury his head in the sand while someone else sorted out this mess for him, found a child murderer and delivered him or her into the hands of the law with a file full of irrefutable evidence.

Only one of those needs was likely to be met this morning.

'Do you want a coffee, Ruby?'

She shrugged and winked. 'I'd fancy a coke more, DI Simmons.' *And not the fizzy kind.*

Marilyn turned to Workman. 'Do you mind going on a coffee run, Sarah?'

Workman shook her head and stood.

'How do you like your coffee, Ms Lovatt?'

Ruby raised an eyebrow. 'Ms Lovatt. I can't remember the last time anyone called me that. Actually, I can't remember the last time anyone called me anything other than bitch. Milk and two sugars.' A pause. 'Please.' Her voice sticking on that last word as if it left a bad taste on her tongue.

Workman left the room and Ruby winked at Marilyn. 'People are going to start talking, you and me alone in here, DI Simmons,' she teased.

102

'The only thing they're talking about is Jodie Trigg.' The statement sounded unnecessarily abrupt, even to his own ears.

Ruby shrugged and her gaze slid from his, but not before Marilyn caught the hurt that flashed in her eyes. Her carapace was no tougher than when he had first met her, nearly fifteen years ago, despite the act she was putting on. She'd been working on that act virtually since birth, and she'd got it to RADA standard by the time she was fourteen. She had been beautiful back then, he remembered, the first time he met her in that grotty interview room in Portsmouth Central Police Station. Beautiful and horribly damaged. She still was beautiful, if you could see past the pallid, sweaty skin, the hollowed-out eyes and the sullen expression. Still beautiful and still horribly damaged, no doubt. Damage like that didn't heal. She was only in her late twenties, he knew, though her lifestyle and the drugs she took made her look a good fifteen years older.

'Did you see anyone else out there on the beach?' he asked, pulling his mind back to the present.

'No.'

'No one?'

'When I got back near the café, there was a few staff leaving. It was closed by then.'

'Anyone else?'

She raised her gaze to the ceiling, drawing an image to mind.

'Someone running. A woman, running. A while before I found the girl.'

'Near the girl?'

'Yeah, pretty near.'

'What was the woman wearing?'

She rolled her eyes. 'Whatever the hell women who have the time and inclination to run wear to run.'

'Colour?'

The eyes rising again. 'Dark. Dark blue or black top and bottom.'

The door opened and Workman came back in, three vending-machine coffees balanced on a hardback notepad in her hand. She slid the notepad on the table and handed out the coffees.

'What did she look like?'

'Who?'

'The woman,' Marilyn said. 'The runner.'

Ruby lifted a hand and pinched a strand of her hair, rolling it between her fingers. 'Blonde, like me, 'cept hers was probably natural.'

She dropped her hand and snaked it across the table, palm upwards.

'Do I get a cigarette with my coffee, DI Simmons?'

Marilyn's gaze tracked from the rough skin on her slender fingers and hopscotched up the black needle marks on her forearm. Drugs, it was always hard drugs that the truly depressed took to anaesthetize themselves against life, nothing else strong enough, reliable enough, persistent enough. His gaze moved to meet hers and he shook his head.

'We can't smoke in here, Ruby. You know that. It's the law.'

The hand snaked back. 'For Christ's sake, the law is a fucking ass. You know *that*.'

She was right. He did know that. His mind returned to the first time he had met her, in that interview room in Portsmouth Central Police Station, him still a constable, itching to move up the ranks on to something more exciting, and putting every hour God sent into his work and networking – drinking, in other words – with his colleagues, his family life imploding.

Ruby and another fourteen-year-old girl had been imprisoned for six days in a 'trick pad', a temporary brothel set up in an empty house right in the middle of Portsmouth. She was locked in an attic room that contained nothing but a double bed. Thick plyboard had been nailed over the one small window so that she couldn't call for help, and the handle on the inside of the door had been removed so that she couldn't escape. She had been raped by dozens of men who were prepared to pay to have sex with underage girls. The children's home she lived in had known that she and the other girl were missing, but hadn't bothered to report their absence to the police. Out of sight, out of mind; plenty of other deeply disturbed, attention-seeking kids to deal with.

One of the men – of the hundred or more who had raped her over the six days – had salvaged a conscience from some part of his psyche, because he had phoned the police, after he'd forcibly had sex with her. He hadn't left a name, had melted back to his family, returned to tuck his kids into their beds and watch *Strictly* with his wife, perhaps salving his conscience with the fact that his call had saved her. God knew how the minds of men like that worked, men who you'd walk past in the street, stand behind in the queue at the supermarket, share banter with in the office. It never ceased to amaze and depress him how people who considered themselves to be upstanding members of society could be so inhumane. Justification in that their victim was marginalized, beneath contempt, perhaps? None of the men who had kidnapped and imprisoned Ruby or the men who had paid to rape her were caught. History was left to repeat itself with countless other vulnerable girls, and the thought made him sick to his stomach.

A judge had sent Ruby back to the care home. She was too old to be wanted by people looking to adopt, or fosterers, too young to live on her own. A child like thousands of others who fell between all the stools. She had spent most of the two years that followed until she was sixteen and legally allowed to live on her own, playing truant from the children's home and from school, sliding deeper and deeper into the underworld, further from help.

Within a year of Marilyn's first encounter with her, she had a pimp and was hooked on heroin. He later heard she'd been knocked up by one of her clients, and then dumped by her pimp for refusing to get an abortion. He had no idea what had happened to the child, but their paths had crossed a few times since and each time a little more of that feisty, furiously proud but sad and deeply damaged girl he had first met had been replaced with shadow. Numbness. Lifelessness. He wasn't sure when she'd wound up in East Wittering or where she was living. He'd need to know the latter at least.

Movement across the table brought him back to the present. Tilting back, Ruby slid her hand into the front pocket of her skin-tight jeans and pulled out a half-smoked cigarette and an orange plastic Bic lighter. Marilyn put his hand out for the cigarette. With his other, he reached into his suit jacket pocket and pulled out his own packet of Silk Cut, held them out to her.

'Swap.'

He ignored the look that he was sure Workman was

casting him, twisted in his chair and tossed the half-smoked cigarette Ruby dropped into his hand towards the bin by the door, watched it bounce on the rim and hit the floor. Sport had never been his strong point. He'd pick it up later.

'I always knew that you were a softie, DI Simmons,' Ruby said with a grin, scooping up the packet, opening it with a practised flick of her index finger and shaking out a cigarette. She slid the rest of the packet and the lighter into one of the bulging pockets of her olive-green army-style parka that was hanging on the back of her chair.

'The smoke alarm will go off,' Workman said.

Standing, Marilyn moved his chair to under the smoke alarm, climbed up and yanked out the battery. Returning his chair to the table, he sat back down, avoiding Workman's gaze, *again*. He felt unsettled, disconcerted. There was something about being in Ruby's presence that made him feel as if he had been trapped in a time machine and transported back fifteen years. Glancing down at Jodie's file, he forced himself to focus.

'Why didn't you call us earlier?' he asked. 'When you first found the girl's body?'

Ruby shrugged. 'She wasn't going anywhere, was she?'

Workman sat forward, elbows on the table, her fingers linked together to form one big fist with her hands. 'She might still have been alive.'

Ruby curled her lip. 'She wasn't.'

'How did you know that for certain?'

'I didn't come down with the first shower . . . Miss . . . Mrs . . . '

'Detective Sergeant Workman,' Workman said.

Marilyn thought that Ruby might sneer again, make some

snide remark about Workman's use of her rank, but she didn't.

'I've seen enough dead bodies in my time, Detective Sergeant Workman. I know what one looks like.'

'And it didn't occur to you that her mother might be wondering where she was? That people might be worried?'

'She wasn't, was she?' Ruby snapped. 'You didn't even know who the poor little sod was until hours later, did you? Even I would have made a better fucking mother than that, if I'd wanted to keep my sprog – which I didn't.'

Shoving the cigarette into her mouth, she lit it, sucking hard, blowing the smoke slowly out of her nostrils, her eyes fixed on Marilyn's face, daring him to object. He wasn't about to. Ruby was right. He could murder a cigarette himself, was tempted to snatch it from her slender fingers and take a few desperate drags. The air in the room felt stifling, not the product of the smoke. If he'd had a knife he could have sliced it.

'Tell me what you remember seeing, Ruby. When you found her, when you found Jodie? Walk it through in your mind. Tell me everything, just as you saw it.'

18

Jessie saw Carolynn immediately, sitting alone on the stony section at the top of the beach, a newspaper flapping in her hand. She wasn't reading though, just staring out to sea, absolutely motionless, the paper the only animation. Jessie knew nothing about her, beyond what Carolynn had told her in their five counselling sessions, the core of it lies, she now knew. The address she had given, an address in Chichester, was a fake. She had always paid for her sessions in cash, Jessie had found out this morning from the practice receptionist, because 'my husband has one of those cash-in-hand jobs'. The woman like quicksand.

Sand.

The only certainties to build on in her search for Carolynn this morning, the dusting of crystal white sand she'd noticed on Carolynn's feet yesterday and the memories she had shared with Jessie about watching container ships plough their way up the Solent to Portsmouth or Southampton Docks with her daughter, how she watched them every day now, alone. And she had run once, she'd said a couple of weeks ago, sprinted, a horse cantering close by her on the sand, feeling superhuman, almost as if she could outrun it. *That was a good moment, one of the few.* Lies too, perhaps, but Jessie thought not. She had no reason to lie about those details. Only Bracklesham Bay and East Wittering allowed horse riding on the beach during the day in the summer months, so Jessie had decided to start with those. Carolynn hated the confines of her house, particularly when she was stressed or upset, as she would unquestionably be today with this second little girl's murder. It wasn't a ridiculous notion to believe that, if Carolynn lived in or close to East Wittering, Jessie would bump into her at some point if she spent the day here, searching.

She had parked in the municipal car park and walked along Cakeham Road, looking in all the shops and cafés, fruitlessly; turned into Shore Road and did the same, again without result. She bought herself a takeaway coffee at one of the cafés and walked on towards the sea, planning to sit for an hour or two on the beach, to see if she could catch Carolynn on one of her many runs.

Draining her coffee, tossing the cup into one of the bins by the Fisherman's Hut, a cabin selling fresh takeaway seafood, Jessie crunched on to the pebbles at the top of the beach, walking casually towards the sand and sea beyond, silently rehearsing the excuse she'd formulated to explain her presence at the beach. Would Carolynn ignore her, turn away and hide, or would she call out? Jessie wanted her to make the first move, so that their meeting felt like Carolynn's idea, not something forced on her. She would be feeling extremely vulnerable and sensitive, her antenna tuned to hyper-suspicion.

Jessie had just set foot on the sand at the bottom of the

110

pebbly bank, when she heard Carolynn's voice, calling a tentative, 'Dr Flynn?'

She kept walking, pretending that she hadn't heard.

'Dr Flynn?'

Turning, she pasted an expression of surprise on to her face. 'Laura!'

She retraced her steps, as Carolynn rose to her feet, the paper folded now and clutched to her chest, only the back page, sports coverage, visible, Jessie noticed. 'What on earth are you doing here?'

'Oh, I live just down the beach,' Carolynn said, pointing east in the direction of Bracklesham Bay. She broke off and raised a hand to cover her mouth, like a child who has just unwittingly blurted out a secret she'd promised not to share.

'I'm so envious that you live by the sea,' Jessie said brightly to take the heat from the moment. 'I would love to live by the sea, but I've never had the opportunity. One day, hopefully.' She smiled. 'Can you see the water from your windows?'

'Oh, only from upstairs. There's a shoulder-high concrete wall, a sea defence, between the beach and the road in front of my house. It's ridiculous. I live right by the sea and I can't see it!' Her initial tentativeness replaced now by that Technicolor 'game-show host' tone, her gaze focused on the expanse of sea over Jessie's right shoulder. 'What are you doing at the beach, Dr Flynn?'

'Jessie. Please call me Jessie. It's my mother's wedding next weekend and I wanted to make her a present. I don't have any client appointments today, so I thought I'd come to the beach, collect some shells and make a picture frame for her. I've got a lovely picture of my brother and I when we were kids, playing on the beach in Cornwall, to put in it. I wanted to do something unique, something personal.'

She had formulated this excuse precisely because it was mother, daughter, and personal. She needed to get underneath this woman's skin in a way she hadn't during their sessions if she was going to win enough trust to persuade her to contact Marilyn. The first step was turning herself from Dr Flynn into Jessie, a woman with a life outside her professional persona, even if that life was little more than fiction. The contradiction wasn't lost on her: lie to win trust.

'I'm starving,' she said. 'Will you join me for lunch, Laura?'

'I've eaten.'

Jessie doubted that Carolynn had eaten a proper meal for months. She was so thin in her sheer running tights and vest that Jessie could see the contour of her bones underneath her skin, as if she was a skeleton hanging off a hook in a biology lab.

'Keep me company then?'

The only free table in the café Carolynn led her to was round, three chairs, placed at elliptical angles to each other. Not ideal. Jessie would have preferred to sit directly opposite her, so that she could try to force the eye contact she'd failed to achieve in their sessions or on the beach. They sat down and Jessie ordered a pancake and a tea and Carolynn a black coffee.

'You live in Bracklesham Bay, you said?' Jessie began.

Carolynn hesitated; Jessie shrugged off her question, playing the psychology.

'Don't tell me if you don't want to.'

'No, of course I do, there's no reason I wouldn't.' Emphatically the game-show host again. 'Yes, we're . . . we're renting a house in Bracklesham Bay. Not very glamorous, I'm afraid. There's a derelict house on one side and the gates to a huge static caravan park on the other side.'

'By the sea though, at least?'

'By the sea,' Carolynn acknowledged, relaxing slightly, when she realized that Jessie wasn't going to press her, wasn't interested in exactly where she lived. *Small talk.* Jessie was just making small talk. It had been so long since she'd sat opposite someone in a café and just chatted, that she felt rusty, a conversational Tin Man from the *Wizard of Oz*. She mustn't be so uptight; she wanted, *needed*, to make this work. She really enjoyed Jessie's company, would love a relationship beyond the professional, a genuine friendship.

Roger's warning voice rose in her mind: *You're paying her, Caro. Actually, let me correct that:* I'm *paying her. That's why she's listening to you.*

No, he was wrong. She would prove him wrong.

The food and drinks arrived. Carolynn watched Jessie struggle to hold the fork, an expression of intense concentration on her face, as if she had to focus on sending the electrical signals to 'grip' from her brain to her left hand. It was badly scarred, an angry gash across her palm that had been stitched. She'd noticed it before during her counselling sessions, had wanted to ask about it, but she had been stopped by professional distance. Reaching across the table, she laid her hand on Jessie's.

The unexpected contact of Carolynn's chill fingers made Jessie flinch. She recovered quickly, smiling to gloss over her discomfort.

'What happened?' Carolynn asked.

'Huh?'

'To your hand?'

'Oh, uh, just an accident.' *Why am I lying? I don't need to lie about this. I'm as bad as she is.* 'Actually, not quite an accident. I used to be an army psychologist and I was attacked by someone. He had a hunting knife.' She held up her ruined hand. 'This was the result. Not pretty and not functional, but it's getting better.'

'You had to leave the army because of it?'

'I was invalided out five months ago.'

'Do you miss it?'

'Very much. Though I am in a relationship with a military policeman, so I got something good from it at least.' Callan would be furious if he knew that she was sharing information about their relationship to build bridges, force a deeper connection, with Carolynn.

'What's his name?'

'Callan. Ben Callan.'

'Is he hot?'

'Beautiful.' Jessie smiled; genuinely, she realized, for the first time since she'd met Carolynn. 'Truly. I'm very lucky.'

Carolynn nodded wistfully.

'What's your husband called?'

'Roger.'

'How did you meet him?'

'Through friends, years ago now. We've been together for twenty years, married for seventeen.'

'Wow, you get less for—' Jessie broke off. *You get less for murder.* She couldn't believe what she'd been about to say. The café was a crowded surf café with a chilled, fun vibe. She was relaxing too much herself, she realized, lulled into a false sense of security by the atmosphere. She needed to get a grip, get to the point and then excuse herself.

Carolynn raised an eyebrow. 'Less for what?'

'No, nothing. Laura, there's, uh, there's something I need to talk to you about.' Reaching across the table, Jessie unfolded

114

Carolynn's *Mail* and opened it to page five. 'I saw your photo on the television this morning. You're called Carolynn, not Laura, and Zoe didn't die in a car accident, did she?'

Carolynn picked at the corner of the sky-blue paper napkin that had come with her coffee. The colour, what little there'd been, had drained from her face.

'I'm sorry. I shouldn't have lied to you.'

Jessie shrugged. She worked with patients who lied all the time. It was an occupational hazard. Usually, though, she could see through them, recognize the lies. Why hadn't she with Carolynn? What had made her so convincing? It was the fact that she had swallowed Carolynn's story whole that disturbed her the most.

'You had a horrible time, Carolynn. Can I call you Carolynn?'

'Please do.'

'And irrespective of how Zoe died, the emotional fallout is similar.' *Not strictly true.* 'You still lost a child.'

'You're not angry with me?'

'Of course not. I have no reason to be.' *Again, not true.*

She thought back to what Callan had said this morning. *She could be a child killer. She could have murdered her own child.* Her flippancy – laughing it off.

'But I lied to you.'

'Everyone lies sometimes.'

'White lies.'

'White lies, black lies and every shade in between. You've had an incredibly tough time and it was not unreasonable that you wanted to disappear, become anonymous.'

Carolynn's lips drew back from her teeth in the type of smile a toddler pulls for a photograph. It was as if she had forgotten how to smile naturally.

115

'Thank you.'

Her cold hand found Jessie's. 'I won't lie to you again.'

Jessie nodded, forcing herself not to recoil from the chilly touch.

'There's something I need to ask you to do,' Jessie said. There was no easy way to broach the subject, no easy words. 'Detective Inspector Bobby Simmons is someone I've worked with before. I think you should call him and tell him where you are. I'm sure that he just wants to get in touch so that he can let you know about this other little girl's death personally, out of courtesy. He would have hated to know that you'd read about her in the paper.'

Carolynn looked horrified. 'I couldn't. I really couldn't. You won't tell him you've seen me, will you?'

'No. *No,* absolutely not. I would never, ever break patient confidentiality. But I do think that you're only making it worse for yourself if you carry on hiding. Mentally worse for yourself, if nothing else. Living your life with such secrecy is very stressful.'

'You have no idea what I went through when Zoe died, and afterwards, with the police and the trial. *That* was mentally destructive.'

'You're right, I have no idea, and I do understand why you want to hide from society, but hiding from the police is different.'

Carolynn bent her head and gave a faint nod. She was twisting the strip that she'd torn from the blue paper napkin in her fingertips. Jessie watched her, the emotions ticker-taping across her face, only half the information she'd usually have access to as she still hadn't been able to make eye contact, every second line in the story missing.

'This little girl's death could be connected to Zoe's. This

might be your chance to finally get justice for her and clear your name.'

Carolynn's fingers stilled and she nodded again, distractedly. Her gaze had moved from the napkin to the newspaper that Jessie had spread across the middle of the table. The overhead lights cast shadows where her eyes should have been, so that Jessie couldn't tell exactly where she was looking. At her photograph again? At something else?

Carolynn sensed Jessie watching her. She knew that she should look up, catch Jessie's eye and smile, chat, work on the friendship she was determined to establish, but her gaze was gripped by a photograph that she hadn't noticed before. It was the photograph of a necklace. Her necklace. *Hers*. A 'new mummy' present from Roger when Zoe had arrived. It was a silver locket carved with the imprint of two sets of footprints walking alongside each other as if on a beach, one pair an adult's and the other a child's. It had been too mawkish for her taste and she'd hardly worn it, hadn't noticed its absence until a few days ago. She had no idea when it had gone missing.

'Give DI Simmons a call, Carolynn,' she heard Jessie say. 'Tell him where you are.'

She tore her gaze from the necklace. She felt disorientated, horribly claustrophobic suddenly, as if the floor was rising and the ceiling falling, trapping her in between. *You must have mislaid it around the house somewhere. It's bound to turn up*, Roger had said, a few days ago, as they'd stood in their spotless bedroom, no clutter within which to lose personal items.

Something else occurred to her suddenly.

Oh, God – prints. She hadn't worn the necklace since forever, but it might still hold her fingerprints. The police had them and her DNA on file from Zoe's murder. If the necklace did bear her prints, how long would it take the police to match them? Anything connected with a child murder would be expedited through the system.

Jessie watched the woman across from her, the look of abject horror on her face. Something fundamental had changed. Was it something she'd said – her urging Carolynn to contact Marilyn? Or had Carolynn seen something in the paper? Or nothing? Just her being uptight, over-sensitive? The tabletop was a mess, Carolynn's empty coffee cup sitting in a puddle of black sludge, the dregs of her chocolate pancake spread across her plate, like a mud fight. Threads of tissue from the napkin that Carolynn had shredded were dancing across the tabletop, animated by the breeze from the open café doorway. Looking at the detritus, Jessie felt the familiar hiss of the electric suit travel across her skin. If she were alone, she would scoop up the loose threads and stuff them into the coffee cup, call a waitress over to clear up the china and cutlery. But she was supposed to be the professional here, inspire confidence, and she couldn't let Carolynn glimpse that damaged part of her psychology.

'Are you OK, Carolynn?' she asked.

'Yes, of course. It's been a lovely lunch.' A bright, brittle laugh. 'I don't mean to be rude, but I don't think that I need any more sessions.' That stilted smile again. 'I . . . I've enjoyed talking to you here far more than I did in your office. It's so nice just chatting like this. I feel as if we're getting on so well. I'd love to keep in touch, not on a professional basis, but as . . . as friends.'

Jessie returned Carolynn's smile, hers feeling as fakely plastered to her face as Carolynn's looked.

'Call DI Simmons,' she said, matter-of-factly. She felt

intensely uncomfortable suddenly. Something about that twisted smile, Carolynn's tone, her words, made Jessie think again of what Callan had said.

She could be a child killer. She could have murdered her own child.

He was wrong. She was sure that he was wrong. Even so, she had thought that she would be able to breeze through this lunch, persuade Carolynn to contact Marilyn, or not, but at least she would have tried, and then shrug off the meeting, maybe even find a B & B and have a relaxed evening by the beach, drive back to Surrey in the morning to spend the rest of the weekend with Callan making amends, put this woman and the two dead little girls to the back of her mind. How naive had she been? She didn't want to be friends, didn't want that level of connection to someone who had lied so compulsively to her, whatever the motivation.

'Tell him where you were,' she reiterated. 'He'll understand. I know that you had a terrible experience previously, but I can vouch for the fact that he is one of the good guys.'

Carolynn nodded. If only Jessie knew the half of it – the torment she'd experienced because of that man – she wouldn't say that he was one of the good guys, wouldn't suggest that she call.

'I'll call,' she murmured, a tiny lie against all the others she had told. She'd been lying so long that she barely knew truth from fiction any more. Sliding her hand across the table, she coiled her fingers around Jessie's and met her ice-blue eyes directly for the first time ever. 'I'll call, but only because *you've* asked me to.'

19

Through a cloud of smoke, Ruby nodded. For a few moments, the only sound was that of her inhaling and exhaling and of Workman turning a page in her notebook.

'She was whiter than white,' Ruby murmured eventually.

Marilyn hadn't expected that. 'Whiter than white? What do you mean?'

'There was an advert for washing powder that I remember watching, years ago, when I was little. Proper little, four or five. A blonde girl in a meadow full of wild flowers. There was some stupid jingly song that went with the advert and that was all I could think of when I saw her.' Ruby started to sing, almost under her breath. '*Little girl, far away in a world of your own, in a world built of dreams that are yours and yours alone—*' She broke off with a smirk, but Marilyn noticed that her eyes were shinier than they had been. The smoke making them water? 'She was so white. The sand is white, isn't it, up there in the dunes? Like white powder. And she was whiter, brilliant white, like she'd been washed.'

He gave an encouraging nod, but didn't speak.

'Her hair was brown and curly. Her eyes were open. She was laid inside that heart of shells and that doll was beside her.'

'Did you notice anything about the doll?'

'It had black marks around its neck that looked as if they'd been drawn on with a felt-tip.'

Marilyn nodded. 'Anything else?'

'Like what?'

Its eyes. The colour? He didn't say it, couldn't lead her. *Did you notice that the doll's eyes were the same colour as the girl's?*

'Anything else notable?' he said.

Ruby shrugged and her gaze slid from his. 'It was just a cheap plastic doll in a shiny pink ballerina dress.'

Marilyn nodded. 'What else did you see?'

'The little girl had a necklace around her neck.'

'What was it?'

'Silver. A silver chain with a pendant hanging off it.'

'Did you notice anything about the pendant?' Marilyn asked.

'It was engraved with footprints. Two sets, big and small.' Her gaze dipped. 'An adult and a child, walking next to each other.'

Marilyn wasn't sure if he imagined that her voice was rougher, as if she was forcing the words around a lump in her throat. The cigarette smoke again?

'Are you sure?'

'Positive.' She took a long drag on the cigarette, funnelled the smoke slowly out of her nostrils.

Marilyn resisted the urge to lean forward, right into her personal space, to surround himself with the smoke. Second-hand stress relief.

Footprints. An adult and a child. She was right.

He was asking, not because he needed to know what the necklace looked like. He had seen it in an evidence bag and it was currently at the lab being fingerprinted, expedited, the child murder shot to the top of the month's 'to-do list', the year's 'to-do list'. He had asked her the question to see how many details she had absorbed, how well he could rely on her testimony.

'It reminded me of God,' she said.

'Why God?' he asked.

'Just something I remember from school. A story about walking on the sand with God. Footprints in the sand or something stupid like that. That's what it made me think of anyway, that necklace. The beach and that necklace.'

Marilyn nodded. Her eyes were the same as he remembered from the first time they had met. Such a soft blue that they were almost violet. The colour of the purplest bluebells. Workman's voice made their eyes unlock and their heads swivel in unison.

'"Lord, you said once I decided to follow you, You'd walk with me all the way. But I noticed that during the saddest and most troublesome times of my life, there was only one set of footprints. I don't understand, when I needed You the most, You would desert me." "My precious child, I love you and I will never leave you, never, ever, during your trials and testings. When you saw only one set of footprints, it was then that I carried you."'

'Do you go to church then, Detective Sergeant Workman? You one of them?' Ruby asked.

Workman shook her head and smiled. 'It's pinned above the kitchen sink in the children's centre I volunteer at every Saturday. I get to do a lot of washing up, so I've read it that many times I could recite it in my sleep.'

Ruby held her gaze for a long moment, without returning the smile. She curled her lip.

'There was only one set of prints when I needed him the most and they were mine,' she hissed. 'He was no-fucking-where to be seen during the saddest times of my life.'

Hands locked into one fist, fingers white with tension, Workman nodded. This interview fell outside her range of experience. Marilyn would have liked to be alone with Ruby, knew that he would be able to get under her skin more if they were alone, but he'd already sent Workman out on a coffee-run once and protocol would throw up its hands in horror if he asked her to leave him to it now, with the undercurrent palpable. His gaze moved from Workman's and found the cross hanging around Ruby's neck.

'No, before you ask,' she said, noticing him looking. 'I don't fucking believe.' She gave a short, harsh laugh. 'Mary Magdalene is the patron saint of prostitutes. That's why I wear it. Got nothing to do with Him, or any other sodding man for that matter.'

'You're not a prostitute any more, Ruby.'

She winked, the armour sliding back into place seamlessly, as if she had never lowered it. 'I could be if you wanted me to be, DI Simmons. I've always quite fancied you.'

Marilyn could feel himself blushing. Not because of what she had said – he saw it for the edgy banter that it was – but because she'd said it in front of Workman. He felt reduced to the gauche PC he had been the first time he'd met Ruby.

'Ruby,' he muttered, shaking his head.

She lifted the cigarette to her mouth again, and his gaze found the pattern of needle marks on her arm.

'Life's tough, DI Simmons,' she murmured. 'Even for you

with your fancy job.' Her gaze moved to Workman. 'Even for you, hey?'

'If you were out there looking for treasure, why didn't you take the necklace?' he asked, dodging her comment.

She lifted her shoulders and gave a wry half-smile. 'I was going to nick it, wasn't I? But not off a dead child. I'm not total scum.'

'Did you touch it?'

'Yeah.'

Marilyn's groan was audible.

'I wasn't thinking.'

He nodded. 'We've got your prints on file. Where are you living now, Ruby?'

'East Wittering. Council flat.'

'What's the address, please,' Workman cut in, flicking to a new page in her notebook.

'Wyatt Court, Stocks Lane.'

'Number?'

'Seven.'

Workman made a note.

Marilyn sat back. 'Anything else that you think might be important?'

Ruby shook her head.

'Thank you for coming in, Ruby. Please don't go anywhere without letting us know. We'll probably need to speak to you again.'

She nodded. 'Got nowhere to go and no money to go there with, DI Simmons.'

Marilyn walked Ruby down the stairs.

'The last I heard, you had a child, Ruby,' he said gently, as they walked.

'Had, yeah.'

'What happened to him or her?'

A careless shrug. 'I got him adopted.'

'When?'

'Ten, eleven years ago now.' She smiled sardonically. 'I had no use for a kiddie.'

Marilyn nodded. 'I'll let you out the back. The press are out front.'

'You mean I don't get to have my fifteen minutes of fame?'

'Up to you.'

'Nah.' A wink. 'The back door's fine. I'm well used to taking it the back way, whether I want to or not.' The carapace firmly back in place.

As they walked side by side along the corridor in silence, Ruby dug in the pocket of her cargo jacket, produced a yellow packet and held it out to Marilyn. He shook his head.

'Rescue Remedy?' he asked, raising an eyebrow.

Another sardonic smile. 'Take a lot more than this gum to rescue me, DI Simmons, but I gotta start somewhere.'

Warm air billowed into the corridor and sunlight flooded the worn wooden floorboards as he pulled the door open for her.

'Take care, Ruby. You know where I am if you need anything.'

'Thanks, DI Simmons.' Standing on tiptoes, she gave him a quick peck on the cheek. 'See ya then.'

Popping the chewing gum into her mouth, she turned away and he watched her clack in her silver stilettos down the concrete steps and across the car park, feeling as if something heavy had dropped hard into his stomach. A dead weight.

20

Taking her ballet pumps off at the top of the bank, Jessie tucked them neatly, side by side behind the Fisherman's Hut and picked her way down the steep, pebbly section of the beach. The sand was damp, a cool salve to her bare soles after the sharp heat of the pebbles. She walked towards the water – two hundred metres away, the tide fully out, the sea's edge a bubbling line of white foam – stopping occasionally to inspect a shell, dig her toe into the sand-spaghetti string of a lugworm cast.

'I'll call,' Carolynn had said. 'I'll call, but only because *you've* asked me to.'

Jessie shivered, remembering those words and the feel of Carolynn's fingers. Her touch had been chill, as if she'd been resting her hand on a block of ice. Used to their roles being clearly demarcated by the professional environment, Jessie had expected that subtle red line to remain intact. But Carolynn had taken their lunch as an opportunity to step over a boundary that Jessie had no intention of letting her cross.

She paused to trace the tip of her toe around the sand-spaghetti trail of another lugworm cast.

I'll call him, but only because you've *asked me to.*

She hadn't believed Carolynn. She had fallen for many of her lies, but now she was wiser and that statement had been accompanied by direct eye contact for the first time ever, an unblinking stare that had unnerved her with its intensity. When most people lied, they broke eye contact, if only fleetingly, but for Carolynn, a woman who had never met Jessie's gaze directly before, the opposite was true. She had forced herself to hold Jessie's gaze unwaveringly, in the mistaken belief that eye contact signalled truth.

What should she do now? She knew what Callan would want her to do, but he was a policeman. It was in his nature, his DNA, to doubt. Carolynn had terminated their professional relationship, so she no longer needed to worry about patient confidentiality, but could she really just hang her out to dry? Squashing the lugworm cast flat with the base of her foot, an unnecessarily destructive action which she regretted the second she'd done it, she walked on until she reached the water's edge and turned right, heading towards West Wittering, a kilometre away, slopping along in the shallows, her feet engulfed in white foam with each new breaking wave.

She had experienced social isolation herself when she'd returned to school after being incarcerated at Hartmoor Mental Hospital for a year, and it had hurt, badly. She'd been a teenager then, unable to escape, had made up for her lack of control by tidying and ordering the fragments of her life contained within her four bedroom walls. How much worse would Carolynn's experience have been – a woman accused of murdering her own daughter? She would have had perfect strangers intimidating her in the street: stalking her, calling her names, spitting on her, shoving and hitting her. Threatening calls at all hours of the day and night, bricks hurled through her windows, her car scratched and dented, its tyres slashed, the walls of her house graffitied.

Unlike Jessie, Carolynn had been able to run and hide, and she'd done just that. Who could blame her? Certainly not a girl who'd been persecuted herself. Persecuted for having done no wrong, for having been a victim. She would have hidden, run, when she was fifteen, if she'd had the chance, but she'd had to stick it out, add the mental scars of bullying and social isolation to the scars of her brother's suicide, her mother's abandonment, her father's betrayal, layer upon layer of psychological damage, like rock strata laid down in her psyche. The outward sign, her OCD and the electric suit that she could feel now skittering across her skin, a tightness around her throat that was labouring her breathing as she walked.

A sudden noise, alien against the repetitive, soothing sound of the lapping waves. Pulling her mobile from her pocket, she glanced down at the name flashing on the screen. Callan. She was tempted not to answer it. She didn't want to argue with him again, and thoughts of Carolynn, of her own past, had put her on edge. It would be easier to just not answer than to have a conversation where she loaded his innocent remarks with a negative essence that they didn't have. As she dithered, her phone went silent. *Decision made.*

Twenty seconds later, it rang again. Perhaps something was wrong?

'Callan.'

'Good afternoon, beautiful Jessie Flynn.' He sounded

happy, though she sensed that his mood was forced for her benefit, that he was making a conscious effort to start the conversation off on a good footing. ' . . . mum just called.'

'Your mum?'

'No – yours. She's arranged a new time for the dress fitting. Monday at ten.'

'Oh, OK. That's fine. Tell her that's fine.'

'I already told her it's fine. She said to tell you that you can't miss it.'

'I won't miss it.' She ducked, as a squawking seagull swooped low over her head. Did they like shiny, or was that just magpies?

Silence on the other end of the telephone line.

'Callan?'

No response. Had she accidentally cut him off while ducking?

'Callan? Are you there?'

'Did you find her?'

'Who? My mum?'

'No, Jessie not your mum.'

'Who, then?'

An exasperated sigh. 'Laura . . . Carolynn . . . whatever the hell the woman's name is.'

Oh shit. Was he just fishing? Could she bluff it out?

'Have you gone mad, Callan?' she said, dodging sideways as the seagull swooped again.

'Wind, waves, seagull. I am a detective and it wasn't the hardest case I've ever worked on.'

She could picture his jaw set into an intractable square, the cynicism in his amber eyes.

'OK, clever boy. Yes, I'm at the beach.'

'Which beach?'

'East Wittering.'

'Is that where Laura's hiding from her adoring public and the law?'

'Carolynn. It's Carolynn. And we've been through this, Callan. She was acquitted.'

'Yeah, we *have* been through this. She was acquitted due to lack of evidence. As I said before, it's not the same thing as being found innocent. Marilyn believes that she's guilty.'

'I don't believe that Marilyn is or was objective.'

'He's a great detective.'

'He is a great detective, but he's not infallible—'

'None of us are infallible, Jessie.'

She ignored the inference, ploughed on: '—and the murder of a child is highly emotive. As time went on in the Zoe Reynolds case, he must have felt under huge pressure to nail someone for her murder – anyone.'

She started walking again, just beyond the reach of the waves, her feet making perfect imprints in the wet sand, a barefoot chain where she had walked strung out behind her like a memory.

'So she's living in East Wittering?'

'Bracklesham Bay. It's the same patch of picturesque British seaside urban sprawl, but half a kilometre east along the beach.'

'And you've met her, spoken with her?'

'I had lunch with her. Or at least, I had lunch and she sat there watching me eat. She doesn't seem to "do" eating.'

'Is she going to contact Marilyn?'

'I asked her to contact him and she said that she would.'

'She's already proved herself to be a pathological liar.'

'She had reasons to lie. Good reasons.'

'So you trust her? You trust her to get in touch with Marilyn?'

'Oh for God's sake, Callan, I'm not a bloody mind reader. Get off my case.'

The white triangle of a yacht's sail, breaking the thin blue line of the horizon where sea met sky, caught Jessie's eye, the cloudy slash of a plane's contrail, heading out across the Atlantic Ocean, above it. People holidaying. Life continuing as normal.

'I'm sure you told me once that you didn't work with people who lied,' Callan said, breaking the silence. She heard the smile in his voice, a forced smile, but even so, she recognized that he was making an effort to lighten the moment, pull back from the argument they were careering towards.

'And you said that I work with people who lie all the time: patients. And she is my patient—' Jessie broke off. 'Was, actually. She said, at lunch, that she doesn't feel she needs any more sessions.'

'So you no longer have an issue with patient confidentiality.'

'I'm not dobbing her in, Callan. Patient confidentiality aside, that would be a horrendous breach of her trust.'

'This isn't a game, Jessie.'

'I'm not treating it as a game.'

'For Christ's sake, you could be sheltering a child murderer. Actually, let me correct that statement: a *double* child murderer.'

'She's innocent.'

'Jesus, listen to yourself. You're sounding as subjective as you're accusing Marilyn of being.' She heard the choppy, tense sound of his breathing. 'And you're worrying me, Jessie.'

'Worrying you? You're supposed to be my boyfriend, not my babysitter.'

'If you don't want a babysitter, don't behave like a baby,' he snapped.

Her thumb found the phone symbol, cutting him off. She stared at the blank phone in her hand for a few moments, half-willing it to ring again, not knowing how she'd react if it did. It didn't ring. *Bastard*. Turning away from the water, she retraced her steps to where the steep pebbly section of the beach met the sand and slumped down, her bottom on the warm, dry stones, bare feet on the cool, damp sand.

When had their relationship become so antagonistic? Her fault, she knew, ever since the injury to her hand had forced her to leave the Defence Psychology Service. Hers for constantly being on edge. Should she just call him back, apologize? Probably. But she knew that she wouldn't, knew that the nugget of her personality that was stubborn and self-righteous had dug its heels in, despite knowing that she was shooting herself in the foot. That she was risking the best thing that had ever happened to her.

21

Though Carolynn couldn't bear to be alone in this dark, claustrophobic little house, images of Zoe and Jodie careering around inside her skull, she couldn't go outside for fear of being recognized. Even with the curtains closed, she felt as if she was inhabiting a goldfish bowl, as if every passer-by knew that Carolynn Reynolds, the woman who had slithered out of a guilty verdict for strangling her own daughter, the woman who was running alone on the beach when Jodie Trigg was murdered, was hiding out behind those dirty white walls. As if she'd peer out through a crack in the curtains and see a crowd in the street, brandishing pitchforks and baying for her blood.

Her pulse pounded in her ears as she paced restlessly from the kitchen to the hallway, to the sitting room with its coiled vine walls, the tension inside her escalating with each step until she felt as if she would combust from its intensity. The house had a smell of its own that she had grown to hate, the tickly scent of dirt and dust that, however hard she cleaned, she could never eradicate, the years of rental neglect ingrained in its every atom. It was a smell she had come to associate with confinement, with claustrophobia, with a miserable, lonely existence.

The sudden blare of the telephone made her jump. Ducking into the hallway, she snatched at the receiver.

'Roger.'

'Carolynn.'

'Where are you?'

'I'm at work. I was phoning to check how you are.'

'The newspapers.' The words rushed out of her. 'Have you seen them?'

'Yes.'

'My face is in all of them. They'll arrest me again, accuse me of killing that second little girl.'

That second little girl.

Jodie Trigg.

The little girl who lived on the static caravan park, who I befriended six months ago when I saw her hanging around on the beach outside the house alone, with nothing to do and nowhere to go. The little girl I never told you about, because I knew that you would stop me from having contact with her.

'It's a coincidence. Her death has nothing to do with Zoe.'

'You *can't* believe that, Roger. She was found in the same place, in a heart of shells, with an identical doll by her side. It must be the same killer.'

She slapped a hand over her mouth, pushing back the bile that rose up her throat, as a horrifying thought occurred to her. If the police found out she was living here and invented a reason to search the house, they would doubtless find some of Jodie's fingerprints. *Oh God.* Where had Jodie been? What had she touched? All the surfaces in the kitchen for sure: she'd drunk orange juice and eaten chocolate biscuits at the table many times, stayed for an early dinner often too. The downstairs toilet. Where else? The sitting room . . . had she been in there? And what about upstairs? Yes, she'd been upstairs a couple of times too. She'd have to clean everything, every handle, every door, every surface.

'Carolynn. *Carolynn.*' Roger's voice cut through her thoughts. 'Listen to me. You were at home when that girl was killed and I was at work. You always have the lights on, even during the day, so someone would have seen you through the window.'

'Yes,' she murmured. She couldn't tell him that she had been out running in the rain, had run down the beach to West Wittering, the beach deserted.

'We'll be able to find someone to testify on your behalf.'

At the word 'testify', Carolynn's stomach knotted.

'But it won't come to that.'

Her legs were trembling. She leaned against the wall for support, clutching the receiver to her ear as if it was a life raft.

'We need to move, go somewhere else, before the police find out where we are.'

'We're not going anywhere, Carolynn.'

'I can't go through it again—'

'Just do what I tell you. Stay at home, don't open the door and don't speak to anyone. I'll be home in a couple of hours.'

Jodie Trigg. I knew her.

'Close the curtains—'

'I already have.'

'Go upstairs and get one of your pills, put the telly on and watch one of those rubbishy chat shows that you like—'

135

'I don't want to take a pill,' she snapped. 'They make me feel drowsy, stupid.'

I need a clear head. I need to think. I grew up in a prison. Spending my adult life in one is unconscionable. I can't do it. I won't do it.

'Can't you come back sooner?'

'I've got a few things I need to finish at work, but I'll be home as soon as I can.'

Before she could answer, the dial tone buzzed in her ear. As she lowered the receiver to its cradle, her legs buckled. Sliding down the wall, she concertinaed herself into a 'Z' on the hall floor, tucked her face between her knees and screamed until her throat was raw.

Zoe.

Jodie.

You were home when that girl was killed.

If DI Simmons found her, how would she explain the missing hours when she'd been running along the coast, the rain cloaking her in solitude, trying to shake the headache, the ghastly images that the second anniversary of Zoe's death had surfaced, like a horror film reel spinning inside her head. He had failed to convict in Zoe's case. He couldn't let a second child murder go unsolved. With Zoe, as time went on, he'd needed a scapegoat and she had been an easy target. Her fingerprints had been on the shells surrounding Zoe's body, all over that hideous doll left by her daughter's side.

Oh God. The necklace. She had forgotten to tell Roger about the necklace. She couldn't tell him that she knew Jodie, but surely when he learned that her necklace had been found around the dead girl's neck, he would agree to leave, to run, to go to ground somewhere else, far from here.

Unwinding herself from her crunched 'Z', Carolynn pulled the telephone from the hall table on to her knee and dialled Roger's mobile. It went straight to voicemail, didn't even ring. He had been hurried when they'd spoken, keen to cut their call short, she'd sensed from his tone, so he must have known that his phone battery was running on empty. He wouldn't have switched it off – surely? – not when he knew how stressed and upset she was.

Once, a couple of months ago, Roger had called his boss from the home phone and when he'd gone upstairs to bed, she'd quickly keyed in 1471 and scribbled down the 'last number dialled'. Roger liked to keep work and home separate and would have been furious if he'd known, but she wanted the number in case of emergencies and was glad now that she'd done it. She needed to tell him about the necklace.

A man answered, his voice deep and sonorous.

'He's not in today, Mrs Reynard.' *Reynard*: their cover surname. Reynard – fox – cunning. Roger had liked the inference. And it was close enough to their actual surname to be memorable, off-the-cuff answerable to:

'Oh.'

'He hasn't been in since Wednesday. Perhaps he's working somewhere else. Some of my guys moonlight at other places for the odd day or two if the pay's right, though he did say that he was off sick.' A deep chuckle echoed down the line, a chuckle that Carolynn could close her eyes and sink into. No wonder Roger liked to spend so much time at work. His boss sounded easy-going, kind. But Roger wasn't there today.

'Did you say Wednesday?'

'Yes, Mrs Reynard. Wednesday was the last time I saw Roger.'

137

'He wasn't there yesterday?' Carolynn pressed.

'No, I told you, Wednesday.' The man laughed again, but with a slight edge this time. 'Tell him, I'm expecting him back on Monday, could you please. We've got a big new landscaping job starting next week for a stately home, so I need him here.'

'Yes, I will,' Carolynn managed.

'And you take care now, Mrs Reynard.'

As she laid the receiver back on its stand, she felt as if a black sinkhole was opening underneath her. Roger hadn't been at work yesterday or today.

You were at home when that girl was killed and I was at work.

22

There was a pale, ragged line of shells where the flat sand of the beach met the steep stony section, as if the tide, when it came in, brought them as far as the pebbles, but couldn't carry them further. With her Judas left hand, Jessie reached for the closest, the multicoloured oil-slick oval of an oyster shell, concentrating hard on sending the signal from her brain to her fingers to command them to curl and grip. It felt like a gargantuan effort: as if she had to will each electrical impulse to travel from her cerebellum down the nerves, visualize them sparking like lightning, like a flash of electricity from the dreaded suit she could still feel coating her limbs, across each synapse. If there had been anyone around, even people she didn't know, she would have deferred to her right hand, picked the shell up in one confident, fluid movement. But the afternoon was petering towards early evening, the beach virtually deserted. She could use her left without feeling self-conscious, practise, train her deadened fingers, do something positive for a change. Pinching the oyster shell between fingertips and thumb, she placed it on a pristine patch of sand to her left, unsullied by footprints or worm casts.

Another shell. A clam, this time. The pinch required smaller, the movement more intricate. Her fingers felt as if they were encased in lead gloves. The muscles were tired already, she realized, the tendons stressed, just by that one fine movement of pinching and moving the oyster shell. She felt close to tears. Not only because of her inability to master the use of her own traitorous hand, but also because of Carolynn, Callan, the feeling that she was floating, anchorless in the world at the moment, the knowledge that her OCD was worsening and that, despite the window into other people's minds that her profession afforded her, she didn't know how to help herself.

Switching to her right hand, she moved the clam next to the oyster. She collected five more shells, arranging them with the others in a curved line, their outside edges symmetrical. Seven shells in all – lucky seven – each one different. An oyster, a cockle, a clam, a mussel and three she couldn't name. Pushing herself to her feet, she wandered along the edge of the stones, following the ragged line of shells, bending and collecting more. Returning to her previous spot, she sorted the shells, selecting seven more, identical to the first seven. She arranged them as a mirror image of the first to form the shape of a heart. Zoe and Jodie's killer or killers had arranged a heart around their bodies and left a doll by their sides. Jodie also had a necklace around her throat. What was the significance of each of those items?

The heart – love? The breakdown of love? Hatred? Jealousy? Betrayal? All different sides of the same multifaceted shape.

The doll? A historically significant item for the children

or for their murderer? A token to keep the dead child company – a tiny glimmer of humanity from the killer – or something left to taunt the living, the bereaved?

And what about the necklace? It had looked from the photograph in the newspaper to have something engraved on its surface, but Jessie hadn't been close enough to see what that was. Why did Jodie have a necklace around her neck and not Zoe? Was it Jodie's necklace or had the killer put it around her neck? So many questions to which, she hoped for the little girls' and their loved ones' sakes, Marilyn had some answers.

She looked back down to her heart of shells. It was beautiful: too beautiful to be associated with tragedy and death. Collecting up the shells, she slipped them into the side pocket of her handbag. Perhaps she would make a picture frame for her mother's wedding. A heart-shaped picture frame to celebrate love rather than death.

23

Workman shivered.

'Are you OK, ma'am?'

'Just someone walking over my grave, DC Cara.'

Walking over the grave of a dead girl.

The street looked the same as she remembered it, exactly the same. The leaves on the small poplars planted at intervals along the pavement, as luscious summer emerald as the last time she'd been here, a mix of black, grey and navy family Range Rover Evoques, Volvos and BMW four-wheel drives and compact hatchbacks, nanny runarounds, parked at the kerb. No nets in any of the windows, not then or now, all plantation shutters or nothing at all, the owners of these smart, five-bedroom, redbrick terraced houses in south-west London, happy to let passers-by glimpse their enviably comfortable lifestyles.

She thought now, as she had thought back then, almost two years ago, when she had first visited this address with Marilyn, how horrifying it would have been for this neighbourhood to have such tragedy as a child murder lurching down these suburban streets, a thing as unimaginable as an alien descending from outer space.

Workman didn't need to be here, Cara was capable of handling it alone, but she'd wanted to come back, unable to shake off the sense that, by being here in person, she'd be able to sniff out the Reynolds' trail on the air like a bloodhound.

'Let's chat with the neighbours,' she said to Cara. 'See if any of them know where the Reynolds have disappeared to.'

Marilyn had tasked Cara with using his 'Millennials' knowledge of all things technology-related to track the Reynolds down via the Internet, and Cara had spent most of last night and today trying to locate them: scanning the electoral roll, mining 192.com, ferreting through all the online friendship and contacts databases he could think of – LinkedIn, Facebook, Instagram – searching credit-card databases, every search returning a blank. He had discovered that they had rented out their old family house in Battersea via an agency who dealt with them purely by email, and transferred the money to an 'Internet only' bank account that had been set up with their Battersea address. Beyond that, there was no trace. It was pitifully easy, these days, to get convincing fake identification documents via the Internet, allowing anyone who had the desire to reinvent themselves, to steal someone else's identity or create a fictional new one. The Reynolds had clearly made a very conscious decision to disappear and had engineered that disappearance with enviable aplomb.

Workman and Cara had just visited the Reynolds' old house. The woman renting it told them that the Reynolds hadn't left a forwarding address, but that she kept a cardboard box in the cellar, adding any mail addressed to them to the burgeoning pile, throwing away circulars or company promotions.

She smiled and shrugged. 'I should probably just throw it all away, but after what they've been through . . . ' She let the end of the sentence hang.

Workman took the box and its contents, telling the woman that she'd pass it on to the Reynolds when they tracked them down, after they'd opened and examined every item of post for clues – she didn't vocalize that last bit.

'I'll take this side of the road, you take the opposite,' she said to Cara. 'Make sure that you show your warrant card, as soon as they open the door.' Her inference clear: even here in the melting pot that was London, the sudden appearance of a mixed-race twenty-two-year-old male on their doorstep in the early evening, many parents still at work, their wives or nannies and children alone in the house, would induce suspicion and mistrust. 'Try not to arouse too much curiosity,' she added. 'We want to chat to the Reynolds out of courtesy, nothing more.'

Cara nodded. He was a good kid and Workman liked him. The Surrey and Sussex forces needed more diversity and switched-on, clever kids like Cara would, as well being fantastic assets in their own right, hopefully encourage others to join. Race should no longer be an issue, but it was: black, Asian and mixed-race kids as rare as hen's teeth outside the big south coast cities of Brighton, Portsmouth and Southampton, and even in those cities, rarely interested in joining the police, the perceived enemy.

A well-preserved, dark-haired woman in her mid to late fifties, dressed in a navy wrap dress and beige wedge-heeled sandals, answered the sage-green door of the house to the right of the Reynolds'.

'I was surprised when they just upped and left with no forwarding address,' she said, leaning against the doorjamb. 'I liked to think that we were friends, but I suppose when something like that happens, worlds shatter and nothing is the same. Perhaps it was naive of me to think they'd keep in touch.'

'You haven't heard anything at all? No emails, postcards, Christmas cards?'

The woman shook her head.

'Something innocuous, that might have slipped your mind?' Workman pressed.

'We're a friendly road, not best friends or anything, but friendly, and as far as I know, no one has heard from them. We haven't talked about them for months, to be honest, but with this second little girl found murdered on the same beach people have started talking again, wondering—' Breaking off, she raised an eyebrow and smiled. Workman let the silence grow. She was here to gain information, not to share it. 'Wondering what happened to this second little girl.' The woman finished. 'It would be good to know, considering how close we were to the whole event. You know how it is.'

Workman nodded. She did know how it was. Jodie Trigg's murder would precipitate an overdrive of wagging tongues. The residents of this tidy suburban street's connection to the Reynolds, however tenuous, would give them a macabre celebrity in the office, at the school gate and in the local coffee shops, which many would, no doubt, exploit with gusto. But she wasn't going to add fuel to the fire by providing information. She held out her business card to the woman.

'Thank you for your time. Please do get in touch if

145

anything occurs to you. The card has both my office and mobile numbers.'

With a final nod of thanks, she turned and clack-clacked her way back down the tiled path to the gate. *Onwards and upwards.* Or onwards at least: another sixteen front doors to knock on.

The clog of rush-hour traffic reminded Workman why she had never felt any desire to live in London or work for the Met.

'Do you mind if we pay another quick visit, Darren?'

Cara shook his head. 'Where to, ma'am.'

'Lambeth Cemetery, please. Blackshaw Road, Tooting.'

He glanced across.

'Zoe,' she said simply. 'Zoe Reynolds is buried there. I'd like to . . . ' She tailed off. *Like to what? Pay my respects? Apologize? Seek inspiration at the grave of a long-dead little girl who hasn't received justice?*

Tilting her head back, she closed her eyes, as much to avoid the searching glances Cara was casting at her as anything else, letting the rev of idling engines, the hoot of frustrated horns fade into the background.

Cara had worked in Traffic for four years before transferring to Surrey and Sussex Major Crimes and so, unlike when Marilyn drove her in that heap of rust and Blu-Tack he called a car – one hand holding the wheel, the other a cigarette, his mind ruminating on some issue that didn't involve getting them from A to B in one piece – Workman felt no need to direct Cara to a cemetery he had never been to or to ask him to keep his eyes on the road.

They'd had no luck with any of the Reynolds' old neighbours. The couple seemed to have successfully disappeared off the face of the earth. Before her daughter's murder, Carolynn Reynolds had been the assistant director of Children's Specialist Services at Wandsworth London Borough Council, had been for years. And after – nothing. Just the investigation and trial, every aspect of her old life in smithereens.

What had her husband, Roger, worked as? A surveyor? An architect? Something to do with buildings, property, interiors. No, not interiors, she remembered suddenly, exteriors. A landscape architect, of course. Workman remembered Marilyn muttering at the time about how ridiculous a name it was for a glorified gardener. *Like calling a cleaner a 'hygiene specialist', or a bus driver a 'transportation facilitator'.*

What was important though, was that it could be a 'cash-in-hand' job, the civilized end of the British black market. The Reynolds could disappear entirely from the radar and still earn a living. So how on earth were they going to find them?

24

Callan fetched himself a bottle of beer from the fridge and went into the garden, slumping down at Jessie's garden table and hefting over a second chair to rest his feet on. It was a warm evening, the sun hovering halfway between sky and land, washing the field at the end of the garden with a mellow orange glow.

He took a swig of beer, his mind tracing back over his phone conversation with Jessie. It hadn't gone as he had planned, not that he'd given much thought as to how to handle the discussion before he'd called her, to be fair. His mistake. He was worried about her and not just because of that woman, Carolynn Reynolds. Since she'd been invalided out of the army, she had developed an armoured carapace of aggression that shielded the hurt and vulnerability underneath. He didn't know how to handle her these days, felt as if he was treading on eggshells, and breaking the majority of them, despite his best efforts.

As he raised the beer bottle to his lips, he caught movement, a shadow, from the corner of his eye: Ahmose, Jessie's elderly next-door neighbour, looking over the adjoining fence. Jessie had told him that she'd bought this cottage, down a single-track lane in the Surrey Hills, surrounded by fields, precisely to avoid unwanted human contact, and that her heart had plummeted when Ahmose had arrived on her doorstep the morning she moved in, proffering a miniature rose, full of advice on how to keep it flowering. But in their three years as neighbours, Jessie had grown to love and rely on this old Egyptian man more than her own parents – certainly more than her father, who she blamed for her brother Jamie's suicide.

Callan and Ahmose had settled into a comfortable relationship of nods, smiles and exchanged pleasantries, since he had as good as moved in with Jessie, the occasional evening spent, the three of them, chatting over dinner and a bottle of wine. But mostly he had left Jessie and Ahmose to it, recognized the depth of their relationship and his spare part in it.

'Do you want some company?' the old man asked.

Callan didn't. He was happy alone, wallowing in morose thoughts.

'That'd be, great. I'll let you in the front.'

He poured Ahmose a glass of red wine, and they returned to the garden together, Callan pulling out a chair, running his sleeve over the seat to brush off the moss before Ahmose sat down.

Ahmose indicated his gardening trousers. 'Wonderful service, but unnecessary.'

'Only the best for Jessie's surrogate family.'

They sat down and drank for a moment in silence. They had never been alone in each other's company and Callan

149

wasn't in the mood for small talk. His dulled brain fished around for a benign, chatty opener.

'How's the garden?'

'Dry,' Ahmose said. 'It's looking forward to the onset of autumn even if my bones aren't.'

Callan nodded. He had already run out of conversational steam.

'Where's Jessie?' Ahmose asked.

'The beach.'

'It was a lovely day for it. You didn't fancy going?'

Callan cast him a sideways glance. 'I wasn't invited.'

'Ah.'

'She went down to talk to one of her patients, a woman called Carolynn Reynolds.'

Ahmose was silent for a moment. 'Why does that name sound familiar?'

'She was on the news last night.'

'The child murder?'

'Yeah. She's the mother of the first girl who was murdered two years ago.'

'Of course, yes. I saw it on the news back then. It was a terrible tragedy. She was tried for her daughter's murder, wasn't she?'

'Tried and acquitted due to lack of evidence. Then she disappeared, went to ground.'

Callan clocked Ahmose casting him a narrowed glance across the table. He'd clearly noted his cynical tone, but when Ahmose spoke his voice was neutral.

'I didn't realize that Jessie knew her.'

Callan rolled his eyes. 'I don't think Jessie does know her. Jessie was treating her and swallowed a pack of lies.'

'So why is Jessie meeting with her?'

'To convince her to contact DI Simmons, who is the SIO for both cases, tell him where she is. He wants to speak with her about Jodie Trigg's murder.'

'And was she successful?'

'No.'

Setting his wine glass carefully on the table, Ahmose sat forward, steepling his fingers. 'And you're debating whether you should let DI Simmons know where this Carolynn woman is living? Go behind Jessie's back?'

Callan met the old man's searching dark gaze. The more time he spent with Ahmose, the more he understood why Jessie so valued his advice. He was clever, perceptive, astute.

'Yes. Should I betray her trust, to put it bluntly?'

Reaching for his glass and taking a long, slow sip, Ahmose nodded contemplatively. Callan kept a lid on his impatience as he waited for the old man to answer.

'I think, generally, that Jessie is a good judge of character,' he said. 'She is good at her job and that job requires an understanding of how people think, an intuition about what makes them tick, that most of us lack. And she likes me.' He paused, winked. 'And you, despite my early reservations.'

Callan nodded, unsmiling. He wasn't in the mood for cheery banter. 'So you're saying that I should respect Jessie's decision, do nothing?'

Ahmose cut him off with a raised hand. 'But . . . I've never seen her like this before. She is strung very highly, very brittle. Being invalided out of the army hit her hard.' He reached over and patted Callan's arm. Callan resisted the urge to pull away, unused to paternal-type contact. 'You need to make good decisions for both of you. That is one of the most important parts of being in a relationship, making good decisions when the other cannot, guiding them when they lose their way.' Ahmose withdrew his hand and lifted his shoulders in a small shrug. 'How do you say . . . feel free to tell me to mind my own business.'

Callan nodded. He had spent most of his life avoiding committed relationships. The army and relationships didn't mix well and he'd been happy to use his job as an excuse to play the field, screw around, for want of a better expression. Until Jessie.

'She doesn't want my help,' he muttered.

'She doesn't know what she wants,' Ahmose countered. 'She is not in a good place right now. She wasn't before this woman. Now, she is even less so, by the sound of it.'

'What would you do if you were me?'

Reaching across the table, Ahmose tapped his finger on Callan's mobile. 'I'd make a call,' he said.

'She'll hate me for it.'

'She will, without doubt, for a while.'

Callan's gaze found the horizon, the sun sinking now, its bottom edge dipping below the line of hills in the distance. The sky was a rainbow of fire colours, red, washing to orange, to magenta and pink high in the sky. Raising the beer bottle to his lips, he drained it.

'Give me a minute, Ahmose,' he said, pushing himself to his feet.

Palming his mobile, he walked to the end of the garden, scrolling through the numbers in his contacts until he found the one he was looking for.

25

'Did you go to her funeral?' Cara asked, as they walked, in the fading light, along the tarmac path that looped around the edge of Lambeth Cemetery.

Workman gave him a brief, tense smile. 'We weren't invited, if that's what you mean. But we kept an eye.' She pointed. 'From there, under those trees, hiding in the shade, as if we were in some Z-list thriller.'

They found the small grave easily, threading through scores of others, littered with cuddly animals, damp from yesterday evening's rain, plastic toys, china figurines and photographs, each the grave of a dead baby or child. Workman couldn't understand why cemeteries grouped the graves of children together, as if the death of one child wasn't horror enough for visitors.

Zoe's headstone was of black marble, the gold inscription simple: *Zoe Reynolds. Taken too soon. Forever loved.* No teddies or Wade whimsies on her grave. Just a plain black marble vase at the base of the headstone.

The last time that Workman had visited, just over nine

months ago, a few days before the end of the trial, when she could see the way it was going, see that they hadn't been able to provide the jury with enough hard evidence to convict Carolynn, she had caught an Uber from outside the Old Bailey, telling Marilyn she was visiting a family friend, unwilling even to open up to him about where she was going. She had felt self-indulgent. What right did she have to feel the child's death more than anyone else on the investigating team?

The vase had been empty then, a thin layer of frost frilling the black headstone, as if it had been decorated with paper doilies. Today it was filled with a spray of pure white roses, almost luminous in the semi-darkness. Workman knelt and fingered one spongy bud.

'They're fresh,' she said.

'What are you thinking, ma'am?'

'I'm thinking that there are only three people in this world who'd put flowers on the grave of this little girl, on the second anniversary of her murder.'

'The Reynolds,' Cara said, more of a statement than a question. 'Carolynn and Roger.'

Workman nodded.

'And the third?'

Her knees clicked as she stood. She wasn't getting any younger and despite regularly admonishing Marilyn for burning the candle at both ends and simultaneously incinerating the middle, she could do with looking after herself a bit more too.

'Roger has an eighty-year-old mother. She was devastated by Zoe's death. Genuinely.' *As opposed to* . . . she didn't say it. 'But I doubt it's her because she was admitted to a home a few months after Zoe died. She may be dead herself.

154

We should check, actually.' She added another line to her mental 'to-do' list.

'So one or both of them have been here,' Cara said, as they weaved their way back through the graves to the tarmac path.

'Yesterday, I'd say. Yesterday would make sense, wouldn't it?'

'The anniversary?'

'Yes.'

'So what does it mean?' Cara asked.

Workman shrugged. 'That one of them is thinking about Zoe at least, thinking and caring, and that they're not too far away.'

Her gaze found the dark space under the trees where she and Marilyn had stood watching the funeral. It was empty. *Of course, it would be.* What had she expected to see? The Reynolds? The ghost of a little girl waiting patiently for justice? The ghosts of two little girls?

26

A black mist descended over Marilyn as he walked into the dissecting room. Jodie Trigg, a little girl who'd once watched *X-Factor* and run on the beach with her friends was laid out before him, a waxy mannequin on a metal dissecting table in the centre of a chilly, white-tiled room, the embodiment of his failure. Her skin was pale and smooth, as if she had been washed clean in a soapy bath – *she was whiter than white* – and there was no smell, no scent of death, as if she was too young, too fresh for that.

The beanpole figure of Dr Ghoshal, his angular features all business, waited for him, flanked by two morticians, the unacknowledged hard labourers of the autopsy, to the pathologist's star turn. The three of them were ranged around Jodie's body, Dr Ghoshal at the head, the morticians either side, a sombre, frozen tableau. The only time that Marilyn had ever seen the pathologist and seasoned morticians behave as they were now, standing in silence, paying their respects, was two years ago, at Zoe Reynolds' autopsy. The sight, and the memory it dragged to the surface, twisted a knife deep in his chest. *Christ, how the hell am I going to make it through the next couple of hours?* He hadn't been blessed with a strong stomach, struggled with the autopsies of grown men, scumbags, who'd met their end at the hands of fellow drug dealers in revenge for trampling on their patch. *God shows no partiality* – it was a quote from the Bible, wasn't it? In the search for perpetrators, he showed no partiality either, believed that every victim deserved justice, however unsavoury they may have been in life, but it wasn't the same in an autopsy, the body stripped down to its rawest. In here, the sight of the naked little girl on that table made him want to kill to avenge her, administer a slow and agonizing death.

Dr Ghoshal gave a nod to acknowledge Marilyn's presence, breaking the sombre reverie. The morticians moved off silently on their rubber-soled feet and set about collecting bowls, turning on hoses, laying out instrument trays.

Dr Ghoshal cleared his throat. 'DI Simmons.' Not Marilyn. Never Marilyn, a nickname that Simmons had acquired on his first day in the force, after Manson, not Monroe, he would always hasten to add, due to their shared heterochromia. Dr Ghoshal wasn't one for ludicrous nicknames or manufactured mateyness. 'Nice to see you again.'

Only someone with antenna quivering as much as Marilyn's would have noticed the accent of tension in Ghoshal's habitually colourless tone.

'Thank you, Dr Ghoshal.'

Goshal indicated Jodie Trigg's corpse. 'What is your theory, Detective Inspector?'

'I'm trying to keep an open mind.'

Ghoshal smiled cynically. 'That goes without saying.'

Marilyn sighed. 'Similarities to the Zoe Reynolds case.

Look for similarities, please. Anything that I can use to link the two cases.'

'You think it's the same killer?'

'Yes, or a very knowledgeable copycat.'

'You favour the former explanation?'

No flies on Dr Ghoshal. Marilyn nodded.

'Why?'

'The age of the victim, the date of her murder, two years to the day of Zoe Reynolds, where her body was found, the heart of shells, the doll.' He paused. 'The method of killing also looks to be the same, though obviously that's up to you to confirm.'

Dr Ghoshal's' hawk-like gaze moved from Marilyn to survey the bruises around Jodie Trigg's throat. 'Strangulation.'

Marilyn nodded. 'The similarities are all very compelling, but circumstantial,' he said. 'I need to find a link between the two little girls' murders that wasn't in the papers, so that I can eliminate a copycat.'

Another cynical smile. 'Did any details fail to reach the papers?'

Marilyn rolled his eyes in response. He didn't mention that the colour of the doll's eyes had matched the colour of each child's eyes – brown for Zoe, green for Jodie. It wasn't relevant to the autopsy and he wanted Dr Ghoshal to believe that he was Marilyn's only hope of unequivocally linking the two girls' killer, a motivational nod to Dr Ghoshal's professional arrogance if nothing else. Also, he didn't know how leaky Dr Ghoshal's ship was, whether either mortician had a loose tongue. He didn't want his only trump card leaked to the press.

'Let's begin,' Dr Ghoshal said.

Positioning himself over the little girl's body, he raised

his scalpel. The sight of the child's soft skin puckering under the scalpel's blade before it bit, the sound of flesh and the muscle layer beneath being sliced, the smell of the freshly opened body hit Marilyn in successive waves, making his insides constrict. He didn't flatter himself that he had the right to feel the horror of this little girl's murder any more than anyone else in the room, but he suddenly knew, for his own self-preservation, for his sanity, that he just couldn't stick this one out.

'Give me a minute, Dr Ghoshal.'

For the first time in twenty years he walked out of an autopsy with no intention of returning.

27

On Marine Drive, one street back from the foreshore, Jessie found a weathered, white-painted bed and breakfast sign, the word 'Vacant' swinging below it. Though she couldn't see the sea, she could still smell it, the scent of salt carried on the wind, so hyper clean that it even made the country air around her Surrey Hills cottage seem clogged. The white-painted house, with its sea-green woodwork, looked as if it belonged on a Cornish clifftop.

The woman who opened the front door was late sixties, coiffed hair dyed a strawberry blonde, a thick layer of tan foundation that had caked into the crow's feet around her eyes, a dusting of blue eyeshadow and pearl pink lipstick. She was of the generation and type who wouldn't be seen outside their own bedroom without having 'done' their hair and 'put on their face'.

She smiled. 'Good evening, dear.'

'Do you have a room available?'

'For one night?'

'Yes.' Jessie lifted her shoulders as the woman's gaze moved to her handbag. 'I travel light.'

'I've got a lovely room overlooking the beach, a double, if that's OK.'

'That's great, thank you.'

'I'm Una Subramaniam,' the woman said, opening the door to reveal a cool, white-painted hallway, wood-framed seascape photographs pulling Jessie's gaze along it to a sitting room with a stunning view, through a wall of glass, to the beach and sea beyond. She led Jessie upstairs, past more framed seascapes, a sign made of driftwood that read, *The sand may brush off, but the memories will last forever*, an old tin notice proclaiming *Ladies on the beach must wear bloomers*. She walked sideways like a crab, stopping every few stairs to fill Jessie in on the story behind one or other of the photographs.

'My husband used to volunteer for the lifeboats,' she whispered conspiratorially, stopping beside the photograph of a group of men standing by the open doors of a lifeboat shed, the red bow of the boat inside extending from the shadows. She jabbed her index finger at the floor. 'Now he sits and expects to be waited on.'

Dazzling orange light cut into Jessie's eyes as Una Subramaniam opened the door to a white and breezy double bedroom, its far wall a huge window overlooking the beach and the evening sun reflecting off the sea. She dropped her handbag on the bed and went to the window. She could see the spot where she had found Carolynn earlier, fancied she could almost see her own footprints strung out along the beach, the indents in the sand made by her perfect heart of shells that were now stowed in her handbag.

161

'It's wonderful, thank you.'

'You're very lucky, lovey. Last weekend you wouldn't have got space anywhere down here last minute, but holiday season's over now for most kids. It's a shame. I like to look out of the window and see kiddies playing on the sand. That's what the beach is for, isn't it? For kids to enjoy.'

Jessie nodded, unwilling to engage in conversation beyond exchanging mild pleasantries. She wondered if Una Subramaniam had heard about Jodie Trigg. She would have done, surely? She probably hadn't mentioned the murder, because she hoped her guest hadn't.

'Thank you, Mrs Subniam?'

'Sub*rama*niam. The husband.' She jabbed her index finger at the floor again. 'Greek, years back, of course. I don't think he's ever been there. Will someone be joining you later, lovey, or are you down here on your own?'

'No, I'm alone.'

The woman raised an eyebrow. 'Now that does surprise me, a beautiful girl like you alone at the weekend. Though men are idiots aren't they? Always like the blondes.' She patted her own strawberry-blonde curls. 'Highlighted, obviously, but yours is far too dark to dye.'

'I've just split up with my fiancée so I wanted to get away for a day or two,' Jessie said. 'To clear my head.'

Una Subramaniam put her hand to her heart and gasped. 'I'm so sorry, my dear. I really didn't mean to pry.'

Jessie shrugged. Why was she being so facetious? Just for amusement after a frustrating day? A frustrating six months? Or because she had her finger firmly on the 'destruct' button – Callan's opinion. That because she was unhappy, she needed to spread unhappiness to others, make them feel as uncomfortable, as marginalized, as she did.

'If anyone comes, would you mind telling them that I'm not here?'

Hand still pasted to her heart, Una Subramaniam took a step back. 'Will he turn up here?'

'I don't think so. Hopefully, he doesn't know where I've gone.'

'Do you have a connection here? One he might know about?'

'We got engaged on the beach.'

Una Subramaniam's mouth popped open.

'But I'm sure he won't put two and two together and if he does he'll probably end up with five.'

Una Subramaniam patted Jessie's arm. 'I'm sure that it feels terrible now, lovey, but you know what,' she lowered her voice to that conspiratorial whisper again, 'they all end up like him downstairs, just getting under your feet. It never lasts, that first flush of love. Really, it never lasts.'

28

Ruby Lovatt stood on the beach alone and cloaked in darkness, watching the dirty white house across the road, the faint shadow of the woman she knew was inside, moving behind the translucent kitchen blinds. The woman had arrived home an hour earlier and as soon as she'd shut the front door she had gone from room to room, quickly lowering the blinds and drawing the curtains downstairs.

Ruby had seen her before on the beach many times, running, always running, pounding the sand, a skeletal automaton, no light in those eyes, no expression on that pale face. Only blankness. It was a blankness that Ruby recognized: the blankness of a destroyed life. A blankness that Ruby saw every time she looked in the mirror.

She had watched the little girl, Jodie Trigg, too. Seen her enter the dirty white house often, the blonde woman wrapping her arms around her, as if she was welcoming her own daughter home from school, ushering her quickly inside, skittish dark eyes grazing over the little girl's head to take in the road beyond, check that no one was watching. But

Ruby was invisible. She had been invisible virtually since the day she was born. It used to hurt, but now her invisibility was like a worn pair of slippers, comfortable and useful.

Watching the woman with Jodie Trigg, she wondered sometimes where her own child was, at that moment when Jodie was being ushered inside a warm house by someone who cared for her. Her child had been a spring baby, born with the lambs. New life had been everywhere when Ruby was mourning her loss, nature, God, taunting her, rubbing her broken heart raw.

Ruby looked back up at the house. If she were a good citizen, she'd tell DI Simmons that she knew where the woman he was searching for was living. That she also knew the woman had spent many hours alone with Jodie Trigg. Mother of the first dead girl; surrogate mother to the second. A coincidence?

Like hell, Ruby muttered to herself with a bitter chuckle.

She liked DI Simmons. She had liked him from the first time she'd met him, in another miserable segment of her miserable life. He was one of the only people she'd ever had contact with who had treated her like a human being, not like a vessel to be used – the men – or something beneath contempt, to be sneered at or ignored – the women. But being a good citizen had served her poorly and, however much she liked him, it wasn't enough. She was wiser now. Older, wiser, tougher and more cynical. She had learned to take her opportunities where she could find them.

How much was it worth to Carolynn Reynolds for Ruby to keep her secrets? How much was it worth to her husband, to learn his wife's? Or she to learn her husband's?

Turning away from the house, she slid down the pebbles

and on to the flat sand of the beach. Pulling off her plastic ballet pumps, she started to walk, feeling the cool damp sand against her soles. Little pleasures. She felt a shiver of anticipation and excitement, and it felt good.

29

A fat, white moon surrounded by stars hung in a clear navy sky, its shimmering image reflected in the sea, shrinking and growing with the motion of the waves. Lights off, Carolynn stood by the bedroom window, knowing that it would be a long time before she would absorb this view again. This panorama of sea and sky that changed by the hour and season was the only thing she would miss about this miserable house. *Big sky country:* she'd heard that somewhere and it felt appropriate.

Headlights suddenly, illuminating the road outside. She shrank back, apprehension drying out her throat. *Roger.* What would she say to him? He had claimed to be at work when Jodie Trigg was murdered, but she knew now that wasn't true. Would she challenge him or let his lie ride? He hadn't had an alibi for Zoe's murder either. Although they had been on holiday at the Witterings, spending that last long weekend at the beach before Zoe started back at school for the new academic year, he'd been stressing about work, had driven to Kingley Vale in the South Downs, he'd said, hiked to the top of the nature reserve and sat down on the crest of the hill with a flask of tea to mull over the issues. He'd been there for hours, watching the changing day reflected in the Solent below him. There had been no mobile reception and the police hadn't been able to reach him for hours to tell him that his daughter had been murdered and his wife taken into custody. Had he lied about his whereabouts then too?

No.

She was thinking the unthinkable. She *couldn't* let her mind go there. She had been with Roger for twenty years, knew him better than she knew herself – *surely* – didn't she? And Zoe had been their only child, hard fought for, hard won. Though he hadn't been the one accused of Zoe's murder, he had supported her unfailingly throughout the trial, had been tarred with the brush of hatred by association, lived with the vitriolic fallout, his enviably perfect life disintegrating alongside hers.

No, there *had* to be a reasonable explanation for his lying to her about his whereabouts these past two days. She would have liked longer to work out how best to broach the subject. He was unsettlingly tense nowadays.

The car drew up against the sea wall opposite and Carolynn breathed a sigh of relief. It wasn't Roger's car, but an ancient-looking BMW Z3. *God*, she hadn't seen one of those in forever. The car's headlights were extinguished and a man climbed out. The afterimage of the moon and the car's headlights lingering on her retina, she couldn't make him out beyond his height, medium, and build, skinny. Slowly, her vision acclimatized to the dark and she saw that he had black hair and was wearing a black suit. Instead of heading towards the caravan park as she'd expected him to, he moved into the middle of the road and surveyed the house.

A chill gripped Carolynn as if the temperature in the room had suddenly plummeted. She shrunk against the wall to the side of the bedroom window, unable to move, to breathe even.

It was *him*.

That horrid detective inspector with the pale face and those weird mismatched eyes. Those piercing eyes that had stripped her raw every time she'd been pinned beneath their unrelenting stare.

He had found her. So quickly. *He had found her.*

She remembered with cold clarity the look he had given her when she'd left the Old Bailey nine months ago a free woman. She had seen him at the kerbside, standing apart from the heaving press and protestors, alone and static. Their gazes had locked, just for a fraction of a second, as Roger had shepherded her into a taxi. He had nodded his head, the cynical expression in those odd eyes unchanged, the same expression they'd held throughout her trial. She knew then that he was still unequivocally convinced of her guilt.

And now he was here, outside her safe house, shattering the anonymity she and Roger had so painstakingly constructed. She stood frozen, almost dizzy with tension and watched him study each window in turn. Could he sense her? Hear the ragged sound of her stressed breathing through the walls?

She wanted to scream, howl, cry, rip her skin from her own bones in utter desperation. How had he found her? Had Jessie Flynn betrayed her trust? Had she? *No*, Carolynn was sure not. Jessie had looked horrified at lunch when she

169

had asked her if she'd tell DI Simmons where she and Roger were living. And besides, they were friends now. Genuine friends.

Carolynn held her breath as his gaze lingered on the bedroom window, on her motionless form, though she was sure that he couldn't see her. A tense balloon of air emptied from her lungs as he moved around to the side of the house. He must have switched on a torch, because she saw a disc of light moving in jerky arcs across the bedroom's side window, reflecting off the ceiling above her head. The torch beam moved away and she caught glimpses of it tracking across the ceiling of the landing, the bathroom across from her and Roger's bedroom. Thank God that she had locked her car inside the garage, so that he couldn't see it, take down her registration number. One small mercy. The torch moved back to the front of the house and then disappeared, switched off.

The sudden clang of the letterbox made her cry out. She clamped a hand over her mouth, sure that he must have heard her. But a moment later he was crossing the road to his car, casting a last look over his shoulder at the house, before climbing into the driver's seat.

Carolynn remained at the window for a few minutes more, staring at the blank space where he had parked, too stressed and upset to move. She couldn't let herself be thrust back into the public eye again, stomach the leering accusations, the vicious online trolling, being chased down the street by perfect strangers, pushed, slapped, spat at. No. She *had* to protect herself.

30

Jessie felt almost as if she was lying on the floor of a planetarium, the view of the sky and stars was so all-encompassing through the bed and breakfast bedroom's picture window.

She had laid out the shells she'd collected on the carpet in an identical pattern to the way she'd arranged them on the beach, a perfect heart, each half of the heart, seven shells – *lucky seven* – each half an identical mirror image of the other.

A perfect heart, to signal love.

She'd forced herself to use her damaged left hand without respite this time, moving every shell with her unresponsive fingers, fashioning the heart's perfect curve and checking its symmetry, checking seven times, the heat from the electric suit hissing and snapping with each frustration and disappointment, falling with each minor triumph. Pathetic, she knew, but she refused to switch to her right hand and be done with it.

Sitting on the floor, cross-legged like a school child, her gaze found Gemini, her birth sign. For the first time in as long as she could remember, she felt lonely. Lonely and guilty. Una Subramaniam had left a standing invitation to pop down and have a drink with her and 'him downstairs', but she didn't feel like engaging in polite chitchat. Retrieving her mobile from her handbag, she climbed into bed, leaving the curtains open so that she could still see the sky, and dialled Ahmose's number. Though she hung on for a full minute, picturing him shuffling stiffly from his reading chair in the sitting room to the phone in the hallway, the ringtone continued, unbroken. Where was he? He was hers, the one entirely reliable, unchallenging constant in her life, as she tried to be the same in his. He was her port in a storm and she felt unreasonably upset that he had gone somewhere without her.

Who else should she call? Callan? Her mother? She had argued with Callan and then cut him off and she had let her mother down a week before one of the most important days of her life. *God, I'm such a cow.* Would either of them want to speak with her? Because she knew that Callan was right. The need to behave self-destructively was like a parasitic organism that had burrowed itself under her skin, an organism that was hell-bent on goading her into wrecking everything that was good, everything she loved.

She had dealt with many patients who displayed self-destructive behaviour, from negative thinking that trapped them in a downward spiral, leading them to become anorexics, bulimics, over-eaters, self-harmers, alcoholics, drug addicts . . . Why was she refusing help from people who had her best interests at heart, people who loved her?

31

Nine months ago, after the collapse of the trial, when she
and Roger had decided to run, they had both wanted to
come to the Witterings, where they'd spent some of their
happiest times as a family holidaying, and more importantly
where people would least expect them to go to ground – the
location of Zoe's murder. The place itself, a seaside holiday
destination, had worked in their favour too: crowded and
anonymous in summer, shuttered and battened down in
winter. They had changed their surname, bought fake IDs
off the Internet, opened a PO Box in Chichester under their
new false name of Reynard, for the limited Internet purchases
that they made. The house was rented, cash-in-hand, from
a dodgy landlord who had no interest in knowing anything
about them, beyond their ability to pay the rent. The
Witterings had worked well for them for nine months. But
no longer. Not now that Jodie Trigg had been murdered
and Carolynn's name, her face, had been thrust back into
the spotlight. This time it would be sensible to choose
crowded anonymity in a big city, Birmingham or Manchester.

It wouldn't be easy, setting themselves up again, but they could do it. And now that DI Simmons had found them, Roger would agree to leave, he'd have to. They had no choice.

She started to think, plan, directing her anxiety into productivity. They would need a suitcase of clothes, warm stuff for the nights, a wash bag and towels. They'd need to be totally self-sufficient for a while, until they set themselves up again, so sleeping bags and a tent. Where would they be? The loft of course, along with the suitcases they hadn't used since Zoe's death.

Pulling herself from the window, she fetched the hooked pole and opened the loft hatch, stepping sideways to dodge the flurry of dust the descending ladder dislodged. She knew this house, her hated prison of the last nine months, so well that she could function perfectly in the dark.

As she reached the top of the ladder and stepped into the loft, seeing nothing but lumpy, unformed shapes in the darkness, the smell of dust and decay was elemental and unnerving. She hadn't been up here since the day they'd moved in, since she'd helped Roger carry the detritus of their old lives and stow it up here, too raw to decide yet what to keep and what to throw away.

Moonlight from the single velux window cast a milky glow into the centre of the loft, dimming to near blackness at the edges. Carolynn waited until her eyes had accustomed to the graduating shades of darkness and then looked around her. The suitcases were stacked against the far wall, by the brick chimneystack, the tent and sleeping bags piled on top. All their travel gear parked in one dusty, neglected heap.

As she moved across the loft, stepping over taped-down cardboard boxes filled with trinkets salvaged from their old life that no longer held any importance, feeling dust grind under her soles, her eye was caught by a glint.

She froze, her breath catching in her throat.

Oh God, what is it?

An eye? It looked like the eye of a night creature trapped in headlights.

Her heart beating so hard it was almost punching its way out of her chest, she stepped forward and, as though it were a separate being, watched her hand reach out and lift the flap of the box.

A pale face, gelid eyes, a cheap, pink ballerina dress stretched tight over a plump body.

A doll.

The box contained a doll. Its blue eyes catching the moonlight and reflecting it back at her, the frozen, glassy eyes of horror films and nightmares. A doll that she recognized. Carolynn laughed – she couldn't help herself – a startled horrified laugh, halfway between a bark and a yelp.

She reached for the doll, then stopped, her hand hovering, unable to force herself to touch it, unable even to catch her breath. The doll was identical to the one that had been left by Zoe's body and by Jodie Trigg's.

Rearing back from the box, Carolynn jammed her eyes shut, trying to erase the images of the doll and the memories it had surfaced in her mind.

Why is there a doll next to her? She's not a girly girl. She hates dolls.

Reaching for it, pushing it away from her daughter, leaving her fingerprints all over its disgusting, bloated body.

Backing away from the box, she skirted quickly around the edge of the loft, grabbed the tent and sleeping bags in one hand, the largest suitcase in the other, desperate now

175

to be out of this cramped, stuffy space, desperate to escape. Escape from this house, from the crumbling edifice of her life.

With Roger though or without? Could she trust him? Did she really know him at all?

32

Jessie's mother's tone rose in surprise when she heard her daughter's voice on the line. When had she last telephoned her mother? She couldn't actually remember.

'Did you manage to deal with the emergency, darling?'

Emergency? It took Jessie a moment. 'Yes, all sorted.'

'So you're back at home? That's good.'

Should she lie? It would be easier, but she'd telephoned her mum to build bridges between them and lying wouldn't be a great start.

'No, I'm at the beach.'

'With Ben? For the weekend?'

Her mother had only met Callan once, the day that she and Richard had announced their engagement. She had called Jessie the week before to say that they were visiting friends in Guildford for lunch and could they pop in for tea on the way home. *Pop in.* Her and Jessie's relationship still too fragile, too distant for her just to ask if they could visit for the day without fabricating an excuse. Jessie had long since given up trying to analyse their relationship, as each attempt raised too many memories of Jamie, of life before his suicide, of an uncomplicated happiness she barely remembered before a piece of her heart was permanently severed. She had been alone for so long that self-reliance was woven into her DNA. She felt as if she was no one's daughter any more, Ahmose the closest thing to family. Ahmose and now Callan, if she didn't screw it up. *Continue* to screw it up.

'No, I'm alone, Mum. Ben's not here.'

A surprised intake of breath echoed down the line. 'Where is he?'

'In Surrey, at my cottage.' *Unless he's gone back to barracks in a temper, which I can't rule out given our last conversation.*

'It's Friday night, darling . . .'

'Yes.'

'So . . .' The single word hung between them in the ensuing silence.

Oh, God, just say it, Jessie wanted to scream. Shouldn't you be with your boyfriend, working on your relationship? Her mother was sixty: had grown up in a traditional family with father's role as the breadwinner and mother's as the housewife clearly demarcated. She had aped that example in her own disastrous marriage and though she professed pride in her daughter's doctorate, Jessie knew that she'd far rather see her daughter ape that model too: settle down to married life and start producing the next generation, despite the fuck-up that her parents had made of the current generation.

'Why aren't you with him, darling?'

'I was working, Mum, but I'm done now. I'm driving back tomorrow morning.'

178

Another intake of breath.

'I'm driving back tomorrow morning,' she repeated. And she was. She was done here now. She'd accomplished what she had set out to do: asked Carolynn Reynolds to call DI Simmons. Her part in this tragedy was over.

'He told you that I've rearranged the dress fitting for Monday, ten a.m.?'

'He did.'

'It's really the furthest I can push it.'

'I'll be there, Mum, I promise—' She broke off. There was a whole world of things she had planned on saying – that she was looking forward to getting to know Richard better, and his daughter and granddaughters, but most important, that she hoped the wedding would act as a reset button for the two of them. Instead, all she said was, 'I better go, Mum.' *Why can't I open up?*

'Were you calling about something specific?'

'No, nothing specific. Just to say hi.'

'I'll look forward to seeing you on Monday then, darling.'

'Night, Mum.'

The line went dead. Jessie lowered the phone to the bed. *I was just calling to say that I wish everything between us was different. Everything about me was different. That's all.*

33

Carolynn lay rigid in bed as she heard Roger's footsteps reach the top of the landing, the loose floorboard he had been promising to fix since they moved in, groaning under his weight. Her heart thumping, she waited for the bedroom door to open.

It didn't. What was he doing on the landing? She had closed the loft hatch, hadn't she? Put the hooked pole back in the corner of the landing? Now, on the spot, she couldn't think, couldn't remember. All she could visualize was the bloated plastic body in that box in the loft, the glassy, horror-film eyes.

Unable to settle, she had paced around the house for what had felt like hours, her heart leaping into her mouth with the sound of every car that drew up at the gates of the caravan park, thinking that it was that vile detective back again, or Roger, that she would have to face him, smile and kiss him, make small talk while his lies and the doll in the loft were clamouring for attention in her brain, grabbing a vice-like hold of her thoughts.

You were at home and I was at work when that girl was killed.

He hadn't been at work.

You must have lost the necklace somewhere around the house.

She hadn't lost it. The accusation was ridiculous. The house was spotless, a sterile mausoleum. She could close her eyes and visualize every square centimetre.

She had finally looked at her watch – ten p.m. Too late to leave now, she had nowhere to go. She'd leave in the morning, as soon as he left for work. When they'd lived in London together as a couple, *before*, when they'd called themselves DINKYs – Dual Income No Kids Yet – Roger had liked to choose what she wore to dinners out or parties. He liked her to look nice, to *make him proud*. She would have preferred to choose her own clothes – she wasn't a child – but the fact he cared so much had made her feel loved and so she'd let him. So many people weren't loved, weren't wanted. She hadn't been, as a child, and she had been determined that her adulthood would be different, that she would be adored.

Nowadays, they never went anywhere and he had no cause to open her cupboard, showed no interest in what she looked like. His only interest lay in keeping her calm. That was how he demonstrated his love nowadays, by moderating her alcohol intake and feeding her pills.

Light from the landing washed over Carolynn suddenly as the bedroom door opened. Eyes jammed shut, corpse-like in her stillness, she listened to him move around their bedroom, removing his clothes, laying them on the chair, every movement, every sound so familiar. She tried to soften her breathing to the regular timbre of a sleeper, but each

181

breath caught in her throat, meeting the air in a stressed, hosing gasp.

The tilt of the mattress as he sat on the edge of the bed, a chill puff as he lifted the duvet and slid in next to her. Would he touch her? She wasn't sure she could bear it if he did.

The lies.

The dolls.

The necklace.

Tomorrow was a Saturday. *Oh God*, she hadn't thought. Roger wouldn't be going to work tomorrow. Wouldn't even be pretending. She only had one choice now. To wait until he was asleep and leave. It was her only chance to escape.

34

The woman who opened the door matched to perfection Marilyn's image of the archetypical seaside bed and breakfast owner: early-sixties, coiffured hair highlighted in honeyed shades and set immovably; orange foundation caked into skin overly lined from too much exposure to the sun and wind.

'I'm looking for Dr Jessica Flynn,' Marilyn said.

Her expression shifted from one of welcome to one of suspicion. Tilting her head, she gazed at him through narrowed, powder-blue-lidded eyes.

'I don't have any guests by that name.'

Marilyn held up his warrant card, indicated with his other hand Jessie's mini parked on the drive behind him. The woman's mouth popped open, a fish gasping for its last breath.

'I'll wait for her on the beach.' Sliding his warrant card into his pocket, Marilyn crunched back up the gravel, calling over his shoulder. 'Detective Inspector Bobby Simmons, lovely to meet you.'

He was standing on the concrete walkway above the beach, smoking and gazing out to sea when Jessie stalked down the garden and joined him.

'Bastard,' she said.

'Good morning to you too.'

'Not you. Though I doubt if you'll take long to earn that moniker today either.'

'You wouldn't be down here if you didn't have a niggling doubt,' Marilyn said. 'Callan did the right thing.'

Shutting the garden gate behind her, Jessie swung round to face him, hands on her hips. 'He did the right thing for you. He betrayed me. Bastard.'

'Lots of B's being bandied about this morning. Let me think of another one. Breakfast? My treat.'

Jessie rolled her eyes. 'What's the old adage? "There's no such thing as a free lunch." Make that, "There's no such thing as a free breakfast" – I assume you'll want something in exchange.'

'I'll take you for the best pancake you've ever had and it will be worth whatever I ask for in return.'

'The surf café? I went there yesterday.'

'With Carolynn Reynolds?'

'With Laura.'

Marilyn looked momentarily crestfallen. 'Is that what she's calling herself nowadays?' he said, as realization dawned.

'For my sessions, yes. In public? I didn't ask.'

'And she's living in Bracklesham Bay?'

'My my, Callan was a thorough stool pigeon.'

Though it was barely past seven a.m., the sun was already high in the sky, reflecting off the hull of yet another container ship ploughing its way towards Portsmouth docks. How many a day? Scores of them, enough to keep up with the relentless British consumer. It promised to be another hot day, a day for pottering on the beach, collecting more shells for her mother's wedding. She'd planned to call Callan, ask him to join her here for the weekend. Her room in the B & B was free tonight, she'd already checked in anticipation. Not now, though.

'I've already found her,' Marilyn said.

Jessie's eyes swung back to meet his. 'Fast work, Detective Inspector. I'm impressed.'

'I got the team to put the hard word on all the cash-in-hand, ask-no-questions-and-I'll-tell-you-no-lies landlords we know who own properties in Bracklesham Bay.' He winked. 'I've been in Surrey and Sussex Major crimes for twenty years and many of my team have been in it far longer. We know most of the low-level scrotes on our patch and know how to push their hot buttons when we need to. The threat of a tip-off to the Inland Revenue works wonders.'

'The perils of living in a small town.'

'They probably should have chosen to hide out in Birmingham or Manchester, though to be fair, this place has worked well for them for the past nine months. Seaside towns have a certain transient, touristy anonymity . . . ' He paused. 'And this place has connections for them, doesn't it? History. Something I'd like to talk to you about. I don't understand why they'd choose to come back to where Zoe was murdered.' Marilyn held out his arm. 'Shall we? I'm starving.' Grinding out his cigarette on the top of Una Subramaniam's garden wall, he tossed the butt into the bushes at the end of her garden.

'Biodegradable,' he muttered, in response to Jessie's admonishing frown.

'No, they're not.'

'Thick bushes. They'll never see it. Serves her right for lying to me.'

They walked side by side along the promenade towards the Fisherman's Hut and the start of Shore Road, which would take them from the beach to East Wittering village centre.

'She was looking out for the emotional welfare of one of her guests,' Jessie said. 'I told her that I'd just broken up with my fiancé and had come down here to get away.'

Marilyn laughed. 'And who did she think I was? Your fiancé's grandfather, or did she think you'd left your white stick in the car?'

Tilting sideways, Jessie nudged his shoulder with her own. 'Don't be so harsh on yourself, Detective Inspector. You have a certain weathered charm.'

'Am I supposed to take that as a compliment?'

They fell silent, the only noise the flap of Jessie's summer dress against her bare legs. Though she was still furious at Callan's betrayal, another emotion had seeded itself alongside the first, an emotion she recognized as relief. She realized now how much the dilemma of whether to tell Marilyn about Carolynn had weighed on her mind – not that she was going to admit that to either him or Callan.

At the surf café, they found a table in the high-walled rear patio, so they could talk without being overheard and Marilyn could smoke. Jessie ordered a breakfast pancake and a latte, and Marilyn the same to eat with a strong black coffee, two sugars.

'Thanks for coming, Jessie. I do appreciate it.'

She gave a non-committal nod. 'Just don't do anything that is going to make me regret taking you up on your offer of breakfast, however good the pancakes are.'

35

Carolynn was tying the laces on her running shoes when she heard the sound of knuckles against glass. Looking up, she saw Jessie Flynn, wearing black run capris and a sky-blue vest that matched the colour of her eyes, standing at her kitchen window.

'Come for a run,' Jessie mouthed through the glass.

Carolynn joined her outside. 'I didn't know that you ran.'

'I don't, but you can motivate me. I spend far too much time sitting on my arse talking and listening. Come on!'

They jogged across the road, climbed on to the wooden sea defence wall and jumped down the other side, landing on the beach in unison. Though the sun had risen, the early morning air was chill and Carolynn noticed goosebumps on Jessie's bare arms.

'Let's run,' Carolynn said, meeting Jessie's smile with one of her own, a smile so genuine that she felt as if she would burst with it. 'Warm you up.'

Jessie was lithe and strong and though she had said that she wasn't a runner, her movements were fluid and confident and their pace and strides matched as they ran across the flat sand. Jessie's jet-black ponytail was streaming out behind her like the tail of that galloping horse Carolynn had raced on the beach a few weeks ago.

'You're flying,' Carolynn called out, laughing.

'It's you, Carolynn! It's being with you. You make me feel amazing.'

She felt Jessie's hand close around her own, and then they were sprinting, hurtling across the sand towards the sun, hand in hand like a couple of schoolkids at break time, running and laughing out loud. Carolynn felt an incredible rush: the rush of lactic acid building in her leg muscles as their pace outstripped her lungs' ability to provide oxygen, the rush of the endless empty sand, the rush of knowing that she'd been right, that she *was* friends with Jessie Flynn.

Knuckles on glass again and the sun shining brightly, too brightly, right into her eyes. The morning sun's rays magnified by the curved glass of her windscreen, she realized as she forced her eyes open. The knocking, not Jessie, but a man, banging his clenched fist against her passenger window. Her body telegraphed a message of discomfort to her brain, not only her legs, but her arms, neck and back as she struggled to sit up in the cramped space, raising her hands apologetically, ducking her head so that he couldn't see her face.

'You're blocking the slipway,' he shouted. 'I need to launch my fishing boat.'

'I'm sorry,' she shouted back, her voice hoarse with sleep.

Shucking out of the sleeping bag, she squeezed herself between the front seats and sank into the driver's seat. Zoe's cat was still asleep, curled up in a tight doughnut on the passenger seat. Half-asleep still herself, Carolynn turned the key, which she'd had the good sense to leave in the ignition so she could find it easily. Thankfully the engine caught first time. Lifting a hand, she signalled a final apology, hoping that the man would be too caught up with launching his boat to wonder why she had been parked there. She would head for the A3 now and join the rush-hour traffic heading towards Guildford and London. Blend in, make herself invisible.

'Did I ever tell you that I was married?'

Jessie met Marilyn's gaze over the rim of her coffee cup. 'That was unexpected. And, no, you didn't, but you already know that you didn't.'

'Are you going to ask why I'm telling you this?' he said, with a wry smile.

She shook her head. 'I'm sure your reasons will reveal themselves.'

The waiter arrived with their pancakes, and they fell silent while he arranged the plates in front of them, set out napkins, knives and forks.

'So what happened?' Jessie asked, when the waiter had disappeared back inside. 'To your marriage.'

'I screwed around and she left me.'

'It's typical in the police. Broken relationships.'

'Unfortunately, it is. When we first got married, we used to watch all my colleagues in Brighton having affairs, betraying their wives or husbands, splitting up. We were so smug back then. We always said that it would never happen to us.'

Jessie took a sip of her coffee, didn't say anything. They had developed a solid professional relationship over the past year of working together intermittently, and Marilyn had become a friend of sorts, but she had never opened up to him or he to her before and she sensed that whatever she said at this point would halt, not encourage his flow. She also sensed that there was a point to his opening up to her, that it wasn't just a sudden burning desire to unburden his soul. He wasn't the type who needed to share.

'How many affairs did you have?'

'Two she found out about and one she didn't.'

Jessie gave a cynical half-smile. 'Well done, you've earned it – the moniker, bastard.'

Marilyn lifted his shoulders in an apologetic shrug. 'I wanted to stick with it, but she had grown up with parents who hated each other and she had no interest in repeating their mistakes.'

'And you were the one having your cake and eating it, while she was the one at home with no cake, but lots of shit.'

'Thanks for the support.'

'You can always contradict me.'

'But I won't, of course, because you're right.'

'And she knew that you wouldn't change your ways, whatever you promised. Old dogs, new tricks and all that.'

'I wasn't such an old dog in those days.'

She smiled. 'Leopards and spots?'

He didn't smile back. 'I was convinced that it was a one-off.'

'A three-off.'

Marilyn ploughed on. 'And that I'd change, but she knew that I wouldn't, and she was right. Fundamentally, the whole marriage thing didn't suit me.'

'How did you meet her?'

'She was a civilian worker with the police, but she gave up when we had our first child.'

Jessie raised an eyebrow. 'I didn't know you had children.'

'A twenty-six-year-old son and a twenty-three-year-old daughter. We had them young. I was only twenty-two when we got married and she fell pregnant on the honeymoon. I very quickly found her, our whole life, stultifying. She was obsessed with the children, had no interest in going out partying any more, so I started going out partying with my colleagues, one thing led to another and the rest is history.' He drained his coffee and raised his hand to summon the waiter for another. 'With the benefit of hindsight, I can see that she was only trying to provide a loving, stable family life for our children. I was the one who was out of order. I didn't want to face up to my responsibilities, so I dumped them all on her.'

'Relationships are hard. God, I know that and I've only been in one for five minutes. Marriage was invented to protect women and children when women were totally reliant on men, when hardly anyone lived beyond the age of thirty-five and adventure meant travelling more than five miles away from home. Monogamy was never intended to last for fifty or sixty years. It just makes you human, Marilyn.'

'Fallible.'

She smiled. 'Fallible and human. So you left Brighton and came to live in civilized Chichester to reinvent yourself, start afresh?'

'The only problem with new starts is that they end up looking very much like the old ones after a while.'

'You can take the boy away from temptation, but you can't take temptation out of the boy.'

'Something like that.'

'Did you still see her and your children?'

He nodded. 'She is and always has been very civilized. I only see her three or four times a year, but we talk on the phone every week or so. They all still live in Brighton. My son is like his mother, solid and reliable. He's a criminal lawyer.'

'Prosecution, I hope?'

Marilyn smiled. 'He inherited one thing from me, at least.'

'And your daughter?'

'She's a dancer.'

'Ballet?' Jessie asked, noting the expression on Marilyn's face in response to her question, knowing his answer before he spoke it.

'Pole. Stripping.'

'Ah.'

'A dancer, a drinker and a druggie.'

'Lots of Ds.'

'Better than Bs?' The ghost of a cynical smile crossed his face. 'She inherited too much from me and not enough from her mum. She's a disaster. My fault, of course.'

'Is that what your ex-wife says?'

'That's what *I* say.'

Jessie laid her knife and fork on the empty plate. She had felt slightly nauseous since she'd woken, probably the result of another disturbed night's sleep. She hadn't thought she'd eat much, but she had polished off the lot and felt better for doing so. Resting her chin on steepled fingers, she met Marilyn's gaze. 'Why are you telling me all this, Marilyn?'

'Because I want you to know that I'm not just a machine.'

Her gaze moved pointedly from the black coffee with two sugars in his right hand to the cigarette in his left. 'I already know that you're not a machine, Marilyn.'

He rolled his eyes. 'Remind me never to have breakfast with a psychologist.'

'Or lunch. Or dinner.'

'What I mean is—' he broke off.

'I know what you mean. You want me to know that you have a life, a perspective, outside the police. That it – Carolynn, Zoe, Jodie Trigg – is not just about a result, that you can be objective.'

He gave a wry smile. '*Had* a life, maybe. But it is important that you understand where I'm coming from. I went after Carolynn Reynolds hard because I believed that she murdered her daughter. The only DNA on little Zoe's body was hers. Her fingerprints were all over the doll, the shells, her footprints, leading up to and around the murder site, the only ones we could identify.'

'Finding her daughter's body, as she claimed, would leave the same forensic traces,' Jessie cut in. 'And if the killer was smart and forensically aware, it's probable that they would have left very little, if any forensic trace, which Carolynn then smothered with her own.'

'It wasn't just forensics. Her whole demeanour didn't fit with the mother of a murdered daughter, Jessie. I've seen many parents whose kids have been killed, whether accidentally or deliberately, and real grief doesn't look like that.'

'You can't expect people's reactions to conform to some textbook standard. Everyone's different.'

Marilyn gave a weary half-nod, half-shake of his head. 'I still believe that she murdered her daughter and Jodie Trigg, but I need help to prove it. I need to nail the killer this time, Jessie. I failed last time and I can't fail again. Both those little girls need justice.'

'They do both need justice, but I believe that you're wrong about Carolynn, Marilyn. She's not a killer.'

He ploughed on, ignoring her comment. 'I need your help, Jessie. I need someone as intransigent as I am to work with.'

'Work against, don't you mean? Yin and yang.' She lifted her shoulders. 'I'm here, aren't I, so talk away.'

Marilyn shook his head. 'Officially, on an ongoing basis, as a consulting clinical psychologist. We have a budget for freelance advisors. You are freelance these days, aren't you?'

Her involuntary exit from the army; another thing Callan had shared with him, without asking her. Bastard.

'Freelance, yes, but not ready to prostitute myself to the highest bidder just yet.'

Marilyn smiled. 'I can guarantee that Surrey and Sussex Major Crimes won't be the highest bidder.'

Sitting back, Jessie folded her arms across her chest. 'We're at opposite ends of the spectrum on this case, Marilyn. You're convinced of Carolynn's guilt and you're determined to prove it, and I'm convinced there is no way the woman I got to know over five hours of clinical psychology sessions murdered her own child.'

'You'd add balance to my thinking.'

'Either that, or we'll end up wanting to kill each other.'

'I'm willing to take that risk, if you are.'

Jessie chewed on her lip, didn't answer. Was she willing? She liked Marilyn, rated him hugely, but she felt that, with regard to Carolynn Reynolds, and despite all the circumstantial evidence he'd laid out in front of her, he had lost objectivity. She wasn't interested in being involved in a witch-hunt. But then he was right when he said that she could add balance. And he was also right when he said that the little girls deserved justice.

'I can't share anything that Carolynn told me in our sessions with you,' she said finally. 'I can't renege on that patient confidentiality.'

'I won't ask you to.'

'And I am not willing to be used just to back up your case. The case you've already made up your mind is correct. That Carolynn is guilty.'

'I won't ask you to do that either.' He extended his hand across the table and after a moment, Jessie shook it. 'I told you that you'd be willing to do anything for one of those pancakes!' Pushing his chair back, he stood. 'Come on, Dr Flynn, we have a house call to make.'

37

Roger opened his eyes to a quiet room and the sense that he was alone.

He stretched out, star-fishing across the bed, appreciating the opportunity to spread. Carolynn's side was cold. Rolling on to his stomach, he pressed his face into her pillow. Also cold, and her scent barely there. Yawning, he rolled back and fumbled his watch from the bedside table. Nine a.m. – *Christ,* much later than he'd thought. Carolynn was doubtless out running again, must have left even earlier than usual for the pillow and sheets on her side of the bed to be so cold.

Shrugging on his navy towelling dressing gown, tying the cord in a neat bow at his waist, he went downstairs and made himself a coffee, strong, with a splash of milk and one level teaspoon of sugar, just how he liked it.

As he wandered from the kitchen into the hallway, sipping his coffee, the shoe rack caught his eye, specifically the buttercup yellow of Carolynn's running shoes, stowed on the bottom shelf. His gaze rose to the key hook above the hall table. Her door key was on its hook, but her car key was missing. Why would she take one and not the other, particularly when she knew how important it was that she get inside the house quickly? Waiting on the doorstep to be let in risked attracting unwanted attention. *What the hell is she playing at?* With the furore surrounding this second kid's murder, he'd told her not to leave the house at all. His blood pressure hiked at the thought of her stupidity. A solitary early morning run was just about forgivable – much as he hated her obsessive running, he knew how much she relied on exercise to calm her – but a trip to the supermarket, the only other place she ever went, was madness. Rubbing shoulders with nosy locals who would be reading the front page of their Saturday papers straight off the shelves and standing around gossiping, only one subject on their lips.

Draining his coffee, he placed the cup in the sink and headed upstairs, taking the steps two at a time. He'd throw on some clothes and drive into East Wittering, find Carolynn and get her to come straight home, stay inside, stay hidden. As he crossed the landing, grit ground into his bare soles. Carolynn hoovered the upstairs carpets daily. Cleanliness was important to him, to both of them, and cleaning gave her a focus, structure to her days. Crouching, he ran his hand across the carpet and his palm returned coated in dust. Looking up, he saw that the loft-hatch was closed, but his gaze snagged on a dusty cobweb hanging from one corner, twinkling in the sunlight.

In the loft, Roger scanned the sunlit boxes. All closed and taped shut as he'd left them when he'd stowed them here nine months ago. Apart from one, a small, rectangular box, and he knew what was inside it. Nothing obviously moved or disturbed, but a trail of shoe prints led across the dusty floor. For a moment, he could see nothing but lumpy unformed shapes in the recesses at the edge of the loft where the light from the single velux didn't stretch. As his vision adjusted, he realized that the tent, a sleeping bag and one of the suitcases was missing from the pile by the brick chimney breast. His jaw twisted and his cheeks burned red. She wouldn't have just upped and left him, surely, knowing how much he'd done for her, what he'd sacrificed?

As he descended the loft ladder, stewing with impotent fury, the doorbell rang. He'd almost forgotten what it sounded like, it was used so infrequently. So Carolynn had returned, changed her mind, realized her error. *Not before time*. Taking a deep breath to cool his anger, he jogged down the carpeted stairs on silent feet.

38

The dirt drive that led down the side of the house to the garage was empty, but a black VW Golf was visible through the open garage doors. The house itself looked neglected, typical low-end seaside rental, white pebbledash peeling in places and mottled green with lichen in others. The front garden was 'low-maintenance seaside', bare of planting, just a protective evergreen laurel hedge lapping over the rotting fence. Curtains were drawn across the upstairs windows, but a dim light shone from behind one. All the other rooms upstairs and down were in darkness.

'Looks like they're in,' Marilyn said, indicating the car and the light.

Jessie crouched at the end of the drive. 'They have two cars though, or at least two cars have been using this drive because there are two different tyre tracks.' She pointed. 'These are from the Golf and these from a smaller car.'

Marilyn clapped a hand on her shoulder. 'We'll make a copper of you yet, Detective Flynn.'

Straightening, Jessie rolled her eyes. 'You didn't buy me

a big enough pancake for that. Carolynn likes to run, early. She might have driven somewhere to run.'

'Run,' Marilyn muttered. 'You said it. Did you notice what she drove when she came to your sessions?'

'No. Usually, I had appointments before and after so I collected her from the clinic's waiting room. The one day we left at the same time, a man in a black Golf was waiting for her.'

'That black Golf.'

She shrugged. 'I'm not a detective, Detective, so I didn't memorize the registration plate.'

They skirted along the narrow garden to the front door. Standing to one side of the doorstep so that his face wouldn't be framed in the magnifying spyhole, guiding her to do the same, Marilyn jammed his finger on the doorbell.

'That's sneaky,' Jessie murmured with a smile.

Marilyn didn't smile back. Badly concealed tension radiated from him like heat. 'With all these windows overlooking the road, they may have already seen us, but if they haven't, I'd prefer that they don't get to decide they'd like to continue hiding from me.'

Marilyn's ring elicited no visible signs of life. The same dim light continued to shine from behind one of the upstairs curtains, no new lights were switched on, they saw no movement from inside, heard no footsteps. He raised his finger to the doorbell again, but Jessie caught his arm.

'They would have heard it. If they're going to come, they'll come. Ringing it again is too demanding, it says officialdom.'

With a nod, he slid both his hands into his pockets. His sole drummed a tense tune on the concrete path.

There was the sudden sound of a bolt being drawn back and the front door swung open in one fluid movement to reveal a big man in a navy towelling dressing gown, pale blue pyjama legs protruding beneath, feet bare. Despite his state of undress and the bed hair, Jessie recognized him immediately as the solid, dark-haired man she had seen waiting for Carolynn a few weeks ago. It was clear from the way his eyes widened fractionally when he looked from Marilyn to her, that recognition was reciprocated. Not ideal.

Stepping forward, Marilyn held out his hand. Glancing down, Jessie noticed that he had planted one suede Chelsea boot firmly over the threshold. He wasn't taking any chances.

'You remember me, Mr Reynolds?'

'How could I forget?' His grey eyes were cold. He made no move to take Marilyn's outstretched hand. 'What do you want?'

'Can we talk?'

'We have nothing to *talk* about.'

'You've heard about the young girl found dead on West Wittering beach on Thursday, I presume? Jodie Trigg?'

'I'd have to be living on Mars not to have done, but it has nothing to do with us.' His tone was measured, a 'poker' tone, if there was such a thing.

'She was strangled.'

Reynolds lifted his shoulders. His expression remained unchanged. 'I'm very sorry for her parents, but as I said, it has nothing to do with us.'

'Like Zoe, she was strangled.'

Reynolds didn't react.

'Her body was found very close to where your daughter was found, two years to the day, lying in a heart of shells with an identical doll left by her side.'

202

'What are you implying, DI Simmons?'

'I'm not implying anything. I'm here purely out of courtesy, to assure you that finding your daughter's murderer is still one of my key priorities. I *will* find out who killed her.' There was an edge to his tone that was at odds with the reassuring message.

'I sincerely hope that you do find out who murdered my daughter. My wife and I have been waiting two years for a result. Waiting in vain.'

'Is your wife in, Mr Reynolds?'

'No.'

'Where is she?'

Reynolds shrugged. 'Out running, probably.'

'Does she often go running early?'

'Most days, I believe.'

'Her car is missing.'

Marilyn waited for Reynolds to contradict his statement. Another shrug. 'Shopping then.'

So Jessie had been right – they were a two-car family.

'Does she like to shop?'

Reynolds' wrinkled his nose. 'Don't all women like to shop?'

Jessie would have liked to interject in the negative, but kept silent. Her feminist principles would just have to let that one go.

'What car does she drive?'

'Small, silver.'

'Like about five million others then?'

Reynolds suppressed a smirk.

'Make, model and registration plate?' Marilyn asked.

'I'm not good with cars, DI Simmons, so I don't remember.'

'Where are your ownership documents?'

'I can't recall where I left them,' Reynolds said. 'I'll have a think and get back to you.'

'How predictably convenient,' Marilyn snapped. 'What time did she leave?'

'I was working late last night and slept late. I only woke up a few minutes before you rang the bell. She was gone when I woke.'

Reynolds' appearance validated his story.

'Where do you work?'

'None of your business.'

'I'm sure I can find out.'

Jessie gave a subtle warning shake of her head, but Marilyn didn't notice, wasn't looking at her. He was eyeballing Reynolds, and Jessie could almost see the hackles raised, like a dog sizing up for a fight. This wasn't the approach they had agreed on. The plan was to go softly, softly, engender cooperation, however obtuse Roger Reynolds tried to be. Marilyn was letting his bias guide his actions, but however much she wanted to, she couldn't pull him up in front of Reynolds.

'Where was your wife the day before yesterday, between three and five-thirty p.m.?'

'At home.'

'Any witnesses?'

Reynolds' knuckles whitened as he tightened his grip on the front door. 'This is sounding suspiciously like an interrogation, DI Simmons. Should I call my lawyer?'

Jessie stepped forward. 'No, Mr Reynolds, you don't need to speak with your lawyer. As DI Simmons said earlier, we're here out of courtesy, to ensure that you had heard about Jodie Trigg and to inform you that the police believe the two murders are linked.'

Reynolds eyeballed her, unsmiling. 'Very uncourteous courtesy. And you are?'

Jessie was tempted to tell him that she was well aware he knew exactly who she was.

'My name is Dr Jessie Flynn and I'm a psychologist working with the police. I've been counselling your wife.'

'Poacher turned gamekeeper.'

'I've worked with the police on a few other cases. It's another aspect of my job and one that ideally doesn't overlap with my freelance clinical psychology work. I give my assurance that nothing your wife told me in our sessions will be shared with the police. I take patient confidentiality very seriously.'

Reynolds' lip curled. 'Back when our daughter died, we trusted. *Everyone* we knew let us down. Forgive me if I don't believe a word you're saying, Dr Flynn.'

Jessie continued to look him straight in the eye, though it was an effort. Fury and mistrust pulsed from him.

'I understand why you wouldn't believe me, but my word *is* good.'

She sensed Marilyn shift beside her.

'Can we come in, Mr Reynolds?' he asked.

'Why do you want to come in, DI Simmons?'

'To continue our chat in comfort and privacy.'

'We're done chatting.'

Reynolds moved to shut the door. It bounced off the toe of Marilyn's boot.

'I can arrest you,' Marilyn said, extending his arm to hold the door open.

'What the hell for?' Reynolds hissed.

'Living under a false name, non-payment of taxes. I'm sure I can think of something that will stick.'

205

'Jesus Christ, you really are scum.'

'I'm just trying to do my job, and I could do with your cooperation.'

'And you think this is the way to achieve it, by coming here and throwing out accusations? After all you've done, all the harm you caused before?'

'I'm concerned that your wife may have gone. *Run*, for want of a better word.'

'She wouldn't have gone anywhere without me.'

'Are you sure about that?'

'Positive.' Reynolds said it with the tone of a man who had been brought up to believe in himself.

'I'd like to look around,' Marilyn said. 'I don't have a search warrant, but if you give me your permission, I don't need one.'

Reynolds nodded. His mouth twisted. 'I give you permission to go fuck yourself, DI Simmons.'

Slapping Marilyn's arm away, he shoved the door closed, bouncing it hard against Marilyn's toe until he withdrew his foot. The force of the slam rattled the door in its frame.

39

Anxiety was knotted in Carolynn's muscles, had hitched her shoulders up around her ears, though the tension was beginning to drain with the miles she put between herself and East Wittering. Between herself and Detective Inspector Simmons. Herself and Roger.

It had taken her an age to escape from the house early this morning, sliding the suitcase silently from under the bed as Roger slept, holding her breath as she inched her cupboard doors open, as if her own silence would mute the creak of their hinges, snatching just the basics, a couple of bras and a handful of knickers – they wouldn't match but she didn't care about that now, she could buy new when she was settled – a few T-shirts, a jumper and a pair of jeans, reaching up from where she was squatting on the floor, below Roger's eyeline if he happened, half-asleep, to open his eyes, to pull a couple of practical day-dresses from their hangers. As she had reached the bedroom door, the suitcase in one hand, the tent wedged uncomfortably under her arm, he had muttered and stirred. She'd frozen, every one of her muscles screaming with the agony of maintaining such stillness, her chest caving in from denied breath. If he opened his eyes now, he would see her framed in the doorway, a glowing statue lit by the moonlight cutting in through the landing window. But his eyes had remained closed and after a few more mumbles, he'd settled, still and silent again. Downstairs, she had grabbed her handbag from the hall table and unhooked her car keys from the key rack. She didn't need her house keys any more, had no intention of ever coming back to this ghastly little prison.

Outside, the front garden and drive had been pitch-black, the walls of the house seeming to suck every lumen of light from the moon. A strong breeze had been cutting in from the sea, raising goosebumps on her bare arms and legs. She moved silently down the garden to the drive, to her car, but as she was lifting the tailgate to stow the suitcase and tent, a sudden movement had caught her eye. She had stopped, her hand hovering, her breath caught in her throat.

Roger? No – it couldn't be. He was asleep upstairs; she would have heard the front door opening.

That detective inspector, hiding out, waiting for her? No, she was being silly, fanciful, her nerves playing tricks.

Relaxing on an out breath, she stowed the suitcase and tent, shut the tailgate and moved around to the driver's door. But as she'd slid the key into the lock, something had brushed against her bare leg. Gasping, she spun around, her pulse rate rocketing.

Oh God. The cat. Zoe's fucking *cat.*

She breathed out, furious at herself for how terrified she had been in that split second. Furious at herself. But more furious at him.

God, how she hated that *fucking* cat.

Opening the driver's door, she stood back, giving him space, knowing that he wouldn't come close if she was standing right there. But he was curious, always had been, and she knew that he couldn't resist an open door. It was only a matter of waiting and she was patient. Patience had served her well in the past and it would serve her well now. A moment later, a splodgy streak had shot past her legs, into the car. The cat had started to miaow and paw at the window as she backed out of the drive, but she had swiped at him hard with the flat of her hand, knocking him into the footwell, where he'd crouched trembling, wide-eyed and frightened. *Good.* Because she hated him, even more than he hated her.

But he had been Zoe's pet, her best friend, and so she would take care of him. Just as she had taken care of the seagulls that had landed on her bedroom windowsill when she was a girl.

40

Jessie and Marilyn walked back to his car in silence.

'Passengers get in the other side,' he said, pulling the driver's door open.

'You handled that badly, Marilyn.'

He turned to face her. 'I don't need your advice.'

'You told me an hour ago, at breakfast, that you did need my advice.'

'On the case. I need your advice on the case.'

'I'm giving you my advice on the case. There was no need to go in all guns blazing like that. It was counterproductive.'

Marilyn sighed heavily. 'I had them both up to here.' He laid his right hand on top of his head. 'Actually, no . . . to here,' he corrected, stretching his arm straight above his head, 'when I was trying to find their daughter's murderer.'

'They were grieving.'

Marilyn shook his head. 'I found her.'

'Who?'

'Their daughter's murderer.'

'Oh, for God's sake, Marilyn.'

Ignoring her admonishment, he reached into his glove compartment, pulled out a map and unfurled it on the soft-top roof.

'What am I supposed to be looking at?' Jessie asked, stepping forward, her arms still folded across her chest, sending Marilyn a body language message as negative as her feelings.

'Here.' He placed his finger on a stretch of road that ran parallel to the beach. 'We're here, right.'

She traced her gaze from the centre of East Wittering, along Stocks Lane, right into Bracklesham Lane and right again into West Bracklesham Drive. She ignored the sound of Marilyn drumming his fingers impatiently on the roof next to the map.

'Can't you just take my word for it?'

'No.' A moment later. 'Yes, we're here . . . there . . . where you said.'

'Right, so Roger and Carolynn are hiding out here, where we are now.'

'Yes.'

He moved his finger, a centimetre to the right. 'Jodie Trigg lives— *lived* here, five hundred metres away.'

'Half a kilometre away, on a caravan park with how many hundreds of homes on it?'

'She could walk past this house every day.'

Jessie took a moment. 'Her school is in East Wittering. She wouldn't need to walk past Carolynn and Roger's house to get to school. In fact, she'd go in the opposite direction, down the beach, most probably, as that's the most direct route.'

'She had hours alone every day after school to wander. I believe she would have passed this house regularly, and it's

211

not beyond the realms of possibility that she saw them, met them, knew them.'

Jessie stepped back from the map. 'You're right, Marilyn: it is not beyond the realms of possibility that she knew them. She could have come out of the caravan park and wandered past this house many times. But you need evidence, Marilyn, not subjectivity and conjecture. *Evidence*. That's what a good case is built on.'

'Thanks for the 101, Dr Flynn.'

'Pleasure.'

Folding the map, he tossed it into the glove compartment. 'Hop into the car and let's chat on the way back to the office. Perhaps we can swing by the Co-op and get a bottle of gin to share. I could do with some alcoholic anaesthetization.'

'I'm not coming with you.'

He threw up his hands. 'Oh, come on, Jessie, I wasn't *that* bad with Reynolds.'

'And I'm not *that* juvenile, Marilyn. I want to walk around the caravan park to get a sense of where Jodie lived. I'd also like to look in her room, at her things, if I may. I have a vague sense of Zoe from my sessions with Carolynn, though most of it was probably lies, but I have no sense whatsoever of Jodie.'

Marilyn nodded. 'I'll radio the PC guarding the Triggs' caravan and let him know that you're coming. I'm sure he could do with some company to break the monotony. I have some other things I'd like you to look at too. I was going to give them to you when we got back to the office, but it would be useful for you to have them now.' Opening the boot, he produced two brown paper files and an iPad and held them out to her. 'One file is Zoe's, the key information

212

from the ten-metre-high stack we amassed. The other file and the iPad are Jodie's. Take a look at her Instagram account. The password is Odie, like the dog in Garfield.'

'Do you take these everywhere with you?'

'Those and all my mental whips for self-flagellation. I was going to leave the files and iPad with you at the B & B if you refused to help.'

'Guilt me into it?'

'I was pretty sure the crime scene photos would succeed if my rhetoric failed.'

With a roll of her eyes, Jessie took the files and iPad from him. 'Is Jodie's mother at the caravan?'

'No, she's gone to stay with her sister in Guildford. I'll drop you.'

'I'll walk.'

'To get a sense?'

'We'll make a psychologist of you yet, Dr Simmons.'

He shook his head. 'I didn't buy you a big enough pancake for that.'

41

The sign said 'Breakfast Van'. Nothing solid had passed Carolynn's lips since breakfast yesterday and she was famished. Easing her silver Fiesta from the slow lane of the A3 into the lay-by, she parked behind the van. Roger had chosen the Fiesta for her, as it was one of the most common cars on the road, in the most common colour. Though it had been purchased precisely to blend, she had felt far from invisible since leaving the slipway an hour ago, must have checked her rear-view mirror a hundred times expecting to be dazzled by flashing blue lights, seeing only singletons like her, couples and families staring blankly through their windscreens as they ploughed through the morning traffic towards London.

An eighteen-wheeler lorry, curtains drawn around its cab, was parked beyond the breakfast van and a small silver hatchback had pulled into the lay-by behind Carolynn, a woman, she noticed, her heartbeat slowing with relief. She watched the blonde occupant flip down the sun visor and apply mascara to her lashes, blusher to her cheeks, getting ready for a coffee with friends or to see a boyfriend, perhaps? Carolynn felt a twinge of sadness. She couldn't recall the last time she'd had cause to apply make-up. The trial, *of course*. Another twinge, sharper, which she quickly suppressed. She had worn make-up, nothing too showy, completing her look with a plain navy work suit, white blouse and sensible low-heeled navy court shoes, as her barrister had instructed.

Juries hate glamorous female defendants. Handsome men typically receive lighter sentences than ugly men, but the opposite is true for attractive women. Juries like to make attractive women pay. We're aiming for neat, reliable, dowdy.

She had also applied make-up when she'd been to see Jessie Flynn, she remembered now. Not for the first session: she'd thought her psychologist would be a frump, but for the second. She hadn't consciously acknowledged why she'd done it, but as she was leaving the house, she'd turned back, gone upstairs and pulled her make-up bag from the bottom shelf of the bathroom cupboard, dust motes flying as she unzipped it, smudged some concealer over the black rings under her eyes, coated her lashes with mascara and added a touch of pink sorbet lipstick. Nothing too glamorous – still playing the role. *Neat, reliable, dowdy.* But then she didn't want to look too dowdy for Jessie. She wanted to look more like her old self, a bird of a feather. Dragging her eyes from her rear-view mirror, from the woman, from the unsettling glimpse of normality, Carolynn climbed out of her car, locking the door, leaving Zoe's cat curled up on the passenger seat.

The young man behind the breakfast van's counter had oily black hair and custard-headed acne spots peppered his jaw. The thought of him preparing food made Carolynn want to spin on her heel, but she was here now and it would have been too rude, too obvious, to turn away.

'A bacon sandwich, please,' she said.

The man tossed the red-top newspaper he'd been reading on to the counter next to the grill. Carolynn's eyes widened.

The photograph on the front page was her. Not the beach or Jodie Trigg any more, but *her*, from that bloody 'godparents and close friends only' christening. She reached out, an involuntary movement, to spin the paper around so that she could read the headline above the photograph, her hand freezing in mid-air as her brain engaged. The man's hooded gaze flicked from her face to her photograph and back.

Carolynn licked her lips, which were suddenly bone-dry. *Look him in the eye. Hold his stare.*

42

Buena Vista was a cream-coloured static caravan, jammed amongst acres of others that varied in shade from white to over-stewed tea brown. Each caravan was anchored on one side by a tarmac parking area, on the other by a narrow garden, which some owners had demarcated with flower borders, low bamboo screening, or ankle-high picket fences. A group of children were skateboarding in the road, tackling jumps made from bricks and wooden planks, a row of smaller kids cheerleading from the grass verge. Jessie could hear the voices of other children, carrying from different areas of the caravan park and from the beach, which must be about fifty metres away to the south. It was hard to remain orientated, given the densely packed sameness surrounding her. Though she'd never met Debs Trigg, Jessie was relieved that she was staying with her sister in Guildford. There were too many children here, too much joy.

The uniformed police constable guarding the caravan looked hot and bored. Stepping over the low white plastic picket fence, she joined him in the front garden and held out her hand.

'I'm Dr Jessie Flynn. DI Simmons radioed to say I'd be coming.'

The PC – Miller, Jessie read from his nametag – obviously new to the job and just a kid, nodded. 'Yes, ma'am. I'll let you in.'

Unlocking the front door, he held it open and followed her into the cramped kitchen.

'I'd like to be alone, please,' she said, easing the message with a smile.

Miller hesitated, clearly unwilling to risk screwing up his first major assignment.

'Radio Maril— Detective Inspector Simmons, if you're unsure. Forensics have already been through the place, and I'll be careful not to disturb anything.'

'Fine, OK, ma'am.' He backed down the steps and, with a last nervous smile, pulled the door closed.

Quiet. The children's voices and the grind of their skateboard wheels on tarmac muted now, as if she was listening through ear defenders. Moving into the middle of the kitchen, she turned a slow three-sixty, taking in dark wooden kitchen cupboards set with a small oven, a double hob and sink ahead of her. To her right, a corridor led to what looked like the master bedroom, a crumpled white duvet sagging half-off the bed, a pile of clothes and wedge-heeled gold sandals discarded on the floor visible through the open door, two other doors opening off the corridor, a bathroom and Jodie's bedroom, she supposed. A built-in beige sofa wrapped around the far end of the caravan to her left, net curtains covering a window above it, smothering the sunlight in their dusty grey folds.

The air in the caravan was hot and stuffy and Jessie could smell the lingering scent of cigarettes. So Debs Trigg was a smoker: not unusual and irrelevant to the case. To have a vice was part of being human and, at their extreme, human vices were what kept her in a job. Her own vice was alcohol, Sauvignon Blanc, to be precise. Sauvignon and her dirty secret – OCD.

She opened one of the kitchen cupboards to reveal a jumble of cereal boxes, their tops roughly torn open, jars of jam and spreads leaking their sticky contents, tins of fruit and vegetables, an open bag of spilling fusilli. Though the electric suit fizzed as she surveyed the cupboard, she resisted the urge to clean, restack, order. She had to keep a lid on her OCD while she was here, irrespective of the triggers, and focus her mind on what was really important. Stepping back, she shut the doors – out of sight, out of mind – a policy that failed more often than it worked, but this time, with so much else of importance on her mind, the heat from the suit subsided.

She checked the other kitchen cupboards, equally as crammed as the first; the sitting room, more stuff; Debs Trigg's bedroom, the same. The whole caravan evidenced the disorder of a woman with too many other pulls on her time. Finding nothing of particular relevance to Jodie or her murder, Jessie was stepping back out of Debs' bedroom when she heard the telephone ring. A click and the hum of an answering machine from somewhere at the far end of the caravan.

Hello, this is the Trigg residence.

It took her a moment to realize that she was listening not to Debs Trigg's voice, but to Jodie's, each word carefully enunciated, the tone earnest, but clearly that of a child.

I'm sorry that we can't come to the phone right now, but if you leave your name and number after the tone, we will phone you back very soon. Thank you and goodbye.

Now that she had heard Jodie's voice, she wanted to see her, feel her, understand as much about her as she could from whatever she could find within the four walls that the little girl had once called her own.

There was something eerie and toxically sad about intruding into a dead child's room, opening her cupboards and drawers, handling her possessions. Clothes, toys, books, pictures . . . nine years of life snuffed out, leaving behind a room filled with things that had sustained her daily, things she had valued, others she'd loved, the totality of which would hopefully explain a life.

A life and a death.

43

The photograph was of her old self, a woman even she struggled to remember. Unrecognizable to a stranger, surely? The skin on Carolynn's lips stretched and cracked like parchment as she smiled. Sudden understanding leant a gleam to the oily van-man's feral eyes. Wrapping the bacon sandwich in a paper napkin, he held it out to her.

'That'll be twenty quid,' he said.

Carolynn sucked in a breath, biting back the – 'What the hell?' – growing on her lips. *Fine.* It was worth it to her. Opening her handbag, she looked for her purse, couldn't see it. Her handbag's interior was shadowed by the van's blue-and-white striped awning. Stepping back into the sunlight, she held her handbag open and rummaged inside. Car keys, hairbrush, powder compact, mascara, a lipstick, mirror, 'pay-as-you-go' mobile phone, a collection of coins for parking clinking in the bottom. But no purse.

Oh God. She remembered now: taking her purse out of her bag to give £2 to a charity collector who'd knocked on the front door selling cupcakes yesterday. Then what had she done? Left it on the hall table? Carried it with her into the kitchen, and put it down on the work surface while she emptied the cakes into the bin? She couldn't think. Looking up, she met the man's hooded gaze.

'I must have left my purse at home.' She tried to keep her voice even, mask the thread of desperation. 'But I've got £10 in my pocket, here—' She held it out to him. 'And some change.' Raking her fingers along the bottom of her handbag, she scooped up the change, a couple of pound coins, three fifties, a few other silvers and some coppers, all covered in downy lint. She laid the pile of coins on the counter.

The man grinned, a wet red hole gaping at the centre of his mouth where both of his incisors were missing.

'Like I said, the sandwich costs twenty quid, lady. Cheap at the price, I'd say.'

'And I've just told you that I've forgotten my purse.' Carolynn held up her bag to him, open so that he could see. She was close to tears. What else could possibly go wrong? How else would she be punished? Hadn't she been punished enough for what she had done? Punished over and over and *over*.

Scooping up the money, the man winked. 'I'll let you off the rest, lady, 'cause I'm nice like that. You have a good day now, won't yeh.'

44

On her way from the Reynolds' house to Buena Vista, Jessie had sat on the beach wall and studied the crime scene photographs of little Jodie's pale body, her head surrounded by that halo of curly brown hair that looked like seaweed, a mermaid from a child's fairy story washed up on the beach in her heart of shells. She had looked at Zoe's too, the staging of the dead girls identical, the differences only in the children themselves, Zoe blonde and brown-eyed, Jodie green-eyed and dark-haired. But despite those differences and the divergence in their backgrounds and lifestyles, she didn't believe that either girl had been randomly chosen. Each item of the stage set, so carefully constructed, had meant something to the killer. She would review all the material that Marilyn had collected during the investigation into Zoe's murder later, but for now her focus was on Jodie. If she could get into the little girl's mind, understand how she thought, how she behaved, perhaps she could uncover the reason for her death and learn something valuable about the person who killed her.

So who was Jodie Trigg? Her job to find out.

On the surface, she was the nine-year-old daughter of a single mother. Her father had left before Jodie was born, leaving Debs with no way of funding her daughter beyond relying on the government or on herself. Though she would no doubt be vilified as a chaotic and uncaring mother in the press, she had chosen to rely on herself, and that one act alone spoke volumes to Jessie about who Debs Trigg was and who she would have wanted her daughter to grow up to be. Two nights ago, she had got back from work late – seven and a half hours after Jodie had left school, between six and seven hours after she had been murdered in the dunes – and found her bed empty. No doubt she would forever be haunted by the fact that she had been working, oblivious, while someone was wringing the neck of her baby girl.

Zoe, conversely, was the privileged daughter of affluent married parents, her lifestyle comfortable, her education private, her future, if she had lived to take it, assured in a way that Jodie's would never have been.

As she twisted the handle and pushed the door open, Jessie held her breath, almost expecting a child with dark, curly hair to come bouncing across the room, grab her by the hand and pull her through the doorway, talking, explaining, picking things up and showing them off to her, doing handstands on the beds. But the room was empty and silent – *of course it would be* – east-facing and flooded with morning sunlight, no nets in here to diffuse its brightness. Jessie wondered if Jodie had slept with the curtains open as she did, letting the night come into the room with her, counting stars.

45

A uniformed PC waved Marilyn to a halt as he drew up to the entrance of West Wittering beach car park, then stepped back apologetically, hands raised when he recognized the car's driver.

'Any luck?' Marilyn asked.

Four uniforms had manned the entrance from dawn until dusk since Jodie's murder, stopping every car, quizzing the occupants as to their whereabouts on Thursday afternoon between three and five-thirty p.m., showing them Jodie Trigg's photograph, asking if they'd seen her, any girls who looked like her, might have been her, even a slim chance, in the vicinity of the beach on Thursday afternoon. Questioning them as to whether they'd seen her in the few days preceding her murder either alone or in company. Or if they'd seen anyone, male or female, acting suspiciously on Thursday afternoon or any of the preceding days. Other uniforms were strung out along the beach from West Wittering to Bracklesham Bay, outside the Reynolds' rental house, showing the same photograph and asking the same questions. He had

PCs on the roads in and out of the Witterings, stopping all the cars, others going from house to house. He was leaving no stone unturned, and still they had turned up nothing useful.

'Nothing,' the PC said, hastily adding, 'So far, sir, so far,' in response to Marilyn's crestfallen look.

West Wittering car park was routinely packed to capacity throughout the summer weekends, the kilometres of white sand a magnet for holiday-makers and day-trippers from London. This afternoon, though, it was barely a tenth full, murder bad for business, only the ghouls drawn by it. He drove until the tarmac road that cut through the car park petered to a sandy cul-de-sac, then parked. It had been here, at the far end of the beach car park, that he had first set eyes on Carolynn Reynolds clutching Zoe's lifeless body and howling. Great playacting, he'd always thought, the woman as cold as a dip in the Solent in January. Hypothermia-inducing cold.

'What have you found?' Marilyn asked, ducking under the 'Police – Do Not Cross' tape a few minutes later to join his lead CSI, Tony Burrows, in the dunes on the deserted peninsula.

'Nothing,' Burrows muttered. He looked tired and wind-swept, his bald spot sunburnt to a wince-inducing smoked salmon. 'Or everything.'

Marilyn raised an eyebrow. 'Everything?'

'A bin-lorryload of discarded food wrappers; assorted kids action figures; one green-and-purple Furby; three beach towels; two pairs of ladies knickers and a pair of gents boxers, stripy – quite natty ones, actually; a pink lacy bra, courtesy of M&S's Autograph Collection, whatever that is; twelve condoms at the last count; and a significant amount

226

of faeces.' He shuddered. 'Both dog and human. Makes me never want to sit on a beach again.'

Marilyn smiled grimly. 'Sounds like the *Generation Game*, Brucie.'

'And next on the conveyor-belt . . . '

'Is some luck.' He couldn't imagine being lucky on this case, however much he crossed his fingers and promised God he'd be an upstanding, clean-living citizen in exchange for a break.

His gaze moved past Burrows to survey the deserted dunes, still taped off, still officially a crime scene. Nearly forty-eight hours since Jodie Trigg's body had been found and a few hardy journalists were hanging around outside the cordon, hoping for a juicy tit-bit, testament to how high profile his Zoe Reynolds debacle had been, how Jodie Trigg's identikit murder had them smelling 'massive circulation' blood. At least the seagulls seemed to have worked out that they'd get no joy here and had moved on.

'I can't afford to fail this time, Tony,' he murmured.

Without making eye contact, Burrows laid a slightly awkward hand on his shoulder. 'Everyone fails, Marilyn.'

Marilyn nodded grimly. 'Only the once though. Only the once – and I've had my once,'

46

Workman and DC Cara crunched side by side up the gravel drive, past a lime green Lamborghini, to the front door.

'I thought those cars only existed outside Harrods,' Workman said.

'Or in my dreams,' Cara replied.

He had started off his police career in Traffic because he loved cars, he'd told Workman as they trudged, sweating, from house to house, past Mercedes SLs and SLKs, top-of-the-range BMWs, a couple of Porsches, all in silver, grey or black, muted, distinguished tones, expensive statements, but not tacky ones. The owner of the Lamborghini wasn't so circumspect.

'If you save half of your salary for the next ten years, you might be able to afford this,' Workman said to Cara, indicating a metre-by-metre patch of flowerbed by the front door.

'How long for the Lambo?'

'Until you're my age.'

'Another half-century then.'

She met his grin with a roll of her eyes.

They had already visited twenty houses – palatial residences, more accurately – on the bankers' ghetto of West Strand, houses that fronted on to the beach and would leave no change from £5 million. So far they'd had no joy in finding anyone who had seen Jodie Trigg, either alone or with her killer, on Thursday afternoon. Most of the houses were owned by weekending financiers and their families, and the few who had been in residence on Thursday hadn't been looking out of their windows at school girls from the cheap end of town passing by on the beach.

Was it really possible for a nine-year-old girl to walk to her death on a summer afternoon and for no one to notice?

47

Jodie Trigg's small bedroom was dominated by two single beds, both covered in purple duvet covers scattered with pink and white butterflies, both neatly made up. The bed by the window must have been the one that Jodie had slept in as the other was crammed with stuffed toys – all cuddly cats, Jessie realized after a moment, in different sizes and colours, all tucked side by side under the duvet, their fluffy heads resting on the pillow. No dolls in the collection on the bed or anywhere else, she noticed, thinking of the plastic doll in its pink nylon ballerina dress that had been left by the dead little girls' sides. What had been the significance of the dolls? Significance for the killer, Jessie thought, not for the child, or not for Jodie at least.

Had the same been true for Zoe? Carolynn had told her, in one of their sessions, that Zoe had hated dolls and Jessie had had no reason to disbelieve her, not then, at least. And now? Had Marilyn asked her that question, received an answer? Pulling her mobile from her pocket, she pressed voice record and spoke into it, reminding herself to check with Marilyn about the dolls.

Sliding her phone back into her pocket, she opened the single wardrobe to reveal an interior that reminded her of the cupboards of new army recruits or of her own wardrobes – *perhaps not quite that extreme* – the few summer dresses hanging creaseless, jumpers, jeans and T-shirts carefully folded and stacked, colour coded, with their own kind, pants, socks and tights neatly layered in a plastic basket on the bottom shelf. Though she was loath to deal in stereotypes, they could usefully provide an initial frame of reference that could be embroidered or picked apart as more information was gathered. This wasn't the room of a stereotypical nine-year-old girl, the type of messy, disorganized nine-year-old that most of her friends and she herself had been, before Jamie's death and the advent of her OCD. There were no clothes strewn on the floor, no books scattered on the bedside table, no posters of ponies, actors or musicians on the walls. Even the cuddly cats were ordered in their slumber in the spare bed, ranged from large to small, but not large at one end, graduating to small on the other, Jessie realized. Jodie had arranged them so that the large cats were at the edges of the bed, the smaller further in, and the smallest, a pale blue kitten with a navy and white polka-dot bow around its neck, right in the middle. Looking at the arrangement, the word *protected*, occurred to her, the bigger protecting the smaller.

Sitting on the end of Jodie's bed, Jessie pulled the iPad that Marilyn had given her from her handbag.

Instagram, he'd said. *Have a look.*

Typing in the password 'Odie', Jessie pressed 'enter'. *Wrong password*. She tried again, typing carefully. Access

231

still denied. She texted Marilyn. 'What was the password to Jodie's iPad?'

A few moments later, her phone pinged. *Oddie. The dog in Garfield. As I said before!!*

Jessie texted back. *Thank you. Btw. The dog in Garfield is called Odie!*

Another ping. *Smartarse.*

The little girl's Instagram page was short, just twelve photographs and two videos. Most of the photos showed her on the beach with her mother, a few with friends. A couple of photographs, selfies from the closeness and angle, showed Jodie cuddling a peculiar-looking, splodgy black, tan and cream cat. It made the farm cat that was forever attempting to prostrate itself on Jessie's under-floor-heated kitchen tiles look like a super-model feline, though from the way it was cuddling up to Jodie, it looked friendly enough. It was impossible to judge the location of the photographs, as little background was visible, but in one the cat was sitting on the bonnet of a car, a slash of silver paintwork beneath its paws, the reflection of the edge of the iPad visible in the windscreen over Jodie's left shoulder.

The last photograph was one of Jodie sitting on her bed, drawing. For a moment, Jessie thought that Jodie had drawn one of her cuddly toys, but when she turned the iPad upside down, so that she could look at the drawing the right way up, she realized that Jodie had drawn the ugly tortoiseshell cat. The cat was sitting on a black-and-white tiled floor, tiles that reminded her of a butcher's shop. The cat didn't have a collar. Whose cat was it, if anyone's? Did it matter?

48

Walking, determinedly, head bent, along the beach towards the car park, ignoring the few journalists trailing in his wake, hoping his *no comment* had been a joke, that he'd suddenly feel a burning desire to unburden his soul, give them the journalist's equivalent of manna from heaven, Marilyn mentally reviewed everything he'd achieved, or more accurately, failed to achieve, since Jodie Trigg's murder two days ago, and what already felt like a lifetime of lost sleep and self-recrimination. He had once watched a film in which a man in a suit had committed suicide by walking into the sea. Just walking, calmly and purposefully, as if he was perambulating along the pavement in the City of London, until he had disappeared under the waves. He had pulled a few suicides from the freezing sea when he'd served in Brighton, the grim reality so different from the stylized film. And yet, when he had seen little Jodie's pale, broken body on the beach, he'd had the overwhelming urge to walk down the sand and into the sea, keep walking across the Channel to France, emerge into a shiny new life. Buy a small vineyard and start a winemaking business, perhaps. Working with alcohol would suit him, as would pottering down to the pension in the local village to drink espressos, smoke Gauloise cigarettes and shrug his shoulders, impervious to the march of the rest of the world. Leave the demons that he had amassed from his time in Surrey and Sussex Major Crimes behind. Over the past two days, he had thrown everything at the Jodie Trigg murder, but still they had achieved nothing concrete.

What had he missed with Zoe Reynolds? Why had he failed so spectacularly to nail anyone for her murder? Carolynn's DNA had been all over her child, all over the doll left by her body, all over the shells. Her footprints had surrounded the crime scene, obscuring any others, if there were others to obscure. The forensic case had been impossible and beyond that, despite tens of thousands of man-hours, they'd found nothing solid enough to hang a conviction on.

Before the little girls' deaths, he would have thought a touristy beach a crazy place to commit murder, but he now knew better. Was the killer as forensically smart as he or she seemed to be, or had he or she just been lucky? Yet another question to which he had no answer. It was becoming a nasty habit.

49

The back of Jessie's neck prickled as the first of Jodie's two Instagram videos began to play. From the angle of the video, which took in the doorway, the end of Jodie's bed and the whole of the second bed, it was clear that the little girl had propped the iPad on the windowsill. The film must have been recorded in the winter, because she was wearing jeans and a thick red jumper.

'They were in a mess,' she said, bouncing down on to the spare bed and wrapping her arms around the pile of soft toys in its middle. 'So I'm rearranging them, tucking them under the covers so that they'll be warm and safe.' She mocked shivered. 'Because it-is-freeeeezing in here.' One of her upper incisors protruded at a forty-five-degree angle. She'd need braces . . . would have needed braces, Jessie corrected herself. Watching the video, it was almost impossible to believe that the little girl who was hugging and kissing each cuddly toy before she slipped them under the covers, spinning an orange tabby cat around to face the camera, holding its paw and waving to the viewer, was now a chilled eviscerated mannequin in Dr Ghoshal's morgue. Almost impossible and impossibly heartbreaking.

'It's important that the little ones get looked after,' she said. 'That's why I put them in the middle.' Jumping up from the bed, she pirouetted on one leg and grinned at the camera. 'So that the big ones can look after them. Like Mum does for me.' Another grin, this one lopsided, lacking the conviction of the first. ''Cept it's kind of the other way around. Well, both ways around, I suppose. She looks after me and I look after her, because it's just the two of us.'

She pirouetted across the tiny room, looming large as she reached to switch off the video.

The second video was shot in the summer: Jodie and Debs Trigg walking on the beach, probably filmed with an iPhone that Jodie was holding on a selfie stick. Her other hand was clasping one of her mother's and she was walking slightly in front of Debs, leading her, instructing her to be careful not to stand on the worm casts – *because you'll squish the worms underneath* – guiding her around the collected puddles of seawater. After a minute or so, Debs reached into the pocket of her shorts and pulled out a packet of cigarettes and a lighter.

'Not here, Mum, not on the beach. You can't smoke when the air is so clean and lovely.'

Jodie took the cigarettes from her mum's hand, pushed them back into her pocket and started walking again, dragging Debs behind her, holding the selfie stick jerkily out in front, chatting, making jokes, her voice too high now, forced jollity, a tone that Jessie recognized from her own childhood, trying to break the tension in her parents' marriage by clowning. She felt an intense twinge of sadness for the little girl. Debs looked puffy-eyed and tired, her dark hair limp

236

and greasy, her skin wan and pasty. Jessie knew that if Marilyn resorted to putting her on an appeal, she wouldn't make good TV. Unlike her daughter, she wasn't photogenic. Jodie must have got her good looks from the father she had never known.

The video continued to play, but Jessie's mind had moved to wonder who Jodie had been walking on the beach with two days ago. No selfie stick video of that walk to save them all the pressure and pain of an investigation. From the crime scene photographs, the only bruises on her body had been the strangulation marks around her neck. If she had been dragged along the beach against her will, she would have had bruising to her arms or torso. The rain had washed the footsteps around the little girl's body to formless indents, but still Tony Burrows had found a trail that he thought could be the footprints of an adult and child walking side by side towards the site of her murder.

So Jodie had most probably walked voluntarily with her killer along the beach to meet her death. Perhaps, as they had strayed further from civilization, she had become concerned. Perhaps she had stopped and asked where they were going, why they needed to walk so far. Or perhaps she hadn't. Perhaps she had been entirely comfortable in her killer's company, at ease and unworried. Or perhaps, Jessie thought, her gaze fixing on the frozen image of Jodie on the beach with her mother, the video finished now, her killer had been someone she'd felt she needed to look after. Perhaps she had walked, as she walked with her mother, holding her killer's hand, playing the child carer.

Jessie liked Jodie Trigg. She wished that she hadn't looked at the crime scene photos, that she could just hold an image of the living girl from the videos in her mind instead.

237

Impossible now: the images of death would forever eclipse the images of life. It had been the same with her little brother, Jamie. That final static image she had of him hanging by his neck from the curtain rail in his bedroom dominating the seven years of moving images she had from his life.

Pressing the off switch on the iPad, Jessie stood. She smoothed her hand over the crumples in the duvet, erasing the imprint of her seated self, wanting to leave the little girl's room exactly as she had found it. But as she cast a last look around Jodie's bedroom, her gaze fell on the little kitten tucked in the middle of the bed – protected – and something stirred in her memory.

The kitten, a cat. *The* cat. That spoldgy black, tan and cream cat. Something niggled – what?

Switching Jodie's iPad back on, she found Instagram again, that photograph of Jodie's drawing. But it wasn't the cat in the drawing that Jessie focused on. It was the tiles in the background. Black-and-white tiles that reminded her of a butcher's shop. And instead of the cat, surrounded by that black-and-white checkerboard, an image of Marilyn's suede Chelsea boot wedged firmly over a threshold rose in her mind.

I give you permission to go fuck yourself, DI Simmons.

50

Past

Little girl, far away in a world of your own, in a world built of dreams that are yours and yours alone.

The girl stood very still and watched the seagull as it balanced on her bedroom windowsill and snatched at the torn segments of bread she had left out for it. She had spent countless hours over the years watching the seagulls swooping past her window, soaring out over the sea in the distance, silvery clouds billowing behind the fishing boats as they chugged back into the harbour with their catch.

She had promised herself many times that, one day, like those seagulls, she would escape. Live right by the sea in a proper house, have money. Money and a good life.

The seagull on her windowsill had webbed feet, like her feet. But the seagull was free to go where it wanted and she was trapped in this shitty flat with only her mother and the television, that smug blonde girl in the advert, for company, and the view from her bedroom window, a knife sliver of cobalt sea in the distance between the grey stone tower blocks.

When she was little, she had loved the blonde girl in the advert, had wanted to be her, wear that white broderie anglaise dress, run in that field of wild flowers. She had loved her mother too back then. But now that she was older and wiser, she hated them both. Hated the smug blonde bitch for having what she didn't and despised the weakness in her mother that had stranded them both here, that made her put her next hit above her daughter's welfare.

She had never known her father. Her mother told her that he had been a sailor and that the relationship hadn't lasted, that he'd left before she was born. But she didn't believe that. She was twelve now and she believed none of that shit any more. Her father was one of the men who her mother fucked for drug money. At night, she lay in bed and listened to her mother's headboard slamming against the dividing wall, the grunts of the men, her mother sucking and wheezing while they fucked her, as if she was punctured.

The girl had known from a very early age that she was alone, that she could only ever rely on herself.

In the cramped, dirty kitchen, she peeled another slice from the white loaf and returned to her bedroom. The seagull was still perched on the windowsill, but as she approached, ever so slowly, the bread held out in front of her, he shied away, stretching out his wings and taking flight.

As she watched him circle on the wind and head out to sea, envy twisted her bitter heart even more out of shape. She wanted to be as free as that seagull. She wanted to be that seagull. She wanted to steal his power and his liberty.

51

The doorbell's ring, muted through the huge, carved oak front door, sounded like a bee buzzing under a towel. The house was modern; cubist, it would probably be called if it were a painting, blocks of whitewashed concrete embedded with huge rectangular plate-glass windows. Workman and Cara had given up hope of finding a 'live one' inside and were turning away, when the door was opened by a middle-aged man wearing baggy jeans rolled up to mid-calf, and a grey kite-surfing logo T-shirt. His clothes said 'ageing beach bum', but his salt-and-pepper buzz-cut, the enquiring focus in his grey eyes and the Lambo said banker or successful entrepreneur. Which was it, or a combination of all three? They would probably never find out. Workman extended her hand.

'Detective Sergeant Sarah Workman and Detective Constable Darren Cara from Surrey and Sussex Major Crimes.'

'Anthony Moore. How can I help you?'

'You may have heard that a young girl was found dead

on the beach on Thursday afternoon, around the corner, on the peninsula,' Workman said. 'We believe that she was murdered sometime between four and five p.m. We're looking for witnesses.'

Moore nodded. 'Thursday? Yes, I heard about the little girl and yes, I was here. Come on in.'

The room they stepped into was spectacular, a double height open-plan space painted a soft, dove grey, a wall of glass overlooking the garden, the beach and Solent beyond. Titanic-sized white sofas were arranged around a driftwood coffee table this end of the room, a glass dining table seating twelve at the far end. It was a masterpiece of seaside minimalist chic. Moore noticed Cara looking at the telescope lined up in the middle of the picture window.

'So my kids can watch me kite-surfing when they come to stay. It's inspirational for them, seeing their old dad getting out there doing stuff.'

Cara nodded, thinking that he was sure Moore's kids' attention would be rapt by the sight of their father blasting up and down two hundred metres out to sea. *Not.*

'I'm divorced. Kids live with their mum in Belgravia. Good for them to come down here and experience real life occasionally.'

Real life. Cara's parents had divorced when he was six. Real life for him when he went to stay with his father had been a trip to William Hill. He turned from the window and the view, pushing a lid down on his envy. Though he didn't earn much, he loved his job and he knew that his lot could be worse, much worse.

'As my colleague mentioned, a nine-year-old girl, Jodie Trigg, was murdered on the beach on Thursday afternoon,' Cara said to Moore. 'We're looking for witnesses, anyone who could have seen her before she was killed, walking on the beach perhaps, either alone or in company, or seen anyone else on the beach around that time.'

'I was out kite-surfing that afternoon,' Moore said. 'It was windy, raining, no one else out on the water. I love it when it's like that. I get too much of people in the office.'

'Did you see anyone on the beach, sir?'

'Two people. A woman and a child, a girl.'

'Together?'

'Yes, walking together.'

A 'live one' finally. Cara pulled a photograph of Jodie Trigg from his suit jacket pocket and held it up. 'Was this the girl?'

'Do you know what speed you can reach kite-surfing on a windy day?'

Cara shook his head, swallowing the facetious comment that was sitting right in his voice box. 'No, sir.'

'Fifty, sixty kilometres an hour. And you're a hundred, two hundred metres out to sea. No way I could tell if it was her.'

'So what did you see, sir?'

'Blonde.'

'The child?'

'The woman. Blonde hair, shoulder-length or longer. Long enough to swish.' He smiled. 'Could be an advert right?'

As far as Cara could remember, it was already an advert. 'Long enough to swish?'

'To stream out.' Moore flapped his hands around his head. 'Behind her in the wind.'

Cara made a note. 'And the child?' he asked, looking back up.

'Probably not blonde.'

'Why do you say that?'

'Because I didn't notice her hair. I noticed the woman's hair because it stood out against their clothes.'

'What were they wearing?'

'Dark. Grey, navy blue, black, those kinds of colours, both of them.'

Jodie Trigg's school uniform was a navy-blue trouser suit.

'Trousers? Skirts?' Workman cut in.

Moore shrugged. 'Too much detail.' He paused. 'Only the woman's hair was flapping though, so maybe they were both wearing trousers.'

'Who was closest to you?' Workman asked.

'The woman.'

'What time did you see them?'

'I went out just after three fifteen and I was out for an hour or so. I saw them about halfway through my session, give or take.'

'So around three forty-five?'

'I don't wear a watch out there, so it's a rough estimate.'

'How did they seem?' Workman asked.

Moore raised a quizzical eyebrow. 'What do you mean by "seem"?'

'Did the girl seem as if she was being coerced? Forced?'

'No. As I said, I was two hundred metres offshore and going like the clappers, but nothing stood out to me. If she'd been being dragged or been screaming, I would have noticed that and I would have contacted you guys after I heard about the dead girl. I remember thinking that they were mother and daughter, out for a walk.'

Workman nodded. 'Which direction were they walking in?'

'Towards the mouth of the harbour, the peninsula.'

'And where did you first see them?'

'Walking along the beach outside my house. That's why I noticed them. I was looking at my house from the water and I saw them walking past it. Then I saw them a few more times, while I was steaming back and forth, before they disappeared around the corner.'

'On to the peninsula?'

'Yes.'

'Did you see anyone else?'

'No, just them. It was a shitty afternoon. It was just me and them out there. No one else, not that I saw, anyway.'

52

Trying to suppress the look of smug satisfaction that had taken possession of his face the moment Workman had called to tell him that a credible witness had seen a girl walking along West Wittering beach on Thursday afternoon with a blonde woman, the smugness intensifying when Jessie called about the splodgy cat and the black-and-white tiles, Marilyn held up the hastily obtained search warrant. He felt as if he had been shown a chink of light in an otherwise pitch-black tunnel – not before time. And he was going to sprint for it like a lunatic, even if sport wasn't his strong point.

Taking the search warrant from Marilyn, Roger Reynolds scanned it briefly. Screwing it up, he dropped it at Marilyn's feet and drew back, pulling the front door wide open. Bending at the waist, he swept his arm in a broad arc, a mockingly regal gesture.

'Welcome to my humble abode, Detective Inspector Simmons. We had nothing to hide two years ago and we have nothing to hide now.'

'*We?*' Marilyn hitched an eyebrow. He couldn't help himself. 'Where is your wife, Mr Reynolds? Still running?'

Without answering, Reynolds turned his back and disappeared into the kitchen. Marilyn heard the vacuum suck of a fridge door opening and then an equally familiar sound as Reynolds pulled the ring on a can of beer. A Carling Black Label in his hand, Reynolds crossed the hallway to the sitting room without glancing at Marilyn, Jessie, Tony Burrows and his CSI team who were trooping up the front path, all clad in forensic overalls and overshoes. Slumping down on to the sofa, he turned on the television.

'Please stay where you are and don't touch anything, Mr Reynolds,' Marilyn said, raising his voice to be heard over the football commentary.

Marilyn's 73, a marked police car and the van of the forensic investigation team, parked nose to tail along the sea wall outside, had already drawn gawkers. Seeing the swelling crowd, Jessie felt intensely sad for the Reynolds. Those rubberneckers were the first tear that would make ripped shreds of their new life. Ushering the last of Burrows' team into the house, she closed the front door, shutting out their inquisitive gazes. The action felt akin to rearranging the deck chairs on the *Titanic*.

Reynolds was sitting on a beige corduroy sofa facing the television and the window beyond. He didn't seem to have noticed the people lining the sea wall, but Jessie knew that he must have done, was feigning indifference, just as he was now feigning indifference to the sound of feet creaking on boards above his head, of drawers being pulled out and rummaged through, cupboards being opened and searched, the creak of what Jessie assumed was the loft ladder being

247

lowered, Burrows' team locust-like in their speed and thoroughness.

'Can I join you?' Jessie asked.

Reynolds glanced over. 'My permission is irrelevant, given the circumstances, isn't it?' His gaze flicked back to the football match.

Jessie sat down on to the sofa perpendicular to his, taking the end closest to him and crossing her legs, right over left, mirroring his sitting position. Settling back against the cushions, she tried to adopt a posture as relaxed as his. Playacting – both of them. The only thing she didn't try to mirror was the disdainful curve of his lip.

'Do you know why we're here, Mr Reynolds?'

Without shifting his gaze from the match, he rolled his eyes and muttered, 'Because you have a search warrant?'

'Did you read it?'

'I read the Nazi diktat at the top outlining the fact that I no longer have the right to say who I let into my home.'

'The police are looking for evidence that Jodie Trigg was here.'

'Good luck to them. They'll find nothing. Neither of us knew the child.'

Jessie was watching him closely, the nuances of his expression; it didn't change, not even minutely.

'So Carolynn didn't tell you that she had befriended Jodie?'

His widened eyes met hers for a brief moment before he regained control and the shutters came back down. He was surprised, she realized, genuinely.

'Lies,' he snapped. 'She would have told me if she'd known Jodie Trigg.' His tone had a hard edge to it. 'She tells me everything.'

'Clearly not quite everything,' Jessie said.

53

Past

Paulsgrove, Portsmouth

Breaking off a corner from the slice of bread, the girl laid it on the windowsill. She broke off a second piece and placed that on the top of her chest of drawers, by the open window. A third piece, she laid on the floor. When she had finished, a trail of bread led from her bedroom window to the far corner of her box room.

Ducking down beneath the windowsill, she covered herself with the dirty grey sheet from her bed and settled down to wait. She would wait as long as she needed to. She had nowhere to go, nothing else to do and she was patient. She had learned patience over the years of having nothing to occupy herself but the television and the seagulls, and today her patience would pay off.

A flap of wings and the scratch of claws on wood, as a seagull landed on her windowsill. She felt totally calm, euphorically calm almost, every one of her muscles relaxed, her breathing shallow, just enough to gain oxygen to sustain her, but no more. Another flap and a different timbre under claws now as the seagull scrabbled along the veneered top of her chest of drawers. She could make out its ghostly shape through the sheet, as it flapped from the chest to the floor, following the trail of bread that she had laid into the far corner.

Bursting up from under the sheet, she slammed the window closed as the seagull bulleted against the glass and crumpled to the floor, stunned by the impact. But it would only be for a moment and the girl knew that she'd have to be quick. The sheet stretched between her hands, she tossed it over the seagull, following with her body, feeling the bird's frantic struggle underneath her. She lay on top of the seagull as it bit and clawed at the sheet, at her skin in frenzied terror, but she felt no pain. Only an intense exhilaration.

After a few minutes, the struggling ceased, the bird exhausted. She could hear it panting, feel the raised, fearful beat of its heart through the thin cotton. She smiled, enjoying the unfamiliar feeling of power. As she inched the sheet away from the seagull's head, it swung and snapped at her viciously, but she clamped her hands around its neck and yanked its body free of the material.

The seagull was huge and strong in her hands and she felt its vital desperation as it kicked and writhed, fighting for its life. The feathers on its neck were silky, downy, just as she had imagined they would be. She tightened her grip and felt the sinews underneath, felt the blood pulsing in its arteries in time with the panicked beat of the bird's heart.

Its eyes bulged from its head as she gripped even tighter. In a last desperate movement, its body twisted wildly from its neck, webbed feet pedalling the air. Laughing, the girl lifted her legs from the floor and pedalled her own webbed feet in time with the seagull's. Two pairs of webbed feet, one bird, one human. One free, one trapped. But where it had been she who had been trapped before, now it was the seagull. The feeling of power she felt over something that had been so free made her giddy with its intensity. The seagull's will to live was strong, but her will to kill was stronger. The seagull's webbed feet twitched, once, twice and were still.

She sat, cradling the lifeless body in her arms, until it cooled and began to stiffen. Moving to the window, she opened her fingers and watched the seagull fall. Its wings rose out from its body and for one brief second they looked as if they would catch the wind and take the animal out to sea. But then they folded in on themselves and the seagull plummeted to the concrete below.

Now that she had killed, the girl felt good. Elated. Powerful. The seagulls would lose their freedom and she – the girl with the webbed feet – would gain hers. It was only a matter of time and she was patient.

54

'Do you have a cat?' Jessie asked.

'What?' Reynolds' voice was incredulous.

'Do you have a cat?'

'What the hell has whether we've got a cat or not got to do with anything?' He pointed his finger at the ceiling. 'Got to do with this . . . this *invasion*?'

'Just humour me, please?'

Reynolds sighed. 'Yes, Dr Flynn, we have a cat. Did my wife not share that information with you in any of your cosy sessions? How remiss of her.' He raised an eyebrow and smirked, courting a reaction.

'Can you tell me about him or her,' Jessie said evenly, denying him the satisfaction of providing one.

'Him. My mother bought him for Zoe's fourth birthday. A Burmese, because they love people. Zoe adored that damn cat and it adored her. So yes, we have a cat . . .' His voice faltered. 'A legacy cat.'

'What does he look like?'

Reynolds' brow wrinkled. 'He has a head, a body, a tail and four legs.'

'And two eyes, a nose and a mouth.'

Reynolds sighed. 'He's splodgy,' he muttered. 'He's covered in black, brown and cream splodges, like some abstract art exhibition. As if a kid coloured him in, a kid with no artistic talent. Zoe called him Oddie, because he looks odd.'

'We have a photograph of Jodie Trigg stroking a cat which looks as if it could be him. And the password to her iPad was Oddie.'

'Oddie's a tart. He spends half his day on the wall outside, begging passers-by to pet him.'

'Jodie Trigg drew a picture of herself and the cat sitting on a tiled floor that looks very much like the one in your hallway.'

'Have you not noticed the state of this house?' Reynolds snapped. 'It's a nasty, cheap rental. I can't imagine that the hall tiles would be expensive or rare. I'm pretty sure that the butcher's in East Wittering has the same. Why don't you pop down there and ask them about their bloody cat.'

'A witness saw a blonde woman walking along the beach with a child who was most probably Jodie Trigg on Thursday afternoon.'

'Have you nothing concrete, Dr Flynn?' His voice was taunting, though Jessie registered the high note of unease running through his tone.

'It was enough to get the search warrant.'

'Of course it would have been,' he snapped. 'I don't doubt that just our names were enough.'

'I'm sorry,' Jessie said plainly. And she meant it, felt it, genuinely.

Reynolds swung around to face her. There was a vicious light in his eyes.

'Are you, really, Dr Flynn? Because what exactly is your role? To feed that bastard DI information my wife shared with you in confidence?'

Jessie forced herself to hold his gaze, weathering the pulsing hatred. 'As I told you before, everything that your wife shared with me in our sessions is confidential. I have not, and will not, pass any of it to the police, or anyone else, even you. You have my word on that.'

'Your word?' he spat. 'I have learnt from bitter experience to trust no one's word, Dr Flynn, and that decision has served me . . . served us very well for the past nine months. Unfortunately, it seems that my wife didn't learn that lesson well enough.'

Jessie sat forward. 'Carolynn is allowed to associate with people, make friends, Mr Reynolds. Her associating with Jodie doesn't necessarily mean anything significant.'

'*If* she associated with Jodie Trigg, then of course it fucking means something. It means that, whatever the truth is, our lives will get ripped to shreds all over again.' He pointed his index finger at the ceiling. 'This is just the beginning.'

'DI Simmons is very experienced,' Jessie said lamely.

'He's not objective,' Reynolds snapped.

Should she contradict him? She should, perhaps, out of loyalty to Marilyn if nothing else, but she believed that Reynolds was right. Marilyn wasn't objective on this case. He had seized on the information that Jodie Trigg was on first-name terms with the Reynolds' cat with the unbridled glee of a vulture tearing into a fresh carcass. Could she best help solve these murders by defending Marilyn, a lost cause in Reynolds' eyes, or by trying to convince Reynolds of her impartiality? Marilyn was clearly right – Carolynn had run. If Jessie had any hope of convincing Reynolds to help her locate Carolynn before she entirely hung herself in Marilyn's eyes, it had to be the latter.

'I've spent a lot of time with your wife and I don't believe that she's a killer and I *am* objective. But running isn't going to help her case. Please help me find her and convince her to turn herself in before this gets completely out of hand.'

His lip curled. 'Listen, love, I have as much idea of where she is as you do. Now why don't you just run along and join your mates crawling all over my bloody house, so I can watch the football.'

55

Jessie went out into the hallway, each step in the forensic overalls and over-shoes making her feel as if she was encased in a supermarket's plastic bag. The forensic locusts had spread downstairs. She almost tripped over Burrows in his white onesie, squatting by the front doormat, dusting fingerprint powder on to the tiles.

She felt nauseous again. The house was close and claustrophobic: low ceilings, the wall colours dense sixties beiges and browns that shrank the space to doll's house proportions and thickened the air. She wanted to haul open the front door and step outside, gulp in sea air to calm her stomach, but a quick glance around the edge of the kitchen blind told her that the rubberneckers' ranks had been swelled by a few journalists and that whoever ventured out would be fresh kill for the pack.

Skirting back around Burrows, she tried a couple of other doors off the hallway and found the downstairs toilet. Climbing on to the toilet seat, she cracked the window open and pressed her nose to the gap, sucking in air. Feeling no better, she dropped to the floor, lifted the toilet lid, and felt her stomach heave. She vomited twice, took a couple of sucking breaths and vomited again until her stomach felt as if it had been turned inside out. She closed the lid, flushed and washed her mouth out with water from the tap. Emerging from the bathroom, she saw Marilyn descending the stairs, clutching a dusty cardboard box.

'Join me in the sitting room, please, Dr Flynn.' His tone was formal, his voice loud enough to carry and not for her benefit.

Reynolds was still determinedly watching the television, an advert for baby formula now. Marilyn dropped the box on the floor at his feet.

'Don't touch,' he snapped, as Reynolds leant forward. No surprise on his face this time, Jessie noted; he already knew what the box contained. As Marilyn lifted the cardboard flaps with a latex-clad hand, it took all of Jessie's professionalism not to recoil.

The box contained a doll. A plastic doll in a cheap, pink nylon ballerina dress, identical to the ones found by the little girls' bodies. Except that this doll had blue eyes. Brown for Zoe. Green for Jodie. Blue for . . . ?

'You already knew what was in this box, didn't you, Mr Reynolds?' Jessie said, looking from the doll to Reynolds.

'I've only been in the loft once since the day we moved in and that was on Wednesday.'

'You knew,' she pressed.

Silence. Then a sigh, followed by a dull nod.

'How?'

'I saw that box for the first time this week,' he muttered.

'On Wednesday?' Jessie asked.

'Yes.'

257

'Where?' Marilyn cut in.

'In Carolynn's bedroom cupboard, right at the back, hidden behind her shoe rack.'

'What were you doing in her cupboard?'

'Does it matter?'

'Humour me.'

'We . . . Carolynn, kept a shoebox of Zoe's things. Photographs, her favourite teddy bear, her first sleepsuit, first shoes. With the anniversary of her . . . her death the following day, I wanted to have a look through the shoebox.' His gaze dipped. 'Wallow, I suppose you'd call it.'

'And you found the box with the doll in it?'

'Yes.'

'Was it you or Carolynn who moved the box to the loft?'

'Me.'

'Why?'

'Because it's repulsive. Creepy and repulsive. I wouldn't be able to sleep knowing that an identical doll to the one found by my daughter's body was in my bedroom.'

'Did you challenge Carolynn as to why she had it?' Jessie demanded. 'Where it came from?'

'Not when I found it. But I thought that when she realized I'd found and moved the doll, she'd speak to me. I wanted her to talk about it . . . to tell me why she had it. But she never mentioned it and I didn't want to press her.'

'Because the issue was too delicate, particularly given the time of year, the anniversary?'

His gaze locked to the doll in the box, Reynolds nodded.

'So your wife bought it. Is that what you're saying?' Marilyn asked.

'I've never seen it before is what I'm saying. *All* I'm saying.'

'Why were you in the loft this morning?' Marilyn asked.

'I felt dust, grit, on the landing carpet this morning under my bare feet. The only place it could have come from was the loft hatch. I wanted to know why Carolynn had opened it.'

Marilyn eyeballed him. 'And why had she opened it?'

From his stance and tone, Jessie knew his hackles were rising, tried to catch his eye, warn him to keep the conversation civil. Reynolds was cooperating; confrontation was liable to make him clam up. But Marilyn wasn't looking at her – deliberately?

'I don't know,' Reynolds muttered.

'To collect a suitcase?'

'I said, I don't know.'

'There's a rectangular imprint against the brick chimney breast in the loft that is dust free. Below is a stack of suitcases. The imprint says to me that the top suitcase is missing.'

'Does it?' Reynolds lifted his shoulders in studied nonchalance. 'I was only up there for a minute, and then came down because you rang the doorbell. I didn't get as far as the chimney breast.'

Marilyn switched tack. 'Mr Reynolds, you have told us repeatedly that no one apart from you and Carolynn has entered this house since you moved in nine months ago.'

'That's what I thought.' Though the look of studied indifference was still fixed to his face, his body language was as deflated as a week-old party balloon that most of the air – the fight – had leaked from. 'But you're telling me that Jodie Trigg was probably here.'

Marilyn nodded. 'Most of the surfaces downstairs, those that people routinely touch, have been recently wiped clean, including all the door handles, the surfaces of the doors, the downstairs toilet, kitchen worktops, cupboard doors and the kitchen table and chairs.'

'I like things tidy . . .' Reynolds said, hastily adding, 'We *both* like things tidy.'

Marilyn raised an eyebrow. 'However, we have found a child's fingerprints on the hall floor.' He held out his hands horizontally, miming placing them on a flat surface. 'Our CSI thinks the prints were left when the child was sitting on the floor, perhaps putting his or her shoes back on.'

'Are they Jodie Trigg's prints?' Roger asked dully.

'We'll need to compare them to those we've taken from Jodie before I can answer that question. We found another set on the kitchen windowsill, just the left hand. The child must have been standing at the window for some reason and rested her left hand on the sill.'

'The cat sleeps on the kitchen windowsill because it catches the sun, the only place in this godforsaken house that does. The kid probably stood by the window and stroked the cat.'

Marilyn nodded. 'Thank you, Mr Reynolds,' he said. 'We also found two sets of footprints in the loft. A pair of your wife's shoes match the smaller prints. The larger prints were barefoot, size 11. I assume they were yours from this morning?'

'Probably.'

'We'll have to confirm that.'

'I'd expect nothing less, DI Simmons. Dot the i's, cross the t's and miss the big fucking picture altogether.'

Marilyn ignored the goad. 'My CSI, Tony Burrows, is waiting in the loft, if you'd be so kind as to go up now and assist him.'

'Where is the cat?' Jessie asked, as Reynolds stood. 'Where is Oddie?'

260

'I haven't seen him today.'

'Do you usually see him every day?'

Reynolds nodded. 'He's a homebody. The furthest he ever ventures is the garden wall, to court attention from people passing by. I'm sure he'll be back soon.' His dull gaze met hers. 'You can have the cat, Dr Flynn, when he returns, if you want him. There's no love for him here any more and he does so enjoy being loved.'

56

Carolynn pulled off the A3 at the next junction, took a couple of turnings until she found a quiet country lane and cut the engine. Winding down her window, she hurled the bacon sandwich into the bushes. Tears of frustrated anger were sitting right behind her eyes and in the constriction of her throat. But she wasn't going to cry. She had learnt at an early age that crying was pointless.

No.

She could sit here and cry impotent tears or she could take control. She'd had enough of being a victim, enough of letting life get the better of her and it stopped now.

She desperately wanted her old, perfect life back. The life that she'd had, not before Zoe died, but before the bloody child had come into her life at all, when it had just been her and Roger, living in a beautiful house in a civilized neighbourhood, dining in expensive restaurants, weekending in Prague or Palma, having stylish, clever friends, women like Jessie Flynn. And she wanted to look like that woman she'd locked eyes with on the front page of the van-man's newspaper and on the television screen. She had worked so hard, for so many years to transform herself into that well-spoken, well-mannered, cultivated woman, with the gym-toned body, the expensively highlighted hair and the immaculate clothes, unrecognizable to anyone who had known her as a child. She wanted to be, she *would* be, inside that enviable skin once again.

She wasn't deluded enough to believe that she could go back, reclaim her old life to the letter, but she was resourceful, clever and exceptionally determined – she always had been, ever since she was tiny – and she was certain that she could go forward into something good, something better, perhaps, even than before.

Reaching out, she stroked her hand gently down Oddie the cat's body, from his head to the tip of his tail, enjoying the tickle of his silky fur against her palm. She had taken care of him as she had promised herself that she would. As she had promised Zoe's memory. She had taken care of him, as she had taken care of the seagulls who had landed on her bedroom windowsill when she was a girl.

She stroked her hand from head to tail again, pressing harder, feeling the solid knots of his muscles underneath his skin, the ridged lines of his bones. He was cold now. Cold and stiff.

Curiosity killed the cat.

He had always hated her and she had always hated him because he was Zoe's, her best friend, the only thing that she had truly loved. Opening the door, she slid her hand under his doughnut body. His head sagged as she lifted him. His neck was broken – she'd pressed harder than she had needed to and snapped his spine. Careless, when all she had intended to do was to cut off the oxygen and blood to his brain, send him gently to sleep.

No matter. The end result was the same.

Placing him on the grass verge, to sleep in a patch of sunlight, she climbed back into the car and started the engine. A plan had formed in her mind; she'd take the A3 north for a few more junctions. She wasn't going to let anyone or anything derail her plans. She had worked too hard, suffered too much, survived too much for that.

57

Past

Queen Alexandra Hospital, Cosham, Portsmouth

There was a clock on the wall and the girl fixed her gaze on it, though time had already lost all meaning for her. She could only measure its passing by locking on to the rhythmic sound of her own blood pounding in her temple, the hammering beat of her heart and the soft timbre of her baby's tiny heart, that she could hear through the monitor the nurse had strapped to her stomach. With each pulse, each beat, the pain – the biting, twisting agony – of the contractions built, and with each one her fear intensified. She had been shut in a room on her own, not because she was a private patient, but to keep her away from prying eyes. Hide what was to come when her baby was born.

The contractions were relentless now and she could focus on nothing but the pain, each new wave coming faster than the one before, leaving her no space in between to breathe, to cry out. She was terrified and still no one came. She had been alone for most of her short life, but she had never felt as lonely, as abandoned, as she did now. Though she had borne a lot, she was struggling to bear this. But her baby was coming, to be born into wretchedness, whether she wanted it to or not.

The room lightened, daybreak, as the girl writhed there, chewing on her fingers to stop herself from crying out. She wouldn't cry, had learnt, many times, that crying did no good. She sensed now that she was no longer alone, that there were others in the room with her, but the pain was so great that she was just drifting, floating and sinking, with each new wave of agony.

A blur of uniforms, the clash of metal instruments, noise, voices, faces swimming before her. Intense pain and a sudden, desperate need to push, to expel, the only need that mattered now.

'It's a baby girl,' a voice said. A soft voice, with warmth in it. The first warmth that the girl had heard. 'And she's gorgeous. Just gorgeous.'

58

'What?' Jessie asked, shutting the incident room door behind her.

Burrows wouldn't meet her gaze; Marilyn held it directly, throwing down a challenge.

'Tony has dusted that doll we found in the Reynolds' loft for fingerprints and found one clear set,' Marilyn said.

'Whose are they?'

With a slight smile, Marilyn shook his head. 'Whose do you think they are?'

Jessie rolled her eyes. 'I forgot to pack my crystal ball, Marilyn.'

'Guess.'

'Why? So I can be wrong and you can be smug? Because this case is a competition between us, isn't it?'

'That's what we agreed at breakfast: that I need someone as intransigent as I am to work with. As intransigent and with the opposite viewpoint.'

Pulling out a chair, Jessie sat down. She tried to catch Workman's eye, but she was gazing out of the window, faux

nonchalantly, distancing herself from the palpable antago-
nism. *Sensible lady.* Workman was by nature a smoother, a
facilitator, Jessie had surmised from their limited interac-
tions. It was a personality type that would work well with
Marilyn when he was on track, but with this case, and
Zoe's, Marilyn needed a rock to counter his hard place. *My
job.*

'Carolynn's,' she said. 'I think that the prints are
Carolynn's.'

Marilyn arched a suspicious eyebrow. He hadn't been
expecting that response. *Good.*

'Why do you think they're Carolynn's?'

'Because you have a self-congratulatory look on your face
and, as you don't like losing, I assume that the fingerprints
have affirmed your viewpoint.'

'No flies on you, Doctor Flynn.'

'So I'm right?'

He nodded. 'The doll bears Carolynn's fingerprints.'

'And Roger's?'

'No. Just the print of his flat hands on the sides of the
box, and his index finger and thumb on the lid.' Raising a
hand, he pressed his thumb and index finger together. 'Pincer
fingers.'

Jessie took a moment to think. 'Where were Carolynn's
prints?'

'As I've already said, on the doll.'

'Yes, but where specifically? On which part of her— its
anatomy?'

Marilyn narrowed his eyes. 'Does it matter?'

'From a psychological point of view, I think it does.'

Her gaze moved from Marilyn to Burrows. 'Tony?'

'The prints were on the doll's ankle,' Burrows said.

'The ankle?'

'Yes. The doll's left ankle.' He pressed his thumb and index finger together as Marilyn had done. 'Pincer fingers. The index finger and thumb.'

Jessie nodded. 'Did you find Carolynn's fingerprints anywhere else on the doll?'

'No.'

'Is it possible that her prints are somewhere else on the doll that you weren't able to lift, such as on the doll's dress?' she asked. 'The dress covers most of her body.'

'Thanks to my counterparts at the Scottish Police Services Authority and the University of Abertay, Dundee, who pioneered the technique a few years ago, we can now lift fingerprints from some clothing materials using VMD – vacuum metal deposition,' Burrows said. 'The dresses are nylon, one of the materials that works with this technique. There were no fingerprints on the doll's dress, not Carolynn Reynolds' or anyone else's.' He held up his hand, to stop Jessie from interrupting. 'But I have detected fingerprint residue on the doll's hair.'

'You couldn't lift a traceable print?'

'Not yet, but I'm working on it. I need to lay the hairs in exactly the same position they were in when the prints were left, or at least enough hairs to get an adequate section of fingerprint to enable us to match it. I'm working on it.'

Sitting back, Jessie ground the tips of her fingers into her eye sockets. Though she had lain in bed for eight hours in the B & B, the curtains open, surrounded by stars, she had barely slept. There had been too many disturbing images, too much information careering around inside her skull: Zoe; Jodie; Carolynn; Roger, Oddie, that ugly, splodgy cat; Callan; her mother's wedding; the inescapable feeling that she was

269

letting everyone down. She had finally come to the realization that it was fine to let the others down temporarily – but not Zoe and Jodie. She refused to let them down. Whatever it took, however much she'd have to disappoint everyone else, she was determined to get a result for them. A robust result, and justice.

'Revulsion,' she said, dropping her hands.

Marilyn frowned. 'Revulsion? You've lost me.'

'The way Carolynn held the doll. I believe that it signals revulsion.'

As she verbalized the thought, a memory from fifteen years ago rose in her mind: coming home from school and running straight upstairs to her attic bedroom as she had done every day since she had been sent to live with her father and his new wife, Diane. She would shut herself in, make herself invisible, *not there,* for hours, until she heard the sound of her father returning from work.

But on this one day, she had jogged silently up the stairs to find Diane in her room. Diane's arm was outstretched and something black-and-white dangled from her pincer fingers. *Pandy.* She was holding Pandy, Jamie's beloved teddy bear, by its ankle between her thumb and index finger, her arm perpendicular to her body and ramrod straight. Even now, fifteen years later, every detail of the expression on Diane's face was seared into Jessie's memory. It had been a look of pure revulsion. She had thought, back then, a naive, disturbed fourteen-year-old, that Diane had been revolted by how smelly and grey Pandy was. The only reality Jessie still had of Jamie, beyond static two-dimensional photographs, was his scent caught in Pandy's dirty fur and so she'd never washed him. But as an adult, with the benefit both of hindsight and her professional training as a psychologist, she realized that Diane's revulsion had not been directed at Pandy but at everything he represented: her new husband's past, his family, his children, whose existence, if only in memory for Jamie, she could never erase. Jessie had snatched Pandy from Diane's pincer fingers and shouted right in her face: *Get out of my bedroom.*

Diane's response: *It's not your bedroom. It's a room in my house that you have temporary use of until we can find somewhere else for you to go.*

Jessie's: *It's my father's house. He bought it. You don't even have a job.*

The acrimony between them as thick and black as tar. As Diane's angry clatter receded down the stairs, she had tucked Pandy back under her duvet, his ratty head resting on her pillow. Naive. So naive. She should have known then what Diane would do next, how there was no way that she would let Jessie win.

'Revulsion,' she repeated, her gaze travelling from Marilyn's cynical expression to take in Burrows' non-committal one, to Workman who had looked back from the window and was nodding. 'Isn't that the way you hold something if you're revolted by it? If it disgusts you? By the ankle, in pincer fingers.' She reached across to Workman's notepad, the nearest thing to her and lifted it by the corner. 'By the corner, the tip, the ankle, so that you touch as little of it as possible. And holding the doll upside down is dismissive, devalues it.'

Marilyn rolled his eyes. 'Where do you hold a straw if you're clutching it?'

Jessie ignored him. 'What do you think, Sarah? Tony?'

'I can see where Jessie is coming from,' Workman said. 'When my husband leaves his boxer shorts on the floor instead of putting them in the laundry bin, I pick them up by the elastic, with the tips of my fingers.' She immediately reddened, as if regretting the personal nature of what she had just shared.

'When the foxes attack my bins and spread rubbish all over my front garden, I pick the detritus up in the tips of my fingers,' Burrows added.

Marilyn dropped his head to the table and mimed banging it on the wood.

'God help me.'

'You and me both,' Jessie said, sitting forward. 'You and me both, Marilyn, because we're nowhere, are we? It's now . . . what . . . ?' Her eyes found the wall clock. 'Seventy-two hours since Jodie Trigg was murdered, two years and seventy-two hours since Zoe was murdered, and we're still virtually *nowhere*, despite you throwing everything at it. You have all those years' experience as a major crimes detective, you've solved countless murders and yet we're still nowhere on this one. We have a few of Jodie's prints from inside the Reynolds' rental house. But really – so what?'

Marilyn sighed. 'I need certainty, Jessie.'

'Psychology isn't about certainty. It's about probabilities. For heaven's sake, medicine as a whole isn't about certainty, and the brain is the least well-understood organ in the body. I can help you generate theories, possibilities, *probabilities* that we can then turn into certainties by fleshing them out with evidence.'

'So, if your theory is correct and Carolynn was revolted by the doll, why did she have it? Why did she stow it in her bedroom cupboard?'

'There are a number of possible reasons why, the most

unlikely being that she intends to murder another child and wanted to prepare in advance.'

'Enlighten me.'

'A compulsive disorder. She saw the doll somewhere and was compelled to buy it.'

'How do you define compulsion?'

This definition Jessie knew like the back of her hand from her own OCD.

'A compulsion is an irresistible urge to behave in a certain way or do a certain thing.'

Cynicism written all over his face, Marilyn held up the thumb of his right hand. 'Possible reason one – compulsion. Driven by . . . ?'

'Driven by the doll's significance in her daughter's death. Perhaps because it was keeping her dead daughter company on the beach, or that with the exception of Zoe's killer, that doll was the last one to see Zoe alive, and it was the last thing Zoe saw before she was murdered.'

'That would be totally irrational.'

'I don't believe that Carolynn is rational.'

Marilyn raised an eyebrow. His look said: *QED*.

'But it doesn't mean that she's a killer,' Jessie snapped. *I have a PhD in acting irrationally and I've never killed anyone, though at the moment I'm tempted.*

'What else?'

'Perhaps someone sent it to her.'

He held up his index finger. 'Two. Why?'

'The killer, to taunt her.'

'Zoe was also found in a heart of shells,' Marilyn said. 'Where's the box of shells in the loft?'

Jessie sighed. She was finding this discussion hard going. Marilyn was being deliberately obtuse. At times like this, she found it difficult to justify every nuance of her trade. So much of psychology was about constructing and testing straw men, and her men were struggling to stand up in the face of Marilyn's icy arctic gale. She remembered a quote that she had heard from the governor of Broadmoor Hospital for the Criminally Insane, something about how he could let half of his patients out tomorrow and they wouldn't reoffend, the only issue being that he didn't know which half.

'The shells were laid out in the shape of a heart, so I would suggest that the shape has more significance than the materials used to make the shape. The children were murdered on a beach. There are shells everywhere.'

Marilyn nodded. 'So the heart signals love?'

'Love. Hate. Loss. A combination, perhaps. I'd say that they're all different sides of the same multi-faceted shape.'

'Which does suggest that the killer had a personal connection to both children.'

Jessie nodded. 'Certainly to Zoe. But neither of us have ever believed that these killings were random.'

'Why just Zoe?'

'Because she was the first.'

'Meaning?'

She waved a hand in the air, in a gesture that she knew looked as ineffectual as her thought processes felt. 'I'm not sure. But her murder precipitated all this. She definitely has a fundamental connection to the killer, while Jodie might just be fallout.'

'Collateral damage?'

'In a way, yes. Two years is a long time to wait, so I would suggest that the killer isn't a serial killer or he or she would want to kill more often.' She looked at Marilyn for confirmation.

'Typically,' he said. 'And serial killers of children are usually sexually motivated and there was no sexual assault or rape in either case.'

'So I'd suggest that something happened between the two murders, to precipitate Jodie's.'

'Like Carolynn befriending Jodie,' Marilyn said. 'Poor little sod.'

'Yes, like that—' She held up both hands to halt his interruption. 'But that doesn't mean that Carolynn killed her, or Zoe. We need to understand what the personal connection was between Zoe and the killer and why it was so dangerously negative.'

'Motive,' Marilyn said. 'The classic – motive.'

'When you interviewed Carolynn as a suspect in her daughter's murder, did you ask her about the doll?'

Marilyn nodded. 'Many times.'

'What did she say?'

'She repeatedly said that she had no idea why a doll would be left by her daughter's body. She was adamant that Zoe wasn't a girly girl, that she had never liked dolls.'

He glanced at Workman, who concurred.

'She said that Zoe liked teddies, cuddly toys, but that she had never shown any interest in dolls and that she had never owned a doll,' Workman said.

'How did Carolynn know that Zoe didn't like dolls if she'd never given her any?' Jessie murmured, half to herself. She raised her voice: 'Did you speak to the doll's manufacturer?'

'They're made in China, surprise surprise. By a company in Shanghai, to be precise, who has been making those exact dolls since 2001. The dolls are all identical, except for the colour of their eyes. The company manufactures the same doll with brown, green, blue and grey eyes so that children can buy a doll with eyes that match their own, if they so choose. They're shipped to the UK on those floating multi-storeys you see ploughing through the Solent, and they're sold in a number of shops, including Toys R Us, Argos and the Entertainer. It was a dead end.'

'So what conclusion *did* you come to about the doll?' Jessie asked.

'Either that Carolynn had put the doll by Zoe's body as a red herring, to mislead us, or that she had put the doll there because it had significance either for her or for Zoe, or for both of them, and she then lied to us about that significance when we fingered her as a suspect.'

Jessie nodded. 'Or that Carolynn hadn't put the doll there at all, because she didn't murder her daughter. What about Jodie?'

'Debs Trigg said the same,' Workman replied. 'That Jodie wasn't into dolls.'

'There were none in her room,' Jessie said.

'So the doll has a significance for the killer that we don't yet understand,' Marilyn surmised.

'And perhaps that significance is connected with both children or, more likely in my opinion, only Zoe, but by using an identical signature, the killer communicated to us that he or she was responsible for both murders.'

'What about guilt?' Marilyn asked.

Jessie raised an eyebrow. 'Yours or Carolynn's?'

'Ha, ha.'

Sliding her chair back, Jessie stood. The room was hot and stuffy and she felt sick again. As far as she was concerned, the conversation was over.

'Where are you going?' Marilyn asked.

'We're done, aren't we?'

She felt Marilyn's eyes trail her as she walked to the door.

'Why do I feel that there's something you're not sharing with me?' he muttered.

'Paranoia?' She smiled over her shoulder, as she pulled the door open. 'Just because you're paranoid, doesn't mean they're not out to get you, Marilyn.'

'What? What the hell does that mean?'

'You can work it out,' she said, stepping through the door and pulling it closed behind her.

59

Though Jessie knew no one in East Wittering, she was relieved that Boots the Chemist was empty. She felt like a naughty schoolgirl nipping into the sweet shop on her way home from school against her mother's strict instruction, as she glanced guiltily both ways down the street – half-expecting to see Marilyn standing there eyeballing her, one cynical eyebrow raised, or worse, Callan – then ducked through the double doors.

She wandered up and down the aisles, scanning the shelves: hand and body; cosmetics; skincare; hair accessories; deodorants and body sprays; holiday essentials; facial skincare; family planning.

She stopped. *Family planning.* The title laughed at her. *What the fuck have I done?* – would be more appropriate.

As her gaze roved over condoms – *too late for those now* – lubricants, ovulation tests, the electric suit skittered across her skin at how out of control her life had become, how seismically more out of control it would become in an instant, based on the results of a simple two-minute test.

Pregnancy tests.

She had expected there to be only one type, but of course that would have been far too easy. She scanned the multiple boxes and grabbed one that advertised itself as being early detection and 'Swiss made'. The Swiss were renowned for always being on time and her watch had never let her down, so there had to be some quality assurance in that.

As she rose, shielding the box against her chest with her arm, she had the sudden, unsettling sense that someone was standing right behind her. She spun around and stepped back, coming hard up against the edge of the metal shelves. The woman, who she didn't recognize, mirrored her movement, silver stiletto sandals pecking at the lino as she stepped forward, so close that Jessie could barely focus on her face.

The woman arched a plucked eyebrow. 'Who's the father?'

Jessie was so shocked at the directness of the question that she didn't have the self-possession not to answer.

'I don't think I'm pregnant,' she spluttered.

The woman's cracked lips twisted into a nasty smirk. 'You wouldn't be buying one of those if you didn't think you was pregnant.'

Jessie lifted her shoulders. 'My boyfriend, maybe.' She paused. 'I don't mean that it could be someone else, only that I'm probably not pregnant at all.'

Her gaze hardened. 'So you're too good to screw around, are you? Too posh?'

'No, I . . . that wasn't what I meant. I just didn't get the opportunity. I've never been great with relationships . . . with men.' *Why the hell am I justifying myself to this stranger?* She took a step sideways to disengage herself from the shelves, another backwards and held her hand up in front of her, half-wave goodbye, half unequivocal physical

279

signal that she was disengaging herself from this conversation. 'I'm sorry, but I'm in a hurry.'

Immune to Jessie's body language, the woman aped her movements. 'Does he know that you're knocked up?'

'What?' *No. Who the hell is this woman?* This whole conversation was ridiculous and she needed to end it. The thought that she could easily be pregnant and the juggernaut that news would drive through her life – and Callan's – was white noise in her head, the electric suit an itch that had intensified with the woman's intrusion. 'I'm sorry, I really do need to go.'

A blur of movement and the woman's fingers snaked around her wrist.

'I've seen you,' she hissed.

Jessie stepped back, trying in vain to disengage her arm.

'With DI Simmons. I've seen you. Are you police?'

Twisting her arm hard, Jessie broke the woman's hold, no pretence at politeness now. 'No, I'm a psychologist working with the police.'

'You must be clever to have a job like that.' Another spiteful smirk. 'But not clever enough to use contraception.'

A quickly suppressed titter from the direction of the cash till. Jessie had had enough. She was tempted to toss the pregnancy test back on the shelf and sprint for the exit, but Boots was the only chemist in East Wittering and she needed it. She needed to *know*. The woman's voice rose in volume, as she turned away.

'I saw you at that anorexic blonde's house. The woman who used to spend time with the murdered girl.'

Though she had an overwhelming urge to keep walking, Jessie had no choice now but to turn back.

'Jodie Trigg? Are you talking about Jodie Trigg?'

The woman had the most extraordinary lilac eyes, Jessie saw, as she met them again, sunk deep into shadowed, hollowed-out sockets. Jessie had expected the light in them to be hard, calculating, but it wasn't. It was something else entirely, something she hadn't expected. Bereft. Desolate. She realized now, as she focused properly on the woman's face, that she was a good few years younger than she'd thought: late twenties. She would have been extraordinarily pretty, if it wasn't for the pallid skin, the oily hair bleached a hard white-blonde, and that wretched look in her eyes.

'What's your name?' Jessie asked.

'DI Simmons knows. He knows me.'

'Have you told him that you saw Jodie at that house?'

She shook her head. 'There's no benefit to me in telling him.'

'So why are you telling me?'

She couldn't get a handle on the unsettling mix of aggression, sullenness and intense sadness pulsing from the woman. Her fingers found Jessie's wrist again. Perhaps because of the urgent look on her face and the desperation in her eyes, Jessie didn't pull away this time, though she had the urge to claw her nails down her own skin to rid herself of the feel of the woman's fingers, and the electric suit snapping across her skin.

'Don't let anyone take your baby,' she hissed, right into Jessie's ear. 'Whatever they tell you, you'll give your own baby a better life than anyone else can.'

They. Who are they?

Releasing her arm, the woman slipped past her. As she walked to the till, Jessie realized that she was shaking. She paid quickly, avoiding eye contact with the cashier. She felt deeply unsettled by the conversation. All she wanted to do now was to find somewhere private to take the pregnancy test and then finish the case, solve it, help those two little dead girls get justice – too little, too late – before she might have to deal with her own living child.

She *couldn't* be pregnant. What would she say to Callan? A child didn't feature anywhere in her, or Callan's plans. She couldn't look after herself properly, let alone a child, not with her history, her brother Jamie's suicide, and her OCD. She needed to sort out her own brain before she could contemplate bringing a tiny human being into the world, and despite her profession, the window into the mind that it afforded her, her own psyche was more out of control than it had ever been.

60

The telephone-kiosk-sized toilet sported a trendy surf-shack door made from warped, reclaimed driftwood planks that started mid-calf, finished half an arm's length above Jessie's head and opened into the middle of the surf shop attached to the restaurant. She hadn't used the toilet when she'd eaten here with Carolynn or Marilyn and if she'd known how exposed it was, she would have gone elsewhere.

As she inched back the cellophane wrapping and extracted a pregnancy test from the box, she felt as if every shopper and diner were privy to her secret. Her gaze hopscotched down the instruction sheet, picking out the essentials: urine, lay test flat to develop, two minutes. Flipping up the toilet lid, she did the necessary, feeling as if she was performing in a goldfish bowl. As she balanced the pregnancy test on the edge of the sink to pull up her knickers and rearrange her dress, she caught sight of her face in the mirror. Despite the faint tan her translucent Irish skin had somehow managed to absorb over the summer months, she looked as white as the plastic casing on the test, as the porcelain it was resting on. Shell-shocked and ghostly pale. She looked down at the test – no change. Glanced at her watch – only fifteen seconds gone. *Oh God*. She felt as if she'd aged a decade since she'd entered the toilet cubicle.

She knew that countless other women and girls had felt as she did now, alone and sick with anxiety, many of them far younger and much less well equipped to give a child a good life. Even if Callan wasn't interested in being an active father, she had a good job and her child would have a stable family in Ahmose, her mother and Richard, if not in herself. Her mother would be delighted, not just her wedding to heal the family's wounds, but a baby. The ultimate Band-Aid baby, plastering over the canyon-sized fissures in their history.

But what if her baby was a boy? Her little brother Jamie's heart problems, his restrictive cardiomyopathy, had been hereditary, the condition inherited in an autosomal dominant pattern, only one copy of the altered gene in each cell necessary to cause the disorder. Only one. *No*, she couldn't let her mind go there. In that direction lay only madness.

Whispers outside the door suddenly and a young girl's urgent voice, 'I need to go *now*.'

Jessie washed and dried her hands.

'Ask them to come out, Mummy. I'm *desperate*.'

A tentative knock. 'I'm sorry, are you going to be long?'

'No, I'm just—' *Just what*. The desolate face of the strange young woman with the lilac eyes who had accosted her in the chemist rose up before her. *Waiting to see if I'm knocked up*. 'I'm nearly finished.' She looked at the test again – nothing – at her watch – only forty seconds gone.

'Pleaseeeeee.'

If she hadn't felt so close to tears, she would have laughed

284

at the absurdity of her situation. Shoving the test into her handbag, pushing it right to the bottom so that it retained some semblance of 'flat', she unlocked the door, squeezed past the mother and her child, muttering a quick – 'Sorry for taking so long' – as she passed, ducked out of the shop and ran down to the beach.

61

Past

Little girl, far away in a world of your own, in a world built of dreams that are yours and yours alone.

Fighting back the tears that were blurring her vision, the girl began to dress her baby in the pure white sleepsuit she had bought. She thought of the little girl in the advert she used to watch – that perfect, soft-focus blonde child playing in a meadow full of wild flowers – and she felt a sadness debilitating in its intensity. She would never get to see her own child in a meadow, never get to see her play. She would never even get to hear her daughter's laugh or know her voice.

She lingered as she dressed her child, savouring every second, committing each detail to her memory – the feel of her skin, the crease in her brow when she frowned, the grip of her tiny hand, the perfect pink crescents of her fingernails – knowing that by the time the images in her mind began

286

to lose focus and fade, her daughter would have changed beyond recognition. She had only known her daughter for a few hours, but she already knew that no one else would ever know her as she did. Love her as she did.

The door to the hospital room opened. Through the fog of her tears, she saw a woman, blonde like her, and a man wearing a navy-blue uniform. A policeman. Why had the social worker brought the police to take her baby away? What did they think she was going to do?

The blond woman walked to the bed and held out her arms. 'I'll take her now, thank you,' she said. There was no emotion in her voice.

'Anna,' the girl said. 'She's called Anna.'

The blonde woman wouldn't meet her gaze.

'Anna,' she repeated desperately. 'I named her Anna.'

The blonde woman didn't acknowledge that she had spoken. Her gaze was fixed on Anna. 'I said, I will take her now.'

The girl tried to shield her daughter's body with her own, but the pain in her ravaged stomach was unbearable and she couldn't bend.

'Please don't.' Her voice, barely there, was choked with tears that she had promised herself she wouldn't shed. 'Please don't take her from me. *Please.*'

Chill hands slid between her stomach and Anna's tiny body and though she tried to cling tight, her daughter was wrenched from her arms.

'*I'll take her now.*'

62

A cross.

Jessie felt as if she had been punched hard in the gut. Doubling over, she clutched her arms tight across her stomach and rocked backwards and forwards, smothering her growing howl in the dome of her knees.

Oh God, no. A cross, signalling a seismic earthquake in her life.

She checked the test again, knowing that she didn't need to, that her first fleeting, horrified look had told her all she needed to know. There was no one close by her on the beach, the walkway behind her deserted. She could scream, yell, cry all she liked and no one would hear. But it wasn't her style. She had always turned trauma inwards, internalized it, the damage that suppression had caused over the years leaking out through the cracks in her emotional defences in the form of her OCD and the electric suit.

Pressing her head between her knees, she jammed her eyes shut and tried to send her mind to a place of calm, but there was nowhere she could go, no emotional reserves to draw upon and the only thing her mind found was Jamie: a freeze-frame image of her little brother hanging by his school tie from that curtain rail, his beautiful face bloated and purple.

A loud squawk, close by, cut into her consciousness and she raised her head. A seagull was standing on the sand in front of her, so close that she could almost have reached out and stroked its petrol feathers. The pregnancy test on her lap seemed even more alluring to this seagull than her phone had been to the one who had dive-bombed her yesterday. She was tempted to toss it to him. If he carried it away, perhaps that would negate the result and she'd wake up with a sunburnt face, the imprint of beach stones on her back and a sense of intense relief that it had all been a dream. *Wishful thinking.*

The seagull's webbed feet, the same buttercup yellow as his beak, left ghostly fan-shaped imprints in the wet sand as he paced in a semi-circle around her.

'Nothing to see here,' she murmured, wiping away the single tear that had escaped from her eye. She needed to get a grip, stop obsessing about her own problems and focus on what she was supposed to be doing down here at the beach – and it wasn't sobbing into her knees or conversing with local wildlife.

The seagull had stopped pacing. Head tilted to one side, he seemed to be studying her, sizing her up. He must have flown here from the dunes, as pale talcum powder sand dusted his webbed feet. The sight dredged a memory.

'*How was the beach?*'

'*Huh?*'

'*Sand. Your feet.*'

'*Oh, I thought you were a mind reader for a second.*' A

tentative, distant smile. '*I'd hate you to actually be able to read my mind.*'

She had been the antithesis of a mind reader with Carolynn. Five intensive hours spent in her company and Jessie felt as if she had only seen the inside of a fairground funhouse filled with distorting mirrors. Every view that she'd had of the woman a fake one, warped, disfigured.

'*I have scars too. And not just psychological ones.*'

Both of them giving nervous half-laughs, grateful for the opportunity to break the tension, Jessie knowing that the subject matter was minefield-sensitive. Carolynn spreading her toes to show Jessie the pale scar running around their inside edges.

'*I was born with webbed feet, like a seagull. Perhaps that's why I love the sea.*'

Jessie had paid no attention at the time because the content of Carolynn's reveal had seemed irrelevant and she'd realized that Carolynn had only shared in order to elicit an explanation about her own scarred left hand. Anyway, the scars between Carolynn's toes had nothing to do with her psychology. Or so she'd thought.

And now?

'*I was born with webbed feet . . .*'

The memory of Carolynn's words stirred another: a patient from her NHS days, not one of hers, but a colleague's, a conversation she'd overheard at the coffee machine. Dropping the pregnancy test into her bag, she dug out her mobile and Googled, scanned the list that the search returned and found what she was looking for. Her stomach knotted as she read.

Jesus. What if Marilyn had been right about Carolynn all along?

63

'I'm not paying you to spend the day at the beach sunning yourself,' Marilyn said, in response to another loud squawk from the seagull, bereft at the disappearance of the tantalizing white stick.

'You're not paying me at all, yet,' Jessie countered. 'Listen, Marilyn, did you ever check Zoe's DNA against Carolynn and Roger's?'

No response. She waited, knowing that the silence wasn't driven by Marilyn's need to trawl through his memory. Every detail of the Zoe Reynolds murder case had been committed to his memory, an encyclopaedic index at his mental fingertips. She recognized it for what it was, an – *Oh fuck, what is she going to say next?* – pause.

A guarded tone. 'No, I didn't.'

'Why not?'

'Because I didn't need to. The identification box was ticked by Roger Reynolds coming to the morgue and confirming that the little girl's body was that of his daughter, Zoe. Not that we had any doubt before, as we'd found Carolynn

Reynolds on her knees in West Wittering car park clutching Zoe's body and screaming. There was no need to check her DNA. Procedure had been followed, protocol met. Why?'

Jessie had never before heard Marilyn use the terms 'procedure' or 'protocol'. His resort to them now was driven by defensiveness, she recognized. Defensiveness and intense apprehension.

'Do it now, please, urgently.'

'What's going on, Jessie?'

She looked at the seagull. *Her* seagull. They were mates now. He was balancing on one webbed foot, the other tucked into his tummy feathers. He looked happy and relaxed, even a bit smug, perhaps. He'd done his job, helped her out.

'I believe that Carolynn is sterile,' Jessie said.

'What?'

'I've just added the two and two from something Carolynn said to me during one of our sessions and come up with four. I didn't pay attention at the time, because I didn't believe that what she told me was relevant to her psychology, or at least, not relevant to the event I believed was responsible for her psychological breakdown – her daughter's death in a car accident.'

Raising her hand in a 'stay' gesture to the seagull – *Did they share dog psychology? She had no idea* – Jessie stood. The seagull tilted his head and eyeballed her quizzically as she clambered up the pebbles to the concrete walkway.

'I think that Carolynn was born with Turner syndrome,' she continued, walking towards the Fisherman's Hut. 'It's a genetic disorder that affects around one in two thousand females, so it's not uncommon. A girl with Turner syndrome only has one X chromosome instead of the usual two. Sufferers are characterized by a range of physical symptoms, which can include webbed feet. But the most important thing is that girls with Turner syndrome usually have under-developed ovaries and are sterile.'

'Carolynn had postnatal depression, Jessie.'

'Sure, but postnatal depression isn't confined to biological mothers because it's not only caused by hormonal changes. Postnatal depression can be driven by a range of factors such as having unrealistic expectations of the joy of parenting, difficulty in bonding with the child, or being disappointed with the child. The symptoms of postnatal depression in adoptive mothers who experience it are the same as those displayed by birth mothers. Carolynn may well have had postnatal depression, but that doesn't mean she was Zoe's biological mother.'

The sound of Marilyn's tense, choppy breathing echoed down the phone. 'So, if what you're saying is true, Carolynn would have no biological connection to Zoe.'

Jessie reached the Fisherman's Hut and scanned the menu.

'*Jessie*.'

'Yes. No. None.'

'What are you doing?'

'Multi-tasking.'

'What?'

'Never mind, you wouldn't get it.'

'Because I'm a man?'

'I didn't say that.'

Tapping a finger in the middle of the list of 'Today's Catch' chalked on the blackboard, she bought half a pint of peeled prawns in a polystyrene cup.

'Are children who are brought up by parents who aren't biologically connected to them, more likely to be abused or killed by those parents?' Marilyn asked.

'It's a complex and controversial area,' she said, as she slid carefully back down the steep pebbles to the sand. 'Lots of studies have been carried out, but the results have been inconclusive. From a sociological point of view, whatever that's worth, genetic preservation is at the core of human behaviour.'

'And neither Carolynn or Roger had any genes to preserve.'

'Right. But more important than that – much more important, I'd say – is that this was yet another lie, or at least a very major omission of the truth. And an unnecessary one, unless they omitted that truth for a reason.' Another fairground funhouse mirror that revealed Carolynn, freak-show distorted.

Jessie's seagull had obeyed her command and maintained a 'stay'. Balanced on one leg, still happy and relaxed, he tilted his head with interest as he watched her approach with the cupful of prawns. She wished that she could say the same for herself; she felt strung to snapping. She needed to do her job properly now, do it right. Get into Carolynn's head in a way that she had singularly failed to do in their sessions, understand what the hell made the woman tick, and whether that tick was the tick of a time bomb that had already exploded twice, or that of a benign bedside-table clock. Disturbed, but ultimately harmless.

'I'll check the DNA database now,' Marilyn said. 'What are you going to do?'

'Feed a seagull.'

'What?'

'Never mind. I owe him. Call me back.'

64

Tossing his mobile on to his desk with a clatter, Marilyn covered his face with his hands. *Jesus Christ.* He'd lost count of the hours he'd spent since Carolynn Reynolds was acquitted, reviewing each step of the investigation, putting his logic under the microscope, searching for some minute gap in his reasoning, and he hadn't been able to find one. And now it turned out what he had missed was a gargantuan black hole that would swallow him entirely: his career, his reputation – the whole lot, hook, line and sinker – if Carolynn Reynolds had indeed murdered her daughter and got away with it, leaving her free to murder little Jodie Trigg.

But the most damaging blow would be the wholesale destruction of his self-respect. He was a good policeman – a great policeman, he'd venture to say when he was feeling particularly self-congratulatory – and through twenty years on the job he had rarely failed to get a result. His reputation and self-respect had been hard won. Hard won; easily annihilated.

A hand on his shoulder and he almost leapt out of his skin. 'Tea, sir.'

'I need more than a cup of bloody tea, Workman.'

She put the tea on his desk anyway, slipping two milk chocolate digestives next to the cup.

'Are we celebrating something?' Marilyn asked, eyeing the biscuits cynically.

Workman's expression was inscrutable. 'I thought we might need the energy.' She sat down across the desk from him and met his gaze. 'What's the problem, sir?'

'Problem? Is it that obvious?' Massaging his temples with the tips of his fingers, he sighed. 'I've just had a phone call from Jessie Flynn. She reckons we need to compare Zoe Reynolds' DNA against Carolynn's on the database. In haste. Now. Immediately.'

'Why?'

'Because Doctor Flynn doesn't believe that Zoe was Roger and Carolynn Reynolds' biological daughter.'

The expression of horror that crossed Workman's face summed up his feelings exactly.

'And from what she told me, I'm inclined to agree.'

'But there was no indication at all – neither of the Reynolds said anything to suggest she was adopted. Carolynn had postnatal depression. Zoe even looked like her . . . her mother . . . Carolynn.'

'I know, I know, but I should have checked anyway. It was one of the t's I should have crossed. I crossed every other bloody one, whole alphabets full of the bloody things, but not the one that needed crossing.' He shook his head slowly. 'It's on me, this one, Sarah. If Carolynn Reynolds is our murderer, this one is on me. Little Jodie Trigg's death is on me.'

'On *us*, sir. We're in this together.'

'No, Sarah. I'm the SIO. I take the blame, *alone*.' Reaching for his tea, he took a sip, hoping that Workman didn't notice his hand shaking as he lifted the cup to his mouth.

Workman stood. 'I'll get on to it now, sir. Shouldn't take long.'

'Thank you.'

When she had gone, Marilyn demolished both biscuits in four big bites and felt no better for doing so.

This one is on me. Little Jodie Trigg's death is on me.

65

Though Jessie was tempted to keep her finger jammed furiously on the bell until the front door opened, she played the psychology and gave it one short, businesslike ring. Then, instead of stepping sideways as Marilyn had done, so as not to be framed in the eye viewer's circle, she ducked her head so that if Reynolds checked he'd get an eyeful of long black hair, a woman, in his eyes hopefully less of a threat. She hated to be so disingenuous, but she didn't have a choice. She needed to get inside that house and talk to Roger Reynolds, and she couldn't risk him recognizing her through the viewer and deciding that he'd rather shove his head in the oven than answer any more of her questions.

Reynolds had clearly learnt caution; when the door eventually opened, it was only by a fraction. The latched door chain cut across the narrow space, revealing a sliver of pale face and one bloodshot grey eye above it.

'No' was all he said.

Following Marilyn's lead this time, Jessie jammed her foot

in the door. Reynolds looked down at her flimsy summer sandal. 'If I slam it, you risk a severed toe, Dr Flynn.'

'I'll take the risk.'

'Brave girl.' The face withdrew and the door inched slowly closed, as if moved by an invisible force, until it nudged against Jessie's exposed toes.

'Move your foot, Dr Flynn,' a disembodied voice commanded.

'If you won't talk to me, I'll be forced to go and ask your mother about Zoe's biological parentage,' Jessie said. She snatched her foot away, knowing that her words would precipitate either a slam or the door being torn wide open, no scenario in between.

A slam.

Jessie waited. A moment later, she heard the sound of the chain being removed and Reynolds emerged from the concealing darkness of the hallway, blinking furiously in the sunlight.

'You little shit,' he hissed. 'You leave my mother alone.'

She stood her ground and maintained eye contact, though it was an effort.

'No, *you're* the shit, Mr Reynolds. You've been lying from the start. Perhaps your mother might know the value of truth, even if she didn't think to teach it to her son.'

'She's eighty years old, in a home. Zoe's death destroyed her. She loved that little girl.'

'Unlike your wife.'

'Carolynn loved Zoe.'

'Did she? Really?'

'In her own way, she did.' His voice now laced with pain, had lost its force.

Jessie didn't care. 'In her own way?' she said scornfully,

299

raising her voice deliberately. 'What the *hell* does that mean?'

Reynolds glanced past her, aware that people were dawdling in the narrow road outside, that this unprepossessing house had become an unlikely tourist attraction since the police search, the community bush wire buzzing with speculation.

'Come in,' he said, stepping back across the threshold and pulling the door open. 'Come inside the house, now.'

Should she? She hadn't, in her haste, told Marilyn where she was going. Carolynn had given Jessie the impression that Roger was controlling, borderline abusive. Or had that been another fairground-mirror distortion? Probably. The woman was like quicksand; the one thing Jessie was certain of was that she'd been labouring under an illusion, thinking she'd known anything concrete about her former client.

She moved past him into the hallway and was enveloped in darkness as the door closed behind her, shutting out the sunlight. Though Burrows and his SOCO team had finished yesterday, the house still bore signs of the search. A fine dusting of fingerprint powder on the hall floor was slippery under her soles, and in the kitchen, to her left, a couple of drawers hung half open and more fingerprint dust – she could tell from the way the light from the overhead electric spots reflected back at her in sparkles – coated the table. All the blinds and curtains downstairs had been drawn. Outside, a bright summer's day; inside, a chill winter's evening. Her heart was beating too fast. She cleared her throat, trying to play her role.

'Tell me about Carolynn and Zoe's relationship.'

Crossing his arms over his chest, Reynolds leant back against the hall wall. He clearly wasn't going to invite her to sit or offer her tea. *Fine.* She felt more secure staying where she was, a short dash to the front door, even if he was standing between her and escape. She could tell from his hesitation that he was contemplating telling her to shove her questions somewhere even narrower and darker than this hallway.

'What are you going to do with the information?' he asked finally.

'Use it.'

'Against my wife?'

'Potentially. It depends what you tell me.'

'I need to protect her.'

'Like you protected your daughter?' It was a cheap shot, a few centimetres below the belt and it hit home as she had intended it to.

His eyes gleamed angrily. 'Carolynn didn't kill Zoe.'

'Are you sure about that?'

'You've switched sides, Doctor. I was right when I accused you of being a poacher turned gamekeeper.'

'The only side I'm on is that of the truth, whatever it turns out to be. I did defend Carolynn vehemently against DI Simmons' accusation that she murdered your daughter and I'd hate to think that I was entirely wrong to have done so. So what is the truth?'

'You probably know as much as I do,' he muttered.

'I doubt that very much.'

66

Past

Queen Alexandra Hospital, Cosham, Portsmouth

Tears running down her face, the girl held out the doll she had bought for her baby. It was a cheap, plastic doll in a nasty, pink acrylic ballerina dress. It wasn't worthy of her daughter, but it had been all she could afford.

'It's hers. It's Anna's.' She felt desperate. Desperate that the woman, the social worker, understand her. 'From me, from her mother. Something to remember me by.'

The blonde woman wouldn't even look at the doll. Not one glance. With Anna cradled against her shoulder, she reached out and took the doll by its ankle, in pincer fingers. Holding it upside down, away from her body as if it was filthy, she turned and walked to the door. There was a metal flip-top bin by the door, and as she passed it the woman stepped on the pedal to flip the lid open and dropped the doll into the bin.

With a scream, the girl scrambled from the bed, only to

double up as she felt the stabbing agony of her stitches ripping. She staggered, snatching at the bedside table for support, the pain intense, blood coursing down her legs. The policeman stepped forward, stretching out his arms, corralling her. He wouldn't meet her gaze, but she sensed that his reasons were different from those of the blonde woman. She snatched at his arm, trying to pull him around, make him look her in the eye, engage with her. 'Stop her, please.'

'I'm sorry. There's nothing I can do,' he muttered. 'Get back into bed. I'll call a doctor.'

Methodically, his strong fingers unhooked hers, one by one. She wanted him to slap her, punch her, kick her, rape her like the other men had done. Nothing would hurt her more than separation from her daughter.

Beyond the policeman's shoulder, her eyes locked with the blonde woman's.

'Please don't take her. Please.' The girl had begged before, when the men were raping her, and it had made no difference. If anything, it had made most of them crueller, made them revel in hurting her more, and she had promised herself then that she would never ever beg again. Begging made merciless people more savage. But that resolution meant nothing now. She would do anything to keep her baby.

'Please let me keep her. I'll be a good mother. She needs me. I promise, I'll be a good mother. *Please* . . . '

Cool air from the corridor billowed into the room as the woman pulled the door open. As she stepped over the threshold, she glanced over her shoulder, and the cold, blank look in her eyes made Ruby shiver.

'You'll never see her again, so forget that she ever existed. Forget that you ever had a child.'

67

Marilyn glanced up at the sound of footsteps and rolled his eyes. 'Don't tell me you're making up for a lack of love in your childhood by carting that thing around with you.'

'Afternoon, DI Simmons,' Burrows said brightly. Pulling out a chair, he sat down across the desk from Marilyn. His moon face was sunburnt scarlet from his two days combing the beach and his bald patch was peeling. He resembled a particularly unattractive toddler with eczema.

'I've had enough bad news,' Marilyn said. 'So if you've got more, you can keep it to yourself.'

Burrows shook his head. 'I come bearing gifts,' he said.

With a flourish, he laid the doll in its plastic evidence bag on Marilyn's desk. Marilyn looked down at it, but didn't touch. He felt damned enough without cursing himself further by touching that voodoo doll in its hermetically sealed shroud.

'I can do without the gift of a juju curse, thanks, Tony. I seem more than capable of screwing up without any help from the dark side.' Sitting back, he rolled his shoulders and stretched, wincing as his joints cracked at the unaccustomed movement. He'd been sitting motionless, ruminating, his shoulders hitched up somewhere around his ears since Workman had left him forty minutes ago now, he realized in surprise, catching sight of the wall clock.

'Then you'll be pleased to hear that I've managed to extract matchable fingerprints from the hair of this doll that we found in that box in the Reynolds' loft.'

Marilyn sat forward. 'Now you're saying something that I'm interested in hearing.' He maintained a neutral tone, didn't want to jinx Burrows' message with hope. 'A woman's prints?' he continued, thinking of the blonde woman on the beach walking with the child who was likely to have been Jodie Trigg, thinking of Carolynn Reynolds. Trying not to let his thoughts transfigure the neutral expression on his face.

Burrows nodded. 'Yes. The prints were from a woman.'

Marilyn knitted his hands together to stop himself from drumming his fingers impatiently on the desktop. Burrows liked to communicate his findings in a structured way, at his own steady pace. Frustrating, when all Marilyn wanted was the crux.

'I would say that the fingerprints – one finger, one thumb – were left when the doll was lifted or held by the hair, in pincer fingers, to quote your friend Dr Flynn.'

Marilyn nodded, thinking of what Jessie had said. *Perhaps someone sent them to her.*

Why?

The killer, to taunt her.

'And . . .' He held up a finger, halting Marilyn's impending interruption. 'I've matched the prints to someone on the fingerprint database.'

'Carolynn Reynolds?'

68

Rubbing his hands over his face, Reynolds sighed.

'Zoe was never the child Carolynn wanted her to be,' he said. 'She never lived up to the image that Carolynn had of *her* child. She was lively, chirpy, I suppose would be a good way to describe her, but not academic and she could be naughty and difficult.' His gaze rose without meeting Jessie's and drifted around the narrow hallway, his mind seeming to follow it. 'The poor little kid never measured up in the London mother-and-toddler groups. She never *shone*. Carolynn was embarrassed by her, embarrassed by her behaviour and by her . . . ' He paused, swallowed, as if the next word was sticking in his throat. 'By her stupidity.'

'How did you find her? Find Zoe?'

'Carolynn was a senior social worker in children's services, a director, in our local borough council. We'd registered through her department for adoption and she was in a position to oil the wheels from inside. The care and place-ment orders were arranged before Zoe was born.'

'And the birth mother?'

'We requested that she didn't know our identity.'

'And they complied with that request?'

'She was a sixteen-year-old prostitute and druggie from Portsmouth, with a history of violence. So yes, they complied with that. The family courts are secretive. It wasn't a big deal.'

'What was her history of violence?'

'We were told that she attacked a couple of clients.'

'Clients?' Jessie said. 'Tricks, you mean? Men who were exploiting a teenage girl for sex? I'm not sure I'd hold that against her.'

Reynolds sighed and gave a slight, dismissive shrug of his shoulders. 'Whatever. She was deemed to be violent, and she didn't want to give her baby up.'

Jessie thought of the little thing growing inside her. The pregnancy test was still in her bag. She hadn't known what to do with it, but throwing it away had felt wrong. How would she feel when her and Callan's baby was born?

'So Zoe's natural mother wasn't given a choice.'

'The family court decided that the baby's welfare would be best served by being removed from her mother and permanently adopted. The welfare of the child has to come first.'

'Indeed. And so it should.' Though Jessie wasn't entirely sure that it had in Zoe's case. The family court was secretive and had been caught up in controversy before, accused of taking perfectly happy, healthy babies and young children from marginalized parents with no right of appeal, those parents then gagged by the court's absolute rule of secrecy, unable to publicize their plight, however unfairly they felt they had been treated.

'When and where did you collect Zoe?'

307

'Carolynn went to the hospital the day she was born and took her from her mother.'

Jessie frowned. 'Surely that's not policy?'

'As I said before, she was a social worker. One of them had to do it. She went with a policeman.'

'Did Zoe's mother know who Carolynn was? That she was the one adopting?'

'No, she was just a faceless social worker.'

Jessie wondered at the psychology of an adoptive parent who wanted to take a child away from her biological mother in person, from a mother who hadn't wanted to give her baby up. It felt sadistic. Her thoughts must have telegraphed themselves straight to her face, because Reynolds' jaw tightened.

'Carolynn wanted to have her from birth. She said that it made the child more "hers", if you get what I mean.'

Jessie didn't get what he meant, but what she was learning was useful and she didn't want to risk derailing their discussion. He was still loyal to Carolynn for some reason she couldn't begin to guess at – time served perhaps, years invested – and there was nothing to be gained from sharing her newly formed views on his wife. Again, she thought of how completely Carolynn had duped her. Usually, she had a good sense about people. Why hadn't she with Carolynn? The question niggled.

'How did Zoe's mother react when her baby was taken from her?'

His eyes hung closed for a moment. 'Carolynn said that she struggled, fought.'

Fought for her child. Fought and lost. But of course she would have lost. What hope did a teenage prostitute ever have of fighting the system?

'Why Portsmouth?' she asked.

'It's where Carolynn comes from.'

'So she had some misplaced commitment to helping a local child?'

A weak, apologetic half-smile was Reynolds' only reply.

'What kind of family did Carolynn come from?'

'A disadvantaged one,' Roger murmured. 'Very disadvantaged. Single mum – a drug addict. She never knew her father. I'm not even sure that her mother knew her father.'

'Do you think that Zoe reminded her too much of herself? A "herself" who didn't measure up, as she had done? A failure of a mini-Carolynn?'

Roger didn't answer. He looked bereft suddenly.

'People who have escaped are often the harshest critics of people who remain, those who have failed to escape a similar situation, aren't they?' she prompted. 'Just as reformed smokers are the most scathing critics of people who still smoke, who they perceive as being too weak to give up.'

'Carolynn is smart and resourceful,' he said wearily. 'She worked hard, clawed her way up from the gutter. By the time I met her, she'd already polished off the rough edges. I grew up in Winchester, went to agricultural college. Carolynn is far cleverer than I am. She was clever enough for the both of us, and I was privileged and rich enough for the both of us.'

'Who was in control in your relationship?'

Reynolds bridled. Jessie didn't blame him. It was a tough question to ask a man, even tougher for him to answer truthfully.

'Roger?' she prompted.

A heavy sigh. 'Carolynn, initially. She had a very definite

vision of how she wanted our lives to play out, where we should live, how our house should be decorated, what car we should drive, the holidays we should take, who we should befriend.'

The box your child should fit seamlessly into. She could tell by the look on his face that he was thinking the same.

'She *is* very resourceful,' Jessie agreed, her comment the antithesis of a compliment. *A chameleon. A masterful chameleon*. 'And later? After Zoe was murdered? Who was in control then?'

'Being accused of Zoe's murder, the trial and the fallout that followed destroyed her,' Roger murmured.

Of course it would have done. Carolynn's carefully constructed life collapsing around her ears.

'So I took control. It was more important then to be strong, to hold it all together . . . more important than before.'

From his tone of voice and choice of words, Jessie realized that he was trying to salvage some ego.

'Why did you keep the fact that Zoe was adopted from the police?' Jessie asked bluntly. 'Why did you hide it during the trial?'

Reynolds wouldn't meet her gaze.

'Why, Roger?'

'Because we put our names on Zoe's birth certificate as her natural parents,' he muttered.

'Surely that's illegal.'

'It was what Carolynn wanted.'

'Because it made Zoe more *hers*?' Jessie said, her voice laced with sarcasm.

To his credit, Reynolds visibly winced.

'And as the trial progressed?' she asked.

'As the trial progressed, she . . . *we* thought that if we came clean it would negatively influence the outcome. Make us look like liars.'

'You are liars.' *And God knows what else.*

'The lawyers went on and on about Carolynn's postnatal depression. They insinuated that she hadn't bonded with Zoe, that she didn't love her. If we'd confessed the truth about her parentage . . .' he tailed off.

'From what I've heard, she hadn't bonded with her and she didn't love her,' Jessie snapped.

Reynolds was staring determinedly at the floor as if there was something inherently fascinating about the worn black-and-white tiles, though Jessie noticed a muscle twitching involuntarily under his eye.

'Did Zoe know that she was adopted?' she continued, bringing him back to the present with a slight jerk.

He shook his head, a shake that turned into a dispirited half-nod.

'We'd agreed not to tell her, but Carolynn snapped one day and shouted at her, told her that she wasn't even hers. Wasn't ours.'

Jessie winced. *Lovely way for a child to find out.*

'How old was Zoe then?'

'Five,' he said. 'Six, maybe.'

'That insecurity alone would be enough to generate behavioural problems, particularly given that the news was broken to her as a rejection. In her mind, she would have been rejected twice, once by her real mother and again by her adoptive mother.'

And probably not just once by her adoptive mother. If Carolynn had snapped – his words – how many other times had she 'snapped'? And how had each snap manifested itself? Psychological abuse could be as damaging as physical abuse, sometimes more so. Poor little Zoe – Jessie's heart went out her.

'Zoe was a tetchy, irritable baby who grew into a naughty, difficult child. She used to fuss and cry when Carolynn held her,' Reynolds said. He paused, and when he spoke again, his voice was quieter, but rougher, laced with emotion. 'Her behaviour towards Carolynn . . . it was almost as if she knew she'd been stolen from her real mum. That Carolynn . . . that we were imposters. Carolynn has a strong need to be loved and she felt as if Zoe didn't love her in the way she should be loved by her daughter.'

'Zoe wasn't her daughter – or yours,' she said baldly.

When Reynolds only reply was to lift his shoulders, eyes still glued to those worn black-and-white tiles, Jessie asked, 'Who made the decision to run? Nine months ago?'

'We had nothing left in London,' he murmured. 'The fallout after Carolynn was accused of Zoe's murder was vitriolic. We had nothing, no one, just hate.'

She nodded. 'Did Carolynn murder Zoe, Roger?'

69

'The woman whose fingerprints are on the doll's hair is an ex-prostitute, with a charge sheet as long as your arm.' Burrows pulled a sheet of paper from his pocket and glanced down at it. 'Her name is Ruby—'

'Lovatt,' Marilyn cut in.

Burrows' eyes widened. 'Yes, Ruby Lovatt. How did you know that, Uri Geller?'

Ducking his head, Marilyn coughed into his hand in a show of clearing his throat to mask the shock he felt. He looked back up and met Burrows' searching gaze, held it calmly, his heart thumping hard in his chest. 'She's the woman who found Jodie Trigg's body.'

Burrows frowned. 'That can't be a coincidence.'

'She's a . . .' *A what?* 'Unemployed,' he said. 'Always out and about walking on the beach, particularly in the summer months, looking for—' *Looking for treasure.* 'Looking for money, valuables, things that the tourists have dropped. So it could be a co—' he broke off with an unconvincing, unconvinced, shrug.

'I thought you didn't believe in coincidences.'

'I don't. You're right. It can't be a coincidence.'

'So . . . ?'

Marilyn sighed. 'I'd seen a light, Tony.' He held a hand up, thumb and forefinger a millimetre apart. 'I'd seen a tiny light in that pitch-black tunnel I've been floundering around in for the past two years, and you've either extinguished it or lit twenty more flames.'

'Well, good luck with making sense of it all,' he said, pushing himself to his feet.

Marilyn held up the evidence bag containing the doll, by the corner, in pincer fingers. 'Take your dolly with you, Tony. My childhood was fine, just fine, so I won't be needing its dubious comfort.'

Burrows took the bag from his outstretched hand. 'Are you sure about that?'

Marilyn shook his head. 'The only thing I can say for sure is that I'm not sure about anything.'

'You need a long holiday, mate. When all this is over, take yourself off somewhere, chillax.' His sunburnt moon face split into a wide grin. 'Haiti, maybe? Voodoo land.'

70

Reynolds was shaking his head, hands pressed over his ears like a toddler, as if that action would negate the question Jessie had just asked him. She was tempted to grab his forearms and pull his hands away, give him a slap around the face for good measure. But she was alone in his house, he was between her and the front door and he was twice her size. He was also upset and on edge. Fear was a far less predictable emotion than anger: a frightened dog more likely to bite than an angry one, a frightened man more likely to lash out.

'Answer the question, Roger.'

'If I had believed for a moment that Carolynn murdered Zoe, I never would have supported her throughout the trial. She's not capable of killing.'

'Are you sure about that?'

'I've been with her for twenty years. I know her.'

Carolynn was clever, resourceful and a brilliant actress. Jessie was sure she had been whatever Roger wanted her to be, and was equally sure that he'd never known his wife at all. Just as Jessie had never known her, never been able to pin her down, work her out. But there was no benefit to be had in correcting him now. Finding Carolynn was the priority and she needed his help.

'Where has she gone, Roger?'

'I don't know.'

'You need to tell me where she's gone, because I believe that she's . . .' *She's what? Losing it?* On the spur of the moment, she couldn't think of a more professional term. 'She's losing it, Roger.'

He shook his head. 'I need to protect her. I need to protect my wife.'

71

When Burrows and his voodoo doll had departed, Marilyn planted his elbows on his desk and sank his head into his hands. Staring hard into the darkness of his palms, he sent his mind inwards, tuning out the sounds of vehicles and pavement chatter rising up from the street below, the ring of telephones and the clack of keyboards from beyond the glass partition that divided his office from the scrum.

Why would Ruby Lovatt have sent Carolynn Reynolds that doll? It didn't make sense. Unless . . . unless. He thought of her standing on the back steps of the police station two days ago, in her low-cut silver top.

I had no use for a kiddie.

He, she'd said. *A boy.*

He flattered himself that Ruby appreciated their nebulous relationship enough not to lie to him, but he saw now that his sentiment was idiotic, a fool's confidence. He barely knew the woman, knew next to nothing about her. It was he who appreciated the connection, not her: the detective with the common touch. It was a nice moniker; he'd liked

317

it. And he'd liked her, been really taken with her all those years ago when he'd first set eyes on that feisty, fiercely proud, but irreparably damaged fourteen-year-old. Even at that age, she'd already struggled through more shit than most people dealt with in a lifetime. She'd survived, barely, was still surviving, barely, and the reality was that she'd do anything to continue surviving. *Do anything. Say anything. Be anything.* It was human nature.

Was it a coincidence that she had found Jodie Trigg's body? It could have been – she did spend most summer days scavenging on the beach – but now that he really thought about it, he didn't believe it was.

What the hell is going on?

Dropping his hands, he reached for his mobile, dialled Workman's number and spoke as soon as he heard a break in the ring.

'DS Workman, have you run Zoe's DNA against Carolynn Reynolds' yet?'

'Yes.'

'So why haven't you called me?' he snapped, knowing his anger should rightfully be turned inwards.

'I was running more—'

'What's the result?' he interrupted.

'Dr Flynn was right. Carolynn and Zoe Reynolds were not biologically related.'

Oh, Christ. 'Not even distantly?' *Aunt and niece? Second aunt and third niece, four times removed?*

'Not even distantly.'

'And Roger?'

'Zoe wasn't biologically related to him either. She wasn't biologically related to either of her "parents".'

72

A look of torment twisted Reynolds' features out of shape. 'Carolynn didn't kill her. She didn't.' His hands were writhing around themselves, as if they had a life of their own, and his whole body had started to shake.

Jessie couldn't afford to lose him, not now, not yet. She forced a semblance of calm into her voice. 'Where has she gone, Roger? She's out there, alone and stressed.'

He muttered something.

'What? A city? Did you say, a city?'

Without raising his head, he nodded. 'She said that we should go and hide in a city. Somewhere anonymous.'

'London?'

A shrug.

Or was London too close to home? Birmingham perhaps? Manchester?

'Birmingham? Manchester?'

Another shrug.

'If you don't give me useful answers, you know that DI Simmons will be over here in a heartbeat. Surely I'm the lesser of two evils.' Even as she said it, she was sure that it wasn't true. With her out-of-control OCD, the electric suit hissing and snapping and the runaway emotional juggernaut that was her pregnancy, DI Simmons would be a pushover compared to her.

'Roger. *Roger!*' He was still shaking his head and there was a distant look in his grey eyes, as if his mind had closed down, moved out.

'Oh for fuck's sake, have it your way.'

As she fished her mobile out of her handbag, Reynolds roused himself. Pulling something from his pocket, he held it out to her.

'What's that?'

'Carolynn's wallet. I found it on the floor under the hall table. She has no money, no cards, nothing.'

'How much petrol was in her car?'

'I last filled it up for her three weeks ago. She doesn't drive far, but I can't imagine there'd be much left.'

So not Birmingham or Manchester. London was seventy miles away. Did she have enough to get to London? She wouldn't risk running out of petrol and being stranded on the side of the road, would err on the side of caution.

'Does she have any friends left in London?'

'No one she would trust.' His gaze met hers directly, for the first time since she'd entered the house. There was an odd look in his eye, something intense and unsettling. A slight, sick smile crept across his face. 'The only person she trusts is you, Dr Flynn. Where do you live?'

73

Though she hadn't had cause to pick a lock for years, Carolynn opened Jessie's back door with ease, the lock cheap and flimsy, no secondaries to back it up, lax security that only someone who never felt at risk in their own home would choose. Picking locks was a useful skill that she had learnt from the boys on the estate where she'd grown up. It was about the only useful thing that she had taken from her upbringing, with the exception of resourcefulness and resilience. And the knowledge of how to kill.

Stepping into the kitchen, Carolynn pulled the door closed behind her and wiped her feet thoroughly on the back doormat. The kitchen floor was pale grey limestone, matching the dove grey units, and she knew that Jessie wouldn't wear dirty shoes inside, not with her OCD. She wanted to respect her new friend's house, behave as she would.

The sitting room's decor, as with the kitchen's, was straight out of *World of Interiors*. Cool and stylish, it was everything she had hoped it would be: two cream sofas and a reclaimed oak coffee table, white bookshelves bare of clutter, show-home spotless. Only the photograph of the little boy on the cream marble mantelpiece was jarringly out of place, chocolate ice cream smearing his idiotic grin. She was tempted to lay the photograph flat, erase him from her view, write him out of the serenity that was Jessie's home, but she knew who the boy was, knew his and his older sister's history. She had researched her psychologist's history well, chosen her because she had known family tragedy in her past. She had wanted someone who would feel an innate, subjective sympathy for her plight, who wouldn't judge her, as she had been so judged and condemned in the past. She had wanted to see a psychologist on her own terms this time, to help her reclaim her stability, her sense of self, to help her see a way through to rebuild her life after all that she had lost. She had researched her psychologist's background far better than her psychologist had researched hers.

Mounting the stairs, her shoes sinking into the plush pile of the cream carpet, Carolynn found Jessie's bedroom at the back of the house, overlooking the garden and the field of sheep beyond. A crisp white duvet covered the oak-framed bed, a faux silver-fox-fur throw draped the single white chair, and the chest of drawers and built-in cupboards that lined one wall were painted the same soft white as the woodwork throughout the rest of the house.

A second photograph, on the bedside table closest to her, caught Carolynn's eye. But unlike the one of Jessie's dead brother downstairs, this photograph *fit*. The couple pictured were arrestingly attractive. Jessie and a man – her boyfriend – must be.

Is he hot?

Beautiful. Truly. I'm very lucky.

Jessie was right. He was broad-shouldered and long-limbed, blond with the most unusual amber eyes, far more attractive even than Carolynn had imagined from Jessie's description in the surf café. The photograph was a relaxed, fun selfie, Jessie sitting on his knee in a garden, leaning back against his chest, holding the camera in an outstretched arm, both of them laughing. One of his arms was curled around her shoulder, his other hand resting on her thigh, underneath the sky-blue silk of her dress. She could tell from the way the material clung to Jessie's breasts that she hadn't been wearing a bra. Knickers? Perhaps she hadn't been wearing those either. That would account for the smile on his face.

Looking at the photograph, Carolynn experienced a sense of acute envy. She couldn't remember the last time she had felt that happy, that carefree. The photograph was a vignette of the relationship she wanted, how she wanted to feel, the life she wanted. She looked at Callan's hand on Jessie's leg and imagined it on her own, his fingers stroking the soft skin of her inner thigh and felt a fizzing hotness in her groin, sudden and intense. It was a feeling she hadn't experienced in years.

Unclipping the back of the frame, Carolynn extracted the photograph and stroked her hand across Jessie's celluloid face. Her fingers lingered on Callan's, moved to his chest, caressed the muscled arm that led to the hand hidden under the blue silk. She tore the photograph in half, half again, tore and tore until she was holding little more than threads. Opening the sash window, she stretched out her arm and watched the fragments of the photograph scatter on the wind.

74

So Workman had verified the gargantuan black hole in his logic that could swallow his career. Jamming his phone between shoulder and ear, Marilyn sunk his head back into his hands.

'I've run another search on the DNA database to see if Zoe's DNA matched anyone else,' Workman continued. 'Because nowadays, now that pregnancy out of wedlock isn't frowned upon, young girls who get pregnant accidentally tend to keep their babies, don't they? It's often only marginalized people who give up their children for adoption, or have their children forcibly removed. I thought, in that case, that one or both of Zoe's biological parents might have a criminal record and that their DNA might be on the database.'

'Good thinking, Workman,' he muttered into his palms. 'And . . . ?'

'And, I was . . . I was right.' Was he imagining the hesitant delicacy in her tone?

'What is it, Workman?'

'You're not going to like this, sir.'

Marilyn sighed. 'Ruby Lovatt,' he said. 'Ruby Lovatt was Zoe Reynolds' biological mother, wasn't she?'

'How on earth did you know that, sir?'

'Just call me Uri Geller.'

75

Carolynn ran her hand across Jessie's dresses, feeling the roughness of cotton against her palm, the slickness of lycra, the warm bobbliness of wool. The last dress, the pale blue silk dress that Jessie had been wearing in that laughing selfie shimmered as she took it from its hanger. At the bottom of the cupboard, she found a matching pair of pale blue stiletto-heeled sandals.

In Jessie's bathroom, she pulled off her dirty jeans, yanked her stained T-shirt over her head, peeled off her bra and knickers and dropped them into the dirty clothes bin. She tucked her shoes neatly, side-by-side, behind the door. The silk dress was waterfall soft against her skin as she slid it on. The pale blue set off her blonde hair and contrasted stunningly with her dark eyes. In the bathroom cupboard, she found Jessie's make-up bag and made herself up carefully with medium-beige foundation, blusher and coral lipstick. She wouldn't have chosen the blue eyeshadow, but it was all that Jessie had, it matched the dress and at least it wasn't *neat, reliable, dowdy, playing the role*. She had no intention of ever *playing the role* again. It was another woman's turn to play that role now.

Planting her hands on her hips, Carolynn twisted left and right, pouting at herself in the mirror, ignoring how the straps of the dress sat awkwardly over the coat-hanger ridge of her collarbone, how the skirt bagged over her bony hips. She looked good, almost as good as she had used to. *Before.*

A sudden voice, calling up the stairs. A man's voice.

On bare feet, Carolynn tiptoed to the bedroom door and listened. The man again, calling for Jessie. *Callan?*

Smoothing a hand down the dress, fluffing up her hair, Carolynn stepped on to the landing. She had no bra and no knickers on, but who cared? Jessie hadn't had either in that photograph and her boyfriend, Ben Callan, had looked to be enjoying every second.

Jessie would doubtless love her looking like this, would see her as an equal. And Callan? He would love her looking like this too, wouldn't he?

76

From the upstairs bedroom window, Roger watched Dr Flynn spin her car around in the narrow lane and roar off towards the main road.

The only person she trusts is you, Dr Flynn. So where do you live?

He had always been convinced of Carolynn's innocence, hadn't been able to let his mind go to a place where the woman he had lived with for twenty years might have wrapped her hands around a little girl's neck – their little girl, she was still theirs, irrespective of her biology – and squeezed the life out of her. He would never have stood by Carolynn if he had suspected, for one millisecond, that she was guilty. But had he been in denial? Jammed his head, ostrich-like, firmly into the sand. He had let her dominate him for years, he realized that now.

Who's in control in your relationship?

Carolynn, unequivocally. Though when Dr Flynn had asked him so baldly, he had bristled, ashamed to voice that reality. Why had he let Carolynn dictate their lives so comprehensively, when his family's wealth had paid for everything? *God*, when he looked back, *really* thought about it, he realized how pathetically impotent he had been.

He had watched some programme years ago on animal behaviour. He'd forgotten most of it, but the frog had stuck in his mind. Toss a frog into a pan of boiling water and it will leap straight out, save itself, but put a frog in cold and turn the temperature up slowly and it allows itself to be boiled alive.

He had been that frog. The only time he'd railed, tried to climb out of the saucepan, had been when Carolynn had snapped with Zoe, told her that she wasn't their child. He couldn't even remember what the poor little girl had done to precipitate Carolynn's vicious outburst. He'd said something then. He *had* said something. But she had wheeled around and screamed at him: '*Go fuck yourself, Roger.*' Her accent had been different too, all wrong, slipping in that moment of extreme aggression.

Slumping down on the edge of the bed, he put his head in his hands. *I did say something then.* Would that be his moral defence if it turned out that Carolynn murdered Zoe? *I did say something. Once. I DID.* A moral pygmy of a voice, lamely protesting a giant's actions.

If Carolynn really was innocent, why had she snuck out last night while he'd been sleeping?

He didn't feel as if he knew anything any more. Which way was up, which down, what was right, what wrong, who was good, who evil.

77

Past

Queen Alexandra Hospital, Cosham, Portsmouth

Ruby felt desolate. As depthlessly sad as it was possible to be. Her tummy ached and between her legs throbbed, and she sensed the wetness of blood on her thighs and none of that mattered. Twisting on to her side, she curled her knees up, wincing in pain at the movement, hugged the doll that she had retrieved from the bin to her chest, and tried not to cry. An unbearable loneliness engulfed her. She had been alone for her entire life, and yet she had never felt so over-whelmingly alone as she felt now. She had made the most terrible mistake of her life, believing that this baby would signal a change in hers, that she would be able to keep her, look after her, love her. *Of course not.* Good things never happened to girls like her. Girls like her never got what they wanted, never *won*. They just got what people wanted to give them, and more often than not what they got given was shit.

The sound of the door opening and Ruby fixed her gaze on the wall. A soft click and the nurse moved over to the bed on silent feet. The mattress tilted as she settled herself on its edge.

'I'm so sorry, love,' she said, sliding an arm around Ruby's shoulders.

Ruby raised her hand to block the movement. 'Don't,' she said. 'Don't do that. I'll be OK, so long as no one tries to give me hugs or anything like that.' She tried to smile, couldn't muster one. 'I'll get over it. I've got no bloody choice, anyway, have I? Just give me another half hour to get my stuff together, then I'll leave, get out of your hair.'

'There's no hurry, love. You stay as long as you need.'

Ruby nodded. She couldn't meet the nurse's eye, knew that if she did, her resolution not to cry, all that fake strength she had built up inside herself would fracture. Shatter into a gazillion pieces, each fragment so small that she would never ever rebuild herself.

'Like I said, I'm fine. I'll be gone before the hour's out.'

'You'll find her,' the nurse said gently. 'You'll find her again, or she'll find you. When she's old enough, eighteen, she'll come and find you, find her mum.'

Staring hard at the wall as if her life depended on it, Ruby shook her head. 'No,' she managed.

She didn't want to hear it. Couldn't bear to hear it. *Eighteen years.* Two years longer than she had been on this planet and already her life felt interminable. She couldn't bear another whole lifetime of misery before she had any prospect of seeing her daughter again.

And she couldn't bear not knowing where her daughter was, if she was happy or sad, if the people who had her were kind or cruel, if she was playing in the park and riding her bike with friends, or crouching in a corner trying to make herself invisible, terrified of being shouted at, beaten or abused again. She just couldn't bear it.

78

Jessie's cottage looked, as she had expected, deserted. No lights on inside, no cars parked outside, not Callan's or any others. She looked each way down the lane, staring hard into the soupy darkness. Nothing, no one, no signs of life at all.

And yet, she remained motionless in the middle of the lane, listening, feeling a tense tug in her stomach. A stiff breeze brushed clouds over a sliver of moon, intermittently stealing what faint light the moon cast and returning it, rustling the leaves on the hedges hemming the lane.

A sudden, louder rustle in the darkness and her heart rate rocketed. But it hadn't been loud enough to be human, she realized a millisecond after. Just an animal then, a badger or fox, confirmed by eyes shining low to the ground in the lane a hundred yards away, a shine that subdued her pulse, but also brought to her mind the gelid eyes of that doll found in Carolynn's loft.

The only person she trusts is you, Dr Flynn. So where do you live?

A table lamp shone from Ahmose's sitting room, throwing a pale yellow rectangle on to his narrow garden. But when she shifted sideways, so that she could look in through his front window, she saw that he wasn't sitting in his usual reading chair. Pushing his gate open, she walked slowly up the front path, glancing left and right, listening, seeing nothing out of the ordinary, hearing nothing jarring or unexpected. But as her fist connected with his front door to knock, it swung open. Though strangers rarely came down their narrow country lane, Ahmose was careful by nature and he never left his door unlocked unless it was to pop next door to her cottage. *Odd.*

'Ahmose?' Her voice echoed in what felt like a deserted house, but it couldn't be. He was never out at this time in the evening, hadn't been for years, unless it was to visit her, or Callan if she wasn't there.

'Ahmose?' she called again, angling her face so that her voice carried up the stairs. Still no reply.

She stood in the hallway, recognizing the benign sounds that met her ears: the whispered creaks and groans of an old cottage amplified by the silence and her own apprehension; the hiss of water in the radiators, programmed to come on in the evening, even though it was summer, Ahmose, born and brought up in Egypt, hyper-sensitive to the cold; her low-heeled sandals tapping on the wooden floor as she made her way from the hallway into the sitting room – his reading lamp illuminated, a book on gardening spread open on the coffee table – to the kitchen; the creak of the kitchen door as she pushed it open to expose another empty room; the sound of her own breathing, rasping with suppressed tension.

Back in the hallway, she tiptoed up the stairs, flicked on

334

the landing light and checked both bedrooms, empty, the bathroom, also empty. All three rooms upstairs, like those downstairs, deserted. So where was he? Where was Ahmose?

79

Roger Reynolds walked slowly upstairs to his and Carolynn's bedroom and sat down on the end of the bed. The duvet was cold, the room cold and empty. The whole house felt cold and achingly empty, a reflection of what his life had become.

Glancing towards Carolynn's cupboard, he thought of the doll that he had found buried behind her shoe rack, the box he'd moved and stowed in the loft, hating the thought of sleeping in proximity to that grotesque bloated body, that rigid tangle of plastic limbs. The doll in the box identical to the one found by Zoe's body, apart from the colour of its eyes.

He had thought about both dolls – one brown-eyed, one blue-eyed – when he'd driven to Lambeth Cemetery on Thursday to visit Zoe on the second anniversary of her death. He had bought a cuddly tortoiseshell cat to leave on her grave, to keep her company in death as Oddie had kept her company in life. But when he'd got to the cemetery it had been raining, stair rods of water cutting down from a heavy grey sky, and the cuddly animals on the surrounding graves had looked pitifully forlorn. But it had been the dolls left on some graves, like grotesque plastic effigies of the children buried beneath, that had cut him to the core. Tucking the cuddly cat back inside his coat, he had run across to St George's hospital and bought a bunch of white roses from the florist in the reception area, handed the cuddly cat to the woman manning the hospital's main desk to be gifted to the children's ward, run back, soaked by then, and arranged the roses in the black marble vase on Zoe's grave.

That had been Thursday.

And yesterday?

Yesterday, he'd driven into Chichester to consult a divorce lawyer. He didn't want this life any more and he didn't want Carolynn. Their marriage was nothing, a sham. Their lives nothing. Built on lies, deception.

But as he sat on the bed, staring at Carolynn's bedroom cupboard and thinking about the doll, his mind took him somewhere much darker. Took him to doubt, to that pygmy voice in his head, goading him with a question:

What if Carolynn did murder Zoe? What if you let it happen?

80

Marilyn's mobile rang.

'DI Simmons,' he barked.

'Detective Inspector.' The desiccated voice, instantly recognizable as Dr Ghoshal's, echoed down the line as if it was coming from inside a cave. Marilyn's mind filled with an image of the pathologist clutching his phone in one viscera-covered hand, a scalpel in the other, as he multitasked over a dissecting table in the chilled, white-tiled autopsy suite.

'What can I do for you, Dr Ghoshal?'

'This call is about what I can do for you, DI Simmons.'

Other senior detectives in Surrey and Sussex Major Crimes found Dr Ghoshal's attitude patronizing and hard to stomach, but Marilyn had worked with him for so long that everything bar the hard content he delivered, invariably excellent, was water off a duck's back.

'I'm listening,' Marilyn said, pulling the window shut to dampen the sounds of life drifting up from the street below.

'I have completed Jodie Trigg's autopsy. I'm sorry that it

has taken me so long, but I wanted to be absolutely sure of every detail.'

Marilyn waited, in silence, for him to continue.

'I can confirm that Jodie Trigg was, as you suspected, killed by manual strangulation: compression of the ceratoid arteries and jugular vein causing cerebral ischemia. The pattern and size of the contusions around her neck would suggest that the murderer was either a small man or, more likely, a woman.'

Not Roger then. He was big: six-two, with large, calloused workman's hands.

'Are you sure about that last bit? The woman?'

A moment of silence. 'No, I am not *sure*, DI Simmons, but, as I said, it is likely.'

'How likely?'

'If I was a betting man, which I am not . . .'

Was Marilyn imagining the castigation in Dr Ghoshal's dry tone? *Probably.* Since learning that Carolynn Reynolds was unlikely to have been Zoe's biological mother, his paranoia radar had been twitching wildly. *Just because you're paranoid, doesn't mean that they're not out to get you* – he still wasn't sure what Jessie Flynn had meant by that.

' . . . I'd say odds of two to one for it being a woman, twenty to one for a small man.'

'So almost certainly a woman.'

'The child would have fallen unconscious within twenty to thirty seconds,' Dr Ghoshal continued, as if Marilyn hadn't spoken. 'And death would have occurred within a couple of minutes.'

'Would she have been able to scream?' Marilyn asked. Not that it mattered. There had been no one on the beach to hear her.

339

'No. Her death was caused by vascular obstruction, but her larynx was damaged and the hyoid bone in her neck broken, which is consistent with significant pressure being applied to her airways. That pressure would have made it very difficult for her to breathe, let alone to scream.'

'How much knowledge would her killer have needed?'

'The right episode of *Silent Witness*, not even that. Unfortunately, DI Simmons, it is not hard to kill a child via strangulation. Wrap your hands around their neck, apply a reasonable amount of pressure, and there you have it.'

Marilyn had sensed a change in Dr Ghoshal's tone as their conversation progressed, a change that he would venture to say sounded alarmingly like emotion, and he remembered the sombre tableau around the dissecting table on which the little girl's body had lain. Despite a significant weight of evidence to the contrary, there was a beating heart somewhere inside that hypothermic hide of Dr Ghoshal's.

81

Jessie inched the key into the lock and eased open her front door, making no sound. Stepping over the threshold, she stopped, the door open behind her, caught between the silent wall of darkness in front and the whispering wall of darkness behind her in the lane. *Stupid.* Nothing to be frightened of here. This was her cottage, her place of refuge, and it felt empty, just as Ahmose's had. There was doubtless a reasonable explanation as to why Ahmose hadn't been home. Perhaps Callan had taken him out for dinner. Ahmose didn't have a mobile and though she had called Callan's twice on the drive up here, and again a few minutes ago when she'd parked outside, it had gone to voicemail each time. She wasn't Ahmose's keeper, or Callan's, despite the leaden secret growing in her tummy.

Her practised fingers found the sitting room light switch and flicked it on.

The room looked as she had left it, a shrine to her OCD. Closing the front door softly, shivering slightly at the blast of cool air the movement forced into the room with her,

341

she slipped off her sandals and arranged them on the shoe rack, touching her flat hand to the heels to level them – once, twice, three times. She stopped and felt the electric suit surge. She counted on in her head, tapping flat hands to the shoes' heels until she reached seven, *lucky seven*, glancing up to survey the room as she performed the ritual to ensure she was still alone. *Of course I am.* But some lingering sense of nervousness made her check anyway.

As she padded barefoot across the sitting room carpet to the kitchen, her gaze was snagged by Jamie's photograph on the mantelpiece. She stopped frozen to the spot in the middle of the room, her breath trapped in her throat.

The frame had been moved, just a fraction – she saw that immediately. The only thing on display, she always centred it exactly in the middle of the mantelpiece, equidistant from either end and parallel, to the millimetre, with the wall behind. Both Callan and Ahmose knew her sensibilities regarding Jamie and they never touched it.

As she moved closer, the silence surrounding her absolute but for her stressed breath hosing the air, the overhead light picked out a smudge on the glass.

A fingerprint. Too small to be that of a man.

The only person she trusts is you, Dr Flynn. So where do you live?

82

'There was no trace evidence of poison, illegal or prescription drugs or other toxins in Jodie Trigg's stomach contents,' Dr Ghoshal continued. 'So she was not sedated prior to being murdered and wasn't under the influence of alcohol. Neither did I find any prescription drugs, alcohol or other toxins in her blood, and there were no needle marks on her skin, so she wasn't a regular drug user or a drinker.'

'She was nine.'

'Nine-year-olds drink and take drugs, DI Simmons.'

He was right, Marilyn reluctantly conceded, ignoring the condescending tone. He had seen enough of it when he'd worked in Brighton as a young detective: kids hanging out on the beach, mainlining fortified wine or cheap cider, sniffing glue and popping Es. The same, albeit on a significantly smaller, milder scale, in Bracklesham and Selsey. But from what he had learnt, Jodie Trigg wasn't that kind of child. The only accelerated development she showed was an overly mature sense of responsibility, due to her situation.

'We found partially digested sausage, potatoes, carrot,

peas and an apple in her stomach. Lunch, given the time of death. I don't think she had any breakfast on the day she was murdered.' That hint of emotion again in Ghoshal's voice.

'OK. Thanks for all that, Dr Ghoshal,' Marilyn said, trying to quell the disappointment in his own voice.

Everything the pathologist had said so far was basically tick-box, nothing there that would lead him to a killer. The only significant information, as far as he was concerned, was the confirmation that Jodie Trigg, and hence Zoe before her, had been murdered by a woman – a blonde woman, if Workman and Cara's kite-surfing millionaire's long-distance, high-speed vision was accurate.

Not enough.

'In addition to the partially digested food, there was also a piece of masticated chewing gum in the deceased's stomach,' Dr Ghoshal continued.

'Schools often have tuck shops.'

'Indeed they do, DI Simmons. But I doubt that a school tuck shop would be selling this kind of gum. This one is interesting . . . '

83

A sudden shiver ran down Jessie's spine, a strong sense that she was no longer alone. She spun around, her eyes finding both doorways into the sitting room, the front door and the kitchen door snapping from them to the bottom of the stairs, to the spaces where someone small could crouch and hide – behind the sofas, under the coffee table – there weren't many in her Spartan sitting room, her brain knowing almost before she'd finished checking that her sitting room, so familiar to her, was empty. *Knowing* that she was definitely alone in here.

She breathed out, sucked a long draught of air into her lungs, willing herself to relax. But she couldn't shake the feeling that something was wrong. Roger's taunt; Ahmose's absence; the fingerprint on Jamie's photograph, which could have been hers but she was sure not. Too much had been odd.

Soundlessly, she moved to the bottom of the stairway, and looked up. A light shone from her bedroom, so faint that she hadn't noticed it from elsewhere in the sitting room.

Her bedside table lamp, perhaps, or the light in her en-suite bathroom?

And now that she was standing here, she could hear a barely audible rumbling. Low and complaining. The wind? No, because the noise sounded as if it was coming, not from outside, but closer, from within her cottage, within this room. But who or what, and from where?

'Ahmose.' Her voice, barely there, was threaded with fear and she hated herself for it.

Moaning? Now that she really listened, it sounded as if someone, close by, was moaning. Her gaze found the door to the understairs cupboard.

'Ahmose? Is that you?'

No, of course it couldn't be, not in that tiny space. As she moved towards the cupboard, her heart was slamming so hard in her chest that she felt as if it would punch its way out of her ribcage.

'Jessie.'

Jesus.

She spun around. Carolynn was standing at the bottom of the stairs.

'I wondered when you'd come,' she said, smiling.

84

'All chewing gums consist of a gum base, humectant—'

'Humectant?'

'Moisture retainer,' Dr Ghoshal said. 'They also contain flavouring, such as mint oils, sweeteners – either natural or synthetic, depending on the brand.'

'And this gum?'

'Natural. A good quality, if any gum could be called good quality—'

'So what does that tell us?' Marilyn cut in.

'Let me finish, DI Simmons. Let me finish.'

Marilyn bit down on his impatience. He had learnt, over many years, that Dr Ghoshal couldn't be rushed, but at times like this, that knowledge didn't make dealing with the reality any easier.

'It is a myth that chewing gum takes seven years to move through a person's intestine and be expelled, but obviously some of the ingredients, such as mint oils, or softeners like vegetable oil or glycerine are very easily digested and quickly excreted, while others – like the gum base, which is usually made from natural or synthetic polymers – can remain in the stomach for an extended period of time.'

'How long?'

'How long is a piece of string, DI Simmons?'

Christ. Marilyn felt his will to live ebbing away.

'Each manufacturer has its own recipe for the gum base, with the aim of achieving the perfect degree of elasticity—'

'How does this help me, Dr Ghoshal?' Marilyn cut in again, his tone firm. He rubbed a hand across the base of his neck, vainly trying to massage away the stress that had lodged itself in his shoulders while he waited for Dr Ghoshal's measured reply.

'The gum that Jodie had in her stomach also had traces of the following: Helianthemum nummularium, Clematis vitalba, Impatiens glandulifera, Prunus cerasifera and Ornithogalum umbellatum. Do those names ring any bells, DI Simmons?'

85

'Carolynn. I . . . I've been looking for you.' Though Jessie fought to keep her voice even, she sounded a lot like Carolynn when she'd masqueraded as 'Laura', adopting the phony sing-song jollity of a game-show host.

'I hope you don't mind that I came to your cottage without asking you, but friends don't usually mind, do they?' Carolynn's voice, in contrast, was one that Jessie had never heard before: calm, measured, confident.

She met Carolynn's smile with one of her own, a rictus smile that she knew must look twisted and horrible.

'No,' she murmured. 'Of course I don't mind.'

'I love your cottage.' Carolynn's gaze moved admiringly around the room, a frown flitting across her face as it passed over Jamie's photograph. Was the frown driven by the fact that the photograph was of a child, Jessie wondered, or because that dirty smear of chocolate ice cream around Jamie's mouth contrasted so starkly with the spotless room surrounding it? Or both, perhaps?

'It's so chic and calming,' Carolynn continued, her gaze

moving back to Jessie's, no issue with holding eye contact now. 'Exactly how I imagined it would be.'

She looked different too; cool and stylish, entirely at home in this environment. She was wearing make-up, Jessie realized, lots of it, expertly applied: a smooth layer of foundation, blusher highlighting her jutting cheekbones, thick black mascara accentuating her lashes, and blue eyeshadow that highlighted the deep brown of her eyes and matched the dress she was wearing. It took Jessie a second longer to realize that the dress was hers. The sky-blue silk dress that Callan had bought her for her last birthday. She had worn it to dinner that evening, without underwear, to tease him. They had wandered into the garden of the hotel after dinner, sat on a chair on the patio and taken a laughing selfie, before walking deeper into the garden and making love on the dark lawn.

Get it off, she wanted to scream.

'You look amazing, Carolynn,' she murmured.

'Thank you.' Carolynn laughed, a tinkling, carefree sound. 'It's lovely to wear clothes that aren't made from lycra for a change.' Tilting her head, she gave Jessie an odd little smile. 'It's yours. Didn't you recognize it?'

'Wow. No, I didn't. It never looks that good when I wear it.' The words felt bitter on her tongue.

In the moment of silence that followed, Jessie heard another sound, that barely audible moaning again. Carolynn didn't react, didn't seem to have heard. Had she imagined it? She flinched as Carolynn's chill fingers found her arm and squeezed, just lightly, tensed every muscle to stop herself from snatching her arm away.

'How about some wine?' Carolynn asked.

'Huh?'

'*Wine*, Jessie.' Carolynn cocked an eyebrow theatrically. 'I found a bottle in one of your cupboards and put it in the fridge. Sauvignon. It's your favourite, isn't it?'

Jessie nodded dully.

'See, I am a good friend because I remembered. I remembered you saying.'

86

'Well, Dr Ghoshal, if I wasn't thinking that gum in the stomach of a dead child would be a very odd place to find such a thing, I'd say that the bell those names are ringing is flower-related,' Marilyn said.

A moment of silence. 'And you'd be right, DI Simmons. Flowers is right.' Dr Ghoshal sounded unaccountably impressed. 'Flower essences, to be precise.'

'But why the hell would Jodie Trigg have gum in her stomach that contained flower essences?'

'Have you ever heard of Dr Bach, DI Simmons?'

Marilyn racked his brains. 'I can't say that I have, Dr Ghoshal.'

The impressed note had vanished from Dr Ghoshal's voice, replaced by a tone of condescension. *Business as usual.* 'Doctor Bach was a homeopath and bacteriologist who developed a range of remedies – alternative medicine, if you like – inspired by homeopathy. The remedies were derived from flowers and evidently Dr Bach let his intuition guide him as to which flowers had healing powers and which did not. He found that when he treated the personalities and feelings of his patients with his flower-based remedies, their physical distress would be alleviated naturally as the healing power in their bodies was unlocked and allowed to work.'

Sounds like a quack version of Jessie Flynn, Marilyn thought. 'That all sounds like gobbledegook to me, Dr Ghoshal. What relevance does it have to my case?'

'Rescue Remedy,' Dr Ghoshal said simply. 'It's the most famous of the Bach remedies, made up of five flower essences, including—'

But Marilyn had already tuned him out. *Rescue Remedy.* An image had risen in his mind. An image, a feeling, a soft kiss on his cheek, a pale hand fumbling inside a jacket pocket.

Take a lot more than this to rescue me, DI Simmons, but I gotta start somewhere.

87

As she stood in the kitchen watching Carolynn pour two glasses of wine, Jessie discerned that low, rumbling sound again. A vision of Ahmose, folded, bruised and bloodied, into the tiny space under the stairs rose in her mind.

'Did you meet Ahmose when you arrived?' she asked, as casually as she could manage.

'Ahmose?'

'My next-door neighbour.'

A dissatisfied frown moved across Carolynn's brow. 'Oh, the old man. Yes, he popped over.'

'And?' She couldn't risk riling Carolynn, not until she knew where Ahmose was, if he was safe.

'I asked him to leave.'

'OK.'

Carolynn banged the wine bottle back on to the work surface, her mouth twisting with irritation. 'He wouldn't though. He kept asking me what I was doing here. He behaved as if he owned the place, owned *your* cottage.'

Jessie nodded calmly, though her insides were churning. 'Did he leave eventually?'

Though she kept her gaze fixed on Carolynn's, something about her body language must have betrayed her thoughts, because Carolynn's eyes broke from hers and moved past her shoulder to focus on the door to the understairs cupboard in the sitting room.

'Oh, for heaven's sake, Jessie. You don't honestly think I'd shove an old man into an understairs cupboard, do you?' She tilted her head, a hard look, half-disappointment, half-anger flitting across her face. 'What on earth do you take me for?'

Jessie breathed out, trying to calm the swollen knocking of her heart. She needed to be the woman that Carolynn had met two months ago, the woman she respected, the woman she wanted to befriend; cool, edgy, fun, in control.

When did we swap places? When did Carolynn shed Laura's skin and I slip into it?

The moment that Roger asked me where I lived.

She smiled. 'So where is he?'

Carolynn waved a dismissive hand. 'Oh, don't worry. I dealt with him.'

'Carolynn—'

'What?' Her tone one of fraying patience.

'I'd like to see him.'

'He left, Jessie. I told him that we're good friends and that you'd invited me to stay for a few days. He said he was going for a walk to ease his back as he'd been sitting reading all day.' She tilted her head, the look of dissatisfaction mixed with anger, lingering for longer on her face this time. 'Jessie, I came here because I wanted to spend time with you.' Stepping forward she held out the *Happy Birthday, Princess* glass Jessie's dad had given her one birthday, full of wine, brushing Jessie's fingers lingeringly with her own as took the glass. '*You* not your next-door neighbour.'

Stepping back, expanding the space between them, Jessie took a sip of wine, knowing that it was tension, adrenalin, fight-or-flight that had parched her mouth. Ahmose would have spent most of a sunny day like this gardening, not sitting and reading. He never walked alone at night, because the lane was potholed and he was worried about tripping in the dark.

'You won't be offended if I give you a little bit of advice, will you?' Carolynn's voice was soft, her dark eyes locked on Jessie's. 'I used to give all my friends make-up and style advice, before—'

A shake of her head was all that Jessie could manage.

'You should try a little harder, put on some make-up, wear nicer clothes. You're very pretty, but you could look stunning if you tried. You don't want that gorgeous military policeman's eye to start wandering.'

Jessie roused herself. 'Callan? You saw him?'

'Only the photograph of the two of you upstairs.' She smiled. 'You're right, I don't think this dress does look as good on you as it does on me. You need to be a blonde to carry off a dress this colour.' Carolynn clinked her wine glass against Jessie's. 'It's so nice to drink without being judged. Roger hated me drinking.'

Jessie took another sip of wine, her mind working feverishly, spinning through the options, assessing, rejecting, knowing that a mistake in how she dealt with Carolynn now might cost Ahmose his life. *God, I've been so unutterably, arrogantly stupid.*

Callan's words rose in her mind:

The woman could be a killer. You could be putting your-self in danger meeting with her . . .

Her response:

If you had met her, you wouldn't be saying that. She's a frightened, timid, traumatized, middle-aged woman who is so thin she could play hide-and-seek behind a broom handle. She's not a threat to anyone.

Stupid, unprofessional arrogance that could cause the death of one of the people she loved most in the world. If he wasn't dead already.

'Why don't we take our wine up to the bathroom and you can give me a makeover. I don't wear make-up because I don't know how to apply it properly. I'd love you to teach me.'

A plan had coalesced in her mind. She just hoped that she could pull it off quickly enough to find Ahmose and save him. *If he isn't dead already.*

88

Ruby must have been waiting by the window, because she opened the front door to her flat before Marilyn was even halfway down the front path, and came out, leaving the door gaping open behind her. She was wearing the same clothes she had been wearing when he and Workman had interviewed her: that low-cut, thin silver jumper and skin-tight black jeggings. Watching her clack down the pathway towards him in her silver stilettos, he experienced a similar heaviness in his stomach to that he'd felt when she had given him that quick, soft peck on the cheek and tottered away across the car park. But now the feeling was a ton weight that threatened to take the bottom out of his gut. She looked cheap and beautiful, defiant and sad, but mainly just broken. Utterly, irretrievably broken.

As she approached, Marilyn noticed that she was clutching something to her chest.

A doll.

But not just *a* doll. It was *the* doll. Identical to the one left by Zoe and Jodie's bodies, but this one ragged, well-loved, showing its age.

'It's my daughter's,' she murmured.

As she held it out to show him, the rays from the overhead streetlight caught the doll's tatty pink nylon ballerina dress, sending rosy sparkles around the tiny cul-de-sac, skittering them across the pale faces of the crowd of neighbours who had emerged from their flats when they saw the two marked cars and the van of the forensic investigation team pulling up outside.

'It's the doll that I bought for my baby girl.'

'It has blue eyes,' Marilyn said, thinking of the doll Roger had found hidden at the back of Carolynn's wardrobe. *Perhaps someone sent it to her,* Jessie had said.

'All white babies have blue eyes. I wanted its eyes to match my baby's – the colour they were when she was born, at least. I don't know what colour they've turned now, cos I never got the chance to find out, did I? I wanted that fucking bitch cow woman to take it, give it to my baby's adoptive parents, so she'd have something to remember me by. But the bitch just tossed it in the bin without even looking at it. Right in front of me, she threw it in the bin, like it was worthless. Like I was worthless.'

'Did you send Carolynn a doll?'

'Yeah. When I saw her on Witterings beach, six or seven months ago, and recognized her. I followed her home. I bought a doll and laid it on her doorstep one night. I wanted to frighten her, let her know that her daughter's murderer was watching her.'

She jutted her chin and gave Marilyn her best Teflon smile, but her heart wasn't in it because her soft, violet-blue eyes remained fathomlessly sad.

He didn't know what he had expected to see in them: hardness, defiance, satisfaction, rage that she had been caught. But there was none of that.

A few years ago, he'd been called to the site of an accident on the A27, a lorryload of lambs destined for the slaughterhouse that had run off the road and overturned. The sound of the trapped lambs bleating for help had been horrendous. But worse was the look in the eyes of the lambs who were still alive when, hours later, they were finally cut free from the mangled lorry and herded straight into an identical lorry bound for the same slaughterhouse. He could have sworn then that they were fully sentient beings who knew that all they had survived was for nothing. He'd never been able to eat lamb since. Ruby had that same look in her eyes. That same hunted, haunted, hopeless surrender.

And yet there was no excuse for what she had done. The hurt and devastation that she had caused. The lives she had destroyed. She had murdered two little girls, cut short two innocent lives, and there could never be any excuse for that.

Pulling handcuffs from his suit pocket, Marilyn stepped forward.

'Ruby Lovatt, I'm arresting you for the murders of Zoe Reynolds and Jodie Trigg. You do not have to say anything, but it may harm your defence if you do not mention when questioned something that you later rely on in court. Anything you do say may be given in evidence . . . '

89

'It means so much to me that you want to be my friend, Jessie. You're the only person who hasn't shied away, betrayed me,' Carolynn said, as Jessie led her upstairs.

The photograph of her and Callan was missing from her bedside table Jessie noticed when she entered her bedroom, and the duvet was flattened on her side of the bed, a head-shaped indent on her pillow. It made her sick to think of Carolynn lying there, imagining – what? Imagining being friends with her, or of *being* her. Stepping seamlessly into her life, living in her house, wearing her clothes and make-up, sharing a bed with Callan.

A hand on her arm and she jumped. 'You're the only person who understands me, Jessie.'

I don't understand you at all, she wanted to scream, *even though it's my job to do so. I failed miserably.* Instead, she smiled and nodded, going through the motions, buying time, feeling like a bit-part actor in a bizarre horror film trying to second-guess the insane vagaries of the lead.

In the bathroom, she pulled open the cabinet. Her make-up

bag, little more than wallet-sized, was where she'd left it, but the zip wasn't fully fastened. Next to the make-up bag was her nail kit. She glanced quickly over her shoulder. Carolynn was looking in the mirror, rubbing a fingertip under her eye to erase a smudge of mascara. Shifting so that her back blocked Carolynn's view, Jessie palmed her nail scissors into the pocket of her dress. It made her feel infinitesimally more secure to be armed, even with blades so tiny and blunt. Turning, she handed Carolynn her make-up bag.

'There's not much in it.'

'I know. Remember, I've already used it. I put it back as you left it though.' She tilted her head and smiled. 'Because I understand you, Jessie, and I know that it matters.'

Jessie couldn't force a smile in response. She was feeling sick again – sick and dizzy. The baby. She hadn't eaten today, she realized, would have to start being more sensible, taking care of herself and her tiny charge. Sitting down on the edge of the bath, she watched Carolynn arranging the contents of her make-up bag on to the white quartz countertop by the sink. A couple of tubes of foundation in medium-beige and natural-tan – bought on a whim after she'd decided that she was sick of spending 365 days of the year resembling a ghost, but never used – and an eyeshadow palette in five shades of blue; black mascara, pink blusher and a few lipsticks. She knew she should engage Carolynn in conversation, disarm her, but she felt almost as if she was floating above herself, watching this crazy charade from somewhere otherworldly, no sentient body, no mind, no voice.

'You're beautiful, Carolynn,' she managed. 'If you could make me look as good as you, I'd be happy.'

The harsh overhead bathroom lights stripped the gloss from everything, lighting the downy hair on Carolynn's face – a symptom of malnutrition – and accentuating the bony hips jutting through the floaty material of the dress Callan had bought, highlighting the muscles and tendons that coiled like ropes underneath her virtually translucent skin, a skeleton with skin stretched over the bones, emphasizing the cold, calculating light in her eyes.

'Thank you. I feel so much better now I'm away from that house, from Roger, from that pretence of a life. I feel as if anything is possible. Do you know what I mean?'

Jessie nodded. 'What happened with Zoe, Carolynn?' she murmured, her voice neutral, knowing that Carolynn would be hyper-attuned to every nuance of her tone.

'Let's not talk about that now. We're having such fun.'

'Friends talk to each other, share stuff.'

Carolynn didn't reply. She reached to smooth Jessie's hair back from her face, tuck it behind her ears. Jessie dug her incisor into the delicate inside of her lip to stop herself from slapping Carolynn's hand away.

'I didn't like her,' Carolynn said suddenly.

'Huh?'

'My daughter. Zoe. I didn't like her.'

'Not every parent likes their child,' Jessie murmured.

'She wasn't ours, actually. Roger and I adopted her. We couldn't have children of our own, not even with IVF.'

I know, Jessie wanted to yell, right into Carolynn's face. So she'd been right. Had Marilyn checked the DNA database yet, confirmed what she'd told him? What was he doing now? Thinking now? Where was he?

Carolynn's hand moved to cup Jessie's chin, lifting her face to the overhead lights. The electric suit was hissing and snapping, tightening around her throat, making it hard to breathe. She bit harder into her lip, tasting copper, trying to anaesthetize the suit with self-inflicted pain.

'Zoe was stupid and irritating. I suppose I shouldn't have been surprised, given where she came from, but—' Carolynn broke off, and gave a light laugh that made Jessie shiver. 'But I came from the same background and look at me: I'm clever. I just expected that she would be the same, that I would be able to *make* her the same as me.'

'Was it an accident?'

Carolynn looked confused. 'An accident?'

'On the beach, with Zoe. When she died.'

Carolynn straightened. She looked shocked. 'No, no, no, you've got it all wrong, Jessie.' There was a hard edge to her tone. 'I wasn't on the beach when Zoe died – I didn't kill her. I found her, but I didn't kill her.'

Jessie nodded. She didn't believe a word the woman was saying, but she couldn't afford to push further. Ahmose, not the truth, had to be her priority now. It was Marilyn's job, not hers, to find out the truth. She had given him enough. She had to focus on what was important to her, and that was the people she loved. It was too late for Zoe, too late for Jodie.

'Of course I believe you. It's past history, anyway, and you've already been through too much.' Her voice sounded like that of a robotic implant. 'Let's talk about something else.'

She still felt dizzy and sick – really sick. It was a struggle to concentrate, to form coherent thoughts. Leaning forward, she put her head in her hands.

'Are you OK, Jessie?' she heard Carolynn say. 'You don't look too good.'

'I feel a bit sick. Silly of me not to have had any lunch.' She swayed slightly as she stood and reached to the countertop to steady herself. 'The edge of the bath is too low. You're having to bend. Let me grab the chair from the bedroom.'

Holding on to the countertop, she shifted around Carolynn and walked slowly to the door. She wobbled, her shoulder banging against the doorjamb as she stepped into the bedroom.

When she returned with the chair, Carolynn had her back to the door, was painting eyeshadow colours on to her wrist, holding her arm up to the light to compare them. Jessie swayed as she planted the chair by the door, snatched at its back to stop herself from falling. She couldn't focus properly as she reached for the bathroom door handle and began to ease the door closed, making no sound, no sudden jerky movements that might snag Carolynn's peripheral vision in the bathroom mirror. Tilting the chair, she jammed its back under the door handle, kicked the two back legs hard to wedge them securely into the thick pile carpet.

No sound from inside the bathroom, then a tentative, 'Jessie?'

She didn't answer. The chair was solid, the carpet anchoring it deep, but she had no idea how long it would hold. Reeling across the bedroom, she yanked open the cupboard and staggered backwards, almost losing her footing. No Ahmose. Lurching across the landing, she checked the spare bedroom. Empty also.

As she ducked back on to the landing and surged towards the stairs, she heard a roar of fury and something heavy slammed against the bathroom door. Her foot found space where she had been expecting solid floor – *I must have misjudged the stair*, she realized in the split second before she fell. Cartwheeling down the stairs, ricocheting off the wall, smashing her head against the banister, the snap audible as she put her arm out in a vain attempt to break her fall.

She lay at the bottom of the stairs creased up in agony and heard wood splinter.

90

Without making eye contact with the broken young woman in front of him, who would break so many more times over when she discovered exactly who she had murdered two years ago, Marilyn cuffed her wrists together in one swift, practised movement. Laying a firm hand on her back, feeling the tense, elevated beat of her heart against his palm, he shepherded her, as her heels clack-clacked down the path to the road. DC Cara was waiting in the driver's seat of the first marked car, keeping the engine running as Marilyn had instructed him to, aware that the situation – this arrest for child murder in such an incendiary case – in this small, claustrophobic cul-de-sac of run-down council flats, just one narrow road in and out, could turn nasty very quickly. A quick glance at the faces of the assembled rubberneckers told him that they hadn't yet worked out why Ruby was being arrested, but it wouldn't take long for the collective penny to drop. He hoped, at least, that they'd be able to get her out of here before it did.

Workman, whom Marilyn had tasked with securing

Ruby's flat and keeping the neighbours at bay while Burrows and his CSI team went to work inside, was standing stiffly by the gate, three uniforms behind her, supressed tension etched in their expressions.

Marilyn met her gaze. 'Call for backup if you feel you need it,' he murmured, as he passed. 'Don't hesitate.'

Hauling open the rear passenger door of Cara's marked car, Marilyn placed his hand on Ruby's head to guide her inside, averting his gaze from the flash of cleavage her gaping top revealed as she tilted forward to duck, then slid in next to her. A tense balloon of air emptied from his lungs as he pulled the door shut, dampening the swelling noise from outside. A sudden crack as an egg smashed against the windscreen. Another crack, harder, louder as someone launched a stone at the passenger window on Ruby's side of the car.

'Get moving, Cara, before this turns into a proper shit show,' Marilyn shouted, as someone tossed the contents of a dustbin over the car's bonnet.

Sliding his arm around Ruby's shaking shoulders, Marilyn pushed her head down below the level of the window and grabbed the door handle with his other hand to steady himself. Cara pulled hard on the steering wheel and carved a swift U-turn in the narrow cul-de-sac, the rubbish from the bonnet streaking out both sides of the car in the slipstream. He could feel Ruby trembling under his palm, though she made no sound. A volley of cracks against the windows and bodywork as more stones were hurled, hands slapping the car's bonnet and boot, a sudden jeering, contorted face against Ruby's window as a man ran alongside screaming obscenities through the glass before Cara accelerated away, tyres screeching as he spun on to the main road.

Marilyn removed his arm from Ruby's back and helped her upright.

She sat rigid, staring straight ahead through the windscreen, the fingers clutching the doll – Zoe's doll – bloodless.

'You've been good to me over the years, DI Simmons,' she murmured, turning her head stiffly to look across, meeting his gaze. 'And I'm sorry that I let you down. I'm sorry that I never became the person you hoped I'd become. The person you thought I might become back then, the first time we met in that police station in Portsmouth.' Lifting the doll to her face, she breathed, sucking in its scent. Dropping it back to her lap, she gave a choked, mirthless laugh. 'But *Pretty Woman* was never going to happen to me, not where I came from. I was destined to be fucked – literally and metaphorically.'

Marilyn didn't answer. He didn't know what to say. He was tired, strung out to the point of hysteria, and he knew that whatever his dulled brain found in reply would be facile, pointless, not enough. She'd never had a chance, despite what he had hoped for. The course of her life had been mapped out for her at the age of fourteen, when she'd been shut in that trick pad to be used and abused, hot young meat, her body nothing more than a tradable commodity; her mind, her brave, sparky personality, whatever hopes and dreams she might have had for herself, had been an irrelevance to the men who trapped and sold her, those who paid to rape her. There were always the outliers who managed to confound their fate, but beyond those, rare as hens' teeth, were only fairy stories and trite Hollywood endings.

But at the same time he was aware of a simmering fury that he was struggling to keep a lid on. For some reason, he felt furious and unreasonably betrayed, as if she had owed him something, some fairy-tale morality, even though he knew it was a nonsense. He had never felt this way about someone he was arresting. Torn – so ridiculously torn. He would have given anything to have been right about Carolynn Reynolds.

'I told you about that advert I used to watch when I was a kid, didn't I?' she murmured. 'That washing powder advert? That little girl in her white dress in a field of wild flow—'

'Why the fuck did you do it, Ruby?' he snapped, unable to contain himself. 'They were little kids. Both of them – little girls.'

Those soft violet-blue eyes were misted with tears, he noticed now; tears she would fight tooth and nail to hold back.

'Because Zoe was *her* fucking kid. *Her* girl, wasn't she?' she hissed. 'So I did it for revenge. I did it to get even. Fucking simple as that.'

91

Jessie tried to push herself upright, but she couldn't coordinate her limbs, and every time she moved, the room began to spin and she felt a crucifying pain in her left arm. The pounding of feet on stairs and a shape loomed over her.

'It's over, Carolynn,' she managed. 'DI Simmons knows you weren't Zoe's mother. He's coming here . . . in a minute.'

She was slurring her words, but nothing seemed to be working properly: not her brain, her arms, her legs or her lips, and her tongue felt like a wad of damp cotton wool in her mouth. Carolynn's face hung over her, her features blurred, the look in her eyes rabid.

'Everyone I knew betrayed me. *Everyone,*' she hissed. 'I thought that you were different. I thought you'd have a heart buried in there somewhere, because you've known loss as I have, but I can see now that I was wrong.'

Digging her teeth hard into her bloody lip again, trying to use the pain to focus her mind, Jessie pushed herself to sitting with her good arm, shuffled her back against the wall at the bottom of the stairs. Even seated, she knew that she was tipping and swaying like a drunk, but she couldn't seem to keep herself upright in a room that was orbiting around her.

'You haven't known loss. Not a loss that you . . . you cared about,' she slurred. 'You didn't care about Zoe and you didn't care about Jodie.'

It would have been much better to stay quiet, but challenging was who she was, what she was made for. *Fight.* She had nothing to lose now anyway. She couldn't protect Ahmose, wherever he was. She couldn't even protect herself – couldn't run, couldn't *fight* or *flight*. Her brain felt as if it was slopping around untethered inside her skull and she was struggling to focus. It couldn't be just because of the impact of her head on the banister. But she'd watched Carolynn pour the wine for both of them, wouldn't have drunk it if she thought there was a chance it was drugged.

Why did she even feel surprised that Carolynn had screwed her? Stupid. So stupid, yet again, so *slow*. Stuck in the funhouse and still hadn't learned that every view was a distortion.

'You drugged me, didn't you?' she slurred. 'In the glass, before?'

Carolynn had been in the house for hours. She'd put the wine in the fridge, could have slipped something into the princess glass before Jessie had even arrived. *Happy Birthday, Princess.* What a gift. 'Flun . . . Flunitrazzzz . . . ' She paused, sucking in deep breaths, trying to clear her brain, couldn't get her mouth to form the words. 'Rohyp . . . hypnol.' *For anxiety, insomnia – of course – it should have occurred to her that Carolynn would have access to drugs. So easy to buy them off the Internet.* 'Why? We're . . . we're supposed to be fri . . . frien . . . friends.'

'Because you're a lying bitch.' Carolynn's voice had changed, her accent harsh and guttural. 'Roger called me and told me that he wants a divorce. He said that you'd been to the house. He accused me of killing Zoe and Jodie Trigg. It was you, wasn't it? You fed him those lies, turned him against me.'

Jessie shook her head. 'No, not me. I didn't . . .' *Didn't what?* Her mind and body were drifting in a small boat in the middle of the ocean, rocking on giant waves, the sky darkening above her.

'You never believed me, did you? You never believed that I was innocent of Zoe's murder or Jodie's. You tracked me down at the beach on Friday, had lunch with me, pretended that you wanted to be friends – just to trap me, accuse me, lock me up.'

Carolynn stood and for a dizzying second Jessie thought that she was going to move away, but then she saw a blur of movement and Carolynn's foot connected hard with her stomach. She tried to raise her arms, to protect her stomach, the baby, but though her dulled mind willed it, her body wouldn't respond.

A furious scream, another kick, sickeningly hard, and she vomited on to the carpet, coughed and choked, sucking air and vomit back down her windpipe.

Another kick. 'You're all the fucking same.'

Acid daggers as something inside her broke and she felt the gushing wetness of blood between her legs.

'*You're all the fucking same,*' Carolynn screamed. Screamed and kicked, again and again, screaming as she kicked and kicked.

As Jessie slipped into unconsciousness, the pain of Carolynn's kicks receded. Her whole body felt as if it was wrapped in cotton wool, wrapped and protected. But some stubborn, resistant nugget in her brain, a minuscule part that was still under her control, refused to let Carolynn win – not like this. With one last gargantuan effort of will, she fumbled her hand into the pocket of her dress, swung her arm and buried the nail scissors deep into Carolynn's calf.

Her eyes drifted closed and Carolynn's howls of pain faded. She moved her hand to her stomach where her baby had been – *I'm sorry* – and sank into the darkness.

92

No, Marilyn wanted to yell. *Zoe wasn't her kid. She was yours. Your daughter.*

'Why Jodie?' he managed, but even he could hear the thin thread of hysterical exhaustion in his own voice. 'Why her?'

'Because I needed that ice-cold bitch to care,' Ruby spat. 'I fucking needed her to care, like I cared, to hurt like I hurt every minute of every fucking day since she stole my baby from me and gave her away to be adopted. I thought she'd be destroyed when I killed her daughter, but she wasn't. It didn't even seem to scratch that rhino-tough skin of hers.'

'How did you find Carolynn?'

'By chance. They were down here on holiday, her and her wet husband and the daughter, and I was out on the beach, looking for treasure.' She flashed him a bitter smile. 'And I found it, didn't I? Found much more than I ever could have imagined.'

'You recognized her?'

'Of course I fucking recognized her. I've had her image

here' – releasing the doll, she tapped an index finger against her temple – 'for ten long years. The second I saw her, I knew it was her.'

'And when she came back here? After the trial?'

'It's a bit odd, isn't it, coming back to where your kid was murdered?' she said, with a lift of her shoulders. 'Least, it would have been odd if she'd actually loved that poor little sod. I'd been watching her on the television, before the trial, and when it started I hitch-hiked up to London, spent a few months living in hostels, turning tricks up at King's Cross to make money so that I could go to the Old Bailey and listen to her shit. I don't know what I expected to hear, but it was obvious that she didn't care that her daughter was dead. The only thing she seemed to care about was her own precious reputation, her privileged life caving in around her sodding ears. When she moved back down here after the trial, I saw her again, running on the beach. She's always on the beach, running like some insane robot and so am I, walking and searching.' Another bitter laugh. 'Like some insane robot.'

'She looked different from before.'

'She didn't look that fucking different. She still had that same face, that same hard face that's branded on to my brain. Her hair was different, longer and she weighed half what she used to weigh, but I knew it was her.'

'And Jodie?'

'She met Jodie five, six months ago, when the kid was hanging around on the beach with nothing to do. I got the feeling she loved Jodie in a way she'd never loved her own flesh and blood.'

'And that was justification enough for you to kill Jodie?'

Ruby gave another careless lift of her shoulders, though

376

Marilyn sensed that a large part of the carelessness was playacting.

'What chance did the poor little sod have, coming from a home like that? She would have lived a shit life same as I've done, preyed on, exploited, despised There's so many girls like me out there, girls who fall off everyone's radar, and for every one of us there's a hundred men who want to abuse us. I would have preferred to have died when I was a child than to live the life I've lived. Her last hours were spent on a beach, not being screwed by some old man. I did the kid a favour.'

'Why the heart of shells?'

Ruby shrugged. 'Because everyone deserves to be loved, even when they're dead, and I'm not sure that either of those girls had much love in life. Zoe didn't, I can tell you that much. And it made me feel better, leaving them like that, surrounded by love. I'm not hard, DI Simmons. I did feel for them girls – but I had to get revenge. I had to fight back for a change. Just once in my sorry fucking life, I had to fight back.'

Marilyn felt Ruby's eyes searching his face, kept his gaze fixed on the narrow strip of tarmac unfurling in front of them through the windscreen, over Cara's shoulder.

'I dressed my daughter in white, like the little girl in that advert I used to watch when I was a kid. White for purity, white for hope. Anna. I called her Anna. I never told you that, did I? It's such a pretty name, but strong too. She'd never end up a drug-addict whore like her mum, not with a name like Anna.'

Tears were running, unchecked, down her cheeks. She raised a hand and batted them roughly away, a look of fierce pride moving across her face, washed away by a new flood of tears as soon as the first were streaked into the back of her hand.

'I thought that, after a few years, the memory of her would fade. That I wouldn't think about her any more, that she'd just be in my past. I thought the pain would stop. But it hasn't. It's never, *ever* stopped. My Anna is the first thing I think about the second I wake. Sometimes, if I'm lucky, if I've had a drink or a hit, there might be a second or two when I don't think about her, when life is good, just for a couple of seconds. Then the pain hits me, and it stays with me all day, every day, right here—' She laid a hand over her heart, dropped it dispiritedly back to her lap, to clasp the doll in bloodless fingers. 'This is my life.'

Marilyn continued to stare straight ahead through the windscreen. Should he tell her why Carolynn hadn't cared about Zoe? Should he tell her who her baby had become? He felt sick to his stomach with the information he was withholding. Information that would sit on his shoulder, alongside little Zoe's ghost, until he felt the time was right to tell Ruby. It would sit on his shoulder long after the telling. He knew that he would have to tell her at some point, that it would be unforgivably cruel to let it come out at her sentencing hearing, but he couldn't do it now. Not now. Because he knew that it would kill her – psychologically for certain, and probably physically as well. She'd find a way to make it physical. To end her life.

Why did he care so much, after what she'd done?

Because the proud, feisty, broken, fourteen-year-old Ruby he'd met all those years ago deserved so much better? Because so many people, who started off so much nastier than her, had gone on to live diamond-encrusted lives? One of life's great ironies is that it isn't fair. He knew that. He didn't believe in fairness and he wasn't sure that he believed in justice either. In his experience, justice seemed only to serve the privileged.

'I would have made a great mum, if I'd been given the chance,' he heard Ruby say. 'I know that I would, because I really loved her, like my mother never loved me, like that ice-cold bitch never loved her daughter. And that's all that really matters, isn't it, DI Simmons? Love. Proper love.'

93

She had imagined this moment many times over the past two years, since she had been wrongfully accused of Zoe's murder, since the life she had craved so badly as a child, worked hard for so many years to create, had come crashing down. She had designed the perfect stage setting in her mind, toying endlessly with each and every detail. She had imagined that she would be lying on a sun-drenched bed in an airy room, soft white pillows to rest her head on, a smooth white sheet, untouched by human hands, underneath her, another draping her naked body. The window would be open, a breeze billowing the sheer white net curtains into the room and beyond them, a view of the sea. Not the sea at Bracklesham, angry grey for most of the year, but a perfect azure blue sea, the blue of water around a coral atoll, the blue of Greek island postcards. At other times, she had imagined a four-poster bed in a dark, gothic room, gargoyles looking down at her from the cornicing, the bed intricately carved from mahogany or ebony, white drapes shielding her from the world and a soft white bedspread covering her.

White bedding. Always white. For purity, saintliness? Everything that she was not.

Music would be playing in the background, something classical, uplifting. Most often, she imagined that she would be listening to Handel's 'Arrival of the Queen of Sheba' as she drifted into unconsciousness, because she had always wanted that to be played when she walked down the aisle at her wedding. But Roger had wanted something different and she had deferred to his choice. Pretending to be dutiful back then, at the beginning, before they were married. Playing the role.

She pictured herself putting on a floor-length white broderie anglaise nightgown and doing her make-up with extra care; not in the demure fashion she had been forced to adopt in court, but as if she was going somewhere special, for a night out: statement eyes, heavy mascara and pillar-box red lipstick that on her pale face would look startling, shocking, a slash of vermilion blood.

The picture-perfect cinematic moment.

The picture-perfect death.

She had thought that it would be a landmark event that she would need to prepare for. But now that the time had come, it wasn't like that at all. It was just a normal September day, two days after the second anniversary of Zoe's death, two days after Jodie Trigg's.

Though she struggled to feel genuine love for others, she believed that she had felt it for Jodie Trigg. Love, and regret that the little girl was dead. Jodie had been clever, resourceful, determined, old for her years, everything that she herself had been as a girl. Everything that Zoe hadn't been. She had given Jodie the necklace with the footprints of parent and child, the 'Zoe present' that Roger had given her. She'd seen a future with Jodie, a second chance at her own child. But, perhaps it was too late by then for her to have any more chances, just a pipe dream. She had already taken one child from her mother. God, fate, or whatever power was up there, pulling the strings, would never have let her take another, a good child this time, a *deserving* child.

She was tired, sad and lonely, and she'd had enough. Her body felt broken. Her brain felt broken. Her brain had felt broken for a long time now. Perhaps it had broken when she had felt that first seagull writhing in her hands, fighting vainly for its life. Perhaps it had been broken before that. Whatever, whenever, she knew that there was no chance it could ever be fixed. Even Jessie Flynn hadn't been able to fix it, make her normal, content with her lot, hadn't been able to scratch the surface.

She had never done what they had accused her of – she wasn't the one who'd killed Zoe or Jodie – but she had done enough to bring this fate upon her. She had stolen a child from her mother purely because she had wanted her. She had beaten the old man and dumped his limp body in Jessie's understairs cupboard. She didn't care about them, but she did care about Jessie. Perhaps Jessie was dead; she hadn't stayed to check, hadn't wanted to know. Her baby, though, was certainly dead. She hadn't known that Jessie was pregnant until she saw the blood. Would she have behaved differently if she'd known? No, probably not. Her behaviour, the attack, had been fuelled by intense anger and despair that she had been betrayed yet again by a so-called friend. She hadn't been able to control herself.

She couldn't cope with another trial, not after what she'd been through before, couldn't cope with spending years imprisoned. She had grown up in a prison, and the only thing she had ever wanted was to be free, but now she realized that freedom was a myth. No one was ever truly free.

Finding a pad in the bedside-table drawer, she wrote an apologetic note. She wasn't sure if Jessie would ever get to read it, but it felt right to write it anyway, as if she was doing the right thing for once.

In the bathroom, she stood in front of the huge wall-length mirror and stripped off the sky-blue dress, splattered in its owner's blood, dropped it in the bath so that she wouldn't dirty the spotless tiled floor or the fluffy white bath mat.

Purity, saintliness.

She was so thin that she fancied for a moment she could see the neon bathroom lights shining through her translucent skin. It was a ridiculous sight. She was ridiculous. Reaching for the light switch, she extinguished the lights so that she could no longer see herself. In the darkness, she showered and shaved her armpits and legs, sliding her fingers between her thighs to feel for the pubic hairs sprouting at the tops of her legs, shaving them off. She didn't want the pathologist to think that she was dirty, disgusting, that she had let herself go.

Walking back into the bedroom, she extinguished the lights there also. The moon lit the room milky white and for a moment she stood at the foot of the bed and looked at the panorama of the sky above the darkened fields, the stars appearing to ramble away for miles above her head. Not big-sky country, but almost.

She felt completely calm now. She lay down on the bed, Jessie Flynn's bed. She could smell Jessie's scent on the pillow, but perhaps she was only imagining it. It was as close as she would ever get to her now, but still it made her happy.

Take one of your pills, Carolynn.

She emptied the bottle of pills into her palm and fed them into her mouth, one after the other, taking sips of water between so that they slid down smoothly. Though she had put off this moment as many times as she had imagined it, now the time had come, she felt calm, relieved to be finally getting on with it, to be done with life.

Sliding under the covers, Carolynn closed her eyes ready for the long sleep.

94

Shrugging a coat carefully over her broken arm, sliding her feet into her ballet pumps, Jessie let herself out of her hospital room, thankful that understaffing meant the nurses at the station were heads down, too busy to notice one of their patients intent on going AWOL.

Due to the extensive bruising to her abdomen and the cramps in her stomach, she couldn't straighten properly, had to hobble down the corridor in shuffling steps, stopping every twenty metres to lean against the wall and catch her breath. It would take her forever to get downstairs and find a taxi to take her to Guildford Cemetery, but she had all morning. She had nowhere else to go, nothing else to do.

When she reached the cemetery, she followed the tarmac path that led to the chapel and stood on its stone steps, looking out over the expanse of lichen covered graves, her gaze snagged here and there by bright pops of colour – flowers, toys – thinking of Zoe and Jodie, and of her little brother Jamie. Three children who had lost their lives far too soon. She had wanted to come to a graveyard to pay her respects, but now that she was here, she realized that she'd made a mistake. She hadn't known either little girl. They weren't her children, her relatives, and they weren't her fight any more.

And Jamie – she carried him everywhere with her in the torn, ragged section of her heart. She hadn't needed to come here to think of him, to mourn his death.

Turning away, she pulled the pregnancy test from her coat pocket. She hadn't looked at it since that day on the beach, a week ago now, but it had followed her to hospital, tucked in the bottom of her handbag. The cross was still there. A cross for positive. The only tangible sign, now, that her baby had ever existed.

Finding a shady spot under a tree, across the tarmac path from the children's graves, she crouched and dug a hole with her fingers, relishing the feel of the soil grating against her fingertips and the earthy smell of churned grass and soil after the antiseptic smell of the hospital. Dropping the pregnancy test into the hole that she had dug, she smoothed the earth back over it.

'I'm sorry,' she whispered, feeling tears welling in her eyes and, for once, letting them come. It was fine to cry in a graveyard. Everyone cried in graveyards.

Jessie met Marilyn in the coffee shop in the hospital's foyer, later that afternoon. She had expected him to look elated; Carolynn Reynolds, his nemesis of two years, banished, even if she had been innocent of both murders. But he just looked exhausted. Emotionally and physically wrung out. He grimaced when he saw her hobbling across the foyer to meet him.

'Jesus Christ, you make a corpse look the picture of health.'

Lowering herself slowly into the chair that he had pulled out for her, she smiled up at him. 'Thank you for your kind words, DI Simmons.'

'Coffee?'

'Large latte with full-fat milk and a muffin, please. Double chocolate. I need the energy. The two-hundred-metre marathon sprint from my hospital room to here has wiped me out.'

When he had returned with the coffees and her muffin and sat down opposite, Jessie said, 'You don't look happy, Marilyn.'

He hunched his shoulders. 'Do I ever look happy?

'Occasionally. Sometimes. When you're feeling smug.'

He didn't smile, not even a forced one to play along. 'What's up?'

Another irritable shrug. 'It irks me that Carolynn caused all this – the death of those two little girls – by taking a baby away from its mother, so coldheartedly, and yet she escaped. Escaped the fallout.'

'I don't think that death can really be classified as escaping, Marilyn.'

'Still. She chose. She got to choose, to call the shots – again.'

'The trial, the fallout, the destruction of the picture-perfect life that she had constructed was the greatest punishment for her. It's not as if she got off scot-free. Far from it.'

Marilyn nodded. He didn't look convinced. 'I wanted to look her in the eye.'

'I looked her in the eye, Marilyn. And whatever you believe you would have seen – contrition, shame, regret – you wouldn't have seen any of it. Nothing stuck to her conscience, not truly. You would have felt even more angry and frustrated than you do now.'

He sighed. 'Perhaps.'

Jessie touched his arm, sensed him flinch at the unaccustomed physical contact.

'I'm sorry – about Ruby,' she said gently. *More sorrys.*

'There's nothing to be sorry about. She's a double murderer and she'll get what's coming to her. End of.'

'She won't get justice though, will she?' Jessie murmured. 'Because justice doesn't exist for people like Ruby.'

For the first time since she had known him, Marilyn wouldn't meet her gaze. His odd mismatched eyes were fixed on the hospital entrance, as if he was suddenly fascinated by the motley stream of humanity shuffling in through its doors. Something about that woman, Ruby, had clawed its way deep under his skin.

'Will you tell Ruby that Zoe was her daughter?' Jessie asked.

Eyes still fixed on the doorway, Marilyn gave an unequivocally firm nod.

'Yes, of course. It's my duty to tell her.'

'She won't take it well.'

Her words felt like a ridiculous understatement, but she could sense that Marilyn didn't need his nose rubbing in the gravity of the task ahead of him. Jessie couldn't begin to imagine how Ruby would feel when she found out. She had lost a three-month-old foetus, a life that never was, the size of a bean, and she still thought about him . . . her . . . it . . . constantly. It and Jamie. Two little ghosts now, one for each shoulder. She and Marilyn had a lot more in common than she liked to admit.

95

In the five days that Jessie had been in Royal Surrey County Hospital, Callan had erased every trace of Carolynn's visit from her cottage. Carolynn had haunted her fitful, drug-fuelled dreams while she'd been in hospital and she had woken many times, shaking, drenched in sweat, but now that she was home, the woman could have been just a figment of her imagination. She glanced over to the mantelpiece, to Jamie's photograph. Aligned to the millimetre, wiped clean of the smudged fingerprint – he had remembered to do that too – knowing that her OCD would be in hypersensitive mode when she got home, alert to every possible trigger.

Ahmose was still in hospital, would be for a couple of weeks more, recovering from the beating that Carolynn had given him with Jessie's table lamp. Callan had spent much of the past five days flitting between Jessie's hospital room and Ahmose's. He had promised to tend to Ahmose's garden until he was home, prepare it for an autumn that would soon be closing in around them.

A couple of days' stubble shaded Callan's jaw, and his sandy-blond hair curled over his collar, longer than army regulation. He'd need to get it cut before Monday, before he went back to work. He put Jessie's overnight bag at the bottom of the stairs.

'Coffee?'

She nodded. 'I'd love one.'

Though he had spent hours sitting by her bedside in hospital, they hadn't talked about anything substantive, just exchanged pleasantries. They'd talked about her mother and Richard's wedding, which they'd postponed until Jessie was well enough to attend, discussed the mundanities of Callan's job, talked about Marilyn and how he was tying up the loose ends of the Zoe Reynolds and Jodie Trigg murder cases. Now that they were home, the atmosphere between them was tense, polite, akin to new housemates. Her fault, because of the way she had treated him during the case and how she had acted in the five months since she'd been invalided out of the army, like an explosive device that needed kid-glove handling.

She followed him into the kitchen, but he wouldn't meet her gaze directly, his amber eyes flitting around the room as if he was still checking that it would satisfy her extreme sense of order, stave off her OCD.

'I'm sorry, Callan,' she said simply, moving over to the crockery cupboard to extract two cups.

'It's fine,' he said.

'No, it's not fine. I was obnoxious. A complete pain in the arse.'

The Princess wine glass was missing from her collection of glasses on the shelf above the mugs, she noticed. She looked across and he gave a small shrug. Another thing that Carolynn had defiled, banished. He'd ticked every box.

'You were tied up in the case,' he said.

'"Obsessed" is the word I think you're looking for.'

The ghost of a smile crossed his face. 'You do like your obsessions.'

'Yes, it's one of my particularly unattractive qualities.' Setting two cups on the sideboard, she turned to face him. 'I should have listened to you and not trusted Carolynn.'

'You were right about her, though. She didn't murder her daughter.'

'No,' Jessie murmured. 'She didn't. But she was still box-of-frogs crazy, and I didn't see it.'

Her gaze found the scar from the bullet wound on his temple, the stitched skin like the brown petals of a dead rose. She wanted to reach her arm out, stroke her fingers across it, down his cheek, bury her face in the crook of his neck, but the three metres of kitchen floor between them felt Grand Canyon wide.

He didn't know about the baby. That she had lost his baby because of her own stupidity, because she wouldn't listen to the father of that baby. Or Marilyn. Because she was the psychologist and when it came to understanding people, she knew best. Except that in this case – Carolynn's case – she hadn't. She had planned to tell him, to apologize, take whatever fallout came, but now that she was home alone with him, she knew that she wouldn't. She realized, meeting his flitting amber eyes, how much she had missed him, how much she loved him. She would never forgive herself if she screwed up this relationship. What upside was there in sharing with him that she had been pregnant?

None. There was none.

Acknowledgements

It is always hard to know where to start with acknowledgements as the list of people who have helped me, both with this novel and along the way, is long and humbling.

Thanks, as always, to my amazing agent, Will Francis, who has been incredibly supportive throughout my writing career and to the rest of the wonderful team at Janklow and Nesbit (UK).

I am forever indebted to Julia Wisdom, my Publisher at HarperCollins for being such a great champion for the Dr Jessie Flynn Crime Thriller Series. Thank you to Finn Cotton, my fantastic Assistant Editor, for his enthusiasm and conviction, Hannah Gamon and Louis Patel, Felicity Denham, Anne O'Brien who has an unrivalled eye for detail, and the rest of the fabulous team at HarperCollins. It is a privilege to work with you all.

Thank you to my great friend Mel Fallowfield, for all your support for Dr Jessie Flynn and for not killing me (there is still time). I also wanted to mention Bettina and Sean, Laura Deegan (so lovely to be back in touch), Tanya

Carter and Deya Thompson, Galyna for being amazing, Lilia Trigg, Kathleen McInerney, Paul and Katie Creffield for your wonderful friendship and your police and CSI knowledge, and my godson, Will. Huge thanks also to Carolynn and Roger Reynolds for not being horrified!

Thanks also to the Killer Women for being a hugely supportive and fun writing community to be part of.

Love always to my family, Pamela, Maggie, Daan, Charlie, William, Jo, Anthony, Isabel, Anna, Alexander, my late father, Derek, and Oddie the dog.

Most of all, thank you to the readers who pick up *Two Little Girls* – enjoy. You make writing worthwhile.